Why did Rudolph Hess, second only to Adolph Hitler, fly to Scotland?

Why go behind the back of the man he admired and respected most in the world, Hitler?

Why give his name as Alfred Horn when first captured?

Why wasn't Hess extensively interrogated by the British? Is it believable that he was not?

Why did Hitler send SS assassins to Britain to murder Hess?

Why was Stalin so keen to get his hands on Hess?

Why is Hess dismissed in a few lines in the histories of World War II?

Why the conspicuous lack of hard facts?

Why the mystery?

"DRAMATIC . . . THE ENERGETIC, ACTION-PACKED SPECULATIONS PROVIDE PLENTY OF EXERCISE FOR THE MIND'S EYE."
Library Journal

Shadow
OF THE
Wolf

James Barwick

BALLANTINE BOOKS • NEW YORK

Library of Congress Catalog Card Number: 78-31203

ISBN 0-345-28316-3

This edition published by arrangement with Coward, McCann & Geoghegan, Inc.

Manufactured in the United States of America

First Ballantine Books Edition: November 1980

Communiqué authorized by Mr. Duff Cooper, British Minister of Information, and issued from 10 Downing Street on the night of May 12–13, 1941:

Rudolf Hess, the Deputy Führer of Germany and Party Leader of the National Socialist Party, has landed in Scotland in the following circumstances.

On the night of Saturday the 10th inst., a Messerschmitt 110 was reported by one of our patrols to have crossed the coast of Scotland and to be flying in the direction of Glasgow.

Since an Me. 110 would not have the fuel to return to Germany this report was at first disbelieved.

However, later on, an Me. 110 crashed near Glasgow, with its guns removed. Shortly afterward, a German officer who had bailed out was found with his parachute in the neighborhood suffering from a broken ankle.

He was taken to hospital, where he at first gave his name as Horn, but later declared that he was Rudolf Hess.

Prologue

October 2, 1917. Flanders. Midnight. On the rusting strand of barbed wire above his head hung a fragment of cloth with a dented brass button still attached. In the dark he strained his eyes, trying to decide whether the fragment was British khaki or German field gray. It made no difference, of course, but the concentrated effort of decision helped quell the need for muscular movement. It was a trick he had learned long ago in no-man's-land when an English fighting patrol was passing a few yards away in the dark.

He could hear their low whispers now, the squelch of mud and water as they moved slowly through the Flanders mire.

He concentrated on the brass button as the moon emerged briefly from behind a skein of cloud. From the corner of his eye he could see the line of crouched figures, bulky in their greatcoats and flat steel helmets, the feared spiked wooden clubs the Tommies favored for trench fighting held ready in their hands. One movement, he knew, would bring them down upon him, kicking and clubbing with the animal ferocity which all front-line soldiers developed to hide their own fear of death.

A mud-covered boot squelched inches from his face. The skirt of a greatcoat brushed damp across his cheek. Strange English voices cursed softly above him, then passed on.

After a few minutes he rose and unwrapped a small white terrier from the folds of his gray trenchcoat. Then, tucking it under his arm, he scrambled out of the shell hole to stand looking across the broken land toward the banked trench systems ahead.

He found he loved this landscape, the shattered tree stumps, the waterlogged shell holes, the broken wheels of gun limbers, the endless coil of barbed wire. At times like now he would wander with his dog and gun like some Swabian squire walking his acres. On nights like this, when the fighting patrols had all returned and the October mists rolled and parted before him, this was his domain, harsh, ugly, brutal but never to him repellent.

In the entrance to the timber-braced earth bunker which was the forward headquarters of the 16th Bavarian Infantry Regiment, the two officers watched the flashes of gunfire pecking the skyline somewhere far to their right. The sound rumbled faintly toward them.

"British twenty-five-pounders. Well on the other side of the river," the Major said, lifting back the mud-stained blanket that covered the doorway.

Lieutenant Rudolf Hess followed him in. The hurricane lamps swung from the timber supports, gleaming yellow light on the trestle tables and the peasant French potbellied stove.

The Major took his tin coffee cup from the table. "Company reports in yet?" he asked the new adjutant.

"Both reserve companies, sir. The line's down to the forward company. They're sending a runner."

The Major nodded, then smiled as a small white terrier pushed aside the bottom of the blanket hanging in the doorway and scuttled across the earth floor to the warmth of the stove.

A moment later the blanket was lifted aside and the runner entered. "Forward company night report, Lieutenant."

He handed the report to Hess and stood informally, his head held slightly to one side, one hand curling his long mustache.

"There's some coffee on the stove," the Major said. "Warm yourself up before you go back."

"No, thank you, sir."

The Major smiled to himself and turned away. He knew that would be the answer. "As you choose," he said over his shoulder. "Dismissed."

The thin-faced man turned toward Hess and nodded sharply. Then, with a peremptory click of his fingers which brought the terrier to him, the runner turned and left the bunker.

"A strange man," Hess said quietly.

"Crazy," the Major agreed.

But Hess had not heard him. His eyes were still turned toward the hanging blanket through which Adolf Hitler had just passed.

July 20, 1936. Olympia, Greece. As the sun rose above the secluded Peloponnesian vale of Aphios, fifteen Greek girls, the folds of their gowns held at the waist with gilded cord, their fair hair drawn back from their foreheads and gathered in a heavy knot at the nape of the neck, stood unmoving on the marble slab which had marked the starting line for Olympic runners almost three thousand years before.

In the stunning silence of a Greek noon the leading girl touched a polished iron bowl with a narthex wand. A mountain horn sounded eerily. As the straw-bound tip of the narthex stalk began to crackle and smoke in the sun's reflected rays, a young man in loincloth and sandals knelt before the firebearer. Raising the silvery torch in his hand to the now flaming wand, he received the Olympic Fire. Then, turning, he ran —past the broken statues of the gods, the fallen columns of the Temple of Zeus and out onto the ancient road to Athens and the first stage of a three-thousand-kilometer relay to the Olympic Stadium in Berlin.

Through the mountainous Peloponnesus, through the baked, treeless plains of northern Greece, the runners carried the torch, each man covering a kilometer before the flame passed on. From Kula at the border, the Olympic Fire was carried into Bulgaria, then in 238 one-kilometer stages cross-country to Yugoslavia. Through Hungary into Austria the relay continued, and at twilight the runner carried his silver torch high through a Vienna decorated with national banners and Olympic rings. Then on across Czechoslovakia, until at Hellendorf the Greek flame reached German soil.

To Germans it was a homecoming. Saluted by the bells of ancient cathedrals, greeted by swastika-bedecked villages and floodlit monuments, exhorted every kilometer of the way by Wehrmacht bands and companies of the Hitler Youth trumpeters, the flame was carried toward Berlin.

At the kilometer stone of the old Kaiserdamm the final runner took the fire. To a roar from forty thousand escorting Storm Troopers, Otto Schilgen, tall, slim, Nordic-blond and clad in white, turned toward the Reichssportsfeld and the Olympic Stadium.

High in the glass-fronted loge above the packed segments of seated spectators, Adolf Hitler first saw the afternoon sun glimmer on the silver torch as the runner entered the stadium from the eastern tunnel. Massed trumpets flared, twenty thousand white doves rose and wheeled across the sky, Olympic banners surmounted by the Nazi eagle broke out along the stadium's rim and one hundred thousand voices importuned the leader with a repeated "Heil" . . . "Heil" . . . "Heil." . . .

Standing beside the brown-uniformed figure of Adolf Hitler, Rudolf Hess trembled at the magnitude of his Führer's triumph. From all the competitions of the next weeks, from the exhilaration of success and the desolate loneliness of defeat, one victor would emerge above all others. Adolf Hitler had made these

4

Games his own. The world could no longer doubt the power, the organization and leadership of the Nazi State. As the torch touched the vast bronze caldron, capping it with flame, the Führer of the Third Reich declared the XIth Olympiad open.

On the mild overcast morning of August 10, in the chestnut forests beyond the Berlin suburb of Wannsee, the forty-two competitors in the modern pentathlon event were spread across almost half a mile of woodland track as the leaders approached the final marker in the four-thousand-meter cross-country run. Out near the front the slim American, Lieutenant Charles Leonard, and the muscular Italian, Captain Silvano Abba, desperately forced the pace in an attempt to collect maximum points. Both knew this was the weakest event for their main rival, Handrick, the German gold-medal favorite.

About midway down the field Max Bishop, the leading British competitor, saw the fallen log at the bottom of the muddy slope and adjusted his pace to clear it. He could hear at his shoulder the labored breath of the second-string German, Alfred Horn. Four or five times already they had overtaken each other on the narrow pathways through the chestnut woods. Mud-spattered and already reeling with effort, both men knew that this last event was crucial. So close were their total points in the fencing, riding, shooting and swimming events that to lose to the other now would decide their placing at eighth or ninth.

Beyond the log Horn could see the fluttering white three-hundred-meter marker. He knew that if he were going to pull away from the Englishman, he would have to do so now. Sucking air through his teeth, disregarding the dead weight of his legs, he burst level with Bishop as the track widened, and headed for the log.

He could see now that half sunk in the bed of a

stream, it was stripped of bark, dangerously smooth and spattered with mud by the runners ahead.

Shoulder to shoulder, tensed against the looming danger of the log, both men hit the gravel bed of the stream simultaneously and threw their weight upward. Both men's running shoes found the log at the same moment. Then, as their bodies rose, Horn felt the squelch of mud beneath his foot. As his full weight came down, he skidded sideways on the log, sweeping Bishop's legs from under him. His momentum took him four or five paces on. Then, sliding to a halt, he scrambled around to where Bishop lay in the mud below the log.

Behind them, at the top of the slope, they could already hear the patter of running shoes on the muddy path. Horn stood, hesitating. A runner in red vest and shorts was pounding toward him. Two others had just turned the bend in the track. Bishop dragged himself into the scrub beside the path. "Run . . ." he said. "For God's sake." For a moment their eyes met and held. Then Horn turned and ran on toward the three-hundred-meter marker and the finish line beyond.

As Horn bent exhausted, recovering his breath, he watched the military ambulance, summoned by the race stewards, bump its way across the fields toward the chestnut wood. He had met Max Bishop just once, at the athletes' party after the opening ceremony. They had briefly shaken hands, but they had not spoken more than a few words. And now only an Olympic competitor could fully realize what he had done to Bishop. That single second meant not just two wasted years of training; equally important were the years of concentration on the event, the years of ambition—not to win but simply to take part.

And because of Horn, Bishop's chance of finishing the Games had been ruined. The chief steward had been informed of the incident. He would be going across to the hospital to make sure Bishop had no complaint before he posted the results. Horn pulled on his track suit and crossed toward the steward's car.

They had lunch together on the Adlon terrace later that morning, Bishop's plaster-covered foot sticking out from under the table.

"I'd like it," Horn said, "if you'd come and stay at my father's place for a while. See something of the real Germany."

"Isn't this the real Germany?" Bishop gestured at the swastikas lining the Kurfürstendamm.

Horn shook his head. "No. This is the froth. A brash, sometimes crude attempt to show the world we've got our self-confidence back."

Bishop nodded soberly. "I hope you're right. A lot of people in my country feel all this goes pretty deep."

"It's just show," Horn said firmly. "I think this Olympic Games is the turning point. Winning here will be enough. The Germany I know won't need to give the world further proof."

One

April 5, 1941. At five thousand feet above the Dutch island of Terschelling, the flight of black twin-engine Me. 110s banked southeast across the Wadden See toward their Friesland base at Berlikum. The weak March daylight was fading fast now, and ragged patches of mist drifted off the gray coastal waters below them.

At the control of the lead aircraft, Captain Alfred Horn flicked his intercom to speak to his gunner/navigator, Lieutenant Marius Brinkmann: "How about some music?"

"Anything to take the taste of that out of my mouth," Brinkmann said bitterly. "Do we always have to turn and run?"

Horn spun the R/T dial to pick up the BBC. Mantovani had an hour's program of dance music at about this time: not Artie Shaw, but far better than the pedestrian stuff recorded from Berlin's Adlon Hotel. The strains of "A Nightingale Sang in Berkeley Square" crackled through the set.

Berkeley Square. Yes, he had been there once before the war with his mother on their last holiday before she died. A grand old German-American lady who detested the British but always visited their island to buy their clothes and ape their ways.

Berkeley Square. That's where the bombers they

had just left, the Heinkels and Dorniers, were heading. Berkeley Square, Piccadilly, Fleet Street, the East End docks. . . .

"Suicide," Brinkmann said behind him. "And they must know it."

Alfred Horn nodded, although the armor plating at the back of his seat prevented Brinkmann from registering his agreement. The whole Berlikum Me. 110 wing, thirty-six fighters, had just conducted ten squadrons of bombers out across the North Sea. At the limit of the Messerschmitts' fighting range, they had as usual turned back to leave the bombers to fly on alone—also as usual—toward the swarm of waiting Spitfires and Hurricanes glinting in the setting sunlight—twenty kilometers beyond the Messerschmitts' effective range. How many bomber crews, he wondered, would fail to make it back to the Dutch coast tonight?

Horn moved the stick forward to put the Messerschmitt into a controlled dive toward Berlikum. He thought how much he'd like to tell Goering, *unter vier Augen*—"under four eyes," as they said—face to face, what he thought of his insane daylight air tactics. Luftflotte III, the most powerful air fleet in the world, was being whittled away to nothing by the lack of a long-range escort fighter.

The flatlands of Friesland spread below him as he leveled off at two hundred meters. The Berlikum church spire was dead ahead. He dropped the undercarriage, lost another one hundred meters of height and skipped across the canal to touch the concrete strip in a landing which would bring him without taxiing to within a few meters of Hangar 5. Captain Alfred Horn, holder of the Knight's Cross, was one of the Berlikum Wing's most skilled pilots.

After no-contact operations like today's, only the wing leader, Major Thalmann, would attend debriefing with Hans Forster, the station intelligence officer. The rest of the pilots, strolling toward the officers' club now, in their black leather jackets and white silk scarves, were free until tomorrow evening. "Same time, same place," young Brinkmann used to say, "and a hell of a lot of good it does the bomber boys."

But Horn was already thinking of other things. In the little gabled market town of Leuwarden, a few kilometers east of Berlikum, he had recently met a young Dutch widow. Lotte Meering was blond, shapely and one of the few Dutch girls he had met who did not spurn a German lover. He had already decided, high over the North Sea, that he'd have a few schnapps in the club to unwind, then borrow one of the station motorcycles and ride over to Leuwarden. There was nothing like an operational flight to make him, like fighter pilots the world over, feel the need for a woman's company.

In the club he and Brinkmann were first to reach the bar. As Hans, the mess barman, pushed two schnapps toward them, Captain Forster, the intelligence officer, crossed quickly toward Horn.

"Alfred. . . ." Forster drew him aside by the arm.

"Why aren't you in debriefing?" Horn turned savagely on his friend. "Tired of hearing the same old story? Two squadrons of Tommies waiting just out of range?"

Forster shook his head. "I was waiting for you. The Commandant wants to see you right away. He's got an army man with him named Pintsch. Alfred, you haven't been sounding off again about tactics—to that Dutch bit you're screwing, for instance?" Forster looked genuinely worried.

Horn downed his schnapps. From his silver case he took a cigarette. "What makes you say that?"

"The army man has a certain air about him. Treats the Commandant as an equal although he's only same as us, a Captain."

"You mean he's a policeman?" Horn lit his cigarette a little too casually.

"Could be."

"Not SS?"

"No. Abwehr, maybe."

Horn shrugged. Compared with the SS thugs, Military Intelligence were gentlemen. "I'll go and see what he's got to say."

"Let me know," Forster said. "If it's any sort of security matter, I should be consulted."

Horn left the club as the bulk of the young pilots came laughing and pushing through the doors. They were mostly in their early twenties, seven or eight years younger than Horn, whose salad days had been spent in different ways, in training for the Olympics of 1936.

The adjutant knocked on the Commandant's door and opened it.

"Hauptmann Horn, Herr Oberst."

He gave Horn a friendly push.

"Come in, Alfred." The Commandant was long past flying. He had lost a foot in the first days of the Polish campaign and since then grown fat on good food and memories. Today his face was composed and formal. "Alfred, I want to present you to Hauptmann Pintsch. . . ." And as the two Captains shook hands, the Commandant continued, "Captain Pintsch has shown me his credentials. I want to stress that I am completely satisfied by the authority vested in him."

"You are unmarried, Captain Horn?" Pintsch took over without apology to the Commandant. Horn saw what Forster had meant.

"Yes. Unmarried."

"And both your parents are dead?"

"Yes."

"Your mother was an American?"

"German-American. There's a considerable difference."

"You speak English?"

"Of course."

"How well?"

"As well as I speak German."

A silence fell on the darkening room. The Commandant turned on the unshaded electric light and limped quickly to draw the blackout curtains. Pintsch studied the man seated casually before him, one arm hanging over the back of the chair. He was tall for a fighter pilot, dark-haired and with an easy smile when he talked to the Commandant that showed he was no formal, regimental officer. Then few of these fliers were. If he'd been told more about his own mission, Pintsch reflected sourly, he wouldn't be choosing a man in the dark like this. But it seemed to add up to what was wanted: English-speaking, an outstanding flier, a man just into his thirties, a man prepared to sacrifice his life for Germany—as a holder of the Knight's Cross he'd presumably proved more than willing to do that.

Pintsch nodded to himself. Yes, Alfred Horn would be the man.

"I hate to deprive you of your most experienced pilot," he said to the Commandant.

"Am I permitted to know what we are discussing?" Horn said irritably.

"No. I'm afraid that goes beyond my orders," Pintsch said. "I am using my authority to transfer you to Munich. More accurately to Augsburg. This assignment, Captain, is not without considerable danger. By its nature you have the right of refusal."

Suddenly Horn understood. At Augsburg the irrepressible Professor Willy Messerschmitt worked on his fighter prototypes. Test piloting new designs was one of the most rewarding occupations an airman could imagine. It was also one of the most dangerous.

Horn smiled. "Augsburg. Thirty kilometers from Munich and some of the most attractive girls in the world. No. I accept."

Hauptmann Pintsch smiled, too. "There are attractive girls all over the world, Captain. I hear you've even been lucky here in Holland."

Horn inclined his head.

She cried when he told her the news. Not for long—and the tears seemed to dry more quickly as he told her how often his friend Hans Forster had admired her. As he slid from under the duvet for the last time, he promised Lotte he would ask Hans to look after her. She thought Forster a definite second-best to the good-looking Alfred Horn, but it was wartime, and she knew she had to be content.

Afterward he remembered that the car Pintsch brought to drive him to Augsburg first made him think there was something more to his transfer than a tour as one of Willy Messerschmitt's test pilots. It was a powerful supercharged five-liter Mercedes, gleaming brown and beige—five liters when fuel was strictly rationed and taxis, even in Germany itself, all carried a wood-burning gas production unit strapped precariously on an improvised roof rack.

But as his airman servant loaded his cases into the trunk, Horn's questions about the car were bluntly parried by Pintsch. And on the long journey, when Pintsch had cut in the supercharger and the car seemed to glide along the ribbon autobahn toward the south, the conversation remained general, despite Horn's attempts to prize scraps of information from the other man.

He soon found, however, that Pintsch was remarkably well informed about the war. In particular he seemed to understand, as most of Horn's fellow officers simply didn't, the immense productive capacity of the United States. At this point in April 1941 a tiny part of American war potential was reaching Britain—but it was already doing much to keep the island afloat. If America should enter the war against us, Pintsch said, Germany could be fighting for her life within two years. To Alfred Horn, who'd traveled

America as a child, who'd visited the vast automobile plants at Detroit and seen the oil gush in Texas, what Pintsch was saying made sense. He hoped that whatever bigwig put this Mercedes at their disposal understood things as clearly.

On arriving in Munich, Horn was billeted in a small hotel off the Leopoldstrasse and given indefinite furlough, with the proviso that he should never travel more than a hundred kilometers from Munich and that he should keep Pintsch informed of his whereabouts at all times. Before his leave began, he was required to visit a small tailor in Geltendorf who recorded his measurements with great care and refused to say a word about the purpose of the whole visit. Throughout the month of April, as spring struggled to fight off the most severe winter Bavaria had seen for a decade, Horn squandered his pay in the café-clubs of wartime Munich, read Shakespeare and Goethe, skied sometimes and wondered always about the fate Pintsch and his mysterious superiors had in store for him.

Friday, May 9, 1941. As Horn strolled back toward his hotel, the afternoon sunlight, almost for the first time that spring, was warm enough for him to be out without his Luftwaffe topcoat. The girls wore lighter clothes, and the noncommissioned soldiers who thronged the streets looked red-faced and hot in their thick gray serge uniforms.

Lonely and bored by the weeks of inactivity, Horn had tried to keep abreast of the latest war news, knowing enough to realize newspaper headlines like LUFTWAFFE PRESS HOME ATTACKS ON LONDON AGAINST MINIMAL OPPOSITION OR ANOTHER THIRTY-SEVEN ENEMY AIRCRAFT DESTROYED and ENGLAND BUCKLES UNDER GOERING'S HEROES were at best heavily biased propaganda, possibly outright lies.

As he threaded his way through the crowd in front of the Feldherrnhalle, a hand touched his shoulder. He turned to see Hans Forster, the intelligence officer from Berlikum, smilingly extending his hand.

"Hans." Horn grasped his friend's hand.

"Alfred, I've been trying to catch up with you for days."

"It's good to see you. What are you doing in Munich?"

"I managed to scrounge a week's leave."

Horn remembered Forster's parents lived on the outskirts of the city near Forstenried Park.

"How much time have you got left?"

"I'm due back at twenty-four hundred hours tomorrow."

"That gives us time to get drunk and sober up at least twice."

As the waiter served their third beer and second plate of sausage and sauerkraut at an outside table in a small beer garden overlooking the river Isar, Horn studied his friend. He looked older, his face drawn. Something seemed to have faded from his eyes.

"How's the squadron? How's old Wallner?" Horn asked cheerfully.

"The Commandant . . . fatter than ever. I swear he's put on five kilos since you left."

"And Lotte?"

"Lotte's fine, she sends her love. You did me a favor there, Alfred."

"I can see that by your bloodshot eyes, you old ram."

They drank from their steins of beer.

"What about Marius?" said Horn, wiping his mouth. "Who did he team up with?"

"Brinkmann?"

Horn nodded.

The sudden change in Forster's expression gave him his answer.

"What happened?"

"He went down in the North Sea."

They sat in silence. Forster took a cigarette from a gun-metal case.

"It's getting worse, Alfred. We're flying five, sometimes six missions a day, servicing standards are down, the replacement crews are raw recruits, morale's not good."

"This isn't like you, Hans," said Horn, noticing the nervous fingers playing with the unlit cigarette in Forster's hand.

Forster hesitated. "I fixed my leave to coincide with my father's. We've talked a lot in the last few days," he said after a moment.

Horn knew Forster's father was a General in Military Intelligence, well placed to know what was happening on a much higher level than Horn aspired to.

"Apparently quite a number of the General Staff feel we should call it a day here and now," Forster said carefully.

"An armistice?"

"Let's say peace on very favorable terms. We're lining up a formidable list of enemies, Alfred."

"None of them counts for much except Britain."

"Things could change," Forster said.

Horn looked at him across the beer mug. "Something your father told you?"

Forster nodded, already aware he'd said too much.

"You think Germany's in trouble?" Horn asked carefully.

"Some people think we're fighting a war we cannot win," his friend said flatly.

Forster turned away to stare out across the gardens lining the river.

Horn drained his beer mug. "Listen, I thought someone mentioned something about getting drunk."

Die Ringelblume, the Marigold, was the first club they had hit upon. A converted cellar, it was badly lit and overcrowded. Horn and Forster had installed themselves at a table by the tiny stage from which they watched the floor show for the second time around. The tired performers were going through a tawdry routine, an insipid leftover from the brash, brilliant decadence of the early thirties. In those days the libberal attitudes in Germany had attracted a horde of pleasure seekers, degenerates and sexual nonconformists of all kinds, and in the underground clubs and theaters that had sprung up in Berlin they had generated a biting, sparkling series of satirical revues. Then the Nazis had suddenly clamped down, and the artistes and their followers had been forced to scatter. Some had fled to the provinces to start up pale imitations of the original, such as Die Ringelblume.

The actors were nearing the end of a sketch, a complicated affair between a husband, his wife and the husband's best friend. It tried to squeeze humor from tired dialogue which revealed the husband as queer, the wife as lesbian and the friend as a transvestite and culminated with various items of clothing being exchanged among the three.

Horn found the piece had not improved, seeing it for the second time and several bottles of doubtful champagne later. Except for a few suppressed titters from a group of middle-aged men at the bar, and the occasional roar from a crowd of drunken Wehrmacht cadet officers in a corner, the audience had lost interest and chatted loudly among themselves. With a heavy veil of tobacco smoke choking the air Horn became aware of raised voices as an argument started nearby. It was almost 2:00 A.M. and he thought it was time to leave. Forster was very drunk and busily engaged in slurring his life history into the ear of a plump blonde with a pretty round face and full, overpainted lips. She eyed Horn over Forster's shoulder, pursing the painted lips into an inviting pout.

"It's getting late," Horn said, shaking Forster by the arm.

"What?" said Forster, staring around at him. "What is?"

"I'd better take you home."

"Home. Who wants to go home?"

"Let's get out of here."

"Nonsense. What we need is more champagne."

The girl, who worked on a commission from what she could get the customers to spend, immediately took up the cue and called shrilly, "Herr Ober!"

A bored waiter, serving the cadets with another swilling tray of beer, acknowledged her call with a curt nod.

"Let's go, Hans."

Forster, who had seemed determined to lose himself in alcohol from the moment he walked through the door, waved dismissively, then hiccuped and buried his face in mock shame in the blonde's bosom.

The performers had given up the unequal struggle and retreated from the stage. The cadets broke into a song, their lusty off-key voices croaking with drink.

> A thousand miles from Hamburg
> A lonely soldier lad
> Lies dreaming of the Reeperbahn
> And all the girls he's had . . .

They linked arms and threw their heads back for the chorus "Oh. . . ."

Horn smiled to himself. He was familiar with the tune but knew a Luftwaffe version of the words. Marius Brinkmann used to render it in the mess when the schnapps had loosened his inhibitions. Brinkmann, twenty-two years old—they had flown a lot of hours together. It could be me beside him at the bottom of the sea, thought Horn. Damn the war.

The waiter was at his side. "You wanted more champagne, sir?"

"Why not?" he said.

It was almost midday when he arrived back at his hotel. He had finally got Forster back to his parents' house at dawn, sobered him up with steaming mugs of black coffee, helped him change into a fresh uniform and driven with him by taxi to the Munich Bahnhof.

As they waited for the train, they had said little, and their final handshake had been tentative and awkward. Each felt in some strange way a finality about the parting. Neither mentioned the short conversation of the day before.

In his hotel room Pintsch was waiting, sitting very upright in a chair. "You were told to leave word where you could be found at all times."

Horn stared at him for a moment and then exploded. "Listen to me, Pintsch. I've had enough of this schoolboy treatment. I'm a flier. I came here to test-fly for Messerschmitt, and I haven't even been near Augsburg. So write me some new orders. I want to go back on operations."

Pintsch stood up and carefully smoothed his already immaculate uniform.

"You're going to Augsburg this afternoon," he said. "Your orders have just come through."

Horn nodded in satisfaction. "At last."

"You'll be picked up at fifteen-thirty hours."

In his enthusiasm Horn failed to notice Pintsch's expression was more thoughtful than ever.

At four-fifteen that afternoon a dark green Volkswagen with Munich military district number plates left the autobahn at Augsburg and took the branch road past the low-lying Messerschmitt factory. It was a Saturday afternoon, and apart from a few freely patrolling sentries who stopped and watched the Volkswagen pass, the huge works had a deserted air. But then this was 1941 . . . it would be another two years before German war industry would be working weekends and night shifts in a doomed effort to keep up with the flow of war matériel from the United States.

A few hundred meters farther on, the road ended at a black and white timber boom, the entrance to Professor Messerschmitt's small test airfield. The driver stopped and handed his pass to one of the sentries, who glanced at it, then saluted briskly as he saw the Luftwaffe Captain with the *Ritterkreuz* at his throat sitting in the passenger seat.

The boom rose, and the Volkswagen drove around the asphalt perimeter track to the huddle of wooden administrative buildings on the far side of the field. A single Me. 110 stood on the concrete apron outside the hangars, and even at a distance of several hundred yards Horn could see that it had been modified to carry a pair of bright aluminum fuel tanks slung under each wing. Through the partly opened doors of the main hangar he could make out what appeared to be a British Mark II Spitfire being dissected to probe the secrets of its remarkable performance. A chance to fly Spitfires or the newest long-range Me. 110s . . . for that, Horn decided, the long wait in Munich had been well worthwhile.

At the administration block Pintsch was waiting for him. As he climbed out of the Volkswagen, Horn noticed how anxiously Pintsch glanced up at the cloud cover which was beginning to drift in from the east. Horn slammed the car door behind him and moved toward the other man. They shook hands briefly.

Pintsch led the way through cream-and-green-painted corridors until they reached a small pilots' changing room. To Horn's astonishment the man who rose to click his heels in greeting was the tailor from Geltendorf. He turned to Pintsch with a baffled smile.

"Herr Wirkner will fit you up," Pintsch said briskly. "I'll be in the office across the corridor."

"If the Hauptmann would be so kind. . . ." The tailor lifted his hand to indicate that Horn should remove his jacket. Unbuttoning it slowly, Horn heard Pintsch close the door behind him. He handed the jacket to the tailor, deciding against asking him what all the mystery was about. He would have the answer soon enough—the moment the tailor's cardboard box was opened.

The tailor hung the jacket on the back of a chair and extended his hand. "Your *Ritterkreuz*, please, Herr Hauptmann." Horn unhooked the Knight's Cross from around his neck and placed it on the table.

"And your shirt and tie."

"I'm to get a full outfit then, am I?" Horn said with a smile, but the tailor merely nodded agreement and turned to open the cardboard box.

To cover his curiosity, Horn turned casually away and bent to take his cigarette case and lighter from his jacket on the back of the chair. Lighting a cigarette, he turned again to see the tailor holding out to him a pale brown shirt of the type worn by the Sturm Abteilung, once the all-powerful bullyboys of the Nazi Party until Hitler had clipped their wings and elevated the black-uniformed SS in their place.

Horn put on the shirt, noting its quality and fit, and tied the dark brown tie. Now he was certain. Brown was the uniform color of Nazi Party members. He himself had never been a member, had never wanted to be. "Look," he said to the tailor, "I'm not a Party member. I'm a Luftwaffe officer."

"My orders, Herr Hauptmann." The tailor smiled apologetically.

Horn knew he would have to wait to get the full story from Pintsch. He grunted irritably and walked out across the corridor, wearing the brown shirt and light civilian-type trousers. Over his arm he carried a fur-lined black leather flying suit.

He threw open the door with enough force to make Pintsch and the civilian with him leap automatically to their feet.

"It's time I knew," Horn said, ignoring the civilian and addressing himself solely to Pintsch. "It's time I knew what the devil's going on."

"This is Herr Piel," Pintsch said unhurriedly, "he's the works manager here."

Horn nodded briefly. Then he turned back to Pintsch. "Well, Pintsch? First, what's the point of these extraordinary clothes? I am not a Party member, if that's what they're supposed to indicate. I take no part in politics at all."

"Hauptmann Horn," Pintsch said formally, "your Commandant at Berlikum placed you under my command. You will receive your explanations in due course. Until then I order you to cooperate without question."

Horn glared at him. "So this is what I volunteered for?"

Pintsch nodded briefly. But his expression remained unchanged. "Hauptmann Alfred Horn. I have been commanded to administer to you the Führer Oath."

Horn stared blankly, then shook his head. "I took the Führer Oath when I was commissioned. You don't take oaths twice. What's going on, Pintsch?"

"Please raise your right hand."

Frowning, Horn brought his hand up to shoulder height.

"I hereby swear complete and undying allegiance to Adolf Hitler, Führer of the German Reich and Volk, and to the leadership of the National Socialist Party appointed by him."

Horn dropped his hand abruptly. "Officers swear allegiance to the Führer as Commander-in-Chief. Not as leader of the Nazi Party."

"You refuse the oath?" Pintsch said.

Horn felt Herr Piel stiffen.

"Come on now, Pintsch," Horn said. "We've got to know each other pretty well. You're asking me to swear a completely different sort of oath, and you know it. You're asking me to swear obedience to the leadership of the Nazi Party."

"Those are my orders."

"Who from?"

"Horn, I have to ask you again—do you refuse the oath?"

It occurred briefly to Horn that Herr Piel, watching the two Captains in fascinated silence, might not be the Messerschmitt works manager at all . . . might in fact be a member of the local Sicherheitdienst, the Gestapo's equally unpleasant SS equivalent. At this time in Germany it was not an uncommon suspicion when strangers were present at any vaguely political discussion.

"I accept the oath," he said slowly. "But as a Luftwaffe officer I protest about the form of the oath."

"Good enough," Pintsch said. "Raise your hand."

Horn again raised his hand and this time repeated after Pintsch the formula of allegiance.

Pintsch relaxed into a troubled smile and extended his hand. "I'm sorry about the mystery, Horn. Believe me, it's necessary."

They shook hands. Horn realized by the firmness of the grip that he was being wished good luck. "Get your flying suit on. Herr Piel will take you out to the aircraft. *Auf wiedersehen*, Alfred."

He turned quickly and left the room. The use of first names among German officers was normally restricted to particularly close friends. Alfred Horn felt his throat contract in fear. Pintsch was apologizing for whatever was about to happen to him. Perhaps the Me. 110 out there had been modified to the extreme limits of safety. But then what was he doing wearing this hodgepodge of Nazi Party uniform and, if that's what it was, why no insignia or badge of rank? Why had they carefully retained his Knight's Cross?

"May I show you the aircraft, Herr Hauptmann?" Piel's voice broke across his thoughts. He nodded and pulled on the black leather flying suit. Zipping it to chest level, he followed Piel out of the office, along the cream-and-green-painted corridors and out onto the perimeter road. There was no sign of his car or driver. Instead, an army *Kübelwagen* stood ready to carry them across to the waiting Messerschmitt. Alfred Horn checked his watch as he climbed out of the *Kübelwagen* and stood beside the gray-painted Me. 110. It was 1650 hours. Ten minutes to five in the early evening of May 10, 1941.

He turned to the man next to him. "Herr Piel, I have no flight plan, no maps, no test instructions and not the first idea of what I'm supposed to do."

"If you will take the gunner's seat. . . ." Piel indicated the rear-facing gunner/navigator position.

Horn grunted and swung himself up on the footgrips machined into the fuselage of the aircraft and slid into the seat. He had flown navigator/instructor a hundred times; the position was almost as familiar to him as the pilot's seat.

A light wind caught the wings of the Messerschmitt and rocked it slightly. As Piel handed him up his leather flying helmet, Horn looked out across the airfield and saw the familiar brown five-liter Mercedes follow the perimeter road, then turn out along the concrete runway on which the Messerschmitt was standing. It stopped some twenty meters from the Messerschmitt, out of Horn's line of sight.

Pintsch climbed quickly from the back seat and opened the passenger door. A tall man in black leather flying overalls got out. While he stood looking up at the changing cloud patterns pursued by the freshening wind across the sky, Pintsch took from the chauffeur a blue Luftwaffe weather report folder and waited silently. After a few seconds the tall man drew two brown envelopes from inside his flying overalls and handed them to his adjutant. "The first envelope has your name on it, Pintsch. Wait until we are airborne, then open it. It will give you instructions about what to do with the second, blank envelope."

"I understand, Herr Stellvertreter," Pintsch said.

Without a further word, the tall man took the weather report from Pintsch and with a brief smile walked across to the Messerschmitt.

Alfred Horn felt the plane rock as someone climbed

into the pilot's seat. He spoke over his shoulder as he heard the Perspex canopy slide close. "I hope you know more about this flight than they've decided to tell me."

"Yes," a voice said. "I know a great deal more."

Under the rim of his leather flying helmet Horn raised his eyebrows. The tone of the pilot's voice was certainly not inviting further questions.

Facing backward, Horn heard the familiar contact procedures as the twin Daimler-Benz engines were started and felt the fast forward movement as the chocks were pulled from under the wheels. Within seconds they were bouncing down the runway. Twelve, fifteen seconds until the tail rose, another five before the aircraft lifted clear of the ground.

Standing beside the big Mercedes, Pintsch watched the Messerschmitt climb toward the low cloud. After a few moments he climbed into the back of the car and drew out the two letters. The first was inscribed "Hauptmann Karlheinz Pintsch." He tore it open and took out a folded sheet of white paper.

For a few seconds he stared down numbly at the half dozen lines scrawled on the sheet of paper, unaware that the chauffeur had turned in the front seat to watch him.

Pintsch focused again on the large rounded handwriting. For him, Karlheinz Pintsch, he knew it could be an unwitting death warrant. It read:

> The second letter explains my mission and my purpose to Adolf Hitler. Wait four hours from takeoff, and if I have not returned, deliver the unaddressed envelope personally into the hand of the Führer at Berchtesgaden.

In the Me. 110 the pilot spoke over the radio to the Augsburg field. "We are airborne at one thousand meters."

To Alfred Horn in the rear seat the phrase had

a strangely old-fashioned ring. Surely that was World War I terminology? He twisted in his straps to peer around the armor-plated backing of the pilot's seat. The man at the controls turned his head slightly at that moment and looked down toward the ground below. Alfred Horn had never seen him in person before, but the features were nevertheless unmistakable. They were those of the man who carried the designation Stellvertreter, member of the Defense Council, Nazi Party member No. 7, second only to Adolf Hitler in the German Reich. Deputy Führer Rudolf Hess.

Two

May 10, 1941. Weighed down by an extra fourteen hundred liters of fuel in the auxiliary tanks, the Messerschmitt 110 clawed its way to six thousand feet, its two-thousand-horsepower engines at full throttle. Rudolf Hess was an accomplished pilot. He had served in the First World War, flying the fragile biplanes of the period, and had kept his hand in ever since. At one time he had even considered an east-west solo flight across the Atlantic after Lindbergh's success in the opposite direction. He checked the dashboard compass and set a course for Frankfurt.

Behind him Alfred Horn stared out past the twin tail fins at an empty sky, his mind a tangle of confused ideas. One image kept returning: the moment soon after takeoff when Horn had recognized the Deputy Führer. Hess had felt his look and had turned almost full face to him, and in that moment the gaunt, dark features had been broken by a smile. Horn had seen the hollow cheeks, the piercing, sunken eyes a hundred times before, staring grimly out from newspapers and magazines or caught for posterity by the newsreel cameras. But the shock of that sudden smile had been almost physical. The Deputy Führer had buckteeth.

A voice crackled over the intercom. "Are you all right, Hauptmann Horn?"

"Yes, Stellvertreter." Horn's voice was thick. He felt an urge to clear his throat but suppressed it.

"You were asking about our mission." Hess seemed relaxed and good-humored.

Horn imagined those tight lips parting again in the ridiculous buck-toothed grin. "Yes, Stellvertreter."

"This is the flight plan." Hess handed back a clipboard. On top was a folded map. As Horn took it, he noted the heavy gold identity bracelet on the right wrist, the strong fingers, the thick black hair on the back of the hand.

Horn stared down at the map. The flight path had been drawn in red. It arrowed northwest past Frankfurt and Dortmund and on into Holland. Perhaps that was the answer. It was some sort of proving flight. After all, the Me. 110 had been heavily modified, its guns removed, the additional fuel tanks fitted. It was a long-range test flight. But if that were the case, why the veil of secrecy, why was he required to re-swear the oath, why the unmarked uniform and why was Rudolf Hess at the controls?

The red line continued to the edge of the paper. Horn pulled the map clear of the spring clip and turned it over. The flight path plunged on across the North Sea; then just below latitude 56 degrees north it veered due west and crossed the Scottish coast just above Holy Island, then on to finish in Ayrshire.

Scotland! Horn found it impossible to ask himself even the simplest of questions. In navigation terms the prevailing winds offered difficulties but were not insuperable. But fuel supply—that was different. To correct course against wind force meant extra fuel consumption. And how much were they carrying in the pods under the wings? Again they would clearly be landing on a Dutch coastal airstrip for final refueling before they crossed the North Sea. Last of all, he had no idea what modifications Willy Messerschmitt had developed to improve fuel consumption efficiency. And it was obvious that he wasn't expected to know.

He was on this flight simply as a navigator. That much was clear.

"Any problems?" The Deputy Führer's voice came over the intercom.

"No, Stellvertreter."

The early evening cloud cover promised by the weather report was light and patchy, and navigation over land was no problem. As they flew over the German-Dutch border, Horn recognized familiar ground and noted they were within a few miles of the charted course. The last thirty minutes had passed in silence. Horn had now thought of a dozen questions to ask but said nothing. Hess handed back coffee in a Thermos. As the drab, neat flatness of Holland slipped by below, the intercom crackled to life again.

"Have you a wife?" asked Hess.

"No, Stellvertreter."

"You should have. A man should belong—to a family, to a party, to a cause."

"Yes, Stellvertreter."

A full ten seconds passed. Horn sensed that the Deputy Führer was considering his next pronouncement with great care, weighing the words in his mind.

"We are on a mission of vital importance to Germany. I want you to understand that, Horn."

For the first time since takeoff, Horn tried to force his brain to function normally. "I can believe it, Stellvertreter. I can't yet understand it."

Another long pause, then finally Hess replied.

"Have you heard of the Order of Maria Theresa?"

"I don't think so."

"It is an Austrian decoration, rarely bestowed. It can be won only for extreme bravery in an action in direct disobedience of orders. Do you understand?"

"Direct *disobedience* of orders?" repeated Horn.

"Exactly. We are both about to earn it, Hauptmann Horn. The Führer will pin it on our chests himself."

At that moment Horn looked down. They were passing over the Dutch coast. With a lurch in his

stomach Horn realized they had no intention of refueling in Holland.

Six thousand feet below, the cold gray expanse of
the North Sea stretched to the horizon. Horn had seen
it a hundred times before, looking exactly as it did
now in the soft light of early evening. The cockpit was
cold and cramped. They had already been in the air
for an hour and a half. Horn suddenly realized much
of the padding had been removed from his seat in
an effort to save every last ounce of dead weight.
His back and legs had begun to ache, but now that
they were flying over the sea these minor discomforts
were forgotten. Almost as a reflex Horn had tensed
for action. This was the battleground he knew well;
each cloud might conceal a marauding Hurricane or
Spitfire. Death could come from any quarter of the
sky. Almost every day for the last year Horn and his
fellow Luftwaffe pilots had flown out to do battle, ready to climb and dive in the elaborate, weaving
patterns of the dogfight. He knew that one mistake,
one unguarded moment could result in the aircraft's
plunging in flames toward the gray water below, to
sink forever into the dark depths. He scanned the sky,
feeling totally vulnerable. The Me. 110 was unarmed,
flying toward the enemy's fortress, piloted by a man
who had last experienced aerial combat twenty-five
years ago.

With no landmarks to pinpoint their position, navigation became more difficult. Horn used the powerful
radio that the Messerschmitt carried, tuning alter-
nately to the Luftwaffe's radio beam from Paris and
music from the station at Borgelund in Denmark,
then triangulating their position from these direc-
tional fixes. In some ways he was thankful that the
work kept him occupied: it left less time to think
about the extraordinary situation in which he found
himself. He fed Hess a small course correction over
the intercom. Hess eased the Me. 110's stub nose a
couple of points to the north, then checked his watch.

"Well, Hauptmann, we are at the point of no return."

Horn had received a series of jolting shocks during the course of the last few hours, but this was different. Perhaps it should not have come as a surprise. "Point of no return": the phrase had an ominous ring even at the best of times. The halfway point, the point after which there is no turning back. . . . In that one second Horn understood Pintsch's talk of danger and the insistence on his speaking English; the month of waiting in Munich for some suitable opportunity; mention of the Maria Theresa award. . . . This Messerschmitt had no particular long-range modifications, simply two extra fuel pods slung below the wings—enough to get to Scotland but with nothing to spare for a return journey.

Horn sat staring blankly at the distant Dutch coastline receding at two hundred miles an hour. The man in the pilot's seat was on a one-way flight to enemy territory. Worse, the Maria Theresa Cross meant he was flying without the permission or knowledge of Adolf Hitler. And he, Alfred Horn, was trapped in the navigator's seat.

It was almost 8:30 P.M. when Horn told the Deputy Führer he estimated their position as 55°64' N. Hess acknowledged and banked the Me. 110 onto a new course, due west, then dropped down to an altitude of one hundred feet to fly in below the British radar. The sea was stirring under an increasing swell, the wave tops breaking into flecks of white in a stiffening southwest breeze. Horn shifted uneasily in his seat—the weather forecast from Goering's HQ in Berlin had predicted clouds, but the sky ahead was as clear as a blank sheet of blue paper.

The Spitfire was several thousand feet above them and almost directly astern when Horn first spotted it. All he saw was the glint of light on metal as the sun caught the wings for a fleeting moment, but it was enough. He knew at once they were in trouble.

"Spitfire!" He yelled the word into the intercom.

In level flight the stripped-down Me. 110 could match or even outpace the British fighter, but with the Spitfire's height advantage giving vital extra speed in an attack dive, there was no chance they could outrun it. In aerial combat the mind narrows, excluding every other consideration but the necessity to outfly the enemy. As he watched the Spitfire begin its dive, Horn began automatically to relay information in a level tone: "Dead astern. Fifteen hundred meters . . . one thousand. . . ."

Hess, despite his forty-eight years, had acted fast at the first urgent report of danger. He jettisoned the two cylindrical fuel tanks to gain a few precious extra mph of airspeed; then he took the Me. 110 down to within ten feet of the rolling gray water. There was a chance the Spitfire might play it safe and pull out of its dive too early, overflying the Messerschmitt without getting in a telling burst from its four wing-mounted twenty-millimeter cannon. Or an even slimmer chance that the pilot might leave it a fraction of a second too late and crash into the sea.

Horn felt a tight dryness in his throat and a thin sweat of fear on his brow as he watched the attacker relentlessly closing in.

"Stand by for evasive action," he ordered sharply over the intercom, all thought of deference to the Deputy Führer forgotten.

The Spitfire, perfectly positioned, was holding its fire. Perhaps the pilot had seen that the two rear-mounted guns the navigator would normally have at his disposal had been removed. The British fighter, its powerful Merlin engine at full revs, had leveled out four hundred feet back, dead center behind them, and was still closing. Horn could see the pilot clearly; he had a bright blue scarf tied loosely at the neck. And he was taking his time.

The telltale flashes from the twin muzzles in each wing brought an almost instantaneous "Go left" from Horn. He was gambling. From the way the RAF pilot handled his plane Horn guessed that he was left-handed. It would be easier for a left-hander to follow a sharp right turn; it was one of the tricks of the trade that veterans like Horn had learned the hard way.

Hess went left with a vengeance. The port wing of the Me. 110 clipped the white-flecked top of a wave, and the aircraft shuddered until Hess regained control.

The Spitfire was following hard, but the Messerschmitt's violent maneuver had gained valuable distance. Banking to reengage, the British pilot was forced to make a wider arc, and his first burst of fire seemed to Horn to have been ill-aimed. But he had forgotten his pilot's lack of experience. Where a Luftwaffe fighter pilot would have brought up the nose to avoid the stream of tracer shells speeding toward them, Hess was still struggling to keep the Messerschmitt clear of the waves.

Five shells exploded in the body of the Messerschmitt, tearing holes in the metal skin, but as far as Horn could judge, they had not damaged the vital aileron leads which would make control impossible. Then he smelled aviation fuel.

For five seconds, as the Spitfire maneuvered for a second attack, Horn waited for the Messerschmitt to burst into flame. Then he knew the self-sealing device in the tanks was effective.

In the pilot's seat, Hess stared through the brine smashing against the windshield as it whipped up from the wave tops. A dark mass seemed to loom up toward him, distorted by the water streaming across the curved Perspex. Sea mist or cliff face—in a moment of what could have been fatal hesitation he leaned forward, screwing up his eyes, oblivious of Horn's warning on the intercom: "Left, Stellvertreter. Left!"

He heard one single cannon shell explode somewhere beneath his feet before the dark mass ahead seemed to swoop around them, sucking them in. Behind him, Horn, unaware of its approach, suddenly found the gray sea mist, churned by the aircraft's propellers, swirling around them with elemental turbulence. The Spitfire might have been a million miles away.

But the mist that had saved them nearly evened the score. Suddenly they were clear, heading straight into the blazing face of a setting sun. Hess saw the jagged line of cliffs when they were no more than one hundred yards short. He wrenched the stick back into his stomach with such force it partially winded him. The Me. 110 surged upward and cleared the granite mass with four feet to spare. It was over before Horn realized what was happening. Now they were racing in at treetop height, over the fields, woods, clumps of houses, roads and farms. Two people, standing by a gate, flashed by. Horn watched the figures, a man and a woman, retreating into the distance. They were standing close, waving a greeting to the fliers, until their arms dropped to their sides as they saw the black crosses on the Messerschmitt's wings and fuselage.

"That was close, Horn. Very close," Hess said calmly over the intercom.

Horn didn't feel he needed reminding.

"Providence, Horn. I feel the hand of Providence."

Horn scanned the clumps of cloud forming above them and began to consider seriously the possibility that Rudolf Hess was not entirely sane. It was not an easy thing for a man who had grown up in Germany even to entertain the thought that one of the most senior members of the leadership was anything but far-seeing and totally stable. But the prospect of becoming a prisoner of war loomed large in Alfred Horn's mind. And he could see no intervention of Providence that was likely to prevent that. They held course.

The first sign of trouble was the sudden change of

36

note from the port engine. Hess glanced down at the instrumentation and saw the red warning light at once. "Oil pressure ten and dropping fast," he said as the starboard engine began to cough.

"That last shell," Horn said into the intercom. "What's the temperature reading on the port engine?"

"Both dials are in the red segment," Hess said.

Despite himself, Horn found himself admiring the man's courage. But whatever the real purpose of this flight, Alfred Horn had no intention of dying in a burning aircraft.

"Take her up," he said peremptorily.

"We'll be seen on the enemy radar."

"Take her up while we've still got power. It's our only chance."

Hess reluctantly pulled back the stick. The stricken Messerschmitt slowly toiled up to two thousand feet.

"Get the canopy off. We'll have to jump."

"No," said Hess, for the first time his voice showing the strain of fear.

Horn was tearing loose the canopy fasteners.

"I can't jump." Hess now had his voice under control again.

"You've got no choice. The engines are about to seize up."

The twin engines spluttered and missed in their last moments of life. Streams of blue smoke trailed back past the twin tailplanes.

Horn pushed the canopy free, and it sailed clear.

"Get your straps off, and turn her over," said Horn, yelling at the top of his voice against the screaming rush of air.

Hess did not seem to hear. He sat motionless. Horn yelled into the intercom, "You'll kill us both. Turn her over!" Some of the words seemed at last to get through. Hess, for the moment at least, appeared to regain some kind of self-control. He undid his safety straps, passed a bulky canvas bag to Horn, took a firm grip on a slim briefcase he had carried at his side since takeoff and with a sudden wrench of the controls rolled the plane over on its back.

The trick was to relax. As the aircraft turned turtle, Horn waited, knowing the force of gravity would pull him out. Suddenly he was clear, counting to three before pulling the ripcord in a positive flinging motion out across his chest. The chute opened with a reassuring smack above his head, and he began to take stock of the ground below.

In contrast, every muscle in the Deputy Führer's body had tightened as the Me. 110 rolled over. Now, in utter panic, he clawed at the sides of the cockpit with arms and legs, hanging grimly on as gravity tried to pull him down. Then the red-hot engines ground to a sudden stop. The only sound now was the violent rush of air. The stub nose began to angle down as the plane slowly started into its final dive. Every muscle in Hess's body ached with the strain of clinging on, as blood drained from his head, and the second most powerful man in the world passed out. It saved his life. His grip relaxed.

As the rush of cold air on his face brought him around, Hess realized he was falling, and on the verge of hysteria, he wrenched at the ripcord ring. It was his first—and last—drop.

The deep green foot-high grass of the hayfield crushed under Horn's feet as he landed safely. He quickly smothered the parachute, snapped open the quick release clip and pulled himself free of the harness. Then he looked around for Hess. The hanging light-blue mushroom was drifting down a good quarter of a mile to the west. Even at this distance he could see the Deputy Führer was in trouble. Throughout the Luftwaffe the standard issue parachute was a bad joke. The two main support straps met at a point just above the small of the back, so that the jumper hung like a grotesque puppet twisting in the unstable rig. Unless the parachutist were experienced enough to correct his position with body and leg movements, he would start to oscillate and then spin violently. Horn could see Hess spinning like a top, completely out of control. He would be lucky to avoid breaking half the bones in his body when he hit the ground. Horn set off at a run. Following the line of a hedge, he joined a track that led over an ivy-covered medieval pack bridge. As he skirted a small wood, he could see three or four hundred yards ahead the pale blue smudge of Hess's parachute half draped across a stone wall.

He found Hess leaning against the wall, holding the briefcase protectively to his chest, his face expressionless.

"Stellvertreter." Horn approached him breathing hard from the run across the fields. He could see that Hess was taking his full weight on his left leg. "Have you hurt your leg?"

"Yes." The Deputy Führer's voice seemed strained and distant.

"We must go. The British will have seen the parachutes."

"No, you go on alone."

Horn stared at Hess. Even half leaning against the wall, the Stellvertreter was a tall, imposing figure. His earlier doubts about the Deputy Führer's sanity suddenly dissolved.

"Take off your flying suit," said Hess. "We've not much time."

Horn pulled down the long zip and struggled out of the fur-lined flying suit. Standing there in his pale tan trousers and khaki shirt, he watched Hess lean awkwardly forward and pick up the canvas bag.

"You are to go to Prestwick Airport," Hess said. "Our contact will be waiting."

He delved into the canvas bag. Straightening up, grimacing with pain, he held out a dark brown military jacket and motioned for Horn to put it on. As he did so, Horn saw it had the insignia and bars of a Captain in the U.S. Army Air Force. Suddenly he understood the tan trousers and khaki shirt and tie.

And of course, as he slipped on the perfectly fitting jacket, he understood the point of the tailor in Munich. But that was the extent of his understanding. "Stellvertreter," he said, taking the uniform cap which Hess handed him, "I'm a Luftwaffe officer. In this uniform I can be shot as a spy."

Distantly, beyond the wood they heard voices calling to each other.

"You are now Captain John Vincent," Hess said, ignoring the remark. "You have one hour. You must get to Prestwick before ten-thirty. An American general, General Walker, is waiting there to receive us." With a sudden, almost reluctant gesture he thrust the briefcase into Horn's hands. "Give this briefcase to General Walker . . . unopened. I emphasize *unopened*. I require you to remember your oath."

One piece of the jigsaw suddenly fell into place. Horn saw the reason for the pressure put on him to swear the subtly different oath—to the leadership of the Third Reich, which had obviously always been intended to mean Rudolf Hess.

Both turned to the sound of men crashing through the trees and thick undergrowth of the small wood off to the right from where they stood.

Hess took a leather wallet from inside his flying jacket and handed it to Horn. "All the money you'll need," he said. "Go now."

"You will be taken prisoner."

"It does not matter. The war will be over in a month."

Hess pulled himself up as high as his injury would allow.

"Hauptmann, get that briefcase to Prestwick before ten-thirty. An unfathomable fate has decided that the future of Germany is now in your hands."

"Good-bye, Stellvertreter." Horn turned to go.

"Hauptmann. . . ." Hess's voice was sharp with authority. He raised his right arm. "Heil Hitler," he said quietly. Horn hesitated. As a Wehrmacht officer he had never given the Hitler salute in his life. The deepset eyes of the man opposite him glowed with exigent fervor.

Horn lifted his hand, barely above waist height. "Heil Hitler," he said, and turned to run along the stone wall, looking for the nearest gap.

The approaching men were less than a hundred yards away now. Hess exhaled deeply, then flung the canvas bag as far as he could manage over the wall into the hayfield beyond. Then he unfastened the gold identity bracelet from his right wrist. The front was beautifully engraved with an elaborate "RH." He held it in the palm of his hand for a few moments, then turned it over to see the inscription. His mind slipped back, as it did so easily to the early days. They had been good, although they were in prison. They had been close then, very close. Brothers.

The men were very near now, stumbling out of the edge of the wood. Turning painfully, Hess tossed the bracelet into a ditch that ran along the other side of the wall. For a brief moment before it sank into the mud and slime the reverse side glistened in the low light of the dying sun, picking out the inscription: "With Affection. To R. H. from Wolf."

Alex McLean had been walking with his dog when the Messerschmitt had whistled out of the sky and skidded across a field of young corn one hundred yards from where he stood.

As one wing was torn off and burst into flames, McLean had thrown himself flat. Lifting his head warily, he had seen a single parachute disappear behind the trees about half a mile away in the direction of Eaglesham. Now, having scrambled to his feet, he began to run in the direction of the village.

John Angus had been digging in his back garden when the Messerschmitt had almost hit the chimney of his cottage. He had clearly seen the black German crosses on the silver underwing and the parachutist drifting down in the evening sky. Dropping his spade, he had started across the fields toward Eaglesham when he saw Alex McLean running in the same direction.

Billy Wilson, an off-duty fireman, had also seen the parachute. Now, abandoning his bicycle, he snatched a heavy stick from the hedge and ran across the fields to join the other two men.

Following the line of the stream, they had crossed the main Eaglesham road when McLean spotted first the flutter of pale blue parachute silk and then the tall figure in the black flying suit leaning against the stone wall.

They approached warily, Wilson keeping the heavy stick ready. A few yards away they stopped.

Of the four men, Hess seemed by far the most composed. Finally, McLean spoke in his soft lowland brogue: "Who are you?"

Hess turned away without answering. The three men sensed the contemptuous authority in the movement.

"Maybe he can't speak English," ventured Angus.

Hess turned slowly to face them. "I understand English."

Wilson kept the stick held ready. "Who are you then?" he said.

The Deputy Führer's eyes slowly scanned the faces of the men before him. When he spoke, the voice was low and controlled. "I am Hauptmann Alfred Horn."

Three

May 10, 1941. The wind had freshened, and the promised clouds had arrived at last, sweeping in from the west. Behind their dark mass the sun was setting. Horn had stumbled across a field, over a stone wall and across a second field, a distance of about half a mile from the spot where he had left the injured Stellvertreter.

Horn stopped to catch his breath. Though considerably fitter than the average man of his age, he was still a long way from the pinnacle of physical excellence he had reached in 1936. He pushed his way through a clump of wild gorse, cursing as the thorn tore and stung at his legs through the light fawn gabardine of his trousers, then emerged onto a narrow road. To the right it ran away to disappear in a slow curve behind a line of fir trees; to the left it led down a gentle incline through the fields and gorse. Horn decided to go left, for as far as he could make out that was west, and Prestwick must lie in that general direction.

After about half a mile the road forked, and a white wooden post stood leaning at an angle at the point of the intersection. At the top were two inch-wide slots that had once held the road signs, but like all others throughout Great Britain these had been removed when invasion seemed inevitable. Again the question, which road should he take?

43

Horn tried to remember the flight-plan map. Prestwick was on the west coast, only some thirty kilometers away. But he could recall no details of roads or other names. His watch showed nine-twenty, leaving little over an hour to make the rendezvous. The light was almost gone, and the first drops of rain were in the air. The position seemed hopeless.

The car came up the hill without the need to change down. The old Jaguar side-valve engine was perhaps a little sluggish on the flat but could take even the steepest incline in its stride. Dr. Cross had bought the Standard Avon Special new in 1933. In many ways it was a young man's car, but the doctor had fallen in love with it the moment he saw it. Now fifty-five, overweight and still a bachelor, Cross still got a moment of proud excitement each time he started the engine and heard the deep, powerful roar of the six cylinders.

Peering ahead into the gathering darkness, he started the windshield wipers against the increasing rain. The car's crowning glory were the two huge eight-inch headlights on either side of the radiator, but now their magnificent searchlight beams were covered by blackout regulation hoods, leaving two tiny slits of light by which to drive. The doctor pulled up at the fork in the road as the meager spill of light picked out the figure of Horn. He wound down the side window.

"I'm going to Tarbolton," he offered.

For a moment Horn vaguely considered pulling the man from the car, overpowering him and taking the vehicle. He tried to see into the darkness of the interior to get a clearer view of the figure behind the wheel. He saw what seemed a large man, the round face lit up for a moment from the glow as the doctor pulled on a pipe.

"You'll be wanting the aerodrome at Prestwick?"

"Yes," said Horn quickly. For the first time on this

astonishing journey his luck seemed to have changed.

It was a familiar road, and the doctor, anxious to impress his passenger, drove as fast as the conditions would allow. The rain was now pouring down in great driving sheets. Dr. Cross turned up the rheostat he had had specially fitted to the wiper motors and increased their speed.

"You need a good set of wipers in weather like this." The effort to start a conversation, preferably about the car, was lost on Horn. Although there was no heater, the interior was warm, with a comfortable smell of leather and tobacco. He took off his USAAF cap, which was a little tight, lay back in the seat and tried hard to forget a sudden overpowering urge he felt for a cigarette. Except for the wallet, his pockets were empty.

The car sped on, its wire wheels splashing through the patches of water collecting on the undrained road, through the darkened, silent streets of Cumnock and Ochiltree.

"My name's Cross. I'm a doctor."

"Alfred Horn."

Apart from the car the doctor's other interest was genealogy. He tried to place the origin of the surname.

"Would that be Horn with an *e?*" he asked.

"No, just H-O-R-N."

Horn suddenly felt on his guard. The comfort of the car had lulled him into a feeling of security. The papers he carried would, of course, give his name as Vincent. The fatherly figure beside him was the enemy; he must not allow himself to forget it.

American names were always a problem, the doctor thought. So many had been simplified by the immigration officers when the flood of people from all over Europe had poured into New York to seek their fortunes in the New World. Horn could have come from anything, from unpronounceable Polish to twelve letters of indecipherable Coptic script. He decided to drop the subject. He had considered skirting around Ayr, past Prestwick, then on to Tarbolton. It lengthened the journey by a few miles, but that way he could have dropped Horn at the entrance to the air base. Now the rain had stopped, and he would chance the minor road that branched off right, straight to Tarbolton at the next junction. His untalkative passenger could walk from there.

"I'll be dropping you at the next crossroads, if you don't mind."

"That'll be fine," replied Horn.

"I'd take you all the way, but I'm on my way to a confinement."

That was true, but the mother-to-be was the wife of an old friend, and there was no hurry to get there. The doctor expected to chat and drink a dram or two and get a good night's sleep in the spare bedroom before his services there were called upon. The baby would arrive in the morning, another dram to wet its head, then back to the dark green walls of the surgery in time to deal with the minor ailments of the good Scottish people of the district. They at least would mention his car and tell him how they had seen it on the road to Mauchline and how well it was running.

The Standard Avon Special pulled up at the crossroads, and Horn got out.

"I'd stay on the Ayr road; there's a chance someone will pick you up." Horn thanked him, grateful that the doctor had indicated the road ahead. He recalled from the map that Prestwick was only a kilometer or so north of Ayr, and Ayr could not be far from where he stood.

As the deep whine of the Jaguar engine faded off to the right, Horn started walking. The wind, now almost a half gale, had chased the rain east, but his clothes were still damp. Soon he was shivering with cold. As his eyes got used to the darkness he broke into a jog trot. It was still only nine thirty-five. He was making good progress. He should arrive at Prestwick with a good half hour in hand.

The wind sock beside the single concrete runway at Prestwick Airport pulled at its mast as the wind held it rigidly out. In the distance the North Channel waves crashed onto the shoreline. At the locked main gate Albert Howard crouched in the back of his sentry box and wished he was home in bed.

Until March the airport had slept peacefully among the gently undulating countryside. Even in peacetime it had never been busy, and the few commercial flights a week and the handful of private planes had been grounded since the outbreak of war. All that had suddenly changed, and the change went directly back to November of the previous year.

It was then the American people had elected Franklin D. Roosevelt for an unprecedented third term as President, and in December, despite the mounting opposition of the isolationists and anti-British lobby, he had called on the American people to make the United States "the great arsenal of democracy." Responding to this call, Congress had endorsed the Lend-Lease bill, and on February 8, 1941 it had been passed by the House of Representatives. By April the great transatlantic shipments of arms and munitions by sea and air had begun, and by the late evening of May 10, as Albert Howard sat sheltered from the elements in his sentry box, it was in full swing.

Prestwick had been chosen as one of the reception airports, and weekly increasing numbers of the giant four-engine Fortresses surged in from the Atlantic, scattering the seabirds nesting in the sand dunes and thundering in to land. But tonight all was quiet. Albert Howard blew on his hands and settled down on an upturned box for the long night ahead.

Horn had just climbed over a low fence and was beginning to work his way around the airport perimeter when Howard saw him. By pure chance the sentry had peered out to glance up at the sky and had spotted Horn as he moved silently past the gate inside the base. Although the man was inside the perimeter fence, something in the way Horn was moving, the slightly inclined forward angle of his body, made Albert Howard suspicious.

"Hey, you!"

Horn froze at the sound of the voice, deciding whether or not to run for it. The figure was already walking over toward him, and he could make out the rifle at the ready. He blinked as a sudden burst of light from a flashlight hit his face.

"Oh, I'm sorry, sir," said Howard, recognizing the Captain's bars on the uniform. He lowered the 303 Lee-Enfield rifle, a relic from World War I that had probably not been fired for twenty years, and took a step back.

Horn was amazed at his first sight of the British fighting man at close quarters. He was certainly over fifty, with a thin, weasel face and an incongruous shock of white hair protruding from the sides of his flat steel helmet. The battle-dress top he wore was a good two sizes too large despite at least two pullovers worn beneath it to keep out the cold. On the man's left arm was a band with the letters *LDV,* but this had slipped below the elbow. Horn had no way of knowing that the initials stood for Local Defense Volunteer, the motley, ill-armed precursor of the Home Guard. The attire was completed by a pair of thick green civilian corduroy trousers and a pair of brown, unpolished boots.

"Sorry, sir, but we've had a couple of break-ins lately. After the cigarettes. Everybody's after the cigarettes these days."

He sniffed and rubbed the end of his thin nose with a forefinger, waiting for Horn to respond to the hint.

"Then it's lucky I don't smoke." Horn was careful to exaggerate his natural American accent when speaking English. After a moment he added, "Do you know where I can find General Walker?"

"General Walker? Don't think I know him. Most of 'em have left. I think there's a couple of officers in Hut Three. You could try there." He waved an arm to the right, and for the first time Horn noticed a group of low buildings.

"Thanks," he said, and walked away.

"Tightfisted bastard. They all smoke," mumbled Howard to himself as he wandered back into the sentry box.

As Horn came into the Nissen hut, a voice from the desk yelled, "Shut that goddamn door!"

The USAAF sergeant was seated with his back to the door reading a pinup magazine by the light of a lamp held low over the pages. As he shouted, he dropped the magazine and smacked his hands down on two piles, scattering them all over the room. Horn closed the door, and the sergeant turned in his chair to face him, unperturbed by the fact that he had been yelling at an officer.

"Sorry, Captain," he said casually. "Thought you were one of those goddamn sky jockeys."

"Sky jockeys?" Horn said cautiously, wondering whether he should know the term.

"Civilian ferry pilots," the other man volunteered happily. "Guys who've never seen the inside of an army."

Horn looked around. The Nissen had a newly painted smell. To one side was a line of battleship gray filing cabinets, still in their protective cardboard wrapping. Several packing cases lay unopened around the room. In one wall a dozen wires, waiting to be wired into sockets, protruded from a roughly cut hole, while over in the corner a powerful radio transmitter/receiver was turned to a distant station playing swing.

The sergeant, his dark hair cropped to within an

inch of his head, watched Horn with an easy, confident look, his jaws working lazily on a piece of gum.

"What can I do for you, Captain?"

"I'm looking for General Walker."

"You're out of luck, sir. The General left on the last B-17 out of here tonight."

To Horn, exhausted as much by the events of the day as by the loss of last night's sleep, the blow was almost palpable. He rocked on his heels.

The sergeant looked at him with friendly concern. "Anybody else help, Captain? General Walker left one of his aides here—Lieutenant Hampton. Second door on the right."

Horn inhaled deeply. "Thanks." He turned back into the short corridor, lit by bare electric bulbs. He knew he had to keep a tight grip on himself especially in his present exhausted state.

He knocked on the second door on the right. A woman's voice called for him to come in.

She was sitting on the edge of a camp bed, pouring coffee from an electric percolator into a handleless cup. She looked in her mid-thirties and was blond with strong, regular features.

"I'm looking for Lieutenant Hampton," he said.

"I'm she." She misread his hesitation. She tapped her shoulder flash. "Army Nurse Corps," she said. "Assistant to General Walker. Would you like some coffee?"

"That'd be good. Thank you."

She stood up and crossed to a small table against the wall to get another cup. She was tall, and beneath a well-cut uniform her body moved easily.

"How d'you take it?"

"Black, no sugar."

She handed him the cup, then looked at him with a quiet half-smile until he realized she was waiting for some sort of explanation for his presence.

"I was due to meet General Walker here," he said eventually.

"You're Captain Vincent?"

Horn nodded.

"What happened to the Colonel who was supposed to be with you?"

"His car ran off the road."

"Is he badly hurt?"

"No, but he won't be able to make it tonight."

"He's not the only one, Captain, I'm afraid. General Walker left almost an hour ago."

"An hour ago?"

Hess had stressed the importance of getting here before ten-thirty. He had made good time. It could not be much later than ten-fifteen.

"You were due here at ten-thirty. What time d'you have?" she asked.

He checked his watch. "Nearly ten-twenty."

She shook her head. "Captain, we all do it. Your watch shows ten-twenty, right?"

He nodded cautiously.

"You haven't changed it since you got here?"

He looked at her blankly.

"British *double* summer time, Captain. It throws everybody. We've informed New York a dozen times. But the information never seems to filter through to the guys who need it—the fliers. Over there everybody's still working on the idea of plain, one-hour-forward British summer time. When you get back, give 'em hell."

The careful details of the Deputy Führer's plan had contained one simple error. Germany had moved her clocks forward one hour in March, but in the same month Britain had gone on to double summer time, two hours ahead of Greenwich time and one hour ahead of Germany. Horn sipped his coffee. He was confused.

She caught the worried look on his face. "You'd better go tell Colonel Barker. Where is he?"

"X-rays. They're running a few checks on him."

"That's too bad. Will he make it for Monday?"

"Monday?"

"The next air convoy lands Monday afternoon. The crews fly back sometime after midnight."

Horn tried to think fast. If Lieutenant Hampton was offering to arrange for him to fly to America, a neutral country, at the moment that would suit him very well.

"Is the coffee okay?" she asked.

"Fine. My orders are to go on alone. I would like to leave as soon as possible."

"That's still Tuesday A.M."

The phone rang in the outer office. The sergeant called through: "For you, Lieutenant."

"Please excuse me." She left the room.

Once he was alone, questions and new doubts filled Horn's mind. How much did she know? Apparently very little. Who was General Walker? Did Hess plan to fly to America? And what was in the briefcase Hess had given him?

He found that his heart was pounding hard. If wartime Britain was anything like wartime Germany, it was in the grip of spy mania. Anybody in any way strange was reported immediately to the local Gestapo. If the doctor in the Jaguar had noticed something, some slip he had made, he could easily be with the police now. And like the complete amateur he was, he realized, he had given his real destination.

As Lieutenant Hampton came back, he searched her face for any indication of what she was feeling.

She stopped just inside the doorway. "What is it, Captain? Anything wrong?"

"No . . ." he said hurriedly, clasping his cup in both hands. "The phone call. I guess I thought it might have been news of Colonel Barker."

She looked at him curiously and shook her head. "No, just a routine radar clearance from Northern Ireland. All B-seventeens safely on their way."

He sat down heavily. He realized his cup was shaking.

At any moment a question could throw him completely. What was his serial number? Where had he done his induction training? When had he arrived in Britain? And how? After all, she was entitled to ask him these questions.

He looked up at her. "That's good coffee," he said slightly lamely.

"Like some more?"

"No, thanks, Lieutenant. Sorry if I'm not making too much sense. I'm feeling pretty bushed."

"You look as if you need a good night's sleep."

He nodded. "Is there somewhere here I could bunk down?" He rubbed a hand across his eyes.

The American Lieutenant paused. "Better than that. The General rented a cottage for his staff. You're welcome to stay there if you want."

She crossed the room and took down her uniform coat from the back of the door.

"We're going to have to pick up something for breakfast from the club first. And anyway, you look as if you could use a drink."

"Lieutenant, I could use a drink." He forced a smile.

She smiled back over her shoulder as he helped her on with her coat.

"Kay," she said. "Kay Hampton."

"Horn," he said. "Alfred Horn." And immediately realized his mistake.

Her eyes flicked toward him. "As the General was leaving," she said slowly, "he got into some areas I didn't understand."

Horn waited.

"Perhaps he didn't want me to understand," she added after a moment.

"That could be."

She inclined her head. "I've been assistant to the

53

General long enough to recognize that as a possibility."

For a moment or two she stood in the middle of the room. "Okay, Captain," she said suddenly, "let's go get ourselves a drink."

She led the way across the darkened airfield. The humps of Nissen huts could be discerned around the perimeter, and here and there the outlines of a parked British fighter aircraft.

"How long you been in Britain?" she asked out of the darkness beside him.

"Not long." He knew she was probing.

"Did you get to see London?"

"No," Horn said. "I hear it's quite a mess."

"I was just on the phone to Grosvenor Square—they've got a real heavy raid on there right now."

"Is that so?"

She turned between two Nissen huts, shining her flashlight toward a door marked in big stenciled letters "U.S. personnel only." As she pushed the door, a rhomboid of pale yellow light was briefly thrown across the concrete path. They entered what seemed to Horn a dimly lit tent until she parted the heavy curtaining to reveal a long bar, lined with perhaps thirty bar-stools. There seemed to be no customers for the impressive range of bottles lining the shelves behind the one white-coated barman.

"Evening, miss. Evening, Captain." The barman spoke with a soft Scottish accent.

"What will you have?" She slipped onto one of the stools.

"Scotch and water." Horn took the stool next to hers. Behind the barman's head were at least six different types of whisky.

"Any preference, Captain?" the barman asked. "You're in the only place in Britain where you get a choice these days."

Horn read off the nearest label. "I'll take Black & White."

"And you, miss?"

"The same," Kay Hampton said. She turned toward Horn, pushing an opened pack of Lucky Strikes toward him. "So we've got problems with the Colonel. Will he be able to make Monday?"

"I don't think so." Horn took a cigarette and lit it with a book match from the bar top. "I think you're going to have to let General Walker know I'll be coming alone."

She grimaced. "I don't know what this is all about, Captain—and I'm not asking—but I can tell you the General's going to hit the roof when he hears about this."

"There's nothing to be done," Horn said tersely.

She eyed him, surprised at the tension evident about the gray eyes and in the lines of the forehead. The barman broke the moment, sliding two large whiskies toward them and waving a jug of ice water above Kay Hampton's glass. "To the top," she said, and noticed that this strange Captain had already lifted his glass to his lips, oblivious of the fact that it was straight liquor.

Horn took a pull at the whisky and felt its relaxing warmth. For the first time he noticed the shabby figure of a man in a long black overcoat leaning over one of the tables at the far end of the hut. Kay followed his glance, twisting on the stool. "It's old Mr. Frank," she said. "He's not stealing the club silver, don't worry." Horn saw that the man was wrapping candlesticks and silver cutlery in soft cloths and packing them into a battered suitcase. "He's an antiques dealer," she went on, glad to have something to say. "The airfield commander turns something of a blind eye when the civilian ferry pilots come in from the States, and Mr. Frank unloads a few hundred dollars' worth of silver on them. From what I hear they do well on the deal. Some guys say they've been able to double their money in New York."

Hat in one hand, suitcase in the other, the man approached them along the length of the Nissen hut. He was about sixty, of medium height but stooped. His heavy features suggested, rather than proclaimed, a certain type of Central European Jewishness.

He stopped before them. "Good evening, Lieutenant. Didn't expect to see you still here." His accent was strong.

She smiled. "Some extra work came up." She gestured to Horn. "This is Captain Vincent, Mr. Frank. He's leaving for the States in a few days."

Mr. Frank's eyebrows lifted in mild interest. His kindly eyes surveyed Horn's face. "I deal in silver, Captain. But I'm not the most successful merchant. If you're interested, drop in on my shop in the village. You can't miss it, if only because it has the messiest display window in western Scotland." He shifted his gaze. "May I buy you a drink, Lieutenant?"

"We just ordered," she said. " 'I'm in the chair,' as they say over here. So let me buy you one."

The old man inclined his head in thanks. "A glass of whisky then, if I may."

"How long have you lived in Britain, Mr. Frank?" Horn asked while the whisky was being ordered. He was anxious to divert questions from himself.

"I came here in 1934, Captain," Frank said. "From Germany. By then it was clear there was no place for a Jewish businessman in Hitler's Reich. I took out British citizenship, and if I had been a younger man, I would no doubt be serving now in the British army. All of which is curious. Because in the First War, I spent four years in the trenches, fighting *against* the British army."

He took his glass and raised it. "Perhaps after Hitler is defeated, I shall be able to return."

Horn frowned. "Would you still want to?"

"I'm a German," the old man said simply. "I always

will be. Someday my countrymen will return to their senses."

It was just before midnight as they fumbled their way by the dimmed light of the flashlight to Kay Hampton's jeep. Mr. Frank had left them at the door to the club. "I have the feeling," he had said, shaking Horn's hand, "that you are only the first of many Americans to be involved in this war. The first of many millions."

In the darkness, he was unable to see Horn's jaw tighten.

"Good-night, Captain. Good-night, Lieutenant." Then he had turned and shuffled off.

In the jeep Kay Hampton sat in the driver's seat. She had already inserted the key in the ignition. The moon slipped from behind a heavy cloud mass, and he saw she had turned toward him, her full mouth shaped questioningly.

"What is it?" he said uncertainly.

"You tell me," she said in a perfectly even tone.

"Tell you what?"

"Captain John Vincent? Or Captain Alfred Horn?"

"Alfred Horn," he said.

"Captain?"

He nodded. "Captain."

"And John Vincent?"

"There *are* reasons."

"But should I accept them?"

"Your General Walker was expecting me."

"He was expecting Captain Vincent. *And* a Colonel Barker."

"As far as you're concerned, I am Captain Vincent. If I'm not the man your General is expecting, he'll damn soon know it when I arrive in Washington."

She was silent.

"Your move, Lieutenant."

She turned the ignition key, and the engine fired thunderously. "You look like you could do with a night's sleep," she said. "Whoever you are."

* * *

She parked the jeep in the driveway of the small cottage. A thin chink of light showed through the blackout curtains of one of the downstairs rooms. Horn followed her along a garden path, aware of uncut thick grass brushing his ankles. Ahead was a low door heavily covered with wisteria; she stooped to unlock it, then let them into a darkened hallway.

"Hi," a deep American voice called from a room off the hall. The door opened, and Horn was confronted by an enormous figure ridiculously stooping to duck under the top of the door. He grinned sheepishly, an even, white-toothed smile, then straightened so that the top of his head was brushing the low cottage ceiling.

"Ralph—" Kay came forward—"this is John Vincent—one of the officers General Walker was expecting. I said he could sleep here tonight until we figure out what to do with him tomorrow."

"Sure." Ralph extended a huge hand toward Horn. "Ralph Hampton."

Horn saw that he was wearing dark blue trousers and U.S. Navy tabs on his blue shirt.

"The kitchen is the operations center of this ship, Captain," Ralph boomed cheerfully. "It's where we keep the booze. Right this way."

He ducked under the door again, and Horn stood aside to let Kay through. As she walked into the kitchen, he thought he saw just the faint shadow of apology in her smile.

Horn followed them into the small cottage kitchen and on Ralph's gesture took the seat at a pine table in the center of the room. "Scotland seems full of Americans these days," he said.

Ralph poured Scotch for all three of them. "This is only the beginning, Captain," he said. "The moment America gets properly into this war there'll be more Texans in this island than there are back in Texas."

"You think America . . . you think we will get into this war then?" Horn asked.

"I certainly do," Ralph said. "And when it happens, this administration's going to make sure it's good and ready."

Kay added water to her whisky and sipped at it. "No war talk, Ralph. Come on. It's after midnight."

"Okay." He grinned toward Horn. "I'm all for joining this war just as soon as we can. Kay, she takes the other view. She believes peace and goodwill to all men is possible."

Kay drained her whisky quickly. "Look, Ralph, don't keep the Captain up. He could use some sleep."

"Me too," Ralph said. "I have to be down in Liverpool by early P.M. tomorrow. I have a destroyer to put onto that afternoon tide."

"Isn't that classified information?" Kay stood up.

"Not to a fellow officer." Ralph smiled and poured whisky for himself and Horn. "I'll say good-bye to you, honey," he said, standing up. "I have to catch the train from Glasgow at eight in the morning."

Towering over her, he leaned forward and pecked her cheek.

"Take care, Ralph. And see you back in Washington."

Horn looked awkwardly away as they said their casual good-byes. Then Kay was addressing him.

"There's a sofa in the living room, Captain. Okay if you use that? I'll leave you sheets and blankets."

"That's fine," Horn said. "And again, thanks."

She smiled and closed the door.

"Bottoms up, Captain." Ralph Hampton lifted his glass.

Horn thought wryly that it probably wasn't the most felicitous toast for a destroyer captain, but he said nothing and drank. "What's a U.S. Navy destroyer doing in Liverpool?" he asked as he lit a cigarette.

Ralph looked mysterious, then grinned. "To hell with it," he said. "Within a week of war everybody's going to know anyway. We're doing a speed crossing of the Atlantic. Four days with British and U.S. submarines tracking us all the way."

"I don't quite see the point," Horn said.

"The point is, Captain, that we're a stand-in for the big British liners—the two *Queens*. The day war breaks they become troopships—twenty-five thousand U.S. infantrymen apiece and a four-day lone dash across the Atlantic. The theory is no German U-boat would be fast enough to intercept them. Tomorrow we test the theory."

"I wish you luck." Horn stood up and shook his host's hand. "You don't mind if I hit the sack now do you?"

"Go right ahead." Ralph opened the living-room door and looked through into the room beyond. "Yup, you got blankets and sheets there. I guess you'll sleep well."

At last Horn was able to say good-night and immediately closed the door behind him. He sat for a second on the edge of the sofa, thinking about the amiable giant of a man in the other room and his incredible indiscretions. Throughout Germany posters carried a sinister spy figure and the single warning "Pst . . . !" In Britain they seemed to prefer a bar blonde listening intently to two officers and underneath the legend "Careless talk costs lives." He took off his shoes and stood unbuttoning his shirt. Well, Ralph Hampton would certainly cost lives.

Meanwhile, it looked as if he had fallen on his feet. Or had he? He knew if he could hold out for two days anywhere, it would be holed up in this cottage. Yet by the early hours of this morning the hunt would be on. The two parachutes would have been discovered; the interrogation of Hess would have begun; police and army units would be scouring the countryside for the second German flier.

He turned off the light and drew the curtains. No, it was hopeless. He would be tracked down before Monday night.

He looked out across the dark hills, fully expecting a line of pinprick lights as army units searched the rough scrub. But there was nothing. Just the calm moonlight moving from behind a cloud.

He turned back toward the couch, suddenly exhausted. As he undressed, a thought occurred. You can get shot as a spy for wearing a foreign uniform. But what happens if they catch you naked in bed? Weakly he smiled to himself and fell back onto the couch, drawing the blankets over him. But he could not make the moment last. As he drifted into sleep, he seemed to see the lights approaching the cottage across the hills, he seemed to hear dogs baying, and in a recurring dream a khaki-uniformed sergeant, his features squat and brutal under his flat steel helmet, burst open the door and shouted, red-faced in triumph.

Eight hundred miles away Karlheinz Pintsch stood on the blacked-out platform at the Augsburg Bahnhof watching the locomotive pull into Platform Three. The private carriage of the Stellvertreter Rudolf Hess had already been attached to the end of the train. To Bahnhofmeister Gottmann, Hauptmann Pintsch seemed to move toward the distinctive dark green carriage with all the confidence that association with high-ranking Party leaders generated in National Socialist Germany.

But Pintsch was feeling far from confident. He had met the Führer on six occasions in the past and, like many others, feared his rapid changes from amiability to vindictive dislike. Probably what chilled him most about the man was a story from Hitler's down-and-out days just before World War I in Vienna.

There he had lived in the Working Man's Club, painting cheap pictures of the city's great buildings—pictures that were sold by his only friend in the world at that time, Reinhold Hanisch.

But Adolf Hitler had come to believe that for one particular painting Hanisch had received a few marks more than he had admitted. And a petty court case had resulted from the disagreement—with Hitler bringing a charge against Hanisch for swindling him of maybe ten dollars. Hanisch had spent a few days in jail, but it was not enough for Adolf Hitler. The thing had festered, and when he came to power a quarter of a century later, among all his preoccupations as leader of a great power, Hitler had remembered he still had an account to settle with Reinhold Hanisch. A Gestapo four-man murder squad had been sent after him. And Reinhold Hanisch disappeared from history, throttled in his cheap lodgings in Vienna's Prinz Clausgasse.

On Pintsch's instructions the journey to Obersalzberg took all night, although in kilometers the distance was quite small. But there was no point in the train's arriving earlier. He knew the Führer would not receive him until morning. Alone in the private railcar Pintsch slept little, wandering through the kitchens and dining car where he had lunched with the victorious generals after last year's summer campaign in France or with Himmler and Reinhard Heydrich, his sinister second-in-command. After that particular lunch Hess had taken Pintsch to his private room. "If you are ever in trouble with the SS, Pintsch," he had said (and somehow Pintsch knew that he meant if *he,* Rudolf Hess, was ever in trouble with Himmler and Heydrich), "there is something you should know. A piece of bargaining information that could kill you as easily as it could save your life. Reinhard Heydrich, Obergruppenführer SS, has a Jewish mother. Above her grave the very headstone has been secretly recut to obliterate her Jewish name, Sarah, and replace it with initials. Himmler knows—but Hitler still doesn't." In the struggles of the future (and here Hess clearly meant after Hitler's death) this piece of information might be of inestimable use.

Pintsch paced the Stellvertreter's empty railcar that night, turning over in his mind what his boss, the Brother, Brot herr, the "Breadwinner," as his staff called Hess, had told him that day. He had a feeling that it was a piece of information that he might need to use in the near future.

Four

Sunday, May 11, 8:40 A.M. Alfred Horn drifted slowly to the edge of wakefulness, then, with a start that wrenched his whole body, came fully awake. He was oppressed by consuming sensations of alarm as he struggled to orient himself in the small cottage sitting room.

He was in Britain! He rolled into a sitting position. Last night was still a half-remembered haze: the good-looking Lieutenant, the nice old German Jew, Mr. Frank—was that his name . . . ? Returning to the cottage . . . after that, Ralph Hampton. Then nothing. He must have passed out on the couch.

He listened. There was no sound of movement inside the house. Ralph would have left by now. And Kay Hampton?

He went to the window. It was a soft May morning, with banks of white rounded clouds moving slowly across a pale blue sky. Along the road a group of people, mostly elderly, hurried through a lychgate into a gray stone church. It was almost nine o'clock. The service would soon begin, but the bells in the squat flint tower were silent. He remembered reading that from the outbreak of war they had been that way in Britain, to be rung only in the event of invasion.

A movement across the fields caught his attention, and he looked up to see a horse and rider following the line of a stone wall. Even at this distance he could recognize the expertise as she cantered down the hill and took the corner of the wall in an easy controlled jump. As she dismounted, he let himself out of the back door, and keeping a line of trees between himself and the villagers on their way to church, he reached a stile which connected the paddock to the end of the cottage garden.

"You look like you've done a lot of riding in your time, Lieutenant," he said.

She was wearing boots and denim pants and a red sweater that undulated with the fullness of her figure. Her blond hair was tied back to expose the regular lines of her face.

"Some," she said. "Did you sleep well?"

"Like a drunk. I woke up not knowing which day it was."

She gave him a quick glance, full of questions, but said nothing as they headed toward the cottage.

"Where are you from?" she asked as he handed her over the stile.

"California. Long Beach."

He said Long Beach because his mother had a sister who had lived there for twenty years. He had stayed with this maternal aunt for six weeks in 1932, when the Olympics of that year were held in Los Angeles.

"Were you there in '38, '39?"

"Some of the time," he said guardedly.

She gave him a sidelong glance. "Then we were practically neighbors. I was living nearby at Redondo Beach. Did you ever surf there?"

"Sure."

"And Catalina?"

He shrugged, feeling each question was more dangerous than the last. He had gone to Catalina during his visit, but with a fellow German he had met by chance. Being so far from home, they had behaved like old friends five minutes after they had met. On the boat they talked in German and drank quantities of Budweiser with the idea of impressing on the young American manhood surrounding them that it took a German really to know how to drink beer. As a result, Catalina remained no more than a blurred image of a seawall and a heaving sea. As for the friend, he couldn't even remember his name.

They walked along the garden path side by side.

"You're not the most talkative young guy I've ever met."

"You can drop the young guy bit," he said curtly.

She shrugged. "I'm thirty-five. To me you're a young guy."

They walked on in silence. He had no idea why she had been probing. Surely not for the slim chance they might have met somewhere in California before the war? In any case it was impossible. In 1938 he was already in the Luftwaffe, by 1939 flying in the Polish campaign.

Back in the cottage he asked her to turn the radio on for the early morning news, and while she made coffee, he listened to the end of a program of dance music. Somehow by the angle of his head, by the tension still evident around the eyes and mouth, she knew that he was listening for one special news item.

She stood watching the coffee bubble through the percolator. General Walker had been pretty anxious when Captain Vincent and his mysterious Colonel Barker hadn't arrived at the base. When he finally left, he was convinced they hadn't made it—but made it from where? She'd got nothing from this Alfred Horn. She didn't even know how long he'd been in Britain.

The music came to an end, and after the time signal the voice from the radio was deep and distinctive. "This is the BBC Home Service. Here is the nine o'clock news for Sunday, 11 May, and this is Alvar Liddel reading it."

Horn leaned forward. The first item concerned the previous night's air raid on London, which was described as heavy. Then came reports from the various war fronts, the fighting in Greece, the siege of Tobruk. Horn listened carefully without taking the information in, waiting for news of Hess. But the announcer had moved on to the domestic front, a Colorado beetle scare in East Anglia and a warning for children about butterfly bombs in Kent and Surrey.

Remarkably, there was not a single word about what could be called the greatest British coup of the war so far. He leaned over and turned off the radio. "What's a butterfly bomb?" he asked.

She poured the coffee. "The British have posters up about them in the schools, buses, just about everywhere. They're antipersonnel bombs, open up like a steel butterfly and blow the arms off any youngster who has the curiosity to pick one up. The BBC usually issues a warning after any raid." She looked down at him. His cheekbones carried a dark angry flush. "What is it?" she said.

"I've never heard of these bombs the Luftwaffe are supposed to scatter over Kent and Surrey," he said deliberately.

"Why should you have?"

"No reason." He took the coffee cup. "Still, it seems strange to me anyone should waste valuable bombloads trying to blow the arms off children. I would have thought the armament factories were the first targets."

"Sure." She shrugged, sitting down opposite him.

"So it could just be that this whole butterfly bomb story is a British propaganda invention, yes?"

She didn't feel like arguing with this strange, intense man opposite her. "If that's what you want to believe, maybe you're right. Who knows?"

"Who knows?" he echoed, and Kay got a strong emanation of dislike, immediately and bafflingly dispersed by his self-deprecating smile. "Sorry, Lieutenant. I'm just a little cynical about British propaganda. In the last war they had the German army raping nuns and spearing infants on bayonet points."

"In some wars it's not all propaganda."

"It's got to be a big part of any war," he said shortly.

"Not in Spain. In the Civil War the propaganda found it hard to keep up with the action."

He looked at her set face. "You were there?"

"When the war began in 1936, I joined the American Field Service."

"On the anti-Franco side?"

She inclined her head. "It's true enough," she said after a moment, "I never saw any raped nuns. Although I treated a lot of German boys, mostly in the Communist brigades—but a few Condor Legion prisoners as well. They seemed to me much the same as the injured Spanish or French or Americans. . . ."

"Being in Spain, that decided you on life in the service?"

"No. . . ." She was silent for a moment. "No, I joined much later."

"Why?"

She shrugged. "That, Captain, is a long, long story." She poured more coffee for him. "I have to take the horse back," she said. "Cigarettes in the cupboard and some whisky there, too, if you want it. And it's a pretty little village to take a walk around."

"How long will you be?"

"A couple of hours maybe. I have to be back at the base this afternoon, but I'll be back in time to rustle up some lunch."

"Fine. . . ." He stood up as she made for the door. "And Lieutenant . . . thanks. For the hospitality."

"General Walker's orders," she said, smiling. "And in any case it's a pleasure."

He watched her the length of the garden path. Tall, slim-waisted, agile as she half jumped the stile, she was an intriguing combination of girl and woman. As she mounted her horse and urged it into a canter across the paddock, he turned away from the window. He would have to be careful. He knew himself well. If he was attracted to a woman, he would begin to get careless in the excitement of the chase. And this was no time for carelessness.

He drank his coffee—good American coffee of the sort that had disappeared entirely from Germany in the last year. If it were to be a long war, that wouldn't be the only thing that would disappear from the shops. And yet what had Hess said? That it would be over in a month? Hess. . . . Was it possible the British still hadn't recognized their prisoner? No, he was sure, for some reason they were keeping the announcement from the public. By now they would also know that *two* men had parachuted from the Messerschmitt and would be searching the area for the second flier. They'd have got that far surely.

To Horn it seemed logical to believe that the whole of Scottish Command of the British army was out looking for him. What he could not know was that at nine-thirty on the morning after Hess's capture no one had yet recognized the Stellvertreter in the small cottage hospital to which he had been taken. Nor that the two parachutes had fallen apart, straddling the hillside, so that among the apparently conflicting accounts of the Scottish farmers no one, as yet, had realized that *two* men had jumped from the stricken aircraft. For the moment at least Alfred Horn was safe from everybody but himself.

At Berchtesgaden Bahnhof, Pintsch left the train and telephoned one of Hitler's adjutants, Alfred Bormann, an old friend of Pintsch's and brother of Hess's own Party deputy, Martin Bormann. On the telephone he explained to Bormann that he carried a letter from the Stellvertreter to the Führer. Bormann told him that there was little chance of seeing the Führer before the usual afternoon lunch. Hitler was receiving

Architect Speer shortly after eleven o'clock, and once they started discussing plans for the rebuilding of Berlin there was no chance of anyone's getting into the Führer's study. Bormann suggested Pintsch should come for lunch and hope to get a chance to present his letter then.

In 1941 the mountaintop at Obersalzberg was unrecognizable to anyone who had known it a few years earlier. Then the house Hitler had bought with his royalties from *Mein Kampf* had been a small isolated timber building lost in the pinewoods that clothed the mountainside. Today the house had been enormously extended and renamed the Berghof, the "Mountain Court." Around the house and its three square miles of ground stretched a guarded barbed-wire fence. SS barracks had been built on the sides of the approach roads, and paved walkways now replaced the grassy paths through the woods. He passed through the double barriers in the staff Mercedes which Bormann had sent to collect him from the station, and the adjutant to the second most powerful man in Germany trembled as he climbed out of the back seat.

Alfred Bormann met him in the marble-floored anteroom. It was just after eleven, and the Führer was not yet up. Pintsch recognized the young architect Herr Speer reading on the sofa on the far side of the room. He crossed immediately toward him and introduced himself, explaining as best he could that he needed to see the Führer urgently.

Before Speer could answer, the eyes of the SS attendants turned toward the staircase. The anteroom fell silent. Adolf Hitler, in gray jacket and black trousers, was descending the stairs from his private apartments.

Speer, Pintsch, Bormann and the SS attendants came to attention. The Führer approached Speer and shook his hand. Then, as he turned to Pintsch, his eyes narrowed in inquiry.

"Hauptmann Pintsch, Führer."

Hitler's face relaxed. "Hess's adjutant, of course. My apologies for not remembering."

He moved to turn to Speer.

"I have an urgent message from the Herr Stellvertreter," Pintsch blurted desperately.

Hitler frowned. Pintsch noticed for the first time, irrelevantly, that the Führer's fleshy nose was actually wider than the old-fashioned World War I mustache.

"Herr Speer has already told me that he will wait until I have delivered my message, Führer."

Speer's eyes flickered toward Pintsch, but he remained silent.

Hitler's cold glance made absolutely sure both men knew that it was not for them to arrange his appointments. Then he moved across the anteroom toward his study. "Come with me, Pintsch," he said, the voice floating over his shoulder.

An SS attendant opened the door, and Pintsch followed Hitler into the room beyond. The immediate dominant features were the view across the valley to the Untersberg and the huge desk at which Hitler stood to work. Except for official posed photographs of the leader laboring alone in the night Hitler rarely sat at his desk. By 1941 the demonic energy of his youth had burned out. At fifty-two he was lazy, incapable of sustained periods of work, obsessively retelling stories of the past. Karlheinz Pintsch was aware that the reactions of this man in the next few minutes could deprive him of his liberty or even his life.

On the desk were spread a number of designs for the new opera house at Linz. For a moment Hitler stood over them, the corners of his mouth turned down. Then he turned, smiling, toward Pintsch.

"Well, Pintsch," he said amiably, "where is the Stellvertreter? Except for conferences about party matters he never seems to come to Obersalzberg any more."

"I have a letter for you, Führer." Pintsch hurriedly drew the letter from his pocket.

Hitler nodded, glanced back at the opera house drawings and frowned. Another long letter from Hess, an analysis of the political and military situation in Europe, no doubt. He wished Hess would stay with the domestic area he knew best. But Rudolf Hess was one of the twenty or thirty people, one of the inner ring of the *alte Kämpfer,* of the Old Fighters, that Hitler genuinely hated to offend. "Tell me what's in the letter, Pintsch," he said, taking the envelope and dropping it on the desk.

"I think the Führer should read it himself."

Hitler eyed him slowly. Perhaps one of those strange intuitions which some said he was capable of suddenly came to him; perhaps it was the tension he detected in the adjutant's voice. "Where is Hess now?" he asked quietly.

"Last night," Pintsch said slowly, "the Stellvertreter flew to Scotland. The letter explains his purpose."

On Adolf Hitler's face there was no more discernible impact than if Pintsch had said Hess had flown to Berlin. For one wild, relieved moment Pintsch thought that Hitler already knew. He watched as the Führer took his spectacles and placed them on the tip of his nose. Looking like an Austrian schoolmaster, Adolf Hitler tore open the envelope and began to read, nodding to himself as if in broad agreement with the points made.

When he had finished, he removed his glasses and cocked an eyebrow at the adjutant. "Stay for lunch, Pintsch," he said. "Sit at my table, not with the other adjutants."

It was a dismissal. Pintsch thanked him and left the room. As the door closed, Hitler lifted the phone. "Bormann," he said to the operator. Then, as Martin Bormann answered, Hitler hissed into the phone, "Get Goering here at once. Himmler, too." Then, with biting contempt in his voice: "Hess is on his way to *America* to organize peace in our time."

He dropped the telephone and leaned against the

desk. His eye traveled along the line of photographs arranged on the polished pine shelf. Hitler and Goering on the first anniversary of the Munich *Putsch* . . . Hitler and his niece Geli Raubal, driven to suicide by her love for her brooding impotent uncle . . . Hitler and his chauffeur Emil, who often lunched alone with the Führer and knew state secrets before most ministers. . . . In the last photograph on the shelf, Hess stood next to and, appropriately, half a pace behind his Führer. The scrawled caption in Hess's hand read —"To Wolf from R. H." Hess had given him the photograph on the night of their victory in the 1933 elections, when a National Socialist future for Germany at last became a certainty. To Wolf . . . his old code name in the days of struggle.

Five

That same morning at Air Headquarters Scottish Lowlands, Stirling, Wing Commander David Bruce read the brief interim report from his crash examination team on the Me. 110 that had come down at Dungavel last night. One wing of the aircraft had been destroyed in the high-octane fire, but the fuselage and the remaining wing seemed to indicate that the Messerschmitt had been modified for long-range flight. From a fishing trawler off Holy Island another significant piece of information had arrived earlier in the morning—a bright aluminum fuel tank with a seven-hundred-liter capacity had been found floating a few miles from the coast. Wing Commander Bruce decided even at this stage there was enough evidence of important modifications to the Me. 110 to inform Fighter Command Headquarters at Biggin Hill. So much of the RAF's success against the Luftwaffe depended on the fact that the Germans had so far failed to develop a long-range escort fighter for their bombers that Biggin Hill assigned Wing Commander Bruce's report a high priority. This new Me. 110 could be the expected long-range escort prototype. The information was immediately passed on to the Air Ministry in Whitehall.

Less than a mile away in London's Wimpole Street, whose elegant early nineteenth-century houses were more famous for expensive dentists than counterintelligence evaluators, Major Max Bishop of the Intelligence Corps was awakened from a deep sleep by the telephone ringing beside his camp bed. He struggled wearily into consciousness, reaching for the receiver with his eyes still closed.

It had been a bad night. The Air Ministry report estimated three to four hundred bombers had blitzed Central London, and Bishop had spent the whole night dousing the small lethal aluminum incendiary bombs that had rained down on the Oxford Street area. Later reports would establish that seven hundred acres of the capital had been destroyed, one and a half times the damage caused by the Great Fire of London. At ten-thirty on Sunday morning Max Bishop had finally dragged himself up to his room and climbed into bed.

Now, less than half an hour later, he was grunting his name into the phone. A girl's voice, bright and very crisply English, announced Colonel Henderson on the phone. Bishop lifted himself onto one elbow and blinked the sleep from his eyes. He knew Henderson's name in the Intelligence structure. It was rumored that he had direct access to the Prime Minister's office.

"Bishop . . ." Henderson's voice cut in. "I want you to come over to Admiralty Arch straight away. How long will it take you?"

"Depends how quickly I can pick up a taxi. Most of them spent half the night acting as auxiliary ambulances."

"Get here as soon as you can. I'll be waiting."

Max Bishop replaced the receiver and swung himself out of bed. He was a regular Rifle Brigade officer assigned to the Intelligence Corps, and he had a regular officer's understanding of the army mentality. Get here right away meant hurry up and wait. Extreme urgency meant just try not to leave it until next week. He yawned, phoned down to the mess for a cup of tea and, with a robe thrown around his shoulders, padded off down the once-impressive corridor to the makeshift shower rooms.

The offices at Admiralty Arch were not entirely unfamiliar to Bishop. Early in the war he had been called there from France, where he was serving as a regimental officer with the British Expeditionary Force. A civilian had asked him to write a complete report of the time he had spent in Germany during the 1936 Olympic Games as a competitor in the pentathlon. Bishop had been unable to see what use his information could be to the mixture of civilians and serving officers at Admiralty Arch. But he had dutifully typed for a whole morning, listing the Germans he had met, the number of times he had seen Hitler at the stadium, the Führer's anger at Jesse Owens's triple gold. . . . The report had been read that afternoon, and by the next morning Captain Max Bishop found himself promoted to Major and transferred to the Intelligence Corps. Since then he had spent most of his time on security assessments for the expected German invasion of southern England. What this had to do with the Berlin Olympic Games escaped him.

A shapely Wren in black skirt and white shirt led him up the stairs. In the accents of Cheltenham Ladies' College she completely ignored his superior rank and berated him for keeping Colonel Henderson waiting. Knocking briefly at a heavy mahogany door, she responded to a grunt from within and nodded to Bishop to enter.

A full Colonel with red collar taps, Henderson was in his mid-thirties, barely older than Bishop himself. He looked up from a pile of papers. "You took your time," he said. "We'll work together best when you understand that when I say 'right away,' I mean right away. I can offer you whisky or coffee. Which will it be?"

Bishop chose whisky and watched the Colonel take a single bottle from his desk drawer and pour two careful small measures. A man needed a lot of influence to obtain a bottle of whisky in wartime London.

"First, read the report." Henderson handed Bishop

the Air Ministry document. Rapidly Bishop read the concisely written four-page report. At the end of it he still had no idea why he should have been called because a new Messerschmitt had crashed in Scotland.

Henderson took the whisky bottle from the desk drawer and poured more for Bishop. "At this point," he said, "we still don't know whether we're dealing with a defector, a navigational error—or what. I want you to go to Scotland and find out."

Bishop looked at him in astonishment. "Surely that's a job for RAF Intelligence? I hardly know a Messerschmitt from a Dornier.

"You do, however, know the pilot. This morning our cross-index system on known Luftwaffe pilots brought an interesting report to my desk. It was written by you."

"The Olympic Games?"

Henderson nodded. "The pilot who crashed last night is your old pentathlon rival, Alfred Horn."

Half an hour later Max Bishop sat in the back of the dark green staff car on his way to Northolt, the small military airfield a few miles west of London's sprawling suburbs. Last night's air raid damage was apparent as he drove across the city. Frequent detours were necessary as the staff car made its way along Chelsea Embankment, where fires were still burning the Lots Road area, but by Shepherd's Bush traffic had reverted to its sparse wartime normality, and half an hour later the driver was showing his pass to the RAF Regiment MP at Northolt.

The black shape of a Wellington bomber was standing on the runway on the far side of the airfield, its engines already turning over. Bishop climbed out of his car and, blasted by the slipstream, shouted a greeting to the pilot. Ten minutes later they were bucking the air currents as the Wellington headed north on the two-hour flight to Edinburgh.

Strapped in a bucket seat in the freezing cross-

ribbed fuselage of the Wellington, Bishop recalled
carefully that summer in Berlin five years before, when
he had met Alfred Horn.

In so many of the smaller peripheral events like the
pentathlon he had noticed that many of the German
team were serving members of the SS. Even then they
cultivated a remote, unfriendly manner, confident in
the racial superiority that Heinrich Himmler assured
them was theirs. Alfred Horn had been different.
After the accident in the four-thousand-meter run,
they had enjoyed much of the rest of the Games together. They had, after all, a great deal in common:
one a Luftwaffe cadet, the other in his final year at
Britain's officer school at Sandhurst, both from similar
backgrounds, both almost completely nonpolitical,
their interests wrapped up in the five sports demanded
by the modern pentathlon.

It was on that first holiday to Pomerania when the
Games ended that Bishop had met Horn's sister,
Ingrid, and at the end of just ten days had decided
this was the girl he wanted to marry. Of course, nei-
ther Horn's formidable old father, the epitome of a
Junker general, nor his once beautiful globe-trotting
American mother had any idea of Bishop's intentions.

But Horn, whose own interests were at that time
centered on a young Countess at a neighboring
schloss, nevertheless found time to see the way things
were going between his sister and his friend. The
thunder of the Wellington's engines faded from Bishop's ears as he thought about the German girl, about
the astonishing smile that could move him like music.
The following year he had been all set to leave for
a long summer in Germany when Alfred's letter arrived. His sister, Ingrid, had been killed in a car
crash on one of the new autobahnen between Berlin
and the south. Of course, Bishop's invitation to the
castle in Pomerania still stood. . . .

He had written immediately to Horn's father and
later to Horn himself, but he never went to Germany

again. And as the tension grew between Germany and Britain throughout 1939, he gradually lost touch with Horn until the September cataclysm swept away any last chance of their friendship being recovered. And now Hauptmann Alfred Horn was sitting in Scotland. A navigational error? Bishop shook his head. A defector from the Nazi view of Germany? Much, much more likely. He often thought of a few lines in one of Horn's last letters, written from the United States, the only time he had ever referred to the situation inside Germany: "Most of all, Max, try not to think too badly of us when you read about the anti-Jewish demonstrations in Germany. You cannot judge a whole nation by a handful of hooligans." "A handful of hooligans"—did he mean the window-smashing Sturm Abteilung troopers or their hooligan masters in Berlin? As the Wellington came down to land at Prestwick Airport, Max Bishop confidently expected to have the answer to that question within an hour.

Along the empty roads the dark green staff car covered the twenty-five miles to Craigie Hospital in less than half an hour. Sitting in the back seat, Bishop was surprised to see no evidence of any army guards keeping the pilot of the Messerschmitt in custody. But as the car swept into the parking lot of the country hospital, his eye caught a movement up on the roof and another in a clump of evergreens to one side, and he was aware of being covered all the way to the main doors.

A young Lieutenant rose from behind the reception desk as Bishop entered the lobby. The service cap he lifted from the hook behind him carried the gold cap badge of the Loyal Regiment. He saluted while the two sergeants carrying Sten submachine guns watched impassively.

Bishop pushed his papers across the desk toward the Lieutenant. "Major Bishop," he said. "London will have called you to say I was coming."

"That's right, sir." The Lieutenant looked up from

the papers. "Now if you could just give me your authority . . . ?"

"Henderson, Colonel Henderson."

The Lieutenant led the way along a corridor and stopped outside a room guarded by two more armed sergeants. "You like to be alone with him, sir?"

"Please." Bishop leaned forward and opened the door. He felt a keen sense of anticipation at the thought of seeing Alfred Horn again.

As the door swung open, he was aware of a simple white hospital cot and the humped outline of a sleeping figure. He pushed the door closed behind him and took two paces forward. The man in the bed stirred and turned on his back. He looked up at Bishop without speaking.

For a full five seconds Bishop stared down at the pale face of the man in bed. Then he turned on his heel and walked quickly from the room.

The phone in the Wren secretary's office at Admiralty Arch jangled. Highly conscious of the fixed stare of the young naval officer who was waiting to see Colonel Henderson, she stood up and reached across her desk for the phone. She was proud of her legs and had no prim objections to showing them off. "Colonel Henderson's office. . . ."

Max Bishop came on the line. "Let me speak to the Colonel," he said crisply. "This is Major Bishop."

She was disappointed. She'd liked the look of the young Intelligence Major. A few minutes' personal chat before he asked for the Colonel would have been very welcome.

"He's not in the office at the moment. Can I take a message?"

"No message. I want you to get hold of him right away."

"He's in a meeting with Brigadier Downing. Can you call back in half an hour?"

"What's your name?" he said suddenly.

That was better. "Elizabeth Dundas."

"Okay, Elizabeth—get on to the Brigadier's office and haul your Colonel out. I don't care if you risk the firing squad to do it."

"I'd prefer the firing squad to the Brigadier's temper."

"Get him, Elizabeth. Get him now."

She hesitated.

"That's a direct order." His voice crackled down the line.

"Yes, sir." She put down the phone and stood up, angry with herself. She hadn't meant to call him "sir." She found it put her on the wrong relationship with good-looking young officers.

The Brigadier had already been briefed about the Messerschmitt in Scotland. He took the interruption surprisingly quietly. Along the corridor outside, Henderson and Elizabeth Dundas hurried toward the Colonel's office.

"He was very insistent, sir."

"Maybe Horn has decided to cooperate." Henderson nodded to the waiting naval officer and walked through to his room. "Come in and bring your pad," he said over his shoulder to Elizabeth.

He picked up the phone.

"Bishop? Henderson here."

Elizabeth closed the door behind her. As she came forward slowly into the room, her dictation pad and pencil ready, she saw Henderson's mouth gape. "Not Horn? Who? Rudolf *Hess!* Bishop, are you clean out of your mind?"

Elizabeth Dundas dropped her pad and stared unashamedly at Henderson. He held the phone away and with the back of his free hand wiped his mouth. Quietly now he said, "How sure are you?"

In Craigie Hospital, Bishop hesitated. "In Berlin, in 1936, Hess came to the stadium with Hitler. I was presented to him. The usual brief handshake. In height, age, appearance, it's Rudolf Hess. What more can I say?"

"Has he said anything?"

"So far he maintains that he's Alfred Horn. I'm going back in now to try and talk to him."

"Mr. Churchill must be told right away," Henderson said. "I'll get back to you."

Elizabeth Dundas slowly bent and picked up her pad. Henderson replaced the phone. "I'm not sure yet, Elizabeth—but if Max Bishop's right, this just might call for a small Scotch."

At lunch, Bormann sat as usual on Hitler's left. Eva Braun, on his right, talked animatedly to Albert Speer, who was seated next to her. Hitler ate even less than usual, his head bent to one side to listen to the low murmur from Bormann. As he listened, nodding sometimes, his eyes returned again and again to Pintsch.

For Pinstch it was the most uncomfortable meal of his life. Menaced by Hitler's stare, forced to be polite to Luftwaffe General Udet next to him, Pintsch ate little but drank frequent glasses of wine. At one point Hitler beckoned Udet over to him.

"A Messerschmitt One Ten flying alone from Bavaria—could it reach Scotland?" Hitler asked as Udet bent low over him.

"Unlikely, Führer. First, it would need extra fuel tanks for the aircraft to have any chance of crossing the North Sea. Second, British Air Defense would almost certainly detect its approach. May I ask when this flight took place or is to take place?"

"Last night."

"Then it might have a better chance of escaping detection. We mounted our heaviest-ever bombing raid on London last night. Five hundred bombers. British Air Defense squadrons would have concentrated in the south." He paused. "There is one further consideration."

Hitler raised his eyebrows toward him.

"Because of the prevailing winds, Führer, only an extremely experienced navigator could hope to make landfall."

Hitler nodded dismissal. Walking back to his place beside Pintsch, the astute Udet put two and two together—and made five. Someone on Hess's staff, he concluded, had defected to the British. Never for a moment did it occur to him that it was the Stellvertreter himself who had made the flight.

Hardly had Udet seated himself beside Pintsch when the sort of commotion that had always surrounded Goering was heard in the anteroom. The door to the dining room seemed to fly open, and two hundred and seventy pounds of bemedaled joviality stood, seeking out the man he doted on.

Remembering himself even in this crisis, Hitler courteously apologized to Eva Braun and Speer and rapidly left the table. Martin Bormann saw the two leaders to the door of Hitler's study, then returned quickly to the dining room. With a coarse jerk of the head he summoned Pintsch.

"The Führer has one question," Bormann said when the adjutant stood beside him. "Did the Stellvertreter fly alone?"

"No, Herr Reichsleiter. A Hauptmann Alfred Horn flew as navigator."

Without further word Bormann walked across the anteroom toward the staircase. Before Pintsch closed the dining-room door, he saw two men enter, accompanied by a group of SS adjutants. The smaller was Heinrich Himmler, a fearful enough figure to anyone in trouble in the Third Reich. But the tall man in gray uniform with the black SS collar tabs was an even more frightening arrival. Reinhard Heydrich was, as Pintsch knew, the coldest intelligence in the Third Reich. Tall, blond, he moved across the anteroom with the elegance of the fencing champion he was. His ridiculously high falsetto voice carried to

Pintsch as he closed the dining-room door with a hand that already trembled.

Pintsch returned to the lunch table aware not only that the eyes of everybody at Hitler's table were on him, but that even the Berghof adjutants at the smaller tables by the window were watching him across the room. Only Speer and Eva Braun gave him reassuring smiles. Udet, next to him, said simply, "Good luck, Pintsch," and continued his lunch. It seemed only seconds later that the two SS adjutants were standing at the back of his chair.

He stood, clicked his heels to Eva Braun and followed the two adjutants across the room. At the door one of them gave his arm a friendly squeeze. "Sorry, Pintsch," he said, "but we've just been ordered to put you under arrest."

Six

Sunday, May 11, 2:15 P.M. In Hitler's study Goering was speaking. He gave his opinion that even if Hess did get to America, Roosevelt was as much a warmonger as Churchill and would reject out of hand any peace plans.

Bormann, Himmler and Heydrich remained silent as the Reichsmarschall spoke. Hitler paced from his desk to the window listening intently. When Goering had finished, he asked his advice on what the German counterpropaganda should be. Hess himself, in his letter to Hitler, had concluded: "If my mission fails, you can always announce to the world that I was mad." The Stellvertreter, Goering said, had provided the approach himself.

Goering favored an immediate announcement before the British made propaganda from the Deputy Führer's "defection." Hitler insisted on a delay. The chances were high that Hess had crashed in the sea.

At this point there was a short ring on the telephone. Bormann stepped forward to answer it. He frowned, listened and nodded brusquely to Heydrich.

"With your permission, Führer," Heydrich said, "I have already asked for an item of information central to our discussion." He lifted the phone and said, "Heydrich." For a few moments he nodded, then replaced the phone.

He held the moment with an actor's timing. "I have just ascertained," he squeaked to Hitler and the room at large, "that before the Stellvertreter left Augsburg yesterday, he had visited OKW Bendlerstrasse. There he required of the General Staff to be briefed on all current operational plans."

Hitler turned abruptly to the window. The others remained silent. They heard the Führer say almost to himself, "Hess . . . Hess. . . ."

Only Heydrich realized that he was looking not out across the mist gathering on the Untersberg, but at the last photograph on the shelf and the inscription which bound the two men from the days when they had written *Mein Kampf* together—"To Wolf from R. H."

Hitler placed his hands behind his back. "Obergruppenführer Heydrich," he said, "I am giving you full authority to deal with this matter. You will be answerable only to me."

Goering puffed indignantly. Himmler blinked behind his pincenez. Bormann nodded an agreement nobody required. Heydrich's voice tinkled like a glass chandelier: "Of course, Führer. Of course."

Horn found it impossible to remain still. On the radio he had found both a German and a Swiss news broadcast, but neither of them had mentioned Hess's flight. The BBC Overseas Service news had been equally barren.

In this limbo he paced the cottage, moving back and forth from window to window, rationally aware that he was safer inside but overwhelmed with the urge to get out and assure himself that no cordons were being formed around the village, no groups of soldiers assembling just over the hill.

He let himself out the front door, followed the line of trees and then climbed the garden stile. He saw now that by keeping close to the stone wall he would quickly get clear of the last cluster of village houses. The sun was warm on his back as he slid down the slope and reached the line of the wall. He followed it down till he came to a deep sunken lane. On the other side the hills rose gently away from him; the grass, an unfamiliar blue-green in color, speckled with the bright heads of spring flowers.

At a gap in the wall he scrambled down into the lane and began to climb the bank on the other side.

"Hey, you!" The voice rasped authority.

Through the sparse hawthorn hedge he glimpsed a military vehicle and the stiff red caps of the British Military Police. As he ran, he heard the engine roar behind him, passing him down the lane to fade at the next bend.

He stopped. Tension and fear made it difficult for him to control his breathing. Then the engine seemed to growl and snarl with effort, and a jeep came bouncing across the field toward him. As it slowed to a halt, two redcaps jumped out—tall, white-gaitered sergeants, their pistols swinging from white leather holsters.

At the same moment both men seemed to slow up, and to Horn's surprise he realized that both had raised their arms in a crisp salute.

"I'm sorry, sir," one of them said. "I didn't realize you were an officer. We just caught a glimpse of khaki in the lane and thought you were one of our AWOL lads making a run for it."

Horn struggled to control his voice. "That's okay, Sergeant. No harm done."

"You must be one of the American officers from the cottage in the village, sir," the second man said.

Horn nodded. "Thought I'd take a look around a Scottish village while I had the chance."

"They say the church is worth a look, sir. If you like that sort of thing." They were moving back toward the jeep.

"I'll take a look," Horn said.

"Sorry about the mistake, sir." The two sergeants saluted him again and climbed back into the jeep.

Now that they were obviously about to go, Horn felt a surge of confidence. "I'd have thought you'd have been busy chasing German fliers. They tell me a German plane crashed somewhere around here last night."

The sergeant at the wheel of the jeep grinned. "Quite a few miles from here, sir. And not much chasing to be done. The bastard broke his ankle as he landed. Got rounded up by a group of the local lads with pitchforks."

He switched on the engine and put the jeep in reverse. "Hope we didn't spoil your walk, sir."

He fishtailed the jeep skillfully back to a gap in the hedge, then waved before plunging forward into the lane.

When Horn got back to the cottage, Kay had already showered and changed into uniform. "So you decided to take a walk after all," she said, moving ahead of him toward the kitchen.

"Yes. It's a pretty little village."

"Will powdered be all right? The General finished the last of the regular eggs before he left," she called over her shoulder.

Powdered? He wondered what the devil that could mean.

"Sure, fine," he answered with more certainty than he felt. He went into the kitchen and leaned against the doorjamb, watching the tall blond woman with the shapely body under the severe uniform shirt and skirt as she cooked at the stove. She turned and placed the two omelets on the kitchen table, then paused, looking up as she saw him watching her.

He pushed himself off the doorjamb. He was suddenly desperately anxious to talk—to tell her who he was, how he came to be here in her kitchen, four hundred miles from where he should be in Berlikum flying daily sorties against the RAF. But again he knew it was a moment of weakness, of self-pity. Even as he looked into the gray eyes and the calm line of her mouth, he knew the need to talk had to be suppressed.

He had to act alone until he was safe in neutral America.

He pulled up a chair.

"Sorry about the eggs," she said as they began to eat. He smiled across the table at her, but again she caught him with that look, a long, unhurried question in her eyes.

"Anything wrong?" she asked after a moment.

"No, I guess I'm not too hungry." He had eaten no more than a few mouthfuls.

She offered him a cigarette from a pack of Wills Gold Flake.

"They're English. Hope they're okay."

He nodded and took one. She struck a match a little awkwardly and gave him a light.

"Thanks."

She watched him pull deeply on the smoke, his eyes looking past her at the wall.

"What time are you leaving for the base?"

"Fifteen minutes or so. Are you coming? They run a movie for U.S. personnel Sunday afternoon. You could take that in, then have dinner at the bar. By that time I'll be through myself."

He shook his head. Too quickly, he realized immediately. "No"—he deliberately slowed his speech—"I'll stay on here, if that's all right with you."

"Sure." She watched him stub out his cigarette and rise from the table. There was tension in every movement he made. She dismissed the thought that it was partly sexual. He was appreciably younger—four or five years—than she was. Nobody could imagine, even if they were staying in the house alone together. . . . Abruptly she stood up and began to collect the dishes.

"You were going to tell me," he said, "how come you joined the Nurse Corps."

"I was?" She stopped spooning coffee into the top of the percolator.

He smiled. "Let's say I hoped you were."

91

She looked gravely down at him. "I told you it was a long, long story."

"One you want to tell me?"

"We're passing ships, Alfred. Why do you want to hear the story of the mess I've made of my thirty-five years?"

"Will you stop reminding me how old you are?" He smiled. "Women are supposed to be discreet about such things. It's not *decent* to keep bringing it up. I *know* how old you are—and I've forgotten. Okay?" He paused. "I'm listening, Lieutenant."

"It's practically a life story," she warned him.

"I'd be disappointed with anything less."

"Well, let's see then. . . ." She hesitated. "You're sure you want to hear this?"

"Very sure."

"Okay." She looked away at the coffee percolating on the stove. "I was married, aged nineteen," she said, "to the boy next door. He was tall, handsome and had just graduated from West Point. Even in the peacetime army he was going places—and I was going with him."

"So we're not talking about Ralph," he said.

"No, were not talking about Ralph. So what happened? Six, seven years of promotions, successes . . . for him. Six, seven years for me of something I can only describe as an increasing feeling that I was alone. I lived with my husband . . . and I lived alone."

She nodded to herself. "By then, of course, I knew I'd married for all the wrong reasons." She looked up at Horn. "But I still liked him. I was really fond of the man, even though things just weren't working out. You know. . . ."

"In bed," Horn said.

"Yes, in bed."

"What happened?"

"One day I came back home unexpectedly. I don't remember why. He was upstairs. In bed with a young enlisted man. Strangely I don't think I was surprised too much. Maybe I'd known all along; maybe I just put together all those parties where the Captain would be surrounded by young officers and would hardly speak to a woman all evening. I don't know. Anyway, I spent that evening and all that night trying to tell him—what? That I wasn't going to crack up, I wasn't going to blurt it to my parents or his Colonel. I spent all that night telling him about the way *I* felt. I suppose it never occurred to me to ask how *he* felt. I was trying to be modern. In fact, I was just conventionally dumb. At dawn he went out for a walk. The shot woke me up."

"Look . . ." he began.

She smiled. "Didn't think it was going to be this sort of story?"

"No. I'm sorry I asked you."

"I'm not," she said. "It's good to take it out and dust it every now and again. It stops it from getting in too deep."

"You met Ralph . . . ?"

"Not right away. I went to Europe. Paris. I got quite a name as the wild American girl. Then, I don't know, around the spring of '35 I met Jean-Philippe. He was serious, political, intelligent and a hell of a good bedmate. And in 1936, when Franco invaded the Republic, Jean-Philippe went to Spain. He was dead in exactly fourteen days."

He got up and turned off the stove under the percolator. "So you went to Spain yourself?"

"To bring him back. But there was nothing to bring back. Or at least that's what they told me. So I stayed on because I had no reason to leave. I stayed on as an untrained auxiliary nurse. And I amputated legs and wired shattered jaws and buried children. . . . It was a poor people's war, you see. Neither side could afford the expensive long-range weapons. It was mostly bayonet and grenade and even club."

"How long did you stay?"

"Just a year. I couldn't take more. Just a year. I

came home to a civilian life that I just couldn't live any longer. I tried, but it didn't work. Maybe I joined the corps to prevent my conscience from pushing me back to Spain."

"Then you met Ralph?"

"Yes. At an interservice communications course. He was—well, you've seen him, six-five and about as far from the first guy I married as could be. And maybe even farther from Jean-Philippe."

He let her take her time.

"Ralph and I were married within a month." She looked Horn full in the eyes. "He's a nice guy, too," she said.

One hundred and seventy-five kilometers from Kay Hampton's cottage, the U-boat was making heavy weather of a rising Atlantic swell, driven by a stiff cold wind from the east. Fighting the sea, it lunged up the slope of a wave, hung for a moment at the crest, then plunged down into the trough, submerging the whole of the bow section almost as far as the bridge.

Two lookouts, lashed to the superstructure of the periscope column for safety, constantly scanned the sea and sky with powerful binoculars. Eight feet below, on the open deck of the bridge itself, Captain Günter Kranz checked the eastern horizon ahead with his own glasses. He looked older than his thirty-five years, the dark eyes were tired and the matted oil-stained stubble on his chin was already flecked with gray.

They had sailed two weeks ago, leaving the newly established base at Trondheim in Norway at first light on a bitterly cold morning at the end of April. The order to leave the U-boat pack, convoy-hunting in the Atlantic, had been received at 1400 hours. Whatever the exact nature of the mission, it was important; that much the Captain knew. The radio message had been coded direct from Oberkommando der Kriegmarine in Berlin and authorized by Vice Admiral Otto Schniewind, Chief of German Naval Staff and second only to Grand Admiral Raeder himself. To have any chance of making the rendezvous, the U-boat had been forced to travel on the surface at maximum speed, a hazardous operation in daylight. Submerged and running on its batteries, it could average no better than seven knots.

The Captain changed to the northern horizon and saw it immediately. The Blohm and Voss flying boat with its distinctive gnat shape seemed to hang on the horizon. Kranz calculated it was not more than five hundred feet above the waves, searching for the U-boat among the heaving gray-green walls of water. If it had been a British Sunderland or a Canadian Catalina, he reflected with a twisted smile, bad luck would have brought it over the U-boat right away.

He dropped his glasses to his chest and focused on the flying boat with his naked eye. Only if he lost sight of the flying boat, he decided, would he put up a flare. In these waters there were far too many hostile eyes just over the lip of the horizon.

For a minute or two longer the Blohm and Voss buzzed anxiously on a quartering course until suddenly it lifted in a steep bank and began to bear down on the U-boat. Within seconds now Kranz could make out individual struts and then the black crosses on the underside of its duck-egg-green wings as it swept low across the U-boat, banked tightly and came down across the waves to spume water from beneath its twin floats while it rolled and bucked across the surface of the heavy sea.

Kranz watched for other aircraft in the sky as a shapeless form was hurled from the flying boat to inflate into an orange rubber dinghy. As the U-boat Captain meticulously covered the sky section by section, four men rowed from the flying boat.

Five minutes later Kranz sat in his minute sea cabin opposite the leader of the four men. Like his three companions, Otto Denck was dressed in civilian clothes, a nondescript dark suit and a fawn belted raincoat. Denck himself was an open-faced young man of not more than twenty-two or -three. He smiled apologetically as he pushed his authorization across the chart table to Kranz. "I can guess exactly what you're thinking, Captain, to come under orders to a landlubber like me. But I can assure you this is a vital task."

Kranz exhaled heavily. *"A vos ordres,"* he said.

"We have a rendezvous to make at midnight tonight. Midnight British double summer time, that is."

"And where is the rendezvous to be, Herr Denck?"

Again Otto Denck smiled apologetically. "At a point just off the Scottish coast. In the Firth of Clyde, I'm afraid."

Kranz rubbed at the stubble on his chin. Denck saw that behind his hand the Captain was smiling.

"This rendezvous," Kranz said. "Do we have to surface?"

"It's a rendezvous *with* someone. For that we have to surface," Denck said quietly.

"Then take my word for it, Herr Denck, we shall be blown clean out of the water."

Denck looked at him evenly. "Captain," he said quietly, "if I tell you that I received my orders directly from Reinhard Heydrich in the presence of the Führer himself, will that make you feel any different?"

Kranz eyed the earnest young face, the pleasant line of the mouth and determined set of the jaw. *"Much* different," he said, and to Otto Denck's total astonishment burst out laughing. "Much, much different."

Kay finished the dishes and took down her uniform jacket from the back of the kitchen door. "If you're here until Tuesday and there's nothing out of Prestwick until then, you're welcome to stay on here at the cottage," she said casually.

"I'd appreciate it," Horn said.

"Fine," she said briskly. "In that case I'll make out a requisition at the commissary for rations for you. Things are pretty tough here in Britain at the moment. Even a U.S. Army ration scale gets to look pretty princely in comparison with civilian levels."

Horn hesitated. "I think I'd sooner you didn't," he said slowly.

She slipped into her jacket, frowning. "Why not?"

"Look, as you must have gathered, my presence here is . . . somewhat unofficial. General Walker understands my presence. He'd prefer if I weren't entered on any ration list."

She buttoned her jacket. "Okay." She walked across to the table. "You want some coffee?"

"Thanks."

Her back was toward him. He had no way of knowing what she was thinking. But he felt somehow that the fragile bond of trust they had built up in the last hour had broken. He moved to the window and looked out at the walled garden. The grass needed cutting, and the borders were overgrown.

At the very periphery of his vision he was aware of someone standing in the walled garden. Some instinct compelled him not to move his head. Instead, he glanced right to the open window a few inches from his head. Reflected clearly in the glass was the figure of old Mr. Frank, standing with his hands in the pockets of his long black overcoat, perfectly motionless, watching him.

Horn moved unhurriedly, and the old man began to pick his way across the unkempt garden. "Morning, Captain," he called. "Terrible waste of good growing land, this. Especially in wartime."

Horn moved away from the window and opened the door. "Is the lady Lieutenant in?" Frank asked.

Kay came forward. "She is, Mr. Frank. Only just. Come and have some real American coffee before I leave for the base."

"How could I refuse? Especially as I'm bringing a little of good news for you, I think, Lieutenant."

She paused, percolator in hand, intrigued.

"Yes," he continued. "That salt I sold you the other day—"

"The salt cellar?"

"Yes. I've come across the perfect match for it. What did you pay—fifty dollars? Let's see, then; for another, say, forty dollars you can have a pair worth six times as much as the single."

Horn watched the old man carefully. Mr. Frank claimed last night not to be a salesman, but he certainly had the technique. The old man seemed to be reading his thoughts. He smiled. "The Captain here is thinking this is all a very subtle soft sell. Not so, Captain."

"If it makes the pair I'll buy it," Kay said.

"You won't regret it, my dear, I promise you that. But let's see, I'm off to Glasgow shortly. When will you be able to pick it up?"

Kay turned from where she was counting forty American dollars from a polished leather wallet. "Perhaps you wouldn't mind going down with Mr. Frank?" She was looking at Horn. "You could take the bicycle in the back of his van and ride back."

Horn hesitated, temporarily bereft of an excuse.

"You could also look over my shop for yourself," the dealer said. "If you don't like silver, there just might be something else."

"Sure, I'll pick it up for you," Horn said.

In the small market town of Tarbolton, four miles away, the tiny bell above the front door tinkled as Mr. Frank unlocked his shop. The interior had a faintly musty smell to it, matching the contents, early Victoriana, brass and pewter, odd pieces of china, piles of old books and magazines and one or two nice pieces among the bric-a-brac. There was a finely decorated marquetry table against one wall, and by it a late-eighteenth-century English long-case clock. On the opposite wall hung three or four oil portraits of liquid-eyed minor English aristocrats.

"I've ceased to apologize for the condition of my shop, Captain," Horn's companion said. "I bought it originally from a dealer in junk, and I've never really got around to getting it cleared up. Let's go above. I keep the silver up there."

He started up a flight of rickety, exposed wooden steps leading to a gallery above the shop level. As Horn made to follow him, Frank half turned. "Be careful of your head," he said. It was only as Horn ducked to avoid the heavy low rafter that he realized the old man had spoken in German. His heart beating rapidly, he glanced up to see if Frank had noticed his immediate reaction, but the old man had reached the top stair and was surveying his domain. The whole area was piled high with broken chairs, old doorless wardrobes and piles of ancient newspapers tied with string. Space had been cleared in the middle enough to accommodate a table covered with a green baize cloth. The old man selected a chair from a pile, rocked it on its legs to test their strength and handed it to Horn. Selecting another for himself, he placed it on the opposite side of the table, then turned away to where an ancient Bartram safe stood against the wall. After opening the door, he drew a tray of silver objects from inside. In contrast with the rest of his stock, the silver was immaculately kept. Burnished salt cellars and porringers rose among great piles of ladles and gleaming forks.

Staggering under the considerable weight, the old man placed the tray on the table. "There, Captain," he said as he sat opposite Horn. "English silver is among the most beautiful artifacts of a civilized world." He was watching Horn, his eyes hooded by his heavy lids. "Do you enjoy silver, Captain?"

What would the average American flier know about silver? In fact, Horn's father kept a modest collection among which were one or two English pieces. "I know next to nothing about it, Mr. Frank. All I know is what I see. It looks old, and it looks good."

The old man nodded heavily. He took a cigarette from a bent pack of Players Navy Cut and lit it from a lighter. "This is the piece I'd choose for Lieutenant Hampton. What do you think?"

He reached out and took an eighteenth-century salt cellar between thumb and finger. Like a chess player making a move, he placed it in front of Horn.

Horn shrugged. "Don't draw me into this, Mr. Frank. For all I know it was made last week in Scranton, Pennsylvania."

"Hardly." The old man breathed out cigarette smoke. "The other man," he said suddenly, "the officer who was supposed to be flying with you to the States—what happened to him?"

Horn stiffened, his eyes on the gleaming pieces of silver. "How did you hear about him?"

"The Lieutenant told me she was waiting on in England for *two* American officers."

Horn nodded, aware of the old man's unblinking stare. "The Colonel got involved in a road accident. It'll be a week or so yet before he's fit to fly."

Frank closed his eyes. His head rocked almost as if he were going to faint. Then he reopened his eyes and stared rheumily into Horn's face. "Forgive me," he said. "But you can't imagine how much is at stake."

Horn frowned. "At stake. On what?"

"On my being right." Mr. Frank leaned forward and touched Horn's hand with his index finger. "You see," he said, "I believe you are Captain Alfred Horn. I believe your injured companion is Rudolf Hess, Germany's Deputy Führer."

"What in hell's name . . . ?"

"Don't bluster, Captain." The old man cut him short. "I have received a message from Berlin. . . ." He stood up. "I'll show you."

He dragged a battered chest of drawers from the

front of a cupboard and opened the door. Horn was standing at his shoulder as he pulled out a rusty ironing board and a torn and dusty portrait. There in the back of the cupboard the high-powered transmitter receiver gleamed like something from another century among the dusty bric-a-brac of Mr. Frank's life.

"My message from Berlin was to contact you and Herr Hess. It told me you were on your way to America via Prestwick." He heaved his shoulders, almost apologizing. "Prestwick, of course, is my routine assignment. I sell my little pieces of silver to the ferry pilots and report back to Berlin on the number of Flying Fortresses shipped in each month."

"You took a hell of a risk." It seemed somehow natural for Horn to continue in English.

The old man smiled. "You don't know what a hell of a risk, Captain."

A poacher found the canvas bag while following the line of the stone wall in pursuit of a hare. By 3:00 P.M. on Sunday it had been delivered to the police at Eaglesham, and half an hour later Inspector Jess MacDonald of the Ayrshire Constabulary was examining the contents. A phone call to Scottish Air Command brought him in contact with the security blanket which someone had decided must be thrown over the crash of a possibly new long-range type of Messerschmitt 110. All requests for further information would have to be routed through London. Hours later Inspector Macdonald would still be awaiting an answer to his question—who exactly was in charge of interrogating the German flier who had crashed at Eaglesham on Saturday evening?

Seven

Sunday, May 11, 3:00 P.M. Rudolf Hess sat up in bed. He had already complained about the lunch, the coffee and the general lack of respect shown by nurses and the doctor who had examined his ankle.

After phoning Henderson in London, Max Bishop had returned to the guarded private room. The Lieutenant in command of the sentries had warned him that the prisoner refused to answer all questions. Handing Bishop a mug of steaming tea, the young officer nodded toward the door of the private room. "At the risk of sounding a raving idiot, sir," he said to Bishop, "I don't think that man in there is named Horn at all."

Bishop looked at him curiously. "What makes you say that?"

The Lieutenant put down his tea and drew Bishop away from the sentry along the corridor. "You're going to think I'm mad, sir, but I think I recognize him. From the newsreels. I think he's Rudolf Hess."

He stepped back, waiting for Bishop either to burst out laughing or to shower him with sarcasm. Bishop did neither. He drank a deep draft of the dark tea. "I think you're right, Lieutenant," he said. "But you'll be court-martialed if you breathe one word of this to anyone."

The young Lieutenant could hardly contain his

excitement. "What about the press, sir? The Glasgow *Herald* are already interested. They were just on the phone."

"They've no idea who he is? Or rather who he might be?" Bishop frowned anxiously.

"No, sir. To them it's a straightforward story of a crashed plane and a captured pilot."

"Okay, let's keep it that way for as long as we possibly can."

Max Bishop handed the Lieutenant his half-finished mug of tea and walked between the guards into the private room. He stood for a moment looking at the man sitting up in bed. "I've been assigned to ask you a few questions," he said. "My name is Bishop."

"Sit down, Major Bishop."

"Let's get on to the right foot from the beginning. I was in Berlin for the 1936 Olympics. Alfred Horn was a fellow competitor. You are not Alfred Horn." Bishop drew up a cane armchair and sat down. "Who are you?"

"I am Rudolf Hess," Hess said simply. "I think you recognized me earlier."

"And why would Rudolf Hess have flown voluntarily to Britain?"

Hess was silent.

"A superficial resemblance to Rudolf Hess—"

"I am Hess," the German snapped.

Bishop took a pack of cigarettes from his pocket.

"Please don't smoke in here," Hess said peremptorily.

Bishop took a cigarette from the pack and lit it.

"I requested you not to smoke."

Bishop deliberately ignored him. "If you are Rudolf Hess, what are you doing here in Britain? Until you answer that question, your real identity must remain in doubt."

He had miscalculated. Hess stiffened, staring ahead. "I am not prepared to open discussions with a junior officer," he said.

Bishop looked at the strange theatrical pose, the eyes staring at the blank hospital wall in front of him.

"Do you have any way of proving you're Rudolf Hess?"

If Hess heard the words of the question, the meaning failed to penetrate to a conscious level. His thoughts were on what might have been. On the new Reich Chancellery in Berlin the day he arrived back, triumphantly from America, his mission a spectacular success. The Führer, of course, would be waiting, standing behind his vast desk, the Gobelin tapestry behind him. On either side of the desk in groups of two or three, anxious and depressed at the Stellvertreter's fantastic success, would be the Nazi leadership. Goering, who threatened Hess's position as Hitler's deputy; Himmler, who threatened his power throughout the Nazi Party in the country; Goebbels, who jeered at him behind his back; even his own deputy, Bormann, who was worming his way steadily into Hitler's regard. No, there had been no other course to take. He had been right to risk everything in one massive reminder to the Führer that he, Hess alone, would risk life and reputation for Hitler and Germany.

In his imagination he stood now at the twenty-foot-high double doors of the Führer's office, the black-uniformed SS life guards had presented arms . . . an SS adjutant opened the door—and across the enormous room the Führer stood, the Order of Maria Theresa in his hand. . . .

Lost in his reverie, the Deputy Führer of the Third Reich continued to stare ahead, his jaw jutting, his mouth turned down at the corners. To Max Bishop he looked like nothing so much as a petulant child.

In London, Winston Churchill turned from the window overlooking the garden at 10 Downing Street and fixed his blue eyes on Henderson and the Brigadier. "Gentlemen"—his voice rumbled through the room—"it is unknown in the annals of warfare for a power drunk with victory to sue for peace. A physical similarity to Rudolf Hess is insufficient evidence. Give me proof. And give it to me today."

"With respect, sir," Henderson began, "that is an impossible request."

Churchill drew on his cigar. "It is not a request, Colonel." Even in the small room his delivery was timed for the debating chamber. "It—is—a—command."

A knock at the door interrupted them, and the Number 10 butler entered, carrying a silver tray. Henderson's eyes widened in astonishment. On the tray lay a neatly folded pair of black socks. The Prime Minister sat on the arm of a chair, removed his shoes and socks and wriggled his toes in the carpet. "A man should change his socks several times a day," he grunted. "Fresh air is as important to the feet as it is to the mind." He took the new pair of socks from the proffered tray and, cigar in his mouth, bent over, then started to put them on. "Alexandria," he growled. "Try Alexandria."

Above his head Henderson shot the Brigadier an alarmed glance.

"Alexandria, sir?" The Brigadier swallowed hard.

The butler placed the used socks on the silver tray and withdrew. The Prime Minister stood in his stockinged feet. "Hess was born in Egypt. Spent his early years in Alexandria. Must have seen a dentist. Find him. Get his records. Check them against the man we have in Scotland. Good-day, gentlemen."

At a depth of forty meters, the U-boat was making almost seven knots. Like some giant steel cigar, sixty-seven meters long and with a 6.2-meter beam, it slid through the dark water, every moment taking it deeper into the narrowing neck of the Firth of Clyde. In the control room Captain Kranz hunched over the chart table. He knew this was madness. And within a couple of hours they were due to surface. That would be utter madness.

The massive twin diesels, which could develop twenty-eight-hundred horsepower, lay cold and silent. Underwater the submarine was forced to use its electric motors, powered by the banks of batteries stowed under the control room and galley. To use the diesels would have the same effect as running a car in a closed garage: the fumes would kill everyone aboard.

Otto Denck sat on the edge of a bunk opposite his companions. Like him, they were barely out of their teens. Wearing polo-neck sweaters under their dark suits, they looked even more boyish than their young leader. They regarded themselves as members of an elite not simply because each one had graduated with honors from the SS officer cadet school at Bad Tölz, but because they were part of a hundred-man Sonderkommando attached particularly to the person and orders of Reinhard Heydrich.

In the control room Captain Kranz stared at his watch. On the surface it would still be half light, but he knew he must check their position visually. The planesmen sat with their backs to him at the hydroplane controls, keeping the submarine steady and level, constantly checking the inclinometers.

The Captain decided. "Take her up," he ordered.

"Fore planes up twenty, after planes down five," the Lieutenant said in a harsh whisper.

In the bunk room Denck and the three others felt the submarine angle sharply upward.

"At periscope depth," the chief called.

The Captain, hunched in the saddle seat with his feet on the pedals which enabled him to rotate 360 degrees, followed the sea and sky scan periscope up with his head tight against the rubber eye pieces. The chief ordered tiny corrections to the submarine's trim in a gruff, whispered voice. It was a good depth. The motor hummed as Kranz searched around the surface, then centered on the unmistakable outline of Ailsa

Craig. The granite stump of the old volcano rose more than one thousand feet from the deep blue-green sea. He read off the sight bearing to the Lieutenant standing at the chart table. Now he scanned again and fixed on the southern tip of the island of Arran.

It was almost dark as Angus Gemmel shuffled toward the sixth green. He was a sprightly seventy-two-year-old, thin, wiry and tough, like the scrub grass that grew along the shore of his native Ayrshire. Armed with an ancient Lee-Enfield rifle, he, as a member of the Local Defense Volunteers, had the task of patrolling this strip of shore each night. Troon golf course had been part of his life as long as he could remember, first as a ball boy and caddy, then as a green-keeper and member of the Artisans' team. He had retired two years before but still walked daily over his beloved seaside links.

He carried an old leather golf bag and a few favorite clubs. Each evening before the light failed, he hit a dozen or so shots with his low swing and crablike stance; it was not very elegant, but he still played off a handicap of fifteen. The sun had dropped far below the western horizon, but as Gemmel screwed up his eyes and looked out over the darkening sea, he felt, for a moment, he could make out Goat Fell on the Isle of Arran. It was imagination, he knew that. It was a long way off, almost twenty miles, and the light was fading. He recalled how he had seen it so often in his youth, on those sharp, blindingly bright early mornings of spring, when the sea had the look of a sheet of glass and it had seemed so close he felt he could take out his brassie and sail a ball right across to the other side. He continued on his nightly patrol, whistling tunelessly as he went.

"What was that?" said Horn in a quick whisper.

"I heard nothing." Mr. Frank screwed his eyes up to peer into the darkness.

"Someone whistling."

The old man cocked his head, listening intently. "Just the sea. What time is it?"

Horn checked his watch anxiously.

"They'll soon be here, young man. That's if they're coming at all."

"They'll come," said Horn, pulling the collar of the raincoat up around his neck. They sat in silence, Horn staring out across the glistening black water. He felt strangely relaxed and secure. Soon he would be on his way home. They were crouched on the edge of the beach in a hollow in the dunes. The winds rustled the clumps of grass around their heads.

Without a word both men came to their feet as the dark shape of the conning tower broke the water about 250 yards from the shore. Then, with startling speed, the U-boat rose like some primeval sea monster in a sudden eruption of hissing turbulence.

In the moonlight they could clearly see the water pouring down the sides of the hull.

A boatswain's lamp flashed briefly from the conning tower, its short, low-angled beam reflecting on the surface of the water in a thousand points of broken light. Mr. Frank fumbled in the pocket of his overcoat and produced a flashlight, then answered with three Morse dots: the letter S.

The moon had slipped behind a cloud. It was suddenly quite dark. But Horn could hear the paddles moving in the water as the raft neared the shore. He felt immensely comforted by the idea that the long arm of German sea power could reach out like this across the waters. For a brief moment he wondered about the reactions of the old man next to him. He would be staying, daily facing the possibility of the firing squad for the rest of the war.

Horn turned to him. "You must have a family back home . . . ?"

"Yes." The tone was flat.

"Then let me take them some sort of message."

"That wouldn't be allowed, Captain."

The outline of the men in the rubber boat was quite clear now.

"I'm not talking about rules, Mr. Frank. I'll do it anyway."

His companion looked up at Horn. "In Germany," he said, "we Jews make sure the rules are obeyed. It's safer."

The approaching rubber boat was suddenly wiped from Horn's consciousness. "You mean you really are Jewish?"

"Yes."

"Yet you still work for Germany?"

"I have no choice, Captain. My wife and two daughters are in a camp for racial criminals. While I live and work, they are safe." He turned to Horn, his mouth twisted with bitterness, "Safe, I mean, from the immediate threat of death. Not safe from the sadistic brutes who patrol the compounds with dogs and bull-whips, not safe from the smartly uniformed perverts that run these places."

"You've been in a camp?" Horn's voice was thick.

"Yes, Hauptmann Horn. I was in a camp at Dachau. I was a racial criminal, too, of course. Then, one day in 1934, I was told I was going to England. As a refugee. They had a job for me to do there. And my wife and daughters were to stay in Dachau to make sure I did it well."

"When I get back——" Horn said fiercely.

"When you get back," the old man said, "say and do nothing. Our country is in the grip of criminal per-verts, Captain. Wait and watch. And when decent Germany begins to struggle from its drugged sleep, perhaps a young man like you will be able to help nudge it awake."

Horn stood breathing heavily beside the old man, his breath mistily visible in the cold night air. "I used to think," he said slowly, "that bravery was leading men in battle . . . or flying fighter planes. . . ."

Frank shook his head. "I'm not brave, Captain. Every single day of my life I shake with fear that I'll be discovered with that radio set. Because the day I fail to answer a message is the day my family ceases to be protected." He put his hand inside his long black overcoat and took out a small silver snuffbox. "I brought this along for you, Captain. I know nothing about your mission here, but I flatter myself I know a decent German when I meet one. I've had, after all, such a wide experience of the others. Take it as a memento of anything you need a memento for in the next few years."

He pressed the finely wrought box into Horn's hand.

The rubber boat touched the beach, and the four men jumped ashore. Horn slipped the snuffbox into his pocket. "I promise you this," he said. "Whatever happens I won't forget what you've told me tonight."

"Hurry!" the old man pressed his arm.

The waves lapped sluggishly against the flat wet sand as Denck splashed across the last four feet and led the group ashore. They pulled the dinghy clear of the water and scanned around. The dunes had a ghostly emptiness, shining almost silver in the re-emerging moonlight.

"Stellvertreter!" Denck called the word, his narrowed eyes sweeping around. He called again: "Hauptmann Horn!"

"Over here."

Denck turned to the direction of the voice and waved his men forward. Horn could now see them approaching, stumbling over the fine loose sand. It struck him as strange that they seemed to be dressed in civilian clothes, but he started forward to meet them. They stopped twenty feet away. The man in front felt inside his overcoat as if for a pack of cigarettes: a slow, deliberate, relaxed movement.

Horn saw the flash from the Luger but could remember hearing no sound. Two steps behind him Mr. Frank was hurled back six feet with the impact as the bullet hit him square in the stomach. There was another flash somewhere behind the first. Horn felt the jarring impact as he hit the sand. Some reflex had forced him to hurl himself aside. Now he was crawling, stumbling, running, his eyes full of grit, spitting sand from his gaping mouth.

Denck stared down at Frank's face. A muscle twitched in the old man's left cheek, the blood already soaking up into a widening black patch across the front of the overcoat from the gaping tear in the abdomen.

The two SS men came forward to join Denck.

"Who is he?" asked Hans Richter.

"Quiet!" said Denck. His head was turned toward the dunes, listening.

Horn lay in a patch of foot-high grass fifty yards away. At first he thought he had been hit by the second shot. His left shoulder felt numb as he fought to regain his wind. Old Mr. Frank, dead or dying in the sand—why had they ruthlessly gunned him down without a word? Was it some hideous mistake? But then they had called his name. . . . And Stellvertreter.

A soft metallic click caught his attention. Then, after a moment, heavy nasal breathing. He moved his head an inch to increase his field of vision. Richter stood eight feet away, his square, broad-shouldered figure looming against the night sky. Horn could hear a strange snort in the man's nose, smell the stagnant, clinging odor from the submarine. Richter took two steps closer, pulling on a leather glove, looking out at eye level over the prostrate figure lying almost under his feet. Horn's eyes fixed on the black boots. A spray of fine sand clung to the wetness from the sea; the left lace had been broken and retied in an awkward ragged knot. Now another click as the press stud on the second glove was fastened, and Richter slowly lowered his gaze. He seemed to jump with surprise as he saw Horn but immediately straightened his arm, pointing it down, clamping the left hand over the right wrist to steady the aim. Horn saw the familiar square menace of the Luger in his hand and buried his head, facedown, in the grass.

He heard the shot. Then nothing, no pain, no enveloping darkness, no bottomless pit, none of the half-formed images of death he had contemplated many times. Ten seconds passed. Horn got slowly to his feet. Richter lay dead, shot through the side of the head.

A hundred yards away, old Angus Gemmel moved off across the fairway as fast as an excited, jerky trot would take him. He had seen and heard everything, the submarine, the men coming ashore and the German voices. He could not bring himself to believe it at first, but there it was, happening before his eyes. Germans were landing from a U-boat. Crouching low and watching with his pulse pounding in his ears, he had waited for a chance to slip away unseen. But then this one man, moving through the dunes, had come relentlessly toward him. He knew he was about to be discovered, and remembering the advice of an old World War I veteran, he had slipped the rifle out of the golf bag and got the shot in first. The bullet from the ancient 303 had been straight and true; the man was dead, Angus was certain of that. Now his one thought was to sound the alarm, tell the police, rouse the LDV, warn the army, tell everyone the Germans were here.

Hagen, his massive frame heaving with nausea, knelt in the sand and was violently sick. Denck watched him with ill-disguised contempt, then tensed as someone approached from the dunes. It was Godt, whom he had sent to find Richter.

"He's dead."

"What?" said Denck.

"Shot through the head."

"Signal the U-boat," Denck said. "We're staying ashore."

Frank knew he was dying; there was no pain, just a creeping numbness spreading across and up his body as he lay on his back in the damp sand. He could feel what he took to be his own heartbeat in his temples and at the back of the neck.

Denck bent low over him, hissing the question out from between tight lips. "Who are you?"

"Does it matter?" said Frank.

"Where is Stellvertreter Hess?"

Frank turned his head away, feeling the sand cold and grainy on his cheek.

Denck took hold of his chin and pulled the head back around to face his own. "Where is he?"

Frank stared up at Denck's face and in those unblinking eyes immediately knew the truth. They had mistaken him, Joseph Frank, for the Deputy Führer of the Third Reich, and they had gunned him down. It could only mean one thing: They had intended to shoot Hess; they hadn't been sent to rescue him and take him back to Germany. They had been sent to kill him, and they would do it still if they had the chance. He almost laughed as he saw the final, beautiful irony. He could give them that chance; he could set these killers on to number two in the Nazi hierarchy.

"For the last time, are you going to tell me where Stellvertreter Hess is?"

"Gladly," said Frank, with an inward glow of triumph.

Kay sat in the kitchen at the cottage and stared at the untouched cup of coffee in front of her. A note from Horn lay screwed into a ball in the corner where she had thrown it. Its terse, impersonal tone had upset her more than she could have imagined, but what more did she expect? A strange, intense young man had briefly entered her life, and now he was gone.

He had left the pack of cigarettes she had given him on the corner of the table. She went to take one but found the pack empty and pushed it aside. What was she doing anyway? She hardly ever smoked. No, the answer was a hot bath and bed. It was almost two in the morning. She had been sitting here for almost an hour. Irritated at herself, she saw the coffee was stone cold. As she turned to get up from the chair, Horn stood framed in the back door. It had not been locked, and he had entered without a sound.

"I didn't expect to see you again," she said, quickly recovering from her surprise and walking through into the sitting room.

Horn carefully closed and locked the door, then followed.

"Would you like some coffee? Or there's a bottle of Scotch around somewhere." She waved offhandedly over her shoulder.

"Yes." He nodded. "Scotch. . . ."

She turned to face him. "What is it, Alfred? Are you in trouble?"

"I'm okay," he said shortly.

"What the hell have you been doing?" she asked, noticing the state of his clothing.

"Look, I'm fine."

She turned away, trying to remember where she had seen the bottle of Scotch.

"Well, you don't look fine," she said, her voice edged with annoyance. She searched around the room, opening a cabinet and banging the door shut, and her annoyance increased as she failed to find the whisky. She turned to face him again. "You expect to walk back in here in the middle of the night . . . what the hell do you take me for?"

"Kay, old Mr. Frank. He's dead."

The pain passed like a shadow over her face. "There's been an accident?"

Horn sat down. "No accident."

She stared down rigidly at him.

"No." He shook his head. "It wasn't me."

"Jesus," she exploded. "What are you saying?"

"I'm saying somebody killed Mr. Frank."

"Broke into the shop?"

Horn stared up at her desperately. "Look, maybe in an hour or two I can give you some sort of explanation. But I have to do something first, and I need your help. I promise you, Kay, when I can, I'll explain."

She found the Scotch and poured him one. "Okay, Alfred," she spoke slowly, her eyes never leaving him. "When General Walker left for the States, his orders were for me to give you all the help I could."

She brought a glass for herself and sat down opposite him. "Go ahead."

"A couple of days ago a plane crashed over at Dungavel."

She nodded. "A German plane, I heard about it."

"The pilot was injured."

"I heard nothing about the pilot. I guess I assumed he was killed. What do you need to know, Alfred?"

"I want to know where the German pilot was taken," he said slowly.

"What for?"

He remained silent. After a moment she shrugged. "Okay, I guess he was taken to a hospital if he was injured," she said coolly.

"Which hospital?"

"How could I possibly know?"

Horn passed a hand across his forehead and tried to think. Was it possible Hess had eluded the men closing in through the wood? No, he could hardly stand, let alone attempt to escape. He recalled Frank had confirmed there was nothing in the papers or on the radio about the Deputy Führer, but that made no sense either. Hess would be a prize of enormous propaganda value and would surely be exploited by the British to the full. There was one other alternative. Was it conceivable the British had captured their man but simply did not realize who he was?

Horn knew only one thing for certain. His own situation was impossible. He could surrender to the British and face a firing squad as a spy, or try to escape somehow and get back to Germany, but if the events on the beach were anything to go by, what did he face when he arrived home? He felt suddenly flooded by an immense sense of desperation, almost like a child's bitter resentment at the injustice of the world. He was a Luftwaffe officer. He had obeyed the orders of one of the leading men in his country. And those orders had brought him to the labyrinth in which he now found himself.

He was aware that Kay was watching him closely as he stood up, his mouth moving with a mix of anger and self-pity. He knew he had to talk to Hess. Only Hess could tell him what to do next. But Hess was a prisoner. He swallowed a large gulp of whisky. Hospitals, of course, were not prison camps. And if the British really had not yet recognized the Stellvertreter, perhaps they would not have mounted too much of a guard on a German pilot with a broken leg.

"Kay, do you have any way of finding out which hospital?"

She shook her head, baffled. "The nearest one to Dungavel, I guess."

"Where's that?"

"Ten or fifteen miles down the road past the base."

"Can I take the jeep?"

"Look, it's two in the morning, and I'm guessing. A wild guess; he could be anywhere."

"I've got to try," he said flatly.

The car keys were in the pocket of her jacket. She took them out.

"I'll drive you," she said, moving toward the door.

Although the journey was little more than ten miles, it took Horn and Kay over half an hour to reach the hospital. Navigating the narrow Scottish lanes in total darkness, with no place-names or signposts, had been a slow and frustrating process.

At last the slits of light from the jeep's headlights picked out the gateway. Kay drove up to the entrance to the gravel driveway and stopped outside a stone lodge. The long, low hospital building lay completely blacked out in an open parkland setting.

"Park a little farther down the road," he said as he got out of the car. "I won't be long."

As he entered the lodge, the jeep pulled away.

Inside, it was almost as dark as outside, except for a tiny spill of light from a single low-wattage bulb shaded with a makeshift black paper hood. It was difficult to make out very much outside this weak central glow. A door led off to the left. Horn crossed the polished tiled floor to the desk and lifted the telephone. The line was dead. He tapped the cradle, but there was no response. As he replaced the receiver, he noticed a bell on the wall with a small notice beneath it. He squinted to read it. "Ring for attention." He pressed the bell, and a few moments later an elderly man in a black hospital porter's uniform opened the door on the left. He carried a steaming mug of tea and spoke over his shoulder to someone in the rear room, "You can relax. It's not the sergeant."

As the door closed, Horn leaned forward to catch a glimpse of two khaki-uniformed figures in the back room.

"Can I help you, sir?" the porter asked, placing his mug of tea on the desk.

Horn kept his voice low. "My name's Vincent," he said. "John Vincent. Toronto *Globe and Mail*. You've got a German pilot here."

"We might have, sir." The porter picked up his mug. "Then again—"

"You might not." Horn finished the sentence for him. The porter nodded.

From his hip pocket Horn drew a wad of white five-pound notes and ostentatiously peeled off two. "Do they do anything for your memory?"

The old porter swallowed hard and glanced over his shoulder to check that the door was closed. "A reporter, you say. From Canada."

"The pilot, he's here, right?" Horn pushed the money into the man's hand.

"I could be in real trouble if this came out."

"It won't," Horn said. "Now, whereabouts are they keeping him?"

The porter hesitated. "He was up in the east wing. You'll never get to see him; he's too well guarded. And in any case they're due to move him any moment."

Horn's informant moved over to the main door and opened it quietly, then spent a second or two frowning into the darkness. When he returned, he nodded to himself. "The ambulance is up at the main entrance now."

"Where are they taking him?"

"I've no idea, sir."

"Have you seen him yourself?"

"Aye, when they first brought him in. Big man, tall . . . a Captain. Will his name help your story? I've got it here." He turned a page in his book. "Horn, Captain Alfred Horn."

The telephone prevented the porter from registering Horn's surprise. He leaned over and lifted the receiver. "Mr. Rogers, porter's lodge." He listened for a few moments. "Aye, sir, I understand."

He replaced the receiver and turned back to Horn. "You'll have to be going, sir. The ambulance and escort are just leaving." He dropped his voice. "I'll have to warn the lads having their tea break in there." He gestured at the rear room.

Horn nodded and turned for the door. As he opened it, he heard the splutter of motorcycle engines being started fifty or sixty yards away up the drive. Looking toward the hospital main entrance, he could just make out the shape of the military ambulance and the outline of the red cross on a white background. As the vehicle moved forward, the thin slits of light from its masked headlights swung to face Horn.

Suddenly a voice yelled in German, and the unmistakable hammer of a Schmeisser machine pistol blurted from the darkness beside the drive. While Horn crouched at the lodge gate, a percussion grenade exploded under the front wheels of the ambulance, turning it on its side in the ditch and enveloping the engine in flames. Then more grenades split the darkness around, and a second Schmeisser joined the first.

The shouts were now both in English and German, and as one of the motorcycle gas tanks ignited from a red-hot grenade fragment, the whole confused scene was illuminated by a burst of bright yellow flame. In the twenty seconds before it died, Horn saw two running men shot down by a British sergeant firing a Bren gun from the hip; then the back doors of the burning ambulance burst open, and to his astonishment the unmistakable figure of Max Bishop was pushing Rudolf Hess down into the cover of the ditch. As the Stellvertreter stumbled forward and the flames died, the figure of a man ran through the swirling smoke. Lifting his Schmeisser to his hip, Denck fired a long burst into the ditch before ducking behind the ambulance and running for the woods.

Horn had seen Hess hit, jackknifing forward into the ditch. Now, as the firing died away, he heard the elderly porter shout out from the lodge.

"What happened?"

One of the British soldiers ran back to cover the entrance to the drive. "The bloody German pilot's been killed, that's what's happened."

Horn looked a final time toward the burning ambulance. He could see the tall, hatless figure of Max Bishop looking down into the ditch. He had no time to wonder at the staggering coincidence of his onetime friend's appearance on the scene. He turned and, crouching low, ran for the parked jeep silhouetted fifty yards along the road.

Reaching the jeep, Horn wrenched open the door. *"Schnell, schnell!"* he said, and stopped dead, one leg inside the jeep.

Kay looked up at him. "Get in," she said quietly, and started the engine.

Only when they got him into the hospital reception area was it apparent that Hess was not badly hurt. As a doctor sponged the blood from the German's face, Bishop felt an overwhelming relief.

"That was about as close as you can get," the young Scots doctor said matter-of-factly, "without actually spilling your brain all over the driveway."

"Providence," Hess said coldly. "We die when we are meant to die."

"Aye," the doctor said. "But we get killed when some maniac looses off a full magazine at us."

"You realize they were Germans," Bishop said as Hess shrugged.

"Of course." It was the last allusion to the attack that Rudolf Hess was ever to make, the first and last time he recognized that Adolf Hitler had tried to have him killed.

The Lieutenant in command of the guard came through the swing doors and signaled to Bishop.

"What is it?"

"Telephone, sir. The police at Tarbolton." He glanced across at Hess. "Is he going to be all right, sir?"

Bishop nodded.

The Lieutenant pursed his lips. "Can't say if I'm pleased or sorry."

Bishop crossed to the desk and lifted the receiver. A strong Scottish voice said, "Major Bishop?"

"Yes."

"Major, this is Inspector Jess MacDonald. Ayrshire police. I've had to get London to find out who's in charge over there."

"Go on, Inspector."

"I've been holding a canvas bag which I think you'll find interesting. I think it was abandoned by the German flier who came down Saturday night."

"Can you bring it over right away?"

"I've got a car waiting. One other thing, Major. While I was dealing with all the London red tape, I questioned the local farmers who saw the plane crash. From their descriptions I became pretty sure *two* men jumped from the plane. I've had my men up on the hillside all evening. They've just brought in the second parachute."

Eight

Throughout the whole twelve-mile journey through the dark, twisting lanes she said nothing, deliberately concentrating all her energies on steering the jeep. The thin slits of light released by the wartime headlight masks flickered like fireflies on roadside stones or hedgerow leaves, briefly delineating the tunnel of darkness into which she plunged the car.

Horn glanced at her anxiously. Clearly she was waiting until they got back to the cottage. Clearly the questions would begin then. He lit a Camel and shoved the pack back into his shirt pocket. Twisting in his seat, he looked through the rear window. They had reached a slight rise, and as the moon emerged briefly, the narrow road stretched clear behind them. There was no sign of pursuit.

He faced forward again and felt a wave of exhaustion pass over him. He had no doubt that the Germans at the hospital had come from the U-boat as soon as they had discovered that it was Frank, not Hess, whom they had shot on the beach. Equally he had no doubt that this was the result of an order from the Führer. Hess had as good as told him in the Messerschmitt that Hitler knew nothing of the flight. So where did that leave him, Alfred Horn? Expendable. Easier to kill than to have him recount his amazing story in the fighter pilots' club at Berlikum or Calais. And yet he was a German officer. He was no dissident or social criminal of the type that had made the Gestapo's name feared throughout Germany and the occupied countries. He had met Gestapo men, had drinks with them, and although he didn't much like their special mix of hardness and sentimentality, he had never feared them. Ordinary patriotic German officers had nothing to fear. Except him. Because he had been chosen at random to navigate for a Deputy Führer who could well have been going out of his mind. He exhaled heavily in part exasperation, part self-pity and was immediately aware of her quick glance. But as he turned his head toward her, she was already again looking at the road ahead, her mouth compressed into a hard line.

She turned the car through the cottage gate and braked in front of the lean-to garage. She turned off the engine, got out of the car and walked toward the hedge. She stopped to look up at the dark waving treetops against the moonlit sky.

Horn opened the front door and blundered through to the kitchen to light the kerosene lamp. Then, in the bathroom, he removed the briefcase from under the floorboard and brought it back to the kitchen. She was still outside.

He was not entirely sure why he wanted the briefcase with him. In some vague sense he felt it was his only security, his only proof that he was no more than the navigator on the ill-starred flight only a day ago. And with the Stellvertreter dead he somehow knew the briefcase had to stay close to him.

Looking around the small kitchen, he saw a gap of an inch or two between the wainscot and the back of the oak dresser. He had just shoved the briefcase out of sight when he heard Kay open the latch on the front door.

She came into the kitchen and took off her uniform jacket and hung it behind the door. Then, still without speaking, she turned and reached to open a high cupboard. From it she took a half-full bottle of Scotch and placed it heavily in the middle of the kitchen table. She crossed to the draining board and returned with two glasses nipped together between the thumb and finger of one hand. Drawing up a chair opposite, she slid a glass across the table toward him. He poured whiskey for both of them and added an inch of water from the jug on the table.

"Back there," she said quietly, "back at the hospital, you spoke in German."

Horn inclined his head.

"And Alfred Horn. That could just as well be a German name."

Watching her carefully across the rim of the whisky glass, he again inclined his head.

"A German. . . ." She shook her head slowly.

He looked at the troubled gray eyes. For the moment he would let her put two and two together.

"The German flier—the *other* German flier—he was to be Colonel Barker? Was that it?"

Horn drained his glass and poured whisky for both of them. "Yes," he said, "that was it."

"Wearing an American uniform, in an enemy country—that's a death sentence."

"Only if you get caught."

"Jesus Christ!" She jumped up, her full breasts lifting under her uniform shirt. "What sort of fix have I got myself into?" She stood for a moment breathing heavily, looking down at him.

He was suddenly as angry as she was.

"You think it's a pretty dirty business, huh? You a neutral having anything to do with *Germans*. Fine if you supply the British. Fine if you work over here shuttling bombs and guns to the *British*—sure, why not? But to help a *German*—that's different, huh? That really offends your sense of *neutrality*."

She sat down again and filled her own glass. "I'd like a cigarette." She reached across for the pack of Camels.

"I thought you didn't smoke."

"Tonight I do." She leaned across the table and lit the cigarette from the top of the kerosene lamp. Drawing on it inexpertly, she said, "My commanding general, General Walker, gave me orders to arrange transportation for two American officers to the United States. I now discover that these two officers are German fliers. I have to ask myself if General Walker already knew that."

"He knew."

"How can I be sure?"

"If I can persuade you, do General Walker's orders still stand? Will you still help me to get to the States?"

She grimaced and crushed out the cigarette. "No. I have to speak to the General."

"On the transatlantic phone?"

"Yes."

"Kay"—it was the first time he used her name—"I'm going to try some explaining. I don't have too much in the way of answers, but I'm going to tell you what I can about this mission."

"All I need to know is whether or not you are the two men General Walker was expecting," she said coldly.

"I can't answer that. Because the other man, Colonel Barker, is such top brass in Germany that maybe even your General wasn't told he was coming."

"You mean a high-ranking officer?"

"Way above that, Kay. Second only to Hitler himself. The man in that hospital is Rudolf Hess."

She looked at him in total disbelief.

"The Deputy Führer, Kay. The man we call the Stellvertreter—Rudolf Hess."

"Here in Britain . . . you're out of your mind."

"Don't ask me why he's here. I was along only as the navigator, pulled out of an operational fighter squadron a month ago. Rudolf Hess was on his way to see someone in America—someone a lot more senior than your General Walker. That's why I say maybe even the General doesn't know who was coming."

Her mouth opened and closed. She stared at him, unable to form the words.

"It's the truth, Kay. Whether or not the British know it yet, the man in that hospital is Hess. His destination was the United States. He was injured when we parachuted from the Messerschmitt, so he ordered me to make it to Prestwick alone. Rely on it, he didn't make this trip to see some one-star General. He's the sort of man who deals at the top. The very top."

"FDR . . . he was going to see the President?"

Horn shook his head. "I don't know, Kay. I only know two things—first, that Adolf Hitler did not know the Stellvertreter was making this flight; second, that as far as Rudolf Hess was concerned, this was a mission of peace."

"Look," she said, "this just doesn't make sense. Why come to Britain? To your number one enemy?"

"Once you know that America's the destination it makes a lot of sense."

"Okay," she said, suddenly wary again, "tell me."

He spread his fingers and counted off the points. "First, there is no German bomber capable of an Atlantic crossing. Germany to the U.S. is beyond the range of our Condor four-engine bomber. So what's wrong with flying to Lisbon and picking up an American plane there? Answer: Lisbon has more Gestapo agents than the Kolumbiahaus has in Berlin. Hitler would have had him brought straight back to Germany. So what about a U-boat? Same problem. Orders would be radioed for its immediate return to base. The Stellvertreter wouldn't have made it past Land's End." He paused. "But Britain's different. There were U.S. aircraft here ready to fly him to America. Once at Prestwick, he was safe. And last of all, no Gestapo—at least not until tonight. . . ."

"You mean the men at the hospital?"

"They arrived by U-boat. Their orders were to kill

both of us. The Deputy Leader and myself. Orders that must have come from Hitler himself. Tonight part of those orders was successfully carried out."

"At the hospital?"

"Rudolf Hess is dead, Kay. The shots you heard."

She poured the remains of the whisky into his glass, then rose and took another bottle from the cupboard. "I think I'm getting bombed," she said, unscrewing the cap and filling her glass. "Rudolf Hess flies to Scotland —without Hitler knowing. A peace mission when Germany seems in any case to be winning this war hands down. . . ." Her head was swimming. She knew she had already drunk too much. "Where does all this leave you?" she asked him.

"In your hands," he said. "As far as Germany goes, I seem to be some sort of traitor. As far as the British are concerned, I'm a spy in the uniform of a neutral country. The way I see it, the only way I stay alive is to get to America."

"And what do you tell General Walker?"

"I give him this." He leaned over to lift the briefcase from behind the dresser and dropped it onto the table. Its heavy combination lock looked at her like a single unblinking eye.

"Opened—or unopened?" she said, staring at the Nazi crest embossed on it.

"I don't have the combination. Anyway, I've come to the conclusion that the less I know about affairs of state, the better. I've got to deliver this case locked tight."

He was lying to her. The solution to his own problems had just struck him as he spoke. If Hitler wanted to stop the Stellvertreter's mission so badly that he was prepared to have him killed, then it would be suicide for Horn to go ahead and deliver the briefcase to General Walker. His obvious move was to accept Kay's help to get across the Atlantic and hand in the briefcase unopened at the German Embassy in Washington.

For a few moments she said nothing. Then she looked down, fiddling with her glass. "You're right about my idea of neutrality," she said. "If I'm on any side, it's the British."

"Same language, same traditions. . . ."

"Not just that. I think the Germany Hitler dreams of is a rapacious bully."

"And France and Britain at the time of the Versailles Treaty? What did they do when Germany was on her knees at the end of the last war? They bled her dry."

"Why does it take a Hitler to right the wrong?"

"It takes a strong Germany. And only Hitler was prepared to make her strong again."

"I don't really know you," she said quietly, "but I think you're a good man. How can you support someone who passed the Nuremberg Laws against the Jews? How can you support someone who's turning Europe into one vast compulsory work camp?"

"Look, Kay," he said irritably. "I'm like millions of other Germans. I'm not a member of the Nazi Party. I don't go around kicking Jews or informing to the Gestapo. I'm not interested in politics. I'm interested in Germany."

"Then you'd better *get* interested in politics. Roosevelt wants into this war, and that will be the end of Germany if he gets his way."

"A lot of Americans feel different. They feel Germany had a raw deal from the French and British. They don't want to get mixed up in Europe's troubles."

"I know."

"And you?" he asked. "What do you want? You want to fight Britain's war for her?"

She shook her head. "I've seen a little bit of war. In Spain. If America had been in the First War for the whole four years, it would have been different. Americans would have seen the price of victory—the destruction of an entire generation. Wars should be fought only from dire necessity. Not from some high school sense of heroics."

"And this war?"

She hesitated. "Like I said, I believe Hitler and the Nazi leadership to be deeply evil. Every nation has an appetite for conquest. Like every individual has an appetite for theft. What Hitler has done is to encourage that appetite in the German people. I pray the German people will come to their senses in time."

"What if they don't?"

"Then the United States will have to enter the war."

She looked at the briefcase on the table. "Your Deputy Führer, Hess, you say he claimed to be on a mission of peace."

"Yes."

She lifted her glass and watched the shafts of light from the kerosene lamp penetrate and lose themselves in the amber liquid. "Tomorrow we'll go across to the base," she said slowly. "We've got twenty-four Fortresses arriving about noon. A few hours' rest for the crews and we'll be ferrying them back to the States. I'll get you on a plane."

She pushed herself to her feet. The whisky was at work in him, too. Most of the women he had slept with had been slender actresses from the Berlin film studios or young singers from the Munich clubs. He had never before felt desire for a woman so much older, a woman whose body he found sensuously mature in the yellow lamplight.

He realized he was not disguising the direction of his thoughts. "About tomorrow," he said, "the plane . . . I didn't thank you."

She held his look. Then shook her head. "Not that way," she said sharply.

"Goddamnit!" He was on his feet, almost overturning the lamp, "That's not what I meant."

"Isn't it?" she said bitterly, moving to the bathroom door.

"If you get me to America, you're going to save my neck."

"And you feel grateful enough to offer me the comforts of your bed. Well, I don't need your gratitude. And I sure as hell don't need your bed."

She disappeared into the bathroom, slamming the door behind her. He had seen the tears glistening in her eyes the second before she turned. He realized she had drunk too much, as he had himself. He pushed back his chair, walked through to the living room and threw himself onto the sofa.

After a few minutes he heard her come out of the bathroom and move about in the kitchen. He could hear the coffeepot being filled and the rattle of cups. When the kitchen door opened, she was standing in her dressing gown, a coffee cup in each hand.

"I'm sorry," she said, putting one of the cups on the low table beside the sofa. "It's the booze, I guess."

He raised himself onto one elbow. "If I ever have the good luck to meet up with you in the States," he said, "I warn you now, I'm going to try to get you into bed. It won't be out of gratitude, some way of saying thanks for what you've done. It'll be out of pure honest-to-goodness lust." He grinned. "Got it, Lieutenant?"

She smiled down at him. "I bet you say that to all the girls."

"No. Some like candlelight, soft music, French champagne and romance laid on like a Goebbels film script. Not you. You're afraid of it."

"*I* am?"

"Sure. You're scared I'm laughing at you. The romantic American woman. You're even more scared of laughing at yourself."

"They run female psychology courses for trainee Luftwaffe pilots?"

He swung himself into a sitting position and reached for his coffee. "You're a beautiful woman, Kay. With a body that I find difficult to ignore. I'm scared, I'm lonely and I'm very far from home. Now for Christ's sake, go to bed before I prove to you that five years is not an age difference I give a damn about."

She reached out and touched his head as he bent forward to drink his coffee. "Good-night, Alfred."

He grunted into the coffee cup. Then sat listening as she climbed the creaking cottage stairs. He could hear every movement in the bedroom above. When she got into bed, he knew she was lying there directly above his head.

Nine

May 12, 1941. By late that evening the gray stone mass of Buchanan Castle would become the most heavily guarded establishment in Britain. A battalion of Scots Guards and an armored car squadron of the 4th Hussars had been allocated by the commanding officer, Scottish Command, on the basis of an urgent midnight call from the War Office in London. No one at this stage, in London or Scotland, had been informed of the identity of the prisoner. Scots Guardsmen, in hurriedly dug foxholes scattered across the grounds of the castle, were left to speculate among themselves about the live ammunition, the patrolling armored cars and the man in the heavily escorted ambulance who had arrived during the night.

In the huge medieval kitchen of the castle, Max Bishop had set up a desk and an emergency telephone line. He had chosen the kitchen as the only room in the castle capable of being reasonably heated, and by now two enormous roasting fires had been lit, throwing a warm flickering light across the worn flagstones and the high arched brickwork.

Rudolf Hess's canvas bag stood open on Bishop's desk, the American Colonel's uniform and cap, the leather flying suit and the bottles of homeopathic medicines beside it.

Inspector Jess MacDonald poured himself a mug

of tea from the huge iron kettle stewing over the fire. Adding milk and sugar, he turned back to where Bishop sat.

"An American uniform round these parts would be as remarkable, in the pristine sense of the word, as a full SS dress outfit. You can rely on it, Major," he said in his strong Scottish voice, "that uniform represents a purpose quite other than disguise."

Bishop felt the waves of exhaustion pass through him. He had slept no more than a couple of hours in the two nights and two days. "Okay, Inspector," he said. "Let's run it again. Rudolf Hess and a companion, who may or may not be Alfred Horn, land in Scotland."

"With respect, Major"—MacDonald put his tea aside—"we are still not absolutely certain that the man we have upstairs is Rudolf Hess."

"I am."

"All right. Continue on that premise."

"Hess brings with him—and is very anxious to dispose of it—the uniform of an American army air force Colonel. Why?"

"There are American air force officers not far away, Major," the Inspector said carefully.

Bishop looked at him in astonishment.

"At Prestwick. They operate part of the airfield there, bringing in Lend-Lease supplies from the States."

"Jesus Christ!" Bishop was suddenly wide awake again. "Put two and two together, Inspector."

"In my experience it usually makes five at very best."

"Not this time. I don't think Rudolf Hess was flying to Britain at all. I think his ultimate destination was the United States."

"And your friend Alfred Horn? What uniform was he dressed in, I wonder."

"You're right." Bishop was already lifting the phone. "Get me Prestwick Air Base."

As he replaced the receiver, there was a knock on the door and a Guards sergeant entered. "We have a Mr. Lowry waiting upstairs, sir. He's complaining pretty bitterly about being hauled out of bed."

"Lowery?"

"He's a dentist, sir, apparently."

Bishop turned rapidly to MacDonald. "I'll be back in five minutes, Inspector. If my Prestwick call comes through, get on to the Regimental Police there. Tell them we want a treble security check on everyone entering the base."

Hess turned his head and groaned as the door to the room crashed open. He had been sleeping soundly. The light blazed on overhead, and he shielded his eyes against the glare from the naked bulb.

"What's the meaning of this intrusion?" he said in German, in a voice croaking with sleep.

Bishop stared back at him, hard-faced. He was flanked by a sergeant and a civilian who wore a raincoat over pajamas and a pair of black shoes without socks.

"What do you want?" said Hess, this time in English.

Bishop turned to the civilian and handed him a buff card with a photograph attached. The civilian exhaled deeply in protest and moved to the bedside. He took a dentist's mirror from the raincoat and laid the card on the pillow beside Hess.

"Open your mouth, please." Hess gave him a confused glance, then looked at Bishop for an explanation.

"Mr. Lowry is a dentist. Please do as he asks," said Bishop coldly.

"And if I refuse?"

"We will use whatever force is necessary."

Hess shrugged and opened his mouth. The dentist started his examination, moving to one side to avoid the shadow from his own head. Bishop watched impassively. It did not take long. The dentist straightened up and walked back toward the doorway.

"Well?" said Bishop.

The dentist nodded.

"You're sure?"

"The record shows the teeth of a twelve-year-old. The conformation is known as Class Two, Division One. In other words, both central and lateral incisors protruding."

Hess stared at him balefully.

"The lateral photograph," the dentist continued, "establishes the angle. Less than eight percent of the population exhibit this conformation. In addition, the angles of the laterals are highly distinctive. I have no doubt that the dental record belongs to this gentleman. None at all."

Bishop nodded to the sergeant, and the three men went out into the corridor.

"I'll arrange a car home for you," said Bishop.

"I hope it was important," said the dentist with a trace of belated irritation.

Bishop did not answer. His thoughts were elsewhere. Although from the beginning he had been 99 percent certain it was Hess, there was now no longer any possible doubt. The dental records obtained from Alexandria and rushed up from London had proved it. The implications were awesome.

In the early hours of Monday, May 12, as the second day after his Deputy Führer's flight began to dawn over the massive Nazi Imperial-style Chancellery in Berlin, Adolf Hitler received a visitor.

Dozing alone in his study, a tray with a pot of tea and cream cakes on the low table beside him, he looked up as Heydrich crossed the thirty feet of polished wood floor between the double doors and the arrangement of chintz sofas and chairs around the log fire.

Hitler stood up, rubbing at his face, ignoring Heydrich's formal bow. "Well. Any news?"

Heydrich's face was tense. "None, Führer. The U-boat returned to rendezvous again an hour ago. There was no sign of Denck. We have to assume that he is either dead or a prisoner."

"So both Hess and Horn are still alive?"

"It is possible, Führer."

Hitler nodded to himself. "Barbarossa . . . the Japanese attack on America . . . never has a man in enemy hands held such massive secrets as Rudolf Hess. And a man with secrets can be forced to talk."

"Yes, Führer."

"And yet there are no signs of Russian troops moving up to our border. . . ."

"None."

"No Japanese reports of a regrouping of the American navy. . . ."

"No unusual U.S. naval movement has been reported by the Japanese or any other well-disposed neutral."

Hitler hesitated. "What's the answer, Heydrich? Is Hess dead after all?"

Heydrich remained silent.

"Or perhaps he failed to arrive in Scotland at all?"

"The U-boat captain reported two men on the beach, Führer. One of them was shot down immediately."

"And the other escaped?"

"Yes, Führer."

"Escaped from the elite of the SD that you promised me for this operation."

Hitler took up the long brass poker and turned to the fire. With his back to Heydrich, he began poking listlessly at the logs. "By God, Heydrich," he said slowly, "I must have been mad to entrust a matter of this importance to the hands of a *Jew*."

Heydrich's head moved as if he had been struck a physical blow.

Hitler straightened up. "Remove the name of Rudolf Hess from every hospital, every street and every school in Germany. Leak a first report to one of the Scandinavian embassies that he was suffering hallucinations brought on by overwork."

He tossed the poker into the fireplace and strode across the room to the twenty-foot doors. As he passed through them, the SS guards presented arms. It was to be the last time that Hitler would ever use the sumptuous private study of the Berlin Reich's Chancellery.

General Keitel, Chief of OKW, the Wehrmacht High Command, stepped respectfully from the shadows. He had been waiting in the huge red marble anteroom for three hours while Hitler mused and dozed and daydreamed on the other side of the twenty-foot doors—the Barbarossa attack on Soviet Russia had been set for May 15, just three days' time. The General Staff desperately needed Hitler's confirmation or cancellation of the attack.

As Hitler stopped now, his shoulders hunched, staring down at the polished mosaic floor, he was totally conscious of the impact he was making on the most craven of all Germany's senior officers. As he spoke, without lifting his eyes from the gleaming mosaic, he knew the moment would be recorded in that night's diary. "It is my unalterable decision that the attack on Soviet Russia will proceed. The date however will be reset—if no Russian troop movements are reported on our frontier, Barbarossa will go forward in one month's time."

Even Keitel recoiled at the new date. A June invasion would leave desperately few months to defeat the Russian armies before the onset of winter.

As Kay pulled her jeep to a stop outside the main gate of Prestwick Airport, the difference was noticeable immediately. The airfield had an unmistakable sense of urgency about it. At the gates the ancient

Home Guardsman had been replaced by a squad of green-bereted Royal Marine commandos. One of them, a corporal, moved rapidly across to the jeep.

"Yes, miss?" he said, seeming to ignore the fact she was an officer.

"I work here," said Kay sharply, showing her identification.

"Keep to the perimeter road, please," said the corporal, waving to one of the commandos to open the gate. "The rest of the base is off limits."

"What's going on?" she asked. "We didn't rate marine commando guards yesterday."

"Security."

"Security?"

"Orders, miss."

Kay saw she was not going to get very far with the questions. After putting the jeep into first, grating the gears in the process, she drove into the base.

Outside the line of single-story administration buildings, an unfamiliar black Humber saloon was parked. Kay recognized it as some sort of official car and had the disturbing feeling that whatever was happening at the air base was connected with Alfred Horn.

As she slowed in front of the U.S. commander's office, she heard a mumble of voices from inside; then the door opened and the crew-cut duty sergeant came out.

"And we'll need the personnel files," called the voice of the base commander as the sergeant closed the door. He looked at Kay and rolled his eyes to heaven in a gesture of mock desperation.

"What's the panic?" asked Kay.

"You tell me," said the sergeant, "we've got Limey security crawling over the walls."

"What do they want?"

"Checking."

"Checking what?"

"Everything, right down to the goddamn paper clips."

Kay went to her office and sat down behind the desk. For the first time she felt faintly scared. Alfred Horn had admitted he was a German, a serving Luftwaffe officer. He had told her a great deal, but had he told her everything? The sight of the new guards at the gate had brought the implications of her position home to her with a jolt. She had never considered Horn as an enemy, but the British, who had been fighting an increasingly savage war with Germany since September 1939, would certainly feel no sympathy for her attitudes. She was involved on several levels, as a neutral in a friendly country harboring an enemy of that country, and as a woman with a personable and attractive man. She tried to dismiss the second involvement as trivial but knew now that it was becoming more and more important to her.

She lifted the single black telephone receiver on the desk. She had to contact General Walker and learn the truth. The line was dead. She pumped the cradle, trying to reconnect it.

"Yes, Lieutenant?" The voice belonged to the sergeant.

"There's something wrong with the phone. I wanted a line."

"Right. They've jigged around with the wiring. All calls now have to be routed through this desk."

Kay thought fast. Normally she would have been able to phone through direct to Wardrobe Place in London, get clearance from the British duty officer in charge of all overseas calls and be connected to the States.

"Why the change?" she asked.

"Maybe they think I need the extra work. I just have orders to log all outgoing calls."

Kay suddenly felt things closing in. If all calls were being logged, it was possible, even probable, they were also being monitored. The questions she had rehearsed in her mind to put to General Walker were not for other ears.

"What number d'you want, Lieutenant?"

"Forget it," she said, "my sister's going to have to wait for her birthday call until I get back to New York."

Kay came in the front door of the cottage and slammed it behind her. Horn sat up in the bath, calling cautiously, "Is that you, Kay?"

"Yes," she said sharply.

He could hear her crashing around in the kitchen and settled back. Having read in an old copy of the *Times* he had found under a cushion that the British government urged the public to use no more than six inches of tepid water to save fuel, he had filled the bath to the brim. But the plan to sabotage the British war effort had misfired, for when he climbed into the bath, he found the overflow blocked, and the water had spilled out onto the floor.

"Archimedes was right!" he called. There was no answer, and the kitchen was now silent. Horn nodded to himself and closed his eyes in the luxury of the steam-filled room and the smell of soap.

"I want to talk to you, Alfred." Kay's voice came through the door. He could tell she was close, standing right outside the bathroom. He imagined her pose, leaning forward a little, and he felt a sudden surge of sexual excitement.

"Come on in. The door's not locked." He was careful to keep the tone in his voice ambiguous. She could take it as an offhand remark or as a serious invitation. How strange it was, as a man in an increasingly desperate situation the one thing he wanted above all else at the moment was for Kay to come in through that door. He waited, his desire increasing.

Through the thin bathroom door he could hear strange, baffling sounds . . . grunts of effort, the clatter of metal instruments over on the kitchen table . . .

He listened intently; then after a pause he heard

her heels cross the kitchen flagstones as she approached the bathroom door again.

"Get out of that bath, I want to talk to you," she said peremptorily.

Horn frowned, still puzzled. Climbing out of the bath, he wrapped a towel around his waist and went out into the narrow hallway. The kitchen door was open. Kay sat at the kitchen table. The briefcase Hess had given Horn lay open in front of her, the lock forced with a kitchen knife that had snapped in half in the process. The contents of the case—thick linen-backed maps, documents overstamped with the German eagle—lay strewn across the table.

He stood in the kitchen door, his face white with anger. "What the hell have you done?"

She looked up slowly from the kitchen table. "I've done what I should have done last night. I've taken a look for myself."

"Jesus Christ, you've also just made sure I can never return to Germany while this war lasts."

She looked at him in bewilderment and contempt. "Perhaps you'd better just take a look at what's in this case."

Ten

In his somber stone chamber at Buchanan Castle Rudolf Hess sat alone at a writing table, studying the notes he had made for his first interview with a British minister. Suspicious, almost paranoid by nature, he had refused all food that morning in case it were drugged to make him say more than he intended in this first interview. His notes he had encoded in his own idiosyncratic manner. Under his system London was always written as Berlin, Hitler as Stalin and the Atlantic Ocean became the Baltic Sea. To the professional cryptographer this schoolboy code could be broken in under five minutes; to the amateur it seemed as if Rudolf Hess had taken leave of his senses.

With a loud clack the key turned in the lock, and Hess got quickly to his feet. He had demanded that a full Nazi Party member's uniform be supplied for his interviews, but his request had been bluntly denied. As the door opened, he stood, straight-backed, tall, solemn-faced, in the uniform trousers and khaki shirt of an officer in the USAAF.

Max Bishop entered with a curt "Good afternoon, Herr Hess," and held the door open for a middle-aged man, somewhat above average height and dressed in a dark jacket and striped trousers.

"This is Sir John Simon, the Lord Chancellor," Bishop said. "Mr. Churchill has personally asked him to meet you."

143

"Please sit down." Hess gestured at the simple wooden chairs. "I would have preferred more suitable surroundings for these discussions—but apparently the British government considers it unnecessary."

Sir John Simon's eyes never left the dark, intense face of the Deputy Führer as Hess launched into a long catalogue of complaints against his treatment, the refusal to supply him with a uniform commensurate with his rank and the personal attacks in BBC broadcasts on the character and motives of Adolf Hitler.

While Bishop waited impatiently, the Lord Chancellor allowed Hess to continue. His primary object, as defined by Winston Churchill, was to decide whether or not the prisoner was insane. Only after that was he to discuss the purpose of his flight. And it was a decision Sir John Simon found difficult to reach. As Hess moved on to a review of the war, the causes of the war and the inevitable result of the war, Simon saw much that was soundly analytical in the Deputy Führer's presentation. At the same time the wild references to Providence, historical inevitability, horoscopes, the stars, predictions and visions made him seriously doubt the dark-eyed German's mental capacities, if not his actual sanity.

"I come now to the purpose of my flight," Hess said, sitting upright in his chair. "Let me say, first of all, that my loyalty to Adolf Hitler is absolute. Let me say, secondly, that I would never have undertaken this desperate mission if it had not been for a vision that haunts me nightly. It is of mothers, English as well as German, following the coffins of countless children."

"You mean you believe"—Sir John Simon spoke for the first time—"that this war must continue many years with vast destruction on both sides."

Hess's head twitched in surprise. "The German victory is inevitable," he said.

"But the cost perhaps would be too great?" the Lord Chancellor said gently.

"The cost to Britain, the cost to the Germanic world of which Britain is a part."

"I see."

"The world is upside down, Lord Chancellor Simon." Hess was leaning forward now, his slightly stilted English spoken with an intense, sibilant hiss through his protruding teeth. "The two great Aryan nations are spilling their lifeblood. The real enemy, Bolshevik, internationalist Russia, grins on the sidelines as she watches the spectacle of another Germanic bloodletting. Between Britain and Germany there must be peace. Or only the Slav will benefit."

Sir John Simon nodded as if in complete agreement. "But, Herr Hess"—he frowned suddenly—"we have reason to believe that the ultimate object of your flight was not Britain but America. I've listened to what you had to say with great interest. But how possibly does neutral America fit into the pattern of events?"

Hess grinned slyly; then, as if a dark shadow had passed across his face, he composed his features. Again the Lord Chancellor felt a sting of doubt that the man before him was entirely sane.

"Lord Chancellor Simon," Hess said gravely, "before this year, 1941, is out, the whole world will be at war. Worse, Aryan will be fighting Aryan, instead of the Germanic people's natural enemies, the Slavs and Asiatics."

Simon realized he was on the brink of some major revelation.

"I brought with me a briefcase," Hess said urgently. "It contains the most explosive information of our times."

A heavy silence fell in the cavernous stone room. Max Bishop looked from one man to the other as they sat, not four feet apart, their eyes seemingly locked together. He was aware that Sir John Simon was maintaining his outward show of something approaching indifference only with difficulty, knowing that amid the

145

wild claims of an imminent world war there could perhaps be some kernel of truth.

"America," Sir John Simon asked, "will America be in the war?"

"Of course," Hess said briskly. "A world war, Lord Chancellor Simon."

"And that is why you were going to Washington?"

Hess straightened again in his chair. "You must not try to trick me, Lord Chancellor. I said only that the object of my flight was the United States. I made no mention of Washington."

"My apologies, Herr Hess." He paused. "You mentioned a briefcase."

"Yes." The German glanced automatically at his watch. "It will already by now be in America."

"Taken by Alfred Horn?" Bishop asked.

Hess smiled, tight-lipped so as not to show his teeth. "Yes, Major, taken by Alfred Horn."

Hess stood up and began to pace the room. "We are facing a tragedy of immense proportions. A tragedy created solely by the warmongers Churchill and Roosevelt."

"Which tragedy is this?" Sir John Simon's voice was sharp.

Hess stopped in the middle of the room. "Germany, allied to the Asiatics, will be fighting her racial brothers in Britain and America, who in turn will be allied to the Slavs."

"You mean the world war will be between Britain, America and Russia on one side and Germany and Japan on the other?"

Hess nodded slowly. "A world turned upside down."

"This could only be of Germany's choosing." Simon's acute mind felt its way forward. "You are therefore telling us, Herr Hess, that Germany plans war on Russia, and Japan plans war on the United States."

Hess sat down abruptly. "Only I can prevent this tragedy. The Führer has offered Churchill an honorable peace. Backed by the warmonger Roosevelt, Churchill has felt safe to reject the Führer's offers."

"What would you have hoped President Roosevelt would have done?"

"Cut off war supplies to Britain," Hess said harshly. "And forced Churchill to make peace with Germany. Then the Führer would be free to renounce his treaty with Russia and Britain would help Germany in the great European crusade against the Bolshevik Mongols."

"Was your intention to try to persuade the American President?"

"The American President is as great a warmonger as Churchill himself," Hess said bitterly. "But there are other Americans, powerful Americans, who will see that the crusade against Germany is the wrong crusade. Who will see that Soviet Russia is the enemy, that our crusade must be against Red internationalism."

"And Japan?"

Hess waved his arm woodenly. "Japan is of no importance. Except to Roosevelt. He will use Japan's attack on America as an excuse for entering the war against Germany."

"And if you inform these other Americans of Japan's plans to attack their country?"

"Then Roosevelt will be forced to make a diplomatic solution. There will be no war with Japan—and thus no war with Germany." Hess paused, desperate to extract the last ounce of drama from the situation. "Supplied by the industrial might of America, German and British armies will march side by side against the Mongol hordes that have threatened Western civilization for a thousand years. It is the Führer's dearest wish."

They eyed each other across the table, shocked, suspicious, uncertain. The contents of the black case lay shattered across the kitchen table of the Ayrshire cottage—overprinted maps detailed the cataclysmic "Barbarossa" attack on Russia: the massive three-pronged advance by von Leeb toward Leningrad, von Bock to Moscow and the redoubtable von Rundstedt south to the Crimean peninsula and the oilfields of the Caucasus.

On this cottage table lay the order of battle for more than three million men, thousands of tanks and armored vehicles and a vast Luftwaffe air fleet. Very soon a massive military machine would be unleashed on Germany's Soviet ally.

Even more stunning for Kay was the bundle of papers she had scooped to her side of the table: German Foreign Office copies of telegrams that had passed between Ribbentrop, the German Foreign Minister, and Matsuoka, his Japanese colleague. Hurriedly translated by Horn, they told Kay that by the end of the year the Japanese fleet would launch a single massive and totally crippling attack on the American Pacific base at Pearl Harbor.

"We didn't choose to know all this, Kay," Horn said quietly. "But now that we do, we can't put the clock back. We have to decide what we do with our knowledge."

"For me there's no problem," she said. "Those papers have to go to the nearest senior American government official."

"I can't permit that," he said after a few moments. "Your government will inform Russia, and millions of my countrymen will advance straight into a Soviet trap."

"Jesus Christ!" she said vehemently. "It's a trap of your government's making. It's Hitler who's planning to attack his ally, remember. Not the other way around."

"I can't allow you to take these papers, Kay."

They sat opposite each other, grim-faced.

"And if I tell you I still intend to try?"

"Then I'll stop you."

"You can't stop me from *telling* the American authorities."

He was silent.

"To do that, Alfred, you'd have to kill me."

Something in the desperate anguish in his face cut through her determination. For a moment she saw that next to the simplicity of her own course, his decisions were impossibly complex. To betray his country's greatest single war secret. Or to kill a woman in cold blood.

"Last night," she said quietly, "I said I saw your country's leadership as pure evil. You've read these papers; you must know now what sort of Germany you serve."

He remained silent.

"It's not the Germany you remember, Alfred. It's not your father's Germany. It's led by bloodthirsty men who are *destroying* everything you love about Germany. I don't know you well, but I'm sure, either way, you have to *choose*. To serve this Germany— or to fight against it. The blindfold's off."

"If I let you take these documents I murder hundreds of thousands of my fellow Germans."

"No," she said firmly. "If Hitler's intentions are known to the world—if Japan's plan of attack is known—then they won't dare go ahead." She reached out and touched his arm. "We're two people, small people, sitting in a small cottage in Scotland. But by a bizarre throw of the dice we have it in our hands to prevent a world war."

She stood up. "I'm going to bed."

He looked up, frowning. "Now? In the middle of all this?"

She nodded. "I think you need some time alone. I'll catch a couple of hours sleep before the planes leave."

She turned and walked quickly from the room.

Horn sat among the scattered papers, some already ringed with coffee stains, one burned by a neglected cigarette, and thought of old Mr. Frank. Was it true that in Germany his innocent family would pay for his death? His death at the hands of Germans themselves.

Hans Forster, too, in Munich, had as good as said the same thing. The time would come when German officers would have to choose. Well, for himself, Alfred Horn, it had come earlier than anybody could have imagined.

He stood up and slowly circled the table. Somewhere through the sitting room he could hear Kay moving about. He shivered and gulped at the whisky. More than anything he wanted to be lying next to her in bed. Warm, simple and satisfying—sex had never been anything else for him. The very opposite of the head-splitting decisions facing him now.

He slumped back onto the kitchen chair. It would be a matter of seconds to gather up the papers and stuff them into the kitchen stove. But that still left Kay.

He leaned forward for a pack of cigarettes and noticed for the first time a slim tan leather notebook still inside the case. After taking it out, he flicked through the pages.

The page headings appeared to be conference notes, each dated and with the location recorded cryptically —"University, Munich. 2/25/41." Or "Home—48 Harthauser Str. 4/20/41. . . ." There seemed to be no record of with whom the meetings had been held, and certainly no verbatim report of their proceedings— but emerging strongly to Horn as he scanned the pages was a sense that these were Hess's notes on a continuing argument, a process of persuasion which had taken some months: the disastrous outcome of a war in which Germany fought Britain, Russia and the United States . . . the need to persuade America to stop supplies to Britain until Churchill agreed to peace with Germany . . . the crusade against the Bolshevik, godless East which would unite Europe under the blessing of Pope Pius. In short, the chance for a triumphant Western world united under the leadership of Adolf Hitler's Germany.

And who together stood against this glittering vision? Who were the barriers to the thousand-year hegemony of the Reich? Just two men. The cigar-smoking drunkard in London and Washington's cripple with the brilliant smile. Churchill's reasons for refusing peace were obvious. Hitler would refuse to negotiate with him as Prime Minister; his career would be smashed, his chance for a place in history lost forever. But Roosevelt was a more baffling proposition. Many pages of the notebook were devoted to analyzing the American President's apparent anxiety to draw the United States into the war. In the end no solid answer to the mystery was offered. But Hess's informant clearly insisted that the only hope of achieving his aim was to bypass Roosevelt and to open negotiations with the powerful isolationist movement in America. Underlined in red on the last written page was the sentence "It is suggested that negotiations should be opened directly with no less a person than the Ambassador. For this a visit to America would be necessary."

Kay lay in bed in the small cottage bedroom and stared toward the window. It was unusually early to be in bed, and she found it difficult to sleep. Through the drawn curtains, the fading daylight illuminated the room. Downstairs she could hear Horn moving about, the scrape of a chair, the footsteps on the flagstones, even, she imagined once or twice, the rustle of the stiff wax paper maps. . . . She believed she was right to have left him alone with the bottle of whisky and the evidence of his country's naked belligerence. She believed she was right, but there were many other things she would have preferred to have done. Naked between the warm sheets, she shrugged, smiling at herself. Perhaps after he had made his decisions, she would hear him stumbling up the narrow wooden stairs, muttering, drunk, but feeling for the handle of her room. She reached out an arm into the cold air and found the water jug. This was crazy. Here she was, fantasizing like a schoolgirl. She sat up and poured a glass of water. It was silent below now.

She drank the water but remained sitting up in bed. Of course, he had never really had to face the idea of rebellion. He had no doubt trodden a predictable path through life—private schools, university, Luftwaffe pilot, a course almost predestined by his background and upbringing.

She put the glass aside and slipped down low in the sensuous warmth of the bed. Through the closing veil of sleep she fancied she heard a dull click, no more than a half sound from the foot of the staircase. She was awake immediately, dry-mouthed, listening intently.

In the small kitchen below Alfred Horn was slumped, head on the back of the kitchen chair, asleep. He was dreaming of the Stellvertreter. He saw the gaunt face before him, the features break into the ridiculous smile. As Horn stood stiffly at attention, Hess came forward with the ribbon and cross of the Order of Maria Theresa and slipped it over his head. Then, while Horn, bound by his oath of loyalty, stood immobile, the Stellverteter took the ribbon and tightened it viciously around his throat.

Horn jerked awake, his legs kicking out violently, his fingers clawing at the leather garotte that Denck was twisting around his neck.

Teeth clenched with the effort, Denck stood, feet apart, staring down at the back of Horn's head, tightening the thong, watching him thrash helplessly as his life slipped from him.

Horn could no longer even tear at the garotte. His face, suffused with blood, seemed to swell to bursting point. His vision was clouded by a red mist which, parting suddenly, revealed snow-fields, white and virginal. He had no idea of the object under his hand, no thought but atavistic violence as he watched his own limp arm rise slowly to clap the object against the face bending over his.

The glass ashtray shattered in two pieces against Denck's skull an inch above the right temple. Shocked by the unexpected violence of the blow, alarmed at the stream of blood pouring down the right side of his face, Denck momentarily released his grip on the leather thong. Enough only for two burning gasps of air through the narrowed throat, it was nevertheless enough to keep Horn alive. But the thong, wrapped around Denck's fists, still encircled Horn's throat. Lifting his knee to the base of Horn's neck, Denck hauled again on the leather thong until it cut deeply into the flesh on the back of his own hands.

She had thrown herself out of bed and grabbed her robe at the first noises from the room below. Without precisely identifying a single choking sound she knew with certainty that Horn was being strangled to death.

With trembling hands she took the service Colt that Ralph had left her and pushed forward the safety catch. She ran downstairs and threw open the sitting-room door. The sheer brutality of the scene shocked her immobile. And gave Denck seconds in which to act.

Backing across the room, releasing Horn from the garotte as he ripped the leather thong from around his fists, Denck's eyes were on the huge Colt waving wildly in the woman's hand. Delving inside his jacket, he snatched at the butt of his Mauser, ripping the cloth where the gunsight snagged the inside of his pocket.

"For God's sake, Kay," she heard Horn rasp, and as Denck frantically cocked the slim-barreled Mauser, she pulled the trigger of the Colt. The first shot passed through his stomach and tore three vertebrae from the base of Denck's spine. The second shot collapsed his sternum and disintegrated his heart, and the third hit an aluminum saucepan, hauling it violently across the room. Before the saucepan stopped spinning, Alfred Horn had lost consciousness.

After they had dragged Denck's body into the garage and covered it with tarpaulin, they returned to the kitchen to sit looking dark-eyed at each other across the table, each with a coffee cup held between trembling hands.

"Who was he? One of the men from the U-boat?"

Horn nodded. His voice was weak with effort as he forced the syllables from his swollen throat. "Gestapo, maybe. Or SS."

"They have such people, people prepared to kill like that?" Her lips, too, were trembling.

He nodded and sipped painfully at his coffee.

"How did he find you? Not through Mr. Frank," she said with sudden revulsion.

Horn shook his head. "Not directly. But he must have gone to the shop. This was in his pocket." He pulled out of his shirt pocket Frank's bill made out to Kay.

"Will there be others?"

He shook his head. "I don't think so. Otherwise, they would have come together. No. . . ." He put his hand to his throat. "I think, at the moment at least, we're safe."

She laughed—on the edge of hysteria. "Safe? With those documents, with the British searching the area, with another murder party maybe about to land from another U-boat and with a dead Gestapo murderer in the garage, at the moment he says 'we're safe.' "

"Kay!" His voice was a sharp croak.

She looked across at him. "Sorry. But I don't exactly see myself going back to bed for a quiet night's rest."

"What are you going to do?"

"That depends on you."

He lifted his eyebrows.

"It depends on what you have decided, Alfred. Because I still intend the U.S. government to hear about those documents. That man out there in the garage hasn't changed my mind. Has he changed yours?"

Horn shook his head. "No," he said slowly. "But something has. You, old Mr. Frank, a friend of mine named Hans Forster—I've decided. . . ."

She waited.

"And I think thousands of German officers are going to have to decide the same way. Only difference is, I already have a chance to do something about it."

"You'll give the documents to the U.S. consul, here in Scotland?"

"No. . . ." He looked at her across the table. "It's not as easy as that. In the hands of certain Americans, those documents will be buried deep as Adolf Hitler wants them buried."

"But they show details of a Japanese attack. What American is going to ignore that?"

"One American. President Roosevelt. According to Rudolf Hess's notebook here, only the isolationist movement in America can be trusted to use these documents to keep America out of the war by negotiating a diplomatic settlement with Japan. Roosevelt, he says, is determined to come to Britain's aid. He will find some way to use the documents to bring America *into* the war."

"Can we believe Rudolf Hess?"

"He believed it enough to make this whole crazy flight."

"Crazy . . . ?"

"Somehow I think not, Kay, I've read his conference notes. . . ." He took a deep breath. "Perhaps he's not the brightest man in the world, but somewhere behind him, advising him, there's a considerable intellect. It comes out in the notes, but the man's name is never revealed. From the number of meetings that take place at Munich University I would say he could be an academic. Perhaps even an anti-Hitler academic

155

who has got to a position of influence with Hess and found him sufficiently malleable to press into shape."

"I can't read the notebook," she said. "I'll have to trust your judgment. You're saying we give the documents to General Walker, as originally planned by Hess."

"By Hess or his mysterious adviser."

"And what will General Walker do with them?"

"According to the notebook, they will be handed to someone described only as 'the Ambassador.'"

"With a small or a large *a?*"

"In German it's always written the same way. He could be a real official ambassador or just an ambassador in the sense of a go-between. Let's not worry about that. As I see it, our duty is to get the documents to General Walker."

She drank her coffee. She was calmer now. "It's not midnight yet. The ferry pilots will still be in the bar. I'm going to have to go up to the base and start talking to one of them." She hesitated. "I'll leave you the gun."

"Okay."

She stood up and grinned ruefully. "When the delayed shock of this night really hits me, I have a feeling I'll go down like a deflated balloon."

"Before you go to the base, Kay, we have something to do."

She looked at him in unconcealed horror. "No," she said. "Don't ask me."

"You're tougher than that. You told me you'd seen dead men before."

"Spain was a long time ago, Alfred. All the dead men I ever want to see in a lifetime."

Eleven

May 12–13, midnight. London lay black and silent, the "bomber's moon" obscured by a bank of high, slow-moving cloud. A lone double-decker bus, its interior lit by a single faint blue bulb, threaded its way through the uncleared piles of debris still left from the devastation of two nights before. Sunday's five-hundred-bomber attack would prove to be London's biggest air raid of the whole war. Nearly fifteen hundred people had lost their lives, and thousands more had been injured. Most left no epitaph.

Below the level of the blacked-out streets, huddled together like cattle, men and women from the rows of drab houses in the East End and from the streets of desirable residences in the West End of the city sheltered themselves from the bombs and tried to catch a few hours of fretful sleep on the cold concrete platforms of the underground tube stations.

They had begun to gather in early evening, bringing strange, assorted bundles of bedding down with them, staking their claim to the best places, lying in small groups and watching the passengers board the trains and endlessly rereading the grimy posters: "Careless talk costs lives. . . ." "Is your journey really necessary . . . ?" "Share the shelter, but don't share germs."

By ten o'clock the platforms had become crowded with a cross section of British humanity, old and

young, rich and poor, healthy and sick. There were
few children. As the Blitz increased in ferocity, a high
percentage of the under-fourteens had been evacuated,
sent off to the comparative safety of farms and villages
in the country, to be billeted out on anyone who would
take them. In the early days of the terror bombing,
the tube shelters had been highly jovial meeting places,
animated with a camaraderie and a spirit of "we
can take it." Complete strangers had chatted freely,
sung all the old cockney songs and danced the Lam-
beth Walk long into the night, but after months of
almost continual aerial bombardment, aimed at breaking their spirit, the crowds lay silent.

By midnight the platforms were packed solid, and
the smell of humanity hung in the air like a low, clinging fog. People huddled in the half-light, sitting and
lying as best they could, one person's head against the
next one's feet. Coughing, snoring, mumbling and pro-
testing with no room to move or stretch, they waited
until they could emerge from the subterranean darkness into the gray light of early morning—to see if
their houses were still standing, to read the latest cas-
ualty lists, to begin another day of rationing and re-
striction.

This was the reality of total war, waged not by soldier against soldier but by a faceless enemy dropping
death from above onto the populace of a blackened
and scarred city. "We can take it" was still just true,
but the question was: for how much longer?

Up above, the streets were empty now except for the
steady tread of the patrolling air raid wardens. In the
ARP huts and mustering points the men waited, making endless cups of weak tea, playing cards, trying to
predict when and where the next hail of incendi-
aries would fall. They wore armbands designating
their groups, "Heavy Rescue," "Light Rescue," "Fire
Warden" and the special plain purple band denoting
those who had the gruesome task of dealing with the
piles of mutilated bodies every raid produced.

At the corner of Downing Street a lone policeman patrolled the pavement. Another kept silent watch outside the doorway to Number 10. On the roof of the most famous house in London a group of fire watchers drank their steaming mugs of cocoa and scanned the somber skyline, dotted with the cumbersome outlines of the barrage balloons.

Below, in a second-floor bedroom, Winston Churchill lay naked on a feather bed under a single sheet. His small, neat feet, wearing the third pair of black socks of the day, protruded from the end of the cover. It was almost 2:00 A.M., but he had not retired for the night. On a side table at his right hand lay a plate of cold breast of chicken and a half-consumed bottle of champagne. Still working on the report in his lap, he lit a cigarette. Daytime, the time for meeting people and for being seen, that was the time for the large Havanas that had become part of his charisma. An image must be built and maintained, but not in the privacy of one's own bedroom. Above all else, this rotund man with the cherubic features and, in normal conversation, the slow, uninteresting voice saw everything in the sweeping context of living history. To him the past, the present and the future merged in one great canvas. And the central figure in that canvas, he was determined, would be Winston Spencer Churchill.

He put aside the report and lay back heavy-jowled, staring, at the Constable landscape on the wall opposite. Rudolf Hess could destroy him. This mad visionary could force him, Winston Churchill, into a position where only his presence in 10 Downing Street stood in the way of peace in Europe. But what sort of Europe with Adolf Hitler triumphant? What had Neville Chamberlain called the German dictator—"The commonest little dog I ever did meet"? Winston Churchill smiled grimly. The Europe of his ancestors was not going to be allowed to surrender itself to the Austrian guttersnipe.

He lifted the phone. "When Sir John Simon arrives, show him straight in."

The male secretary told him that Sir John had arrived a few minutes earlier.

"Very well, then," Churchill grunted, and replaced the receiver.

After a few moments he heard footsteps approaching, and Sir John Simon entered, closing the door behind him. "Good evening, Prime Minister."

Neither man saw anything strange in the formality addressed to the man lying on the bed naked but for his black socks.

"Good evening, Lord Chancellor," Churchill rumbled. "I read your report." He sat on the side of the bed, wrapping the sheet around him like a Roman toga.

"Still no word from Germany, sir?"

Churchill shook his head. "Baffling," he said. "Baffling." He began to pace the bedroom. "Your report says that Hess claims to have acted without Hitler's knowledge or consent."

"True. But Hess was nevertheless anxious to stress that he remains totally loyal to his Führer."

"Mmmmm. . . ." Churchill's small eyes glittered. "I suspect Hitler knows of the flight. I suspect he is waiting at this moment to hear that Hess or his associate has arrived in America. I suspect that if Hess's mission fails, Hitler will denounce him as a lunatic."

"In this bizarre situation almost anything is possible, Prime Minister."

"I have spoken by telephone with President Roosevelt." Churchill trailed the ends of his toga across the room. "He agrees with me that the information offered by Hess, especially news of the Japanese attack, must be rigorously suppressed. He agrees with me that Hess's associate in America, Captain Alfred Horn, must be found as a matter of the highest urgency. He agrees with me that our statement on Hess should at no time mention that America was his destination."

"What object will we ascribe to Hess in flying to Scotland?"

"I've given this a great deal of thought, Lord Chancellor. Hess landed at Eaglesham. Nearby is Dungavel House, the home of the Duke of Hamilton. I have spoken to the Duke. As you possibly know, before the war he had a number of German connections. Our statement to the world will say that in his feeble, muddled fashion the Deputy Führer of the Third Reich sought to arrange a peace treaty with Great Britain and that Dungavel House was his destination. His belief was that the Duke of Hamilton, as a peer of the realm, could conduct him immediately to His Majesty the King."

"The general intention is to make Hess look halfwitted?"

Churchill nodded.

"So that no one will take seriously his offer of peace."

Sir John Simon rose as the telephone purred. "When will this statement be issued, Prime Minister?"

Winston Churchill lifted the telephone to be told that General de Gaulle wished to speak to him urgently. He told the secretary to put him on the line.

"*Mon Général,*" he boomed in his execrable French accent, "*que puis-je faire pour vous?*"

It was generally believed that de Gaulle had little knowledge of English. In fact, he spoke it well—and preferred it to Churchill's French. "My sources tell me, Prime Minister, that Rudolf Hess has landed in Scotland."

"Let us say, the improbable is possible," said Churchill, "but tell me, *mon cher compagnon d'armes,* would you be so good as to reveal your source?"

"Certainly," replied de Gaulle to Churchill's surprise. "Hitler leaked the news an hour ago to the Swedish Embassy in Berlin."

"I was awaiting such an announcement."

"If Deputy Führer Hess is in Britain to offer terms

of peace, I wish to inform you now that France will accept no conclusion to this war but the total defeat of Nazi Germany."

Churchill smiled wryly. "And I can assure you, *mon compagnon d'armes,* that the intention of the United Kingdom is precisely similar."

After he had replaced the phone, he turned, wrapping his toga around him, to Sir John Simon. "Hitler's nerve has cracked," he said with a grim smile. "Make our announcement to the world's press immediately."

Kay drove fast, staring intently at the road ahead. Horn could see her hands tight on the wheel and knew she was controlling herself with difficulty. He had let her drive, thinking it would help keep her mind occupied. Denck's body lay wedged in the well of the back seats, wrapped in a piece of old sailcloth Horn had found in the garden shed and tied into an ungainly parcel with a length of rope. There was no moon and it was hard to see clearly as the road narrowed into a hedge-lined lane.

"It should be along here somewhere. On the left," Horn said, peering into the darkness for some sign of the disused quarry he had picked out on the ordnance survey map at the cottage. Kay slowed the jeep, then pulled up with a sharp jolt as the lane disintegrated into a muddy track.

Horn got out and looked over the thick thorn hedge on the left. This was the place. The night air was cold and clear with a breeze from the west moving the new leaves of a line of trees against the horizon. Horn went to the back of the jeep and dragged the body out feet first. Kay came around from the driver's seat to help as the head and shoulders thumped to the ground. She stopped, white-faced, looking down at the shape in the roped sailcloth. "Jesus Christ." She shuddered. "Jesus Christ."

He bent over the jeep and took out the bottle of whiskey he had brought with them. Unscrewing the cap, he handed her the bottle. She took it and raised it to her lips, high so that the whisky spilled around her mouth and coursed across her cheeks.

"And again," he said.

She shook her head and handed back the bottle. "I'm okay now."

Horn nodded. "Take the feet," he said quietly.

They carried the corpse around the front of the jeep and struggled over a shallow, dry ditch and through a gap in the hedgerow. As they passed the dimmed headlights, Horn noticed a patch of blood seeping out in a widening circle across the sailcloth. The ground was strewn with stones and jagged fragments of rock between clumps of coarse grass, and they stumbled on for twenty yards, half dragging, half carrying the load. The wind was stronger on this side of the hedge, and Horn heard the lap of water before he saw the ground falling away into the quarry itself. It stretched off into the gloom like some ancient volcanic crater, filled by the rain over the years.

"I'll take it from here. Go back to the jeep."

Kay nodded and went back the way they had come.

Horn pulled Denck the last few yards to the edge of the rocky incline of the old workings. Ten feet below, the wavelets slapped noisily against the broken stone. Horn relaxed his aching arms. Somewhere behind, an owl shrieked from the line of trees, as with a last effort he manhandled the body forward and pushed it over the edge. It slid down in a minor avalanche of rock and pebble and went into the water with a dull splash. For a few moments it floated out from the bank like a dark, misshapen tree stump, then slowly rolled over and sank. Horn waited as one large, gulping bubble belched to the surface. Then there was only the wind.

"Are you sure it sank?" asked Kay as they drove back along the winding lanes to the cottage.

"Yes. It'll come up again, but not for a few days."

Kay exhaled sharply. Horn glanced at her.

"Maybe I should come with you to the base," he said.

"No, it's an extra risk, and there's no reason for it."

The moon had risen, and the cottage was bathed in an insipid gray light as Kay pulled up outside. "Don't worry, it's all going to work out," she said as Horn jumped down on to the road. She was back in control of herself.

Horn waited inside the gate until the sound of the jeep had faded away toward Prestwick, then went to the front door. As he came into the hall, he felt a strange sense of unease. A man had been killed here. He had been involved in killing before, but those deaths had been remote, unseen, encased in the steel of a Spitfire or Hurricane. When he shot one down, he thought more about the plane, the machine, than about the man inside it. But Denck had been a man without a case of steel around him, in the same room and breathing the same air. Somehow it was different.

He checked all the windows on his way into the bathroom. He switched on the light and saw his hand stained red-brown with dried blood. He washed it under the tap and found it was not Denck's blood but his own; some jagged rock or thorn had torn a small gash at the wrist. Patting it dry with the end of a towel, he glanced in the mirror and was shocked at his own image. He looked drawn and gray-faced, haggard to the point of exhaustion. Lack of sleep and the almost continuous tension had taken their toll. He washed his face with cold water and felt a little better, then went into the kitchen and poured himself a glass of milk.

He took it to the couch in the living room. The curtains were undrawn, and he didn't bother to turn on the light. As he drained the glass, it brought back a sudden, forgotten memory of himself as a small boy, late at night, in a hunting lodge on the edge of the Black Forest with his father and some of his friends. . . . There had been a glass of hot milk there, but flavored with a shot of plum brandy from old Graf von Yorck's hip flask, as he sat watching the sweet-smelling pine logs blazing in an open fire and listening to the men talk of the past, always of the past. . . .

Horn awoke with a start at the sound of footsteps and raucous voices at the gate. He leaped from the couch, ran to the stairs and bounded up into the darkness as the front door crashed open and the light came on in the hallway. The voices were loud—three or four men as far as Horn could judge. He knew he should not have come upstairs. Now he was trapped, and he had forgotten Kay's .45 automatic. Then suddenly he could hear Kay's voice.

"Go on through, boys. Make yourselves at home. I'll be right with you." She was coming up the stairs. As she reached the top, Horn grabbed her arm and pulled her back out of the light from below.

"Alfred!"

"Who are they, for Christ's sake?"

"Some of the pilots."

"Why the hell did you bring them back here?"

"They've tightened security at the base. It won't be easy. There's one who looks like you."

"What?"

"Same build, same coloring. I thought you might be able to take his place."

"That's crazy. How?"

"I don't know. If we can get him drunk enough. . . ."

A Southern voice called up from the foot of the stairs. "Hey, Lieutenant, baby, what's keeping you?"

"Be right down," Kay called.

"It'll never work!" Horn still held her arm.

"We can give it a try."

"How many are there?"

"Four. I tried to get the one who looks like you back here alone, but the others tagged along."

"D'you need any help up there?" The Southern voice called again.

"We'd better go down," said Kay. "It's safe enough.

They're all half plastered. They've been in the bar since they landed."

Tressenriter was tall and gangling with cowboy hat and boots. Scruggs was in his late thirties, shorter, stocky and blond. They were sprawled side by side on the couch. Spinner sat forward in the armchair, his round baby face pale and tight from liquor, gulping in air and closing his eyes in long blinks. Travers, the Southerner, sat alone. He was roughly Horn's size and build but nearly ten years older, the face darker and the features coarser. Horn saw at once there was no more than a very superficial resemblance between them.

When Kay brought him into the room, the four accepted Horn with casual first-name introductions. While Horn put records on the old radiogram, Kay kept the glasses filled. Travers had drunk as much as anyone, but to Horn's concern he appeared arrogantly self-assured and stone-cold sober.

"I think I'm going to throw up," said Spinner, his face suddenly green.

"Get him into the john. Go stick his head down the john," said Scruggs.

"What the kid needs is air," said Tressenriter. "Go out the back, kid, and get yourself some air."

Kay helped Spinner into the kitchen toward the back door to the garden.

Travers moved to where Horn was standing to refill his glass.

"Two's company, six is a crowd, right?"

Horn didn't answer. Travers poured himself a large straight Scotch and held the bottle out to Horn.

"You drinking?"

Horn took the bottle and gave himself a good double. Travers watched him carefully, then with a grin downed his drink in one. The way he did it made it a challenge. Horn found himself disliking the Southerner more by the second, but he defiantly threw back his head and gulped down the whisky. The liquid burned the back of his throat, and although he tried to control it, he felt his eyes filling with water.

"Where you from?" asked Travers.

"Indianapolis."

"Al, isn't it?"

"That's right."

"Well, Al. The boy is sick drunk, and those two will soon be the same way." He indicated Scruggs and Tressenriter as he casually refilled his glass. "That leaves you and me. So one of us is going to have to do the gentlemanly thing."

"What's that?"

"Leave, buddy," Travers said, hard-eyed.

Horn looked at him. "I don't have any plans to leave yet," he said slowly. "I've only just started drinking." He reached forward and poured himself some more whisky. Then, taking Travers's glass, he poured the best part of two inches into the tumbler and handed it back to him. "Where I come from," he said, "we leave the choice up to the lady."

Travers turned away, glass in hand, to where Kay had reappeared in the hall doorway. "You going to show me your garden, Lieutenant?"

She smiled up at him. "At this time of night?"

"Sure."

"Listen," she said, "we'll freeze to death out there. So bring a bottle, huh?"

Travers walked over to get the Scotch, and Kay continued toward the door to the hall. As she was about to go out, Horn took her arm.

"What are you doing?" He kept his voice low.

"Trying to get you on that plane."

She pulled her arm free and went out. Travers gave Horn a mocking shrug and followed her.

Horn went into the kitchen, leaving Scruggs demonstrating to Tressenriter how he had spent the night fox-trotting with a six-foot-three hooker. The lanky Tressenriter spluttered with helpless laughter as Scruggs clasped him in his arms, laid his head against

Tressenriter's chest and looked up at him, rolling his eyes.

The canvas sides of the jeep protected them from the worst of the chill May night air. For Travers, the bottle of whisky did the rest. He sat slumped in the driver's seat, the whisky bottle in one hand, the other draped around Kay's shoulder, the fingers reaching under her uniform jacket.

"You drink too much of that stuff," she said in a carefully calculated challenge.

"Never," he slurred, lifting the bottle and taking three, four mouthfuls before lowering the bottle and baring his teeth to the bite of the spirit.

"You do that again and you'll fall right out of the seat," she said.

He gave her a sidelong glance, lifted the bottle, drank and pushed open the canvas door. "You got a room upstairs?"

"Yes."

"Let's go, then."

In the kitchen Horn heard the hall door slam and stumbling footsteps up the stairs.

As she came into the bedroom, Kay gave a sudden involuntary shiver. The room was lit by a flood of cold moonlight from the window. Travers came in behind her, closing the door. She turned to face him, forcing a quick smile. He reached over and pulled her against him with such force it knocked the breath out of her body, then ground her face into his own in a brutal kiss.

"Take it easy. How about a drink?" she gasped.

"Sure, if you need it."

He held out the bottle. She took it and drank a little, then gave it back.

"Well, now, tell me something." He stretched out on the bed, resting the bottle on his chest and crossing his legs at the ankles. "Why'd you pick me? There were a dozen other guys in the bar; why'd you give me the eye?"

"You came over when I did," she said after a nervous pause.

"Hell, right." He patted the bed, and Kay sat down beside him.

"How about that drink?" she said.

"I don't need a drink. I'm ready." He eyed her breasts under her blouse, then cupped one in a dark stub-fingered hand.

"Just one last slug," she said, pulling away from his touch and taking the bottle. She held it to his lips, but he pushed it aside.

"No drink."

He suddenly gripped her shoulders and pulled her down beside him. The bottle crashed to the floor.

He clamped his mouth over her lips. She tried to wrench free, but he was using his legs to pin her down, swinging his body over onto her, crushing her with the dead weight. She was helpless, suffocating. And now the mouth and hands were probing, forcing her into position under him. She tried to fight him off, a grim, silent, losing battle.

Spinner had come back in from the garden. He looked ashen-faced and shaken. Scruggs and Tressenriter were trying to convince him the best thing to do was to have another drink. Between them they had finished more than a bottle of Scotch, and they swayed on their feet and slurred their words. Horn had heard no sound from the bedroom above since the crash of the bottle hitting the floor. He went into the hallway and climbed the stairs. The door to the bedroom was closed. He waited, wondering whether to go in; then the thought of Travers decided it. As his hand went to the handle, the door suddenly opened and Kay stood facing him.

"What are you doing here?" she said, smoothing back her hair and pulling her blouse closed.

Horn looked at her, surprised at his own sense of shock. "Where's Travers?" he said.

Kay stood back and let Horn into the room. Travers lay under a blanket.

"Get his papers," she said stonily.

Horn went to his jacket on the floor by the bed and found his wallet.

"You'd better get going," said Kay.

He turned back to face her, but she avoided his eyes.

"You'll have to keep him here," said Horn, "at least until we've landed."

"I know."

"We'll be in the air all night and most of the morning."

"ETA thirteen hundred hours British time."

Horn wanted to get close to her, but the sudden gulf between them was too sharp, too recent.

"Will you be all right? I mean, will you be able to handle it?"

"I thought we'd already decided we were trying to do something important."

There seemed nothing left to say.

"Good-bye, Kay."

"Good-bye."

The wheels of the jeep sang out their distinctive whine as Horn drove to the base at Prestwick. He was unused to the gears and crashed them a couple of times, but his passengers didn't seem to notice.

"Where's Travers?" said Spinner. The cold rush of night air had revived him.

"We're all here, kid," said Scruggs, his voice croaking from the Scotch.

"No, Travers is missing."

"Go back to sleep."

"He's right," said Tressenriter. "There were five of us. The kid sat in the back, remember?"

"Okay, that's three in the back and two in the

front," said Scruggs, trying to apply his befuddled mind to the problem.

"And three and two makes five," Tressenriter snorted in triumph.

"The Lieutenant was driving. Four and one dame makes five." Scruggs closed the conversation with a loud hiccup.

In the condition he was in, Tressenriter had no answer to the stark logic of the argument, and Spinner had lapsed back into sleep. Horn had gathered from the talk at the cottage that the three of them had flown over on the same aircraft and knew each other slightly before that. Fortunately Travers was an outsider whom none of them had seen before tonight.

There were two marine commando sentries with rifles and a marine sergeant at the airport gates. Horn braked the jeep to a halt, and the sergeant walked over to the passenger side. He shone his flashlight on Spinner, who groaned and turned his face away.

"Are you Americans?"

"Goddamn right we're Americans," said Scruggs. He screwed up his eyes as the sergeant turned and blazed the flashlight into his face.

"I'll have to see your identification."

"What's the problem?" asked Horn.

"There's a war on," replied the sergeant derisively. He waved one of the commandos over and told him to check the jeep, then started to examine Scruggs's identification papers.

The marine crouched down and shone his flashlight under the jeep.

"What's he looking for?" said Tressenriter.

"Horse feathers. That right, Sergeant?" Scruggs grinned drunkenly, then hiccuped again. The sergeant answered by meticulously checking his face against the photograph on his pilot's license, playing the light from one to the other.

"Hey, you're blinding me with that thing!" protested Scruggs. The sergeant ignored him.

Horn tensed, preparing to make a run for it, knowing his papers wouldn't stand this kind of close scrutiny. There was also the duffel bag Kay had provided, under his seat with the contents of Hess's briefcase stuffed into it. The second commando remained some twenty years away, but he was watching the jeep all the time. Horn decided his best line of escape was to head for the dark patch of bushes off to his right. He judged the distance to be about ten yards, time for the marine to react, aim and get off at least one shot. His chances of making it did not seem good. The sergeant's hand appeared in front of him, the palm open. The others had been checked. It was Horn's turn. He handed over the wallet, leaving Travers's papers inside, hoping the cellophane window over the photograph might distort it a little. He braced himself, ready to leap from the jeep.

"All clear, Sergeant," called the marine, straightening up from the rear of the jeep.

"Right," said the sergeant, and to Horn's surprise and intense relief he handed back the wallet with no more than a superficial glance. The gateway opened, and Horn drove through.

The large main office in the low airport administration building was crowded with men and full of noise and confusion. The twenty B-17Cs destined for Number 90 Squadron of RAF Bomber Command had been flown over from the States by sixty civilians, a pilot, copilot and navigator to each aircraft. Civilians had been used as a sop to American neutrality, but the German High Command knew perfectly well what was happening. In the same way, of course, they knew why the fifty ancient destroyers were transferred by the Roosevelt administration to the Royal Navy in September 1940. The thin excuse at the time had been that the destroyers were in exchange for bases in Newfoundland, Bermuda and the West Indies.

Horn waited with Scruggs and Tressenriter in the middle of the throng. The air was full of raised voices and cigar smoke. Spinner had felt giddy and gone back out for some fresh air.

At the back of the office, near the door to the corridor, two desks had been pushed together. A marine commando Captain, his young, pointed face shining with a thin film of sweat, climbed up onto one of the desks and began to explain the reason for the delay.

"Gentlemen, first I must apologize for the confusion." The Americans greeted him with a stream of drunken jokes and howls of laughter.

The ferry fliers were a colorful assortment. Drawn from a variety of jobs, anything from flying circuses to crop spraying, they were in no mood for apologies. Scruggs and Tressenriter were free-lance pilots, presently employed by the Forest Service, working around-the-clock shifts in the spotter planes. They had ferried the Fortresses over to get away from the routine, and because they knew they wouldn't be at the controls flying back, it was also a perfect opportunity to get drunk.

One of the USAAF Majors who was flying the civilian pilots back to the States appeared from the corridor.

"All right, you men, shut up. We all want to get home tonight." The words lowered the noise level enough for the Captain to explain there was to be a security check. The men would be asked to sign their names, and the signatures would be checked against those on the insurance forms they had all signed for the trip. Horn felt something close to despair. He could see no way he could fail to be discovered.

The checking had already started. The men were being cleared by two American enlisted men sitting at the desks. Behind them the Captain carefully watched the proceedings and the USAAF Major waited in bored silence, chewing on the end of a cigar.

As the men were passed, they went out through the door into the corridor, and those who were waiting pressed forward in a loud, unruly mass. Before he realized it, Horn found himself jostled forward two away from the desks and in a moment of negative acceptance decided simply to try to bluff it out. With his free hand he managed to take out the wallet and glance at Travers's signature. To his horror he saw from the backward slope the American was obviously left-handed. As he came to the desk nearest the door to the corridor, he had resigned himself to the fact he was about to be caught.

Scruggs was immediately in front of Horn. He was about to sign his name when the enlisted man looked up.

"Hi, Scruggs, How you doing?"

"Fine. I'm doing great," said Scruggs between hic-cups.

"Sign here."

"What's all this crap for?"

"I don't know. Some German pilot on the lam."

Scruggs wrote his name, holding his breath as he did so. The enlisted man checked it and ticked the name off a list he had at his side. Now it was Horn's turn. He took the pen and scrawled "B. Travers," suddenly feeling the marine Captain's eyes on him. Scruggs still stood nearby, searching his pockets for a match for the stub of a cigar in his mouth.

"Hey, Scruggs." Horn lurched toward Scruggs as if very drunk and draped his arms around his shoulders, leaning his full weight on the smaller man. The enlisted man was picking up an insurance form, comparing the signatures.

"Take it easy." Scruggs tried to undrape Horn's arms, pushing the duffel bag away from his face. The airman stared at the signatures, turning the card Horn had signed at various angles to try to see some similarity. He looked up. Horn's head was now slumped on to Scruggs's shoulder.

"Is he with you? You know him?"

"Sure," said Scruggs.

The enlisted man gave one last incredulous glance

at the signature, shook his head in disbelief, then waved them away, ticking off the list the name of Travers.

Elated, Horn walked along the dimly lit corridor. Through the doorway at the end lay the tarmac and the aircraft waiting to fly them out. He had almost done it. In ten hours he would be in America. He stopped. Tressenriter, who had been checked earlier, leaned casually against the wall, waiting for Scruggs, but beyond the tall American a knot of men waited at the exit doors. They were being searched by two marine commandos. Horn realized his ordeal was not over. One look at the contents of the bag would be enough. He would not be able to bluff his way out of that. He tried to remember the layout of the building and realized the office where he had first met Kay was on the left.

He came to the door. Scruggs and Tressenriter were a few feet ahead. He slipped, unnoticed, into the darkened room.

As he crossed to the window, he noticed the handleless coffee cup from that first night still perched on the edge of the desk where Kay had left it. Looking out the window to the left, he could see the main entrance leading to the large office. Three commandos with Sten guns stood guard, making sure no one walked around to the runway without going through the security check first. To the right the building continued for twenty yards or so. Around the corner were the aircraft. The problem was the guards.

Spinner unwittingly created the diversion Horn needed. He had been found wandering around inside the perimeter fence by the guards at the main gate. The marine sergeant now led him back. He was almost out on his feet and the sergeant shouted to the sentries to help him get Spinner inside.

Horn saw his chance. He opened the window, threw out the duffel bag and jumped out after it. He picked himself up and then ran flat out to the end of the building without looking back. Safely out of sight, he caught his breath, then slowly joined the scattered line of men coming out of the building.

The wind had now dropped, and the sky had cleared. It was a clear, cold night, and the tarmac had a sheen of dew across the black surface. Horn felt a sudden surge of excitement as he saw the huge aircraft looming up ahead.

The two Boeing Fortresses that were to transport the sixty civilian pilots back to the States belonged to the USAAF. The white stars on the blue circles of the insignia shone out from the dark distinctive green of the fuselages, contrasting with the planes' bellies and underwings, all of which were painted in a pale sky blue. They were huge, impressive aircraft with a wingspan of over one hundred feet.

Assuming it would take off first, Horn climbed the short ladder into the Fortress standing first in line at the end of the runway. Inside, about a dozen men sat and sprawled around, making themselves as comfortable as possible in the austere steel-ribbed fuselage. There was no sign of Scruggs or Tressenriter. They must have boarded the second bomber. As Horn waited for the aircraft to fill, he sat leaning back on a bulkhead and thought of Kay, wondering if he would ever see her again.

It was almost an hour before the last of the men clambered aboard. The three-man USAAF crew took their places, and the hatchway was finally closed. Horn could hear the Major in the left-hand pilot's seat going through the preflight check, and at last the magical words filtered back.

"Start one."

"Starting one."

In turn the four twelve-hundred-horsepower Wright engines crackled to life, the brakes were released and the Flying Fortress lurched forward.

Horn looked out the unmanned dorsal gun turret as the aircraft gathered speed. Lined up along the side

of the runway, floating in a low sea of ground mist
that had rolled in like a slow tide, stood the formidable shapes of the twenty B-17Cs destined for the
RAF.

As the Fortress gained height and swung west toward the Atlantic and America, Horn looked back
down. The line of B-17Cs could still be seen, standing
out like dark crosses against the cotton wool of the
mist. In that moment Horn was more certain than ever
that what he was doing was right.

Through the kitchen window Kay watched the blackbird as it searched for grubs in a patch of wet grass
near the shed. It had been light for almost two hours
now, and she wondered how much longer Travers
would sleep. Just before dawn she had gone upstairs
to the bedroom but had found him lying under the
blanket in the same position she had left him after
Horn and the rest had driven off in the jeep.

The blackbird found a worm, pulled it from the
ground and flew off to its nest in the bushes. No com-
plications in his life. A home, something to eat, a
family. . . . Kay turned from the window and looked
at her watch. Horn would have been flying for almost
five hours now over the endless gray Atlantic. She
found it impossible to accept that he was gone from
her life, probably forever. She poured herself another
cup of coffee and took it into the living room. The
mahogany-cased clock on the mantelpiece lay on its
face. Kay had rushed in as it was striking five and
stopped it by turning it over, afraid the strident one-
tone chime might wake Travers.

A sudden thump from the bedroom above took her
into the hallway. Almost immediately Travers appeared at the top of the stairs. He was already
dressed, except for his shoes, which he carried in his
hand. He came down quickly, his face white and
fixed.

"What time d'you have?" he asked.

"Nine-thirty."

"Jesus!" The word was to himself. He glanced around, trying to adjust to the unfamiliar surroundings.

"Would you like some coffee?" asked Kay evenly.

"Thanks."

He followed her into the kitchen, hopping on alternate legs as he put on his shoes.

They sat opposite each other at the table. To Kay he seemed subdued, the brashness and arrogance gone.

"I've missed the goddamn plane," he said.

Kay had rehearsed her answers during the hours of waiting. "Yes, I know. I must have fallen asleep, too. I'm sorry."

Travers gulped down the coffee.

"Forget it. It's not your fault. . . . Did the others make it?"

"I guess so," said Kay, gesturing a shrug with her hands. This was not the way she had expected him to be.

"Christ! They should have woke me up." He finished the coffee. "That's good coffee."

"Have another."

"No. I have to get back to the base." He stood up.

"What's the hurry?" said Kay, trying to make it an invitation, knowing she had to keep him away from the base until after Horn had landed. He stared at her, unsure of the meaning in her voice.

"About last night," he said after a pause.

"What about last night?"

"I passed out, right?"

Kay didn't answer.

"Big man," he said bitterly. "You must have been pretty pissed off."

Again Kay didn't answer.

"Well, for what it's worth, I'm sorry." He turned to leave.

"What's the hurry?" she said quickly, knowing her

voice lacked conviction. "I'm not holding anything against you."

He looked down at her, for a moment undecided. Then shook his head. "Thanks, but I better get back."

"They took the jeep. Someone's bringing it back later." It was another of her rehearsed answers.

"I'll walk it. I can do with the exercise. Good-bye and thanks."

He was leaving. If he arrived at the base and told his story, they would radio ahead and Horn would be arrested as he landed in the States. Looking around in desperation, she saw the phone. As the door closed behind him, she lifted the receiver.

Travers was halfway along the road to the base when the police car pulled up beside him. A uniformed officer got out unhurriedly. He was tall and stout with a red, bluff face.

"Good morning, sir," he said, eyeing Travers carefully.

"It might be for some," Travers said bleakly.

"Just routine, sir. D'you mind telling me your name?"

"Sure, Travers. Bob Travers."

The policeman took a notebook and pencil from his pocket and wrote the name.

"What's your address, Mr. Travers?"

"You mean my address in America? I'm an American."

"Are you, sir." It was not a question.

The driver was now out of the car. He walked forward and stopped a couple of yards to Travers's right.

"Look, what's all this about?"

"Do you have any means of identification?" asked the first policeman.

"Sure. I have an ID card here." He felt in his pocket. "Jesus—my wallet's gone!"

"Mislaid it?" said the driver, glancing at the other policeman.

Travers turned to look at him. The sun was now in his face, and he shielded his eyes with his hand. He was thinking hard. "I'm not that sure."

"Stolen, perhaps?" the policeman said skeptically.

"It just could have been." He shook his head. "No, last night I really tied one on. I could have lost it anywhere."

"I see, sir," said the driver. "Would you mind accompanying us to the station?"

"For what?"

"So we can clear this up."

"Clear what up? Look, if you checked with American personnel at Prestwick. . . ."

"Yes, sir. We'll do all that at the station."

Travers shrugged and allowed himself to be taken to the car.

The police interview room at Tarbolton had pale green walls and one high window opposite the door. As Travers lit his second cigarette, the door opened and Inspector Jess MacDonald came in.

"Good morning," he said, studying Travers with his quick professional eye.

"Morning," said Travers brusquely.

"The officers tell me, Mr. Travers, you were on your way to Prestwick Airport?"

"Right."

"You're an American who missed his plane and lost his identity papers?"

"I had too much to drink last night. Way too much."

"That may be so, but the fact remains you have no way of proving who you are. Or who you say you are." The inspector watched him carefully.

"I told your two patrolmen, it's not hard to check me out."

"We intend to do that." The inspector turned to leave. He had seen and heard enough.

In the vast kitchen at Buchanan Castle, Mrs. Shand,

the cook, waddled past Bishop to the stove. She was a short, plump woman of sixty who resented the recent upheaval in her routine.

"Ten to twelve and the German's calling for his breakfast," she snorted. "Two eggs, parboiled if you don't mind. And ordinary British folk not seeing an egg from one week's end to the next."

Bishop smiled to himself and went back to his work, shifting through the increasing mass of papers, a statement from the poacher who had found the canvas bag, the report from the Spitfire pilot, a sighting of the Me. 110 from the lighthouse on Holy Island, two memoranda from Churchill with copies sent to Roosevelt. The affair was reaching into the highest circles across the world.

"Would you like some tea?" asked Mrs. Shand.

"If you're making a pot." Bishop turned. The eggs had been boiling for almost ten minutes. "I thought you wanted those eggs soft-boiled."

"Not me; the German wanted them that way. I hope they're like bullets, and I hope they stick in his gullet."

Bishop smiled again and crossed to answer the newly installed phone as it rang. It was Inspector MacDonald.

"I think we may have found your man."

"Alfred Horn?"

"Could well be. He fits the description, and he was picked up within a mile of the base at Prestwick."

"How'd you find him?"

"Someone telephoned, usual thing, 'a man acting suspiciously.'"

"Hold him there. I'll be with you in half an hour."

The clock in the church tower across the street from the inspector's office at Tarbolton struck the half hour. Alone in the musty room Max Bishop checked his watch. It was 12:30 P.M. The moment he had arrived at the police station and seen Travers, he had taken a snap decision and told the American enough of the facts, without mentioning anything of real significance, to convince him of the importance of the affair. Travers, in turn, had told him all the events of the previous night. As Bishop waited for the call he had put through to the USAAF Colonel in command of the unit at Prestwick, he already suspected the truth.

A constable stuck his head around the door and told him the call was through. Bishop went to the polished desk and picked up the phone.

"Colonel, this is Major Bishop, British Intelligence Corps."

"What can I do for you, Major?"

"Two questions. First, have the B-17Cs that flew out last night landed in the States yet?"

"Depends on the headwinds. They're due about now."

"Do you have the names of everybody on board?"

"I have them right here on my desk."

"Colonel, is the name 'R. Travers' on the list?"

"Let's see. Yes, it is. Travers flew out last night. Is there something wrong?"

"I'll explain later, Colonel. Travers is here with me at Tarbolton."

Bishop slammed his hand down on the cradle, held it for a second and released it. "Give me the Transatlantic Call Center, London," he snapped to the police operator. "Clear any line you have to to get through."

The copilot emerged from the cockpit into the belly of the Fortress and shouted above the thudding of the engines, "Landfall in ten minutes, you guys."

Horn opened his eyes and watched the sleeping figures begin to stir as the copilot stepped across the scattered playing cards and empty Scotch bottles and began prodding the men with the toe of his flying boot. "Wake up, for Christ's sake. Logan Field in ten minutes, you drunken bums."

Horn threw off his blanket and reached for his Thermos of coffee. He had not taken part in the night's poker game and had declined the circulating whisky bottle so that now, after a few hours' sleep, he felt clearheaded enough to face the problems ahead.

It was more than three years since he had been in America, but before that it had been his second home. Remaining completely German, he had nevertheless found, as had so many visitors to the States, that it was remarkably easy to adopt the speech habits and mannerisms of the country. That part held no worries for him. More alarming was his serious ignorance of what had happened in America, what changes had taken place in the year and a half since war had broken out in Europe. Was gas rationed? He had no idea. Had the government instituted any sort of identity card? Could a stranger buy a car on a used-car lot in the casual way he used to be able to before the war? Europe's war, that was.

Horn strapped himself into a gunner's vacant blister seat and admired the pilot's skill as he banked the huge airplane and brought it in low across the New England coastline. The Luftwaffe had no plane like this, nothing with its enormous range and bombload. And last night after a few gulps of Scotch his companions had begun to boast about a second high-tailed version, with a bombload of twenty thousand pounds, that would be going into production this year. It was when he thought of German cities, virtually defenseless against such high-flying monsters, that he was confirmed in the validity of what he had decided to do.

The Fortress came down firmly and trundled along the concrete strip toward the clutch of administration buildings at the far end of the runway. The hung-over civilian pilots, adjusting Stetsons and baseball caps, the most eccentric assortment of headgear Horn had ever seen, picked up their bags and, seconds after the plane had stopped, began to swing themselves through the open door to the ground eight or nine feet below.

Two or three jeeps were waiting for them, and Horn joined the others as they clambered onto the back of the vehicles and shouted directions to the drivers.

To Horn's astonishment there were no formalities. No papers were demanded; no debriefing seemed to be required. Smoking cigars, the straggling line of boisterous men strolled through the administration building and out to a line of yellow cabs waiting in front. He could see Scruggs out ahead and the tall figure of Tressenriter beside him.

He decided not to risk another contact. In their sober state they might start asking questions about Travers. Standing just inside the doorway, he watched them climb into a cab.

"What's your problem, boy?"

Horn turned. A master sergeant, not far from retirement, to judge from his graying hair and well-worn features, stood in the open doorway of one of the offices off the hallway. He held a pair of sleek Dobermans on thick plaited leather leashes.

"Just waiting for a couple of guys to get their cab," Horn said. "One more session with those guys and I'm ready for AA."

The master sergeant nodded. "Yeah, I hear those flights are pretty heavy—especially on the Scotch." He looked down at his dogs, then up at Horn. "Vic and Sadie," he volunteered.

He watched Horn, slowly absorbing his lack of response. "Vic and Sadie," he repeated. "Like on the radio show."

"Sure." Horn nodded.

The master sergeant frowned. "You never *heard* of Vic and Sadie?" he said with aggressive incredulity. "It's on every single day of the week!"

Horn shrugged and looked out across the parking lot. "My buddies got their cab," he said. As he bent to pick up his duffel bag, he heard the police sirens.

The dogs' ears pricked in some atavistic reaction to the sounds of the hunt. Or perhaps they really do smell fear? Horn straightened slowly, aware of the master sergeant looking at him, aware of the dogs, aware most of all now of the police cars hurtling into the front parking lot and the men spilling out, corralling the ferry pilots and preventing the taxis from leaving.

"What's the matter?" The grizzled master sergeant was watching him intently. Again the dogs seemed to react, their sharp noses raised toward Horn. Horn moved a few steps back along the corridor. The master sergeant came forward. "You just stay where you are, boy," he said quietly. "Vic and Sadie here can outrun you over any distance." Sensing hostility, the dogs strained forward. "Come into the office. Let's have your ID on the table." He dragged the straining dogs aside.

Horn hesitated. The leather leash was wrapped tightly around the man's wrist. It would take a few seconds to release the dogs. He shrugged and took a pace forward. Through the main door he could see three patrolmen crossing the parking lot toward the administration building. Then he turned and ran.

Before he had reached the end of the corridor, he heard the master sergeant urging the dogs forward and the scrambling patter of their paws on the polished linoleum behind him.

Skidding toward the door at the end of the corridor, he wrenched at the handle and simultaneously hit the central panel with his shoulder. With an impact that knocked the breath from him, the locked door brought him to a dead stop. The dogs were on him, tearing at the rough canvas of the duffel bag, snarling and snapping as they fought to get at him. Swinging the bag, he swept one against the wall, but the second was now clear to fly at his unprotected face. As its powerful back leg muscles tensed, the master sergeant's voice cracked out in the bare corridor: "Vic, Sadie—here! Here, damn you!"

The dogs slunk back to his side and stood eyeing Horn, long tongues falling from their open mouths. "You deserve all you get, boy, running from a pair of Dobermans." He jerked his head over his shoulder. "What the cops want you for? Been doing a little illegal trafficking on the side?" He eyed Horn's duffel bag. "Little whisky smuggling ain't no crime."

"Not whisky." In his pocket Horn felt the snuffbox Mr. Frank had given him. "English silver," he said, taking the ornate miniature box from his pocket and extending it in his palm toward the master sergeant. "Little item like this sells for fifty dollars in Boston. We all bring a few over."

The master sergeant reached out and slowly took the snuffbox. Then with his free hand he motioned toward the office door beside him. His eyes never left Horn. "Through there," he said. "The window's open. You can reach the highway without being seen from the front."

Horn stepped past the growling dogs and into the office. As he closed the door, he could see the patrolmen were just about to enter the front hall.

Twelve

Max Bishop stood by a window overlooking the airfield and watched Colonel Tap Garner as he nervously tidied his already immaculate desk. The Colonel was a career officer due for retirement in under two years. He had wanted nothing better than an easy passage, serving out his time in charge of the USAAF spares depot outside Dayton, Ohio. His sudden posting to Prestwick had come as an unpleasant and unwanted surprise. He liked to work strictly by the book, and the stream of civilian pilots who ferried over the Flying Fortresses were in his opinion an undisciplined rabble and a constant cause of concern. General Walker's sudden appearance had also disturbed him. He took it as some kind of damaging reflection on his work. His record was clean, and he wanted to keep it that way. For this reason Bishop, with his apparent connections in high places, made him nervous.

He was a big man in his early fifties with thinning, mouse-brown hair on a head that appeared somewhat too small for his body. He had acquired the nickname Tap from his habit of drumming his fingers or a pencil on the desk as he checked some paperwork or report. He was happiest with the written page. Words and figures were positive and took no sides, and two and two could always be made to equal four.

187

Someone knocked on the door. The Colonel glanced at Bishop, cleared his throat and said, "Come in."

The door opened, and Kay entered. She saw Bishop from the corner of her eye but didn't look at him directly.

"This is Major Max Bishop from British Intelligence," the Colonel said.

"Major. . . ." Kay turned her head slowly to look at him.

Bishop moved forward from the window. "Sit down, won't you, Lieutenant?"

He indicated a chair facing the Colonel at the desk.

"Major Bishop would like to ask you a few questions," said the Colonel, rising from his seat to vacate the desk and leave the room.

"In that case I'd like the Colonel to stay." She was looking at Bishop as she spoke.

"That won't be necessary," said Bishop.

"Then I'm not answering any questions."

"Lieutenant Hampton . . ." blustered the Colonel.

Kay interrupted him. "Am I here as an officer or as an American citizen?"

She had carefully prepared the question when she guessed she was going to be interrogated. It made the Colonel even more uneasy. The Lieutenant was on General Walker's staff, and the General was his immediate superior.

"You are here," said Bishop, "to answer a few questions that might help us in our investigations."

"You mean we're all on the same side?"

"We'd like to think so."

"Then you can't object to the Colonel's being here."

"If that's the way you want it," said Bishop evenly. He could see Kay would be no pushover and would have preferred the Colonel not to be there if he had to get tough. He took out a pack of Players and offered it to Kay.

"I don't smoke."

"Where's Alfred Horn?" asked Bishop, his eyes on the end of a cigarette as he lit it.

"I don't believe I know him."

"The man you met at the base late last Saturday evening."

Kay looked suitably blank.

"The sergeant who was on duty remembers him well, and the barman."

"You mean Captain Vincent."

"Vincent?"

"Captain John Vincent."

"That's the name he used?"

"That was his name."

"All right, where's Captain Vincent?" said Bishop coolly.

"I've no idea."

"You've no idea he took Travers's papers and used them to fly to the States?"

"Why should he do that, Major?"

"Why was he going to America?"

"I don't understand the question. He's an American; why shouldn't he be going to America?"

"Who was he going to meet?"

"How would I know?"

"Did he have any papers with him?"

"Papers?"

"Documents, maps? A case?"

Kay didn't answer at once. Then she said, "As far as I know he didn't have any papers or any case."

Bishop knew she was lying.

"Considering you spent several days and nights with this John Vincent," said Bishop, emphasizing the word "nights," "you seem to know very little about him."

"Do I have to take this, Colonel?" She turned to Garner.

"Why don't we try and keep this friendly, huh?" said the Colonel. His fingers had started to drum.

"Of course. Let's take Travers. You *do* remember him?"

"Sure."

"You picked him up in the bar."

Kay glared at the Colonel. He gave a slight placating shrug.

"*He* asked *me* to have a drink."

"Several drinks. And later you took him back to the cottage?"

Kay nodded.

"You seem to have been pretty busy since the General left."

"Colonel, I'm not sitting here having dirt thrown in my face."

"Major Bishop. . . ." The Colonel appealed desperately.

"I'm not interested in the Lieutenant's love life. I want to know about Alfred Horn."

"If you mean Captain Vincent, he was working under direct orders from General Walker."

The Colonel leaned forward. He suddenly saw trouble looming up, USAAF top brass trouble.

"You're sure of that?"

"Yes."

The Colonel glanced at Bishop.

"Lieutenant, were you also acting under orders from General Walker?"

Bishop immediately saw the way the Colonel's mind was working: he was angling for a way to get Kay and himself off the hook.

"Indirectly, yes."

Bishop started to speak, but the Colonel stopped him with a raised hand.

"That's all, Lieutenant, you're dismissed. Don't leave the base."

Kay saluted and left the room. Bishop sat down in the chair and lit another cigarette. "I could contact London and ask for a special warrant for her arrest."

The Colonel was suddenly decisive. "Then you'd

better get on the phone fast. There's a plane for the States in thirty minutes, and Lieutenant Hampton will be on it."

Bishop pulled thoughtfully on his cigarette. He knew he could do nothing in that time. But at least he had one piece of information withheld by Hess. USAAF two-star General Thomas Jefferson Walker was involved in this.

He had forgotten how generous Americans were with their company. In the Germany of the thirties a lone man could stand for hours on a forest road without getting a lift. Cars and trucks would rattle by, and if the drivers looked stolidly ahead, it was no special German meanness of spirit but a special German fear that the hitchhiker might somehow be undesirable, politically deviant, a KZ *Lager* escapee—even, God forbid, a Jew.

The driver of the huge chemical truck who had picked him up in the late afternoon just south of Boston was a man of strong opinions and sharp eyes. "English," Jerry Green said, glancing away from the road at the pack of cigarettes.

"Yes . . ." Horn said hesitantly.

"You just been over there?" Before Horn could answer, the driver snapped his fingers. "I got it. Logan! You're one of these ferry guys."

Horn hesitated. "Yes," he said. "We got in at noon."

"So how they doing over there?" The driver drove with his head half turned toward his passenger.

"How's who doing?" Horn said guardedly.

"The good guys. They ready to start handing it right back to the Krauts yet?"

"That's going to take time."

"Not if we do what we ought to have done a year ago."

"What's that?"

"You're kidding! Go right in there ourselves,

is what. You guys are doing your bit flying those planes over, but what do the rest of us do, huh, except sit on our butts and read about how London just took another seven straight nights of air raids? I'm with you, buddy; let's get in and get this war moving. And you're talking to a guy with three draft-age sons."

Horn was silent. "How do your sons feel?" he asked after a moment.

"One's at Fort Benning; the other two're at Fort Bragg. That tell how they feel?"

Horn nodded.

"As an impartial observer," the driver said with unconscious irony, "just tell me how things are looking over there. The British are slow starters, I guess; that's what the papers say. But they certainly gave the Luftwaffe a beating in the Battle of Britain."

Horn flushed angrily. He'd flown more than three hundred sorties in the so-called Battle of Britain. He'd picked up BBC broadcasts on the number of German aircaft claimed to have been shot down. RAF pilots were as prone to exaggeration as Luftwaffe pilots. In the excitement and confusion of a dogfight they tended to claim every enemy aircraft they ever fired a burst at. Yet he was honest enough to admit that if it wasn't an outright British victory, at least strategically the RAF had prevented the Luftwaffe from dominating the skies over Britain. And he at least accepted that that meant the invasion force gathering for "Sea Lion," the invasion of Britain, would be cut to pieces before the first infantryman ever managed to set foot in England. What was it Churchill had said in one of his typically bloodthirsty speeches? "Hitler has said that his army is coming. Let them come. We are waiting for them. And so are the fishes."

"It's going to be a long war," Horn said. "Whichever way it turns out, it's going to be a long war."

The truck thundered on through the gathering dusk, heading south from New Haven, Bridgeport and Stamford toward New York. They would be in Washington, Jerry Green assured him, by morning. Horn slept fitfully between cigarettes, cups of coffee from a flask and bursts of animated conversation from the driver. Somewhere before New York they stopped to eat in a roadside diner. It was a long wooden cabin, a brash, noisy place, full of bright lights and the smell of cooking and the shouted greetings of the truckers, many of whom seemed to know each other.

Horn and Jerry Green collected their twenty-five cents' worth of ham and eggs and carried it to a long table. Behind Horn's head the radio blared, and even the wisecracking truckdrivers stopped to listen to "Chiquita Banana." The first singing advertisement had burst onto American radio that second week in May with more than two thousand exposures coast to coast of the "Chiquita Banana" jingle. By next week it would have achieved the saturation of boredom. Today, Wednesday, it was still a novelty.

Alfred Horn listened to the advertisements in wonder. Du Pont was advertising a completely new stocking material—nylon hose, the advertisement promised, would wear twice as long as silk, look twice as good. Local restaurants competed to cut a cent or two off their forty-five-cent dinners, and the American craze for cars could be satisfied on Lincolns or Chevies or Olds—the last even with a new device that made a gearshift unnecessary. Maybe American society had not yet pulled out of a decade of depression, but its potential energy was immense, and while the American in Horn responded to it, the German part of him shivered in fear at the thought of this energy directed toward his homeland.

The nation through which Jerry Green's truck thundered the night of May 13, 1941, was an America that would be almost completely expunged from memory by the events of the next few years. Of the hundred million adult Americans, Gallup Polls were regularly turning in a figure of 70 to 85 percent against involvement in a European war. Yet at the same time war news filled *Time, Newsweek* and a thousand dailies from San Diego to Vermont and the runaway favorite radio song of this isolationist era was a sugary tribute to Britain and the British, "The White Cliffs of Dover." *The New York Times,* surveying war attitudes, rightly decided the nation was suffering a form of dangerous schizophrenia.

On the extremes, of course, men had already made up their minds. The Eastern Liberal Establishment was pro-British almost to a man, favoring an interventionist policy that would not stop short even of a declaration of war. Others, like Key Pittman, chairman of the Senate Foreign Relations Committee, considered Britain as good as defeated and seriously proposed a peace formula in which the British Isles would be ceded to Germany and the British Empire run from Canada.

President Franklin D. Roosevelt, elected on a no-war platform, presided over a divided nation. A limited draft had been introduced, but barracks throughout the country were becoming daubed with the mutinous threat "OHIO," over the hill in October. A battle tank had been driven through the Neutrality Act by last month's Lend-Lease Act, but still the enigmatic Roosevelt promised peace in his radio broadcasts, peace in his speeches, peace at private luncheons and public celebrations. Only a handful of men in America in that spring of 1941 knew that Franklin Delano Roosevelt had already decided that to occupy the place in history his ambition demanded, he would have to lead the nation into war.

At Roosevelt's home at Hyde Park it was not yet midnight. The President, seated in the long-backed adjustable chair which he found most eased the pain in his back, waited before turning his eyes on his visitor. Director of the Federal Bureau of Investigation since he was twenty-nine years old, J. Edgar Hoover, now in his mid-forties, was already a formidable figure in American public life. He handled politicians with an unsubtle mixture of arrogance and threat, and his secret files on the Washington elite were said to be sufficiently extensive and revealing to ensure that he would hold the Director's job for life.

Yet one man J. Edgar Hoover watched warily. He had no love for the left-liberal policies of his President; he had no love for the politics of the New Deal. But he knew that the man with the pale-eyed charm in the invalid chair opposite was the one man with power and determination enough to remove him from the job to which he had devoted his life.

"Mr. Hoover," the President said, "I can tell you no more. Alfred Horn represents a massive danger to our country. He must be hunted down ruthlessly."

Hoover was suddenly aware that it was the third time in fifteen minutes the President had used the word "ruthlessly" to describe the tracking down of Alfred Horn. He felt the hair on the back of his neck tingle. Was it possible he was being asked to do something much more than discover and arrest the German flier?

"Mr. President," Hoover said slowly, "I appreciate that you cannot, for political reasons, tell me exactly what sort of threat to our country Alfred Horn constitutes. But if he's to be arrested, he has to be charged. And the only charge I see against him at the moment is 'illegal entry.' "

He was forcing Roosevelt's hand. If "ruthlessly" meant what Hoover thought it might mean, the President would have to come right out with it. And J. Edgar Hoover would in that moment have established his ascendancy over the cleverest politician ever to have achieved the White House.

"Mr. Hoover," Roosevelt said slowly, "I have no more to add, except to emphasize again the overwhelming importance of this commission. I wouldn't say crudely that your job depends on it"— he flashed the famous disarming smile—"but I might just say *all* our jobs depend on your success."

Riding in the back of his black limousine back to his house in the suburbs south of Washington, Hoover was aware of having been completely outmaneuvered. The President wanted Alfred Horn dead —Hoover was sure of that. But he had made it clear that Hoover alone was going to shoulder the burden.

In his top floor office in the Federal Bureau of Investigation building, J. Edgar Hoover watched from behind his wide desk as a small, compactly built balding man entered the room. Not a man normally to question his own decisions, Hoover nevertheless was anxious that John Dolyacki was the right choice for this assignment. This morning he had received another telephone call from Hyde Park. Roosevelt's voice had been cool, remote. A British Intelligence officer, a Major Max Bishop, would be arriving at the British Embassy in Washington. He was to be met there by the FBI agent Hoover had assigned to the case. All possible aid and support would be provided Major Bishop. Within the parameters Roosevelt had sketched last night, the British officer would have operational command of the case.

Hoover's head had jerked back in angry resentment at the last sentence. British control over an American investigation in America was unthinkable. He had bluntly refused, but for once it hadn't worked. When Roosevelt wanted to take a hard line, even Hoover was forced to retreat into reluctant, grumbling acquiescence.

Dolyacki came forward into the room and, at Hoover's gesture, took a seat in front of the desk. He had met the legendary Director of the FBI only twice before. By reputation he knew him to be unsubtle, obsessional and vengeful, but he also knew him to be, with the possible exception of the Chief Justice of the Supreme Court, the most powerful figure in American politics outside the democratic processes of American public life.

Hoover drummed the desk top. "Sometime yesterday," he said, "a German officer hopped an American bomber in Britain and flew out to Boston." He leaned back and took a file from his desk drawer. "This is a telephone transcript of what the British have given us on the German. It might be true; it might be half true; it might be a pack of lies."

Dolyacki watched while Hoover contemptuously flicked open the file.

"Telephone report on Captain Alfred Horn of the Luftwaffe. Background: landowning family in Pomerania, father army general, died 1931, mother German-American, died 1938. What the hell's German-American? American-American is the only American I know." He pushed the file away. "A Luftwaffe pilot shot down over Britain . . . escapes to America. Why is he so hot, Dolyacki? Why do I get my instructions directly from the President, Dolyacki? Why is a British Intelligence Major being sent out to take charge, Dolyacki? In short, what the hell is going on, Dolyacki?"

Dolyacki felt a mounting sense of excitement. It was obvious that whatever the exact nature of the assignment, it had international significance. And it was so sensitive that not even J. Edgar Hoover was to be let in on all the details. But as he read Horn's file, Dolyacki's quick intelligence picked up a connection which had totally escaped J. Edgar Hoover—Horn had stowed away at Prestwick Air Base, not fifteen miles from where the Scottish Glasgow *Herald* had just that morning reported that Rudolf Hess had landed in Scotland. Mostly still by instinct, Dolyacki knew he was on the biggest assignment of his career.

John Dolyacki, the seventh child of a Hungarian father and a Czech mother, was born to the peal of church bells ringing from the Alps to the Carpathian Mountains. That the bells were ringing to usher in the first seconds of the twentieth century did nothing to lessen his parents' pride in John Karl, their first boy child after a run of six daughters. Prague, John Karl's birthplace, was, at the turn of the century, one of the great subcapitals of Austria's continental empire, a city of imposing architecture, elegant military display and secure status for those to whom the State offered employment as customs officer, public records clerk or police spy. John Karl's father followed the latter profession—until one day a highly placed victim turned the tables and secured the dismissal of Miklós Dolyacki from the State service and his imprisonment on charges of corruption.

Consumed with hatred of the nobleman who had trumped up the charges and for the Austrian State which had chosen to believe them, John Karl, then fifteen, added two years to his age and joined the 3rd Imperial Regiment of Uhlans serving on the Italian Monfalcone front at Trieste. Every pfennig of his monthly pittance was sent back to his mother and six sisters starving in Prague.

Made obsolete by the machine guns and barbed wire of the Italian army, the splendid officers of the Austrian cavalry sat in their magnificent quarters at the Caserma Rosetti in Trieste and drank champagne, gambled and practiced sodomy while awaiting the cavalry breakthrough which would, they believed, sweep them down into the plains of Lombardy. During the four years of this agreeable war a boy soldier could make a golden thaler on any weekend for a beating session with a party of young officers. Most weeks John Karl sent money home to Prague.

And then the unbelievable happened. The German armies fell in the West, the Kaiser abdicated and the whole ramshackle structure of the Austrian Empire collapsed in a welter of anarchy and self-determination. That year Dolyacki's mother died. His father, re-

leased from prison by the new government, went to
live with a brother in the Tyrol; his sisters married or
joined socialist movements in Prague and Vienna; and
John Karl Dolyacki found that he had humiliated himself for three years to support a family that no longer
existed. Part Hungarian, part Czech, German-speaking
but without attachment to any German-speaking land,
John Dolyacki made his way to America and applied
for American citizenship.

He had never married. The marks of the beatings
he had given and received remained as deeper scars
than he could possibly have imagined. He had had
one brief homosexual affair with a young Austrian
in Washington and another, years later, with an
Englishman, in which Dolyacki had almost killed
the Englishman. Frightened at the hate within himself, from then on Dolyacki had willingly sublimated
all his turbulent resentments in his work for the Federal Bureau of Investigation. Speaking Hungarian,
Czech, German, Italian and English, he had at first
been recruited as a language expert but had moved
on to conduct his own investigations in foreign language areas. Now in May 1941 he had achieved
the rank of Inspector.

Dolyacki looked up from the file. For the moment
he would say nothing about the coincidence of time
and place with the Hess flight.

"My instructions from the President," Hoover said
slowly, "are that Alfred Horn should be hunted down"
—he paused—"ruthlessly." His eyes met Dolyacki's.
"Ruthlessly, Inspector. We want him alive . . . or
dead. Do I make myself clear?"

"Very clear, sir."

"Keep me informed every step of the way."

As Dolyacki left the room, Hoover stared down at
the innocuous-looking buff file he had brought from
his private safe in his own study at home.

J. Edgar Hoover maintained a file on all his top
men. This one contained two strange stories. The first

was of a young Austrian Count, a First Secretary at the Austrian Embassy in 1929. He had been found bound and beaten in his rooms at the Embassy. Agent John Dolyacki had spent the preceding month cooperating with him on a currency swindle investigation. The young Austrian had been unable to help the police with a description of his attacker. The second account in Hoover's private file was of a titled Englishman in New York in 1934, beaten almost to death in an expensive apartment building in Manhattan. The confidential report suggested there was more than one reason for believing Dolyacki was responsible.

They came into the District with the sun dispersing the morning mists. Jerry Green, the dark line of his unshaved jaw jutting, as he pushed the truck through the city traffic, kept up his unending flow of talk. "You got business here, you say, Al, but if you're also looking for some muffin, I can fix you some really great muffin."

What the hell was he talking about? "I guess not," Horn said casually.

"The very best in Washington," the driver assured him. "It don't come cheap. All good hotel trade. Ten dollars minimum. It's not your waterfront three-dollar hooker I'm talking about."

Horn smiled with relief. "Muffin"—he'd have to remember that. "Thanks," he said. "I've been married a month. The way I feel right now I'd turn down a row of young English Duchesses."

"English muffin, you mean?" The driver chuckled at his own joke.

At a street corner near Union Station Horn jumped down from the cab.

"You can get yourself a shave and shower there," Jerry Green said. "And if you want to buy that new suit of clothes, they got anything up to eighty dollars in this area. Keep 'em flying," he said cheerfully with a jerk of his thumb in the vague direction of the Atlantic and rammed the big truck into gear.

By May 1941 Washingtonians had begun to wonder if the strange five-sided building across the Potomac would ever be completed. They knew it was intended as the new headquarters of the U.S. Army and many already referred to it colloquially as the Pentagon. Of the completed sides two were already occupied by military staffs, and the khaki Lincoln Zephyrs carried Generals over the construction site rubble each morning to work in offices overlooking a confusion of cranes, dump trucks and stacked steelwork. When the building was begun in 1940, it had seemed a monstrous edifice to direct the minute American army, but mobilization was changing all that. By the end of the year the Pentagon would control one of the biggest and best equipped armies in the world.

General Thomas Jefferson Walker occupied a first-floor office which overlooked a low red steel skeleton of an uncompleted building across yards of churned mud and concrete foundations. The shouts of the hard hats and the thunder of heavy trucks were the constant background to his working day.

But on this Wednesday morning General Thomas J. Walker had no time to be concerned with the inadequacy of his work conditions. The two men sitting opposite him in the new leather armchairs were both portly, fiftyish and had that unmistakable air of power with which Washington endows its most successful practitioners. Both Ted Markland and John Caspiani were Democratic Senators elected on the coattails of Franklin D. Roosevelt, the President they feared. In Roosevelt's victory they saw the triumph of Eastern liberals and a New Deal program which must finally destroy the independence of the individual states.

"The German radio announced this morning that Hess is missing. That means at least he left Germany on schedule," Ted Markland said.

"Yet there's been no word from the BBC." Caspiani shook his head.

"And if the British had the Deputy Führer of Germany in their hands, surely they'd want the world to know."

"It figures," Walker said gloomily. "So we have to assume his plane crashed in the North Sea. Or worse, was shot down over land."

"What makes that worse?" Markland asked. "Crashed in the sea or shot down by an RAF pursuit plane over Scotland, either way the mission's off."

"What makes it worse is that if the British have Hess in an interrogation center somewhere, it's just a matter of time before my involvement in this comes out."

"So?" Caspiani said. "What's so bad about believing America has to be kept out of this war?"

"What's so bad about *any* political view is that I'm a military officer on active duty. Politics is your business. You could host a quiet poker game between Hitler and Churchill if you chose. But that doesn't go for an officer, and you know it."

"What about your man in Scotland?" Markland ignored the outburst.

"It's a woman. A Lieutenant Kay Hampton. I bypassed her commanding officer, so I can't make direct contact with her. And for some reason she hasn't contacted me." He looked at the two Senators. "We'd better accept it; there's only one explanation that fits the facts."

"And that is?" Caspiani asked coldly.

"The British have Hess. When they captured him, they forced him to talk. As soon as they found out he was routed through Prestwick, they demanded the U.S. commanding officer there investigate Kay Hampton. That's what's going on at this moment."

Caspiani looked at Markland, who nodded slowly. Together they stood up.

"It nearly worked, General. There was nearly a very big deal."

"Wait a minute, gentlemen." Walker's voice made both heads turn. It was a long time since anybody had dared to be peremptory with either of them. "You've always assured me that the man Rudolf Hess was to meet here was one of the biggest names in politics.'"

"That's right, General," Caspiani said coolly. "A big enough name to get Hitler's number two man to try to meet him, however it turned out."

General Walker was gray-faced. "I want the name of the man Hess was coming here to meet."

Markland looked at him in disbelief.

"Forget it," Caspiani said briefly. "You said yourself the deal's off."

"And I carry the can," Walker said bitterly.

"You knew what you were getting into, General," Markland said.

"I'm going to need help from somebody placed to give me help. Who better than the man Hess was to meet?"

Almost in unison the Senators shook their heads.

"Our man couldn't do that for you even if he wanted to." Caspiani's hand reached for the door. "We appreciate what you've done, General, and we'll do all we can to make sure your high motives are recognized. But unless Hess is spilling the beans in England right now, our man's name remains unpublished. Believe me, General, there's too much at stake to handle this any other way."

As they made their way down the empty corridor, Markland shook his head. "There's one General that's never going to make five stars."

"Forget him. About tomorrow night—you coming?"

"This time I think I'll pass."

"Don't be so nervous Nelly," Caspiani said. "The sort of people I get are okay."

"Maybe."

"About ten then?"

"I'll drop by after the committee meeting."

"Great. And this General, let's forget about the whole deal. If we'd pulled it off, it would have been spectacular stuff. As it is, we just deal ourselves a new hand."

"Sure."

The two suntanned men left the building and headed for the chauffeured Lincoln parked outside.

Crossing the vast concourse of Union Station, Alfred Horn made for the row of phone booths. A small group of people stood waiting for a booth to become vacant, mostly men in good-quality light suits and snap-brim hats. Horn joined them and stood examining his reflection in the glass of the phone booth opposite him. In his new lightweight gray suit he didn't look too much unlike them.

The woman in the booth opposite him hung up the phone and pushed at the glass door. Horn stepped forward and held open the door. As the woman smiled her thanks, Horn slid into the booth.

In General Walker's office the ringing phone caused him to turn from his morose contemplation of the construction site below his window. He reached across the desk and lifted the receiver. "Yes?"

"I've a call for you, General," his civilian secretary said. "On behalf of a Lieutenant Hampton, the caller says."

"Put it through." His face flushed with excitement. Perhaps after all, his career wasn't ruined. Perhaps when the story of America's fight to stay out of the European war was finally told, there would be an honorable mention for the General who had risked everything to get the Deputy Führer of the Reich to peace discussions in the United States.

"General Walker, I have to see you right away." The voice was undoubtedly American.

"I understand," Walker said. He glanced quickly at

the copper sunburst clock on the wall. "Let's say in half an hour at my office. Can you make it?"

"I'll be there." Horn hung up the receiver with immense relief. He stood in the booth for a moment, lighting a cigarette, until one of the men outside rapped impatiently on the glass. Then he took up his duffel bag and slid back the door.

After crossing the station concourse, he approached the line of yellow cabs waiting outside. The leading driver leaned one huge arm out of the open window and chewed on a nickel cigar.

"I want the new army building across the river," Horn said.

"The brass-hat palace, sure. People call it the Pentagon."

They rode across the Potomac to what looked to Horn like a vast building site. A guard, waving through trucks loaded with sand and gravel, told them how to reach General Walker's office without even asking Horn's name.

Bouncing over the temporary road surface, they followed the directions given by the guard until they arrived at a still-unfinished concrete building.

Outside, the cabdriver drew to a halt. Horn got out and stood by the window. "I could be some time," he said. "You want me to pay you?"

"When I wait, I'm working," the cabdriver said. "With luck I'll also be sleeping. I'll wait down there in the shade. Take your time."

Horn turned and walked under the stretched tarpaulin that served as a weather canopy and entered the building. He saw nothing extraordinary about the sergeant with the white cap, white belt and gaiters who stood talking to a civilian beside the desk. He walked past them and was about to ask the desk corporal for General Walker when the slamming of an office door momentarily caused him to glance up.

A two-star General was approaching Horn across the entrance hall. Flanked by two MP officers, he gave Horn a rapid imperceptible shake of the head as he walked briskly toward the door, the officers maintaining step across the wide vestibule.

The MP sergeant pulled open the door, and Horn turned casually to the desk corporal. "What's going on there?"

The corporal glanced past Horn as the door closed behind Walker and his escort. "Just what you see, sir. I guess that's the way they put a General under arrest." He looked back at Horn. "What can I do for you?"

Horn was suddenly aware that the MP sergeant and the heavily built civilian had moved up to the desk.

"Who was it you wanted to see?" the corporal asked again. The MP and his civilian companion were now definitely interested.

Horn swung the duffel bag onto the desk. "You," he said to the corporal.

"Me?"

"Why not?" Horn smiled at him. "I'm John Chapman of the Church of Christ the Redeemer. I'm what we call a spokesman for the Faith. Now I have here conclusive evidence which I would like you to study—"

"Not today," the corporal said.

"There's no time like the present," Horn urged him.

"Do me a favor, I said not today." The corporal pushed at the bag. "Anyway, I'm a Catholic."

"Ah. . . ." Horn registered disappointment. Then he turned to the other two men looking on. "And what about you gentlemen?"

"On your way, brother," the civilian said unceremoniously.

"Another Catholic?" Horn asked pleasantly.

"I said on your way. This is a military establishment."

"A military establishment still needs God, friend."

The man pointed toward the door. "Out," he said,

"or I'll start looking into how you got yourself in here in the first place."

Horn shrugged defeat and swung his bag off the desk. As he turned toward the door, the phone rang. Behind him he heard the corporal lift the receiver. Two steps before he reached the door the corporal said to the civilian, "The guardroom says you wanted to be informed of anyone with an appointment to see General Walker. . . ."

Horn hit the swing door with his shoulder. As it burst open, he hurtled forward onto the gravel patch outside.

As men spilled out of the building behind him, Horn took the road ahead. He knew that even though he was carrying the duffel bag, none of the men from the lobby would stand a chance of catching him on foot, but as he ran, he could already hear the sound of car doors being slammed shut behind him.

Ahead a group of construction workers had stopped digging to watch the figure pounding down the road toward them, and one or two were already moving uncertainly forward, shovels in hand, in response to the distant shouts of the men climbing into the cars.

Dolyacki, in the passenger seat of the MP sergeant's jeep, saw that the construction work effectively would keep the running man to the roadway until either the approaching workers or the jeep itself would have him.

Horn, too, saw the trap closing. To his left a bright yellow mechanical digger was excavating a massively impassable foundation trench. To his right, where work had proceeded further, a forest of steel reinforcing rods rose from a forty-yard-long concrete foundation pad. As Dolyacki's jeep closed in, Horn decided. Veering sharply, he hurled the duffel bag over the line of steel rods, checked his pace for a left-foot take-off and, to the open-mouthed astonishment of the construction workers running toward him, kicked up with the right leg, flipped his body over and, with the tops of the razor-sharp rods an inch or two from his face, sailed safely over the obstacle.

The MP sergeant braked, sending up dust from the back wheels of the jeep. Dolyacki knew at that moment with absolute certainty that the man he was pursuing was a natural athlete. That the man he was pursuing was Alfred Horn.

Retrieving his bag, Horn ran between stacked drainage pipes and earth mounds, tarpaulin-covered bagged cement and stacked window frames. Like any other Olympic athlete he knew his physical limits better than most men. But he had never before had to add to his calculation the debilitating effect of fear. As he ducked among the piled construction equipment he could almost hear the crack of a pistol shot behind him and feel the snubnosed bullet sloughing into his flesh.

When he stopped in the lee of a wooden hut he was shocked at the violence of his trembling, at the nausea that surged through his body.

There was a site exit not fifty yards ahead with a line of trucks, their engines running, waiting to be checked through. From where he stood he watched the MPs examining documents and waving the drivers on. The empty trucks received no more than the most perfunctory examination, but in the narrow roadway they were still forced to wait in line to move out onto the highway.

He had no way of knowing whether the exit guards had been warned to look out for him. He walked quickly across the broken, furrowed clay to the temporary road. The MPs, moving down the line of trucks, had their backs turned to him. The last vehicle, a small pickup, was rapidly checked by an MP sergeant. As the MP moved away, shouting to the other drivers to get moving, Horn stepped onto the roadway and jumped into the back of the pickup. Seconds later they were moving forward and more trucks were joining the line, commanding the attention of the MPs.

Sitting in the deep shadow in the back of the pick-up, Horn let himself be carried along the highway and back across the river. All his life he had been a hunter, as an Olympic competitor, as a fighter pilot, even in his relations with women. To be the prey suddenly was profoundly unbalancing. He lit a cigarette as the truck rattled into the city. He had never realized how much easier it was to be the hunter. He knew now he desperately needed to rejoin the pack. He never saw the face of his benefactor. At a stoplight he jumped down, threading his way through the stationary vehicles until he reached the sidewalk.

For almost half an hour he walked rapidly, turning onto any street where the crowds seemed thickest, avoiding bus stations, open spaces and empty sidewalks. Eventually, he knew, the shops would be closing; Washingtonians would be making their way home. Soon a single man with a duffel bag would be a conspicuous figure on the emptying streets.

He could not have felt more vulnerable had he been walking the streets with a ticking bomb. He was reluctant to check the bag in at Union Station—that seemed the obvious place for the police to watch for him. But he felt that it was nevertheless vital to make sure the documents did not fall into the hands of the American police. In some not entirely vague manner, he felt he had at least one ace to trade off . . . if he were captured without the documents on him.

On impulse he turned into a drugstore and bought four large envelopes, then used the corner phone to check Kay's Washington address. At the counter with a cup of coffee in front of him he divided the documents into four equal wads of paper and slipped them into the envelopes. Within minutes the four packages, stamped and addressed, had been consigned to the U.S. mail.

Kay's Washington apartment seemed a safe enough destination. Even if she were now being questioned in Scotland, it seemed unlikely they would be interested in an apartment three thousand miles away. And Ralph, her husband, wasn't going to be back for a few days at least. So tomorrow or whenever he wanted Horn could go to the apartment and pry open the mailbox. Compared with the risk of keeping the documents with him, a minor act of burglary seemed both safe and easy.

As he walked on now, he was aware that the area was changing. More children threaded their way, laughing, through the crowds; more and more the adults on the now-teeming sidewalks were Negroes or poor whites.

It was an area of pawnshops, of garbage-littered gutters, of grimy curtained windows and the rattle of invisible freight trains. It was also an area of dollar-a-night hotels with red neon vacancy signs in the ground-floor windows.

Outside the Chelverton Hotel he stopped. He knew the risk he ran, that he might need to produce draft papers or that the police might already have circulated his description. But he knew he had to have somewhere to spend the night whatever course he decided on.

And he knew instinctively that for a while it would be safer to stay in Washington than to take a highway or railroad out.

He mounted the broken stone steps and pushed at the glass door. In the small ocher-painted lobby a bald man in shirt sleeves sat reading a paper. Without moving the angle of his head he looked toward the door.

Horn dropped the duffel bag below the level of the desk. "I want a room for the night. With a shower if you've got one."

The man laid aside his newspaper. "A dollar forty cents with the shower, mister."

"Okay."

"And a quarter on the key."

"Sure."

He reached below the desk top and pulled out a tattered register. "One night, you say?"

"Maybe longer," Horn said. "I'm not too sure of my plans."

The man grunted. "A dollar-forty-cent room drops to an even dollar if you don't use it afternoons."

Horn frowned.

"We guarantee to keep your sheets, mister. They don't get used."

Horn shook his head. "I'll do without the afternoon trade. I'll pay the full rate."

"Please yourself." The man pushed the register toward him. Horn took up the pencil end attached with string to the broken spine of the book and glanced at the other names. After a moment he wrote "John P. Locke, San Diego, California." Nothing further seemed to be required.

The man took his money and passed over the key to Room 32. "Third floor," he said. "No elevator. This end of the corridor."

Horn took the key and crossed to the staircase. He could see that at one time, perhaps sixty, seventy years ago, the building had been a substantial private citizen's house; but the endless catalogue of travelers and whores had by now worn the once-grand staircase and reduced the banister rail to a state of creaking weakness. He pushed on up to the third and top floor, the staircase growing narrower, the corridors becoming longer and thinner as he reached the old servants' floor.

Number 32 was an attic box room, nine by twelve feet, with an iron frame cot and a closet converted to an unsavory shower. From the window the view was across a wide crisscross of railroad tracks to locomotive repair sheds and freight yards beyond.

He dropped the bag onto the floor. Most of all he needed a drink. And another pack of cigarettes.

Sitting on the edge of the bed, more totally alone

than he had ever been in his life, he knew he was close to breaking. Nothing in his life as an athlete or an officer had prepared him for the horror of outcast loneliness he now felt. For a moment or two his body was shaken with a series of dry, tearless spasms. Then he stood up and let himself out of the room.

Thirteen

Dolyacki stood in the oak-paneled room at the British Embassy's imposing mansion on Massachusetts Avenue and looked down on the red and white marquee spotlit in the center of the enormous lawns below. Around the gardens, lanterns hung in the trees and the chiseled accents of the British diplomatic corps floated up toward him. Among the groups strolling with champagne glasses across the lawn, it was not difficult to pick out the tall stooping figure of Lord Halifax, the ambassador, attended by his ADC's, two elegant young men in the dark green mess jackets and red facings of the King's Royal Rifle Corps.

As he watched the two young men, so entirely reminiscent of those Austrian cavalry officers of his youth, Dolyacki's stomach twisted in lust and hatred. The gilded youth of Europe with its highly colored uniforms, its imperious mannerisms . . . it was the first time for many years that he had felt the chill. He turned away quickly to see that the door was opening. The tall officer in the khaki Major's uniform who extended his hand as he crossed the room was just another of the gilded youth. John Dolyacki detested Max Bishop from the first second he saw him.

"You got my message about General Walker?" Bishop asked after they had introduced each other.

"I had him arrested this afternoon," Dolyacki said crisply. "Did you bring pictures of Alfred Horn?"

Bishop produced them from his briefcase and handed them to Dolyacki. He could feel the deep resentment in the other man's manner, but ascribed it to the President's insistence that Bishop should be in charge of the search for Horn.

Dolyacki nodded briefly. "He was at General Walker's this afternoon. We missed him by a hair's breadth. If you'd radioed those pictures to me, the case would have been sewn up by now."

"You worked faster than I imagined," Bishop said. "Too fast. My object was to have Walker arrested after he had been passed the papers."

They eyed each other across the deep-carpeted room. From the garden below a band struck up— "There'll be blue skies over the white cliffs of Dover / Tomorrow, just you wait and see. . . ." Dolyacki snarled his contempt. The British were pulling out all the emotional stops to keep the support of the Washington politicos.

"Okay," he said. "Suppose you tell me first thing what this is all about. I can't run an investigation without background."

"You're not running it, Dolyacki," Bishop said easily. "I am."

"I still need background."

"I'm only authorized to say what you know already —this is a first-class priority for both our governments."

"When the Deputy Leader of Germany decides to fly to Scotland, I can't see it being anything else," Dolyacki said. And saw immediately the shaft had struck home.

"Okay," he continued, "so we know where we are. Alfred Horn flew Hess across. En route for Washington. But Hess breaks an ankle or whatever. So Horn comes on alone, with whatever these papers are . . . to deliver them to General Walker."

Bishop looked at him in reluctant admiration.

"So we now have two separate missions, Major. First, get those papers, second, get to Alfred Horn."

"Get to . . . ?" Bishop said slowly.

"Get to . . . before he can talk to whoever wants to listen. Silence, Major."

Bishop drew a pack of cigarettes from his pocket, took one and lit it. Exhaling slowly, he said, "My orders are that Alfred Horn should be found and arrested. The U.S. government agreed to facilitate his removal to Canada."

Dolyacki looked at Bishop from under his eyebrows but said nothing.

"If you have conflicting orders, Mr. Dolyacki, I should know."

Dolyacki shook his head. "No conflict, Major. None at all."

"Arrest and removal to Canada. Those are *our* orders."

Dolyacki nodded. "Like I said, no conflict, Major. None at all."

The lines had been drawn. For Max Bishop there was the virtual certainty that Alfred Horn would never survive arrest by Inspector Dolyacki.

"Okay," Dolyacki said after a moment's heavy silence. "I can call on any amount of men and facilities we care to ask for. What, if anything, do we have to go on?"

He had no plan as he walked the streets, none, that is, except at some point to buy a bottle of whisky and a fresh pack of Lucky Strikes. Without the duffel bag he felt no more recognizable as a Luftwaffe officer than half a hundred men of his age who jumped on streetcars or bought papers at the newsstands. He looked at the people jostling past him on the sidewalk, the men mostly without jackets now in this part of town, the women with flowered dresses, short to just below the knee and tight to show off slim hips and full busts.

He thought of Kay in the grim blacked-out island across the Atlantic. Then he hurried on, past a policeman on the corner, past a drugstore, past a movie house and stopped. After turning back on impulse, he entered the theater lobby and bought a thirty-cent ticket to see *It Happened One Night*. Seconds later he was sitting among the bums and the unemployed, the old and the housewives, their heads and shoulders just visible dotted around the half-empty theater. Here, away from the eyes of street-corner cops, he could sit in safety and think about what to do next.

On the screen Claudette Colbert with short, curly hair, smiling the world-famous dimpled smile, compounded misunderstanding with Clark Gable. For minutes at a time Horn found he could watch the film, the thought of what to do next pushed to the back of his mind. After half an hour the end titles rolled, the credits nestling in frames of ribboned satin. A short followed—fifteen minutes of the fruity voice of someone named Fitzgerald as the camera roamed among the rice fields of Japan, visited the great Shinto temples above Tokyo and introduced the audience to the rituals of the teahouse. Not a word about Admiral Yamamoto's carrier fleet training at this moment to demonstrate to the world that Japanese naval air power was invincible.

A Western followed. Tumbleweed, dusty denim jeans, savage Indians and deathbed heroism by the town coward. Ninety minutes later Claudette Colbert was meeting Clark Gable again for the first time.

Horn sat through to the end. Then on through the Japanese travelogue.

Halfway through the Western, he closed his eyes. He was aware of an overwhelming, unassuagable loneliness, a great wave of tremulous self-pity that all this had happened to him. Above all, he felt the need for German voices again, for the warm familiarity of his own language. He had mailed the documents; nobody but Kay had seen them. If he walked now to the German Embassy, less than a mile away, he could lay the whole thing before a senior diplomat, a man like the dozens of diplomats he had met at parties and weddings and receptions, an ordinary civilized German who would see his appalling predicament and support his explanations in Berlin.

And everything he had said to Kay? Everything she and Hans Forster and Mr. Frank had said to him? Well, they could be wrong. Or more likely just part right. Germany wasn't ruled by people like Heydrich and Himmler. The German army could trample the combined Gestapo and SS underfoot tomorrow if it were necessary. The Wehrmacht tradition would never allow an officer like himself to be thrown to the Sicherheitdienst. He would be accorded a court-martial. With a military president and with his peers as members of the board. True, he might have to suppress the death of the Gestapo man in Scotland. . . . He opened his eyes. And what would happen to Kay? Undoubtedly she'd tell the U.S. consul in Glasgow the whole story. And if he believed her—*if* he did—then the German government couldn't possibly go ahead with its attack on Russia. . . .

The shots from the screen cracked and whined among the dusty boulders. He was a German officer, for God's sake! What was he doing playing politics? His duty was clear enough. To go to the Reich Embassy and tell the full story. He stood up and walked angrily from the theater. How the hell had he allowed himself to get caught up in all these gray political areas?

It was dark outside when he hailed a cruising cab and asked for the German Embassy. The driver nodded noncommittally and nosed away from the curb. His radio, turned high, played the Chiquita Banana commercial, and he whistled the catchy tune through his teeth. Uncharacteristically he wasn't in the least disposed to talk.

The cab swept down Massachusetts Avenue, past

the brightly lit British Embassy and on to the squat red-brick building that flew the swastika flag.

Horn leaned forward. "Drive straight in," he said.

The cabbie grunted and swung the wheel to turn through a stop sign at the base of the stone steps. When Horn thrust a twenty-dollar bill into his hand and slammed the door behind him, the cabbie whistled the first bars of the commercial through his teeth. "Heil Hitler," he said, grinning at his good fortune.

Horn pushed open the big black door to find himself faced by a metallic grille. Behind it two men in civilian clothes were already moving forward.

"Can I help you, sir?" one of them asked politely in English. Horn saw the other already had a hand inside his jacket as he eyed Horn carefully. There had been too many Jewish demonstrations outside the German Embassy by May 1941 for the guards to take even a single visitor for granted.

Horn nodded crisply. "Hauptmann Horn," he said, and continued in German, "I want to see the senior duty officer."

"The Herr Hauptmann has an appointment?"

"Obviously not," Horn snapped, "or I should be able to give the duty officer's name. Just do as I say. Open this grille, and send for him."

The tone, accent and manner were immediately recognizable to the guard. He drew the keys from his pocket. "Count von Axhausen," he said to the man behind him.

The key clicked in the lock, and the grille slid back. Alfred Horn stepped into the oak-paneled lobby with an immense feeling of relief.

He stood for a few moments ignoring the guard, his eye traveling along the set of framed photographs on the wall. They were all innocuous and vastly reassuring German scenes—pineclad hills at sunset, a gabled village square, Rhine castles, the smoking chimneys of the Ruhr. . . , Two young men came down the carpeted staircase speaking in German. "When I asked her where she'd really like to lunch, she said out on the terrace of the Tally-ho Tavern! My God, I said, I can do better than that, and I took her to the grill at the Mayflower. . . ."

They crossed the lobby, laughing, and passed through a side door. A moment later the door reopened, and a tall middle-aged man emerged. The guard stiffened. "Count von Axhausen, Herr Hauptmann," he whispered.

Horn stepped forward, extended his hand and clicked his heels. "Horn, Alfred. Hauptmann, Luftwaffe."

Axhausen shook hands with him. "Von Axhausen," he said. "What can I do for you?"

"I need to speak to you privately, urgently. First, I need to establish beyond any doubt in your mind my identity."

"You carry papers?"

"No."

"I see." He hesitated. "Come through to my office."

He turned and led the way through the door, which opened onto a long black-and-white-tiled corridor. "Where from?" he asked over his shoulder.

"In Germany? Wolgast, Pomerania."

Axhausen stopped. "Horn . . . ? Freiherr Horn von Thalberg. . . ."

"My uncle," Horn said. "More accurately, my great-uncle."

Axhausen opened a door off the corridor, and Horn entered a simply furnished office. A photograph of Adolf Hitler hung above the fireplace.

"The duty office," Axhausen said. "Not especially comfortable, I'm afraid." He gestured casually to a chair. "Then you would know the von dem Zeitz-Apolda?"

"Very well. Hunted at the Schloss Bergenfeld many times."

Axhausen smiled. "Yes," he said, remembering.

Horn waited.

"Very good, Horn." Axhausen relaxed, sitting on the edge of the desk. "Tell me, is it a long story?"

"Very, I'm afraid."

"Then we shall need something to sustain us." He slid off the edge of the desk, and while Horn lit a cigarette, he took a bottle of cognac from a cupboard and filled two glasses.

"Compliments of the Diplomatic Corps," he said, handing a glass to Horn. "We're on such an incredibly tight budget here it's about the only thing free you'll get, however long you hope to stay. I take it that's what the trouble is. . . . Robbed in some hotel? Dreadful thieves, some of these American hoteliers."

Horn shook his head. "No, nothing like that." He hesitated. "I'd like you to arrange for me to see the chargé d'affaires."

"Herr Thomsen?"

"Yes." Again Horn hesitated. "Has there been any announcement in Germany about the Stellvertreter in the last day or so?"

Axhausen nodded. "Herr Hess was reported missing, possibly dead. We've had a barrage of calls from the American newspapers, of course. But Berlin hasn't given us much to tell, frankly."

"I flew from Augsburg with Herr Hess last Saturday evening."

Axhausen's composure slipped. "You were with Hess?"

"We flew to Scotland. The Stellvertreter's dead. I have the papers he took with him."

Axhausen leaned back against the desk. When Horn began to speak again, the diplomat raised his hand. "One moment, Horn. I think whatever you have to say should be said directly to the chargé d'affaires. Please wait here."

He walked quickly to the door, then turned back. "Help yourself to the cognac." He smiled.

As the door closed behind Axhausen, Horn sipped

his brandy, conscious of a deep feeling of relief. Even the picture of *Der Schnurrbart*, "the Mustache," as the German Officer Corps sometimes condescendingly called Hitler, did nothing to dispel his rising optimism. He had been right, of course. Germany, even the new Germany, was run by men like Axhausen—men who, if they didn't actually hunt on the von dem Zeitz-Apolda estates at Bergenfeld, at least shared their values of honesty and goodwill.

After a few minutes Axhausen returned. "I've seen Herr Thomsen," he said. "It'll be a little while before he sends for you. Let's have a taste more of this quite passable cognac in the meantime."

He poured for both of them. "Dreadful place to be, Washington. Let's hope you're not marooned here until the end of the war," he said conversationally.

"I always thought Washington was the number one post," Horn said. "At least since London has become undesirable and Paris unnecessary."

"Oh, Washington used to be fine." Axhausen smiled wryly. "But now anybody'd think we were at war with *America*. If you're a German diplomat, virtually no one asks you to their parties, and only Italy, Japan and Romania accept our invitations."

"You mean everybody else has taken sides?"

Axhausen shrugged. "I don't know what you're hearing back at home, but frankly we're far from popular. When this war's over, we're going to have a lot of explaining to do."

Horn nodded, more absorbed in the explaining he had to do himself. "What's happening upstairs?" Horn asked. "Had Herr Thomsen heard of me?"

Axhausen shook his head. "He knew no more about this extraordinary Hess business than I did. Wasn't anxious to know more, either."

The phone rang on the desk, and he picked it up. "Axhausen." He listened for a moment, then nodded. "I'll come up immediately," he said, and replaced the phone.

221

Horn stood up. "Do I go with you?"

"Not for the moment. He's just radioing Berlin for instructions. I'll come down and get you when he's ready."

Horn dropped back into his chair. Radio instructions from Berlin. That would be the Foreign Ministry handling it. Good. He was satisfied so far with the way things were going. A long explanation now to the chargé d'affaires, and that, too, would be radioed back through the Foreign Ministry. Just as long as the Gestapo or SD didn't get into the act too early. Like most Wehrmacht officers, he hadn't had much to do with the police and security offshoots of the SS, and his reaction was still, he knew, again like most officers, more contempt than fear. Except for the beach in Scotland and the killer who had come to the cottage.

Of course, for a civilian it was different. The Gestapo and SD had authority over all Reich civilians—and, as Horn knew, from time to time exercised it with grim brutality.

He lit another cigarette and watched the minutes ticking away on the black marble clock beneath the Führer's portrait. Axhausen must have been gone all of ten minutes. He got up and prowled around the room. A shelf of dull directories in English and German—Who's Who, Wer ist Wer for 1940. He took the latter down and looked up his own entry. "Horn, Alfred Maximillian. Olympic athlete . . . Hauptmann, Luftwaffe, holder of the Knight's Cross for gallantry in the Polish Campaign. . . ."

He smiled to himself. What would they say now? he wondered. He replaced the book after flicking through a few entries on his friends and returned to sit in the armchair. Another look at the clock told him that it was now almost half an hour since Axhausen left.

When finally the door opened again, Axhausen stood with his hand on the door handle. Horn stood and placed his glass on the desk, then, turning toward the door, saw Axhausen's face for the first time. With a sense of shock he saw the drawn lines of fear, the look of haunted, guilty compassion. "Come with me," the diplomat said gently, and touched Horn's shoulder as he walked out into the corridor.

A few feet from the office a narrow wooden staircase led to the upper floors. "This way." Axhausen stepped aside to let Horn ascend.

After passing him, Horn stopped on the lower step and turned. "What is it, Axhausen? What the devil's wrong?"

Axhausen, too, had stopped. "I'm sorry, Horn," he said. "Believe me, please, I'm desperately sorry."

Horn felt his hands tremble. "For God's sake, Axhausen, what is it?"

"Herr Hauptmann," a voice called from the top of the wooden staircase. Horn swung around to see two men standing on the darkened landing at the top. Even in the shadow he could see the metallic blondness of the younger man's hair. Even in the shadow, the ugly self-confidence of the SS training school at Bad Tölz communicated itself.

"I asked to see the chargé d'affaires." Horn turned to Axhausen with a massive effort to keep the fear out of his voice.

Axhausen dropped his head. "Herr Thomsen was unable to make himself available," he said. "He has asked Major Niewig to deal with the matter."

He turned and, watched by Horn, walked back into the duty office.

"This way, please, Herr Hauptmann." Niewig's voice floated down from the top of the steep staircase.

It was a self-contained apartment of perhaps five or six rooms leading off a long black-and-white-tiled corridor similar to the one on the floor below. Niewig led the way into a pleasantly furnished sitting room and gestured to Horn to sit down. The second man, short, broad-shouldered and with long awkward arms, followed them into the room and stood impassively just inside the door.

"We shall speak in English," Niewig said. "There's no point in Stratmann hearing all we have to say." He gestured toward the man at the door. "Not, of course, that there's any question about his loyalty. But the man's an ape—and too stupid to know what's important enough to keep quiet about."

"Then why have him in the room at all?" Horn asked.

Niewig ignored the question with confident ease. "Now, let's get down to your account of the last few days, Hauptmann. As you probably guessed, we radioed Berlin for instructions while you were waiting downstairs. Berlin confirmed the broad outline of what you told Axhausen." He paused. "The instructions came from Herr Heydrich himself."

"What *were* the instructions?" Horn felt calm enough now to take out a cigarette.

Niewig again ignored the question, bending forward to light Horn's cigarette. "Herr Hess took with him certain documents on his flight to England. You claim to have brought those documents to America."

"Yes."

"Where are they now, Herr Hauptmann?" He circled Horn's chair. "Not, I assume, on your person."

"No."

"Where, then?"

"I have them safe, Major."

"My instructions, from Herr Heydrich I will remind you, are that the documents are to be handed over straight away."

He walked back to the desk and sat down behind it.

"Major," Horn said carefully, "I am anxious that you, and others, appreciate my position. I was ordered to make the flight to Scotland by no less an authority than the Stellvertreter himself. In the last four days I have been pitched into the middle of the worst confusion of loyalties any man could come across."

"There is no confusion. Certainly not now. Your duty is to hand over the documents to me."

"I am a Wehrmacht officer, Major Niewig. I have requested an interview with the chargé d'affaires, and this for some reason has been denied. I'm anxious to make a full statement to the senior German official in America. With respect, I cannot understand why I am here discussing these matters with you."

Niewig stood up abruptly. "Where are the documents, Horn?"

He knew from the minute movement of Stratmann's body that the interview was about to take a different turn. Drawing on his cigarette, he stood to face Niewig across the desk. "I'm asking you, Major, to allow me the undoubted privilege of a German officer to put his case in writing to the Adjutant General at OKW in Berlin—and to have my case in the form of a sworn statement, forwarded through the diplomatic bag by the chargé d'affaires."

He barely saw Stratmann move. Certainly he saw no signal from Niewig. But the blow that struck him in the kidneys hurled him forward across the desk. As the numbness receded like a fast, shallow wave, he heard his own scream of pain. At the second blow delivered to the same spot by the knuckles of the vast clenched fist some uncontrollable reflex straightened his body so that he rolled across the desk, his legs clear of the ground, and crashed onto the floor.

He was lying on his back, staring up into the impassive features of Stratmann when Niewig kicked him between his legs. He was probably unconscious for no longer than seconds, and even in that time he was half aware of being manhandled upright and his coat ripped from him. By the time he was fully conscious, half supported by Stratmann against the desk, Niewig was bawling in his face, waving the hotel key before him. "Which hotel, you treacherous scum—which hotel?"

The successful torturer is the one who succeeds first in alienating *himself* from humankind. Only then is the victim paralyzed by lack of hope. The momentum once established, the torturer dare not let up—cooperation from the victim must never abate the mindless fury of the assault.

Niewig and Stratmann had learned their job at Kolumbiahaus in Berlin. . . . Stratmann now hurtled Horn across the room, then pulled open the door. Paralyzed by fear and pain, overwhelmed by the speed of the assault, Horn was impotent to resist as Niewig kicked his legs from under him and both men lifted and swung him into the air.

He saw the white ceiling and the white enamel lampshade; then his head crashed against the side of the bath, and the freezing water engulfed him in the pain of shock.

Held by the hair, no longer knowing or caring by whom, Horn felt his head pushed beneath the icy water, held while his arms and legs flailed wildly, and jerked clear, spluttering, choking streaming water from mouth and nose.

Pulled clear for the fourth or fifth time, vomiting water, he heard the shouted questions above his head.

"Chelverton . . . Chelverton. . . ." He was conscious that he was begging them to understand.

They dragged him from the bath and let him lie, gasping and curled in pain, on the bathroom floor. The Gestapo secretary, in neat white shirt and black skirt whom Major Niewig called from his office to check the hotel address, smiled down at the figure in the puddle of water on the bathroom floor. She, too, had trained at Kolumbiahaus.

At a third-floor window diagonally across from the German Embassy, Agent Stranahan lowered his binoculars and inhaled deeply on a Chesterfield. The room was empty, the curtains and carpet removed, decorators' stepladders and buckets lay stacked along one wall and the air carried the faintly nauseating smell of fresh paint. The window had been whitewashed over, and Stranahan had cleared a small circle at eye level. Now he idly enlarged the circle with a fingernail. It was going to be a long and monotonous vigil. He glanced back into the room where, behind a thick painter's dust sheet, Agent Bill Fry, his colleague on the stakeout, was directing a shielded flashlight beam toward two coffee cups.

"You want it black?" Fry asked. "You'd *better* want it black," he added as an afterthought.

"You forgot the goddamn cream?"

"Right."

Stranahan hated stakeouts—especially the open-ended sort they were engaged in right now. He directed the beam of his pencil flashlight at the photograph pinned to the wooden window frame and the big-print descriptions underneath. "Dark hair, light eyes. Six feet tall, 156 pounds, Age: thirty-one; athletic build." No name, no nationality. That little runt of a briefing inspector, what was his name? Dolyacki . . . he certainly wasn't trusting his guys with too much dope.

He took the paper cups from Bill Fry. Letting the binoculars dangle around his neck, he continued to peer down into the Embassy courtyard below as he sipped the hot coffee. In the two hours since they had set up the stakeout they had seen no movement at all in the main courtyard. In the walled yard at the side of the building they had logged nothing more than the kitchen garbage being put out at 2320 hours.

"This coffee wouldn't be half bad if it didn't taste like paint," he said.

"Jesus Christ," Fry said amiably, then looked at Stranahan, who put down his coffee, spilling it over the paint cans.

A side door had opened in the red-bricked building

opposite. Stranahan ground the butt of his cigarette underfoot and quickly lifted the binoculars. Down below, three men were coming out into the walled yard.

In the light from the open door Stranahan immediately rejected two of the men, one tall and blond, one far too short and heavily built. Between them the third man seemed to rock unsteadily on his feet. Stranahan adjusted the focus. The man's hair was plastered across his forehead. They stood in the doorway, waiting.

Stranahan's teeth were clamped together in the effort of identification. Height and build were right. Age seemed about right, too. But the matted black hair defied even the powerful magnification of the Zeiss glasses. The light from the open doorway behind him shadowed and evened his features.

"What've you got?" Fry said at Stranahan's shoulders.

"Christ knows." Stranahan was willing the man to turn into the light. Then suddenly the headlights of a car swept from somewhere behind the Embassy building into the walled yard, and the beams held the three men in perfect motionless clarity. In that moment Stranahan was certain.

He bent down to the field telephone on the floor at his feet and urgently cranked the handle on the side.

Sitting on a wooden crate in a corridor on the ground floor of the building, Agent Lomax answered the call.

"Our guy. Looks like they're bringing him out . . . side entrance," Stranahan said quickly.

"Got it!" Lomax slammed down the receiver and ran to the door and out into the street.

In the small courtyard Horn coughed and shivered as Stratmann pushed him into the back of the Cadillac. Niewig walked around past the low, hanging cloud of the exhaust to get in the other side. He held a gun lightly in the pocket of his black leather overcoat, but he had no doubt that they had broken the spirit of the shivering, coughing wreck of a man in the back of the car. It never did take long.

Lomax pressed himself back into the shadows as the Cadillac drove slowly out into the street. It turned left to the junction with Massachusetts Avenue, then left again. As soon as it was out of sight, Lomax sprinted to the corner and signaled to Agents Faccini and Chappel, who were maintaining watch on the front of the Embassy from a '39 Ford pickup discreetly parked across the street. The truck started up and swung around in a fast turn. Lomax wrenched open the passenger door and jumped in.

"The Cadillac?" asked Faccini.

"Right," replied Lomax, "and don't lose it or Dolyacki will have our guts."

The twelve-cylinder Cadillac now purred north, the Ford following at a safe distance. Wedged in the rear seat between Niewig and the squat figure of Stratmann, Horn tried to control the spasms of shivering. His shirt and trousers hung cold and wet on his bruised body, but at least they had given him back his coat, and inside that he was just beginning to generate a little damp warmth. For the first time he was able to register the enormity of his blunder. Of course it wasn't the gentle Axhausens or Herr Thomsens who called the tune in the Embassy. When Heydrich spoke from Berlin, they were brushed aside and the real power in the Embassy, the blond SD Major, took over.

He knew he had been a naïve fool. The rights and privileges of a Wehrmacht officer! He felt a hysterical laugh rising in his chest as he thought of Hauptmann Alfred Horn, holder of the Knight's Cross, ready to sell his mother's memory for another split second of gasped air before his head was again thrust beneath the water. Why then hadn't he told them about mailing the papers to Kay? Because the manic sadists hadn't asked. Ask and thou shalt hear all! He felt the hysteria rise again, and he converted the laughter into a spluttering cough.

He knew he had to get control of himself.

The blinds had been pulled down over the back windows of the unmarked limousine, chosen in preference to one of the official distinctive Mercedes with their CD plates and metallic swastika pennants, and as he stared out forward, past the broad back of the chauffeur at the almost deserted streets of Washington, one fact was starkly clear. If Niewig ever got his hands on the Hess documents, he would be killed. A bullet through the back of his neck without a moment's hesitation. In that moment he decided he must never tell them because it was his one chance of staying alive. And there was another reason. Like old Frank bleeding to death on the lonely Scottish beach, Horn decided he would never give these monsters the satisfaction of success. Suddenly he was feeling almost human again.

He now tried to wrench his thoughts in a more positive direction—escape. A trickle of cold water ran down the side of his face from his matted hair. Wiping it away with the back of his hand, he felt Stratmann tense at the movement.

"How much farther?" Niewig asked the chauffeur in German.

"Two or three kilometers, Herr Major," the man said without turning.

In the tailing Ford pickup Dolyacki's voice crackled over the two-way radio. "While they're moving away from the Embassy, we're okay. Just stay with them."

"Yes, sir," answered Faccini.

"We've got men at the airport and covering. . . ." Dolyacki's voice rasped on, but the words were lost in a crackle of static and finally faded completely.

"What did he say?" asked Lomax, leaning forward.

"I don't know." Faccini banged the side of the radio

with the flat of his hand in disgust. "The goddamn thing's never been right since the day they fitted it."

Chappel, behind the wheel, gestured ahead and began to brake the car. "They're stopping."

As the Cadillac pulled up outside the hotel, the bald desk clerk gave it a curious glance through the glass doors, then turned his attention back to the man poised over the dog-eared pages of the register.

"Sign right there," he said in a bored voice, and continued to work on his teeth with a well-worn toothpick as the man nervously signed his name. He had seen the charade taking place in the dingy foyer a thousand times before. The man was in his early forties, modestly well dressed in a conservative way, pinstriped suit, dark tie, wristwatch glinting out from under an immaculately laundered but just slightly frayed cuff. His face had a thin sheen of sweat from drink and embarrassed tension. Behind him the hooker casually leaned against the wall, contemplating a dark stain on the wall above the rows of keys behind the desk.

The clerk spun the register to read off the name. As he did so, the entrance door opened and Niewig came in, followed by Horn, with Stratmann immediately behind. They moved straight toward the stairs. As he passed the desk, Horn looked hard at the clerk, trying his best somehow to convey a plea for help, aware that Stratmann's Luger would be leveled at his back beneath the heavy folds of the SD man's overcoat. The clerk's eyes, which from the long years of experience could see everything or nothing according to will, gave no hint of any understanding. He had already been convinced by one quick glance at the ice-eyed leading figure that in this case he would certainly see nothing.

"Okay, Mr. Baker, Room Thirty-seven, third floor. That'll be four dollars."

The girl lifted her eyes to the ceiling.

"Four dollars?" Baker stammered. "You advertised the room at one dollar."

"Four dollars."

Baker took out his wallet and counted off four dollars. Five more for the girl. And it was all company money.

"And a quarter on the key," the clerk intoned.

Baker reached into his pocket for the quarter and placed it on the desk. Taking the key, he turned to the girl. She flashed her professional smile, took the john's arm and led him to the stairway.

Lomax came out of the alley, running down the side of the hotel, and hurried across the street to Faccini, who stood in a doorway watching the front entrance. "Just a fire escape; no rear exit."

"Good," said Faccini, lighting a cigarette.

"Where's Joe?"

"He went to call Dolyacki. Still couldn't raise him on the goddamn radio."

Lomax glanced toward the drugstore on the corner of the block where Chappel was already phoning in.

"What do we do?" said Lomax, nervously blowing into his cupped hands as if they were cold.

Faccini considered. "Better wait for some backup. German nationals. Might get rough."

"Okay, where's the Caddy?"

"Down the street. Driver's still inside." Faccini indicated to his right, and Lomax could just make out the Cadillac parked with its lights out fifty or sixty yards away. "I'll take the back," he said. "You stay here."

Faccini nodded agreement, and Lomax moved away into the alley to cover the rear of the hotel.

As Stratmann pushed him into Room 32 with a hand between the shoulder blades, Horn could feel his pulse beginning to pound in his temples. The Major carefully closed the door, locked it from the inside, then put the key in his pocket and switched on the light. Stratmann checked that the window was securely fastened, then drew the shabby curtains.

Niewig glanced down at the duffel bag on the floor and then up at Horn, who shrugged. He knew that if he were to escape, it would have to be before they found out that he had mailed the papers to Kay's apartment.

Niewig swung the bag up onto the bed and pulled back the long zipper. All three men watched as the canvas sides gaped open. Niewig lifted his head slowly toward Horn. His face showed surprise, despite himself. He had miscalculated. The spirit was not broken. He turned to Stratmann and made a quick gesture. Then, as the SD man began to search the sparsely furnished room, Niewig, this time to Horn's surprise, drew a pack of cigarettes from his pocket and silently offered one to Horn.

He took one and accepted a light. The two men, of almost exactly equal height, stood smoking wordlessly while behind and around them Stratmann continued his methodical search. His powerful hands ripped open a pillow and groped through the cheap fabric of the stuffing.

"Rubbish! You should always sleep on feathers. Eider is best." They were the first words he had spoken. Neither man reacted. Making surprisingly little noise, Stratmann proceeded to tear the room apart, the mattress on the iron bed, the padded seat of the single chair.

"All right," said Horn suddenly. "I think we should talk."

"Talk?" Niewig's voice was guarded. Stratmann had stopped to listen, but the Major gestured for him to continue the search.

"Bargain," said Horn, pursuing the one idea he had left. Now he felt he could only play for time. He would try to lead them to another fictitious hiding place, a locker at the YMCA perhaps.

"You have nothing with which to bargain, Hauptmann."

In the leading Washington Police Department patrol car Dolyacki yelled at the uniformed driver to make a right turn. Stationed by the pay phone in the drugstore, Chappel had heard the wail of the approaching sirens and rushed out onto the sidewalk. Now, as the convoy of four police cars wheeled past him, their tires squealing when they took the corner, he sprinted back toward the hotel.

Niewig and Stratmann had heard the sirens, too, and the skidding of the police vehicles outside the hotel. As he watched the SD Major, Horn saw for the first time a trace of concern on his face. Stratmann had snapped off the light and opened the window a few inches, and the slamming of car doors and shouted instructions were clearly audible. Stratmann pressed his bulk back against the wall at the sound of running feet. Looking down, he could see men hurrying along the alley below.

Down in the foyer Dolyacki thrust a photo of Horn under the clerk's nose and snapped out the question. "This man, with two others. Where?" The clerk would normally have stalled with any representative of law enforcement, but he saw the purpose in Dolyacki's eye, and from the number of men who had burst out of the cars he realized this was no simple vice raid.

"Room thirty-two. Third floor," he said quickly.

"Pass key." Dolyacki held out his hand.

The clerk handed over the key, and Dolyacki ran immediately to the stairs, with Faccini and Lomax following.

On the third floor, Niewig stood uncertainly beside the hotel room door. He had no reason to believe the police activity below was directed toward them. Outside in the corridor he heard a door slam, running footsteps somewhere down below, shouted orders.

He unlocked and opened the door an inch or two. Now he could hear footsteps pounding up the bare stairs. Still standing near the window, Stratmann covered Horn with his pistol but was giving half his attention to the patrolmen in the alley.

Horn saw his chance and seized it. He clenched his

fist and brought it down with all his strength on the nape of Niewig's neck. The blond head jolted with the impact and crashed forward against the doorjamb. Horn grabbed him by the shoulders and hurled him back at Stratmann, pulled the door open and flung himself out. Slipping on the uncarpeted floor, he regained his balance and found himself running for a window at the end of the corridor leading out onto the fire escape. Behind him he heard the scramble of feet. He could too easily imagine the pistol coming up to aim at his retreating back. Before he could possibly get to the window, pull it open and climb through, he would be gunned down. Then he saw miraculously that the window was already open. Hurling himself the last few feet, he dived headfirst onto the cast-iron fire escape outside.

Dolyacki reached the top of the stairs to the third floor, Faccini and Lomax right behind. Niewig stood by the open door to Room 32, still holding the pistol. Stratmann had burst past him and was running toward the window.

"Stop!" yelled Dolyacki, clamping his left hand over his right wrist to steady his aim. Stratmann ignored the warning. Dolyacki fired. The German was hit somewhere high on the left thigh and skidded down to the floor to crash against the wall below the window. Niewig let the pistol in his hand clatter to the floor, his face impassive.

"I am an official of the Embassy of the German Reich. I claim full diplomatic rights."

Dolyacki ignored him, pushing past into the room.

"What the hell's going on here?" The hooker stood in the doorway to Room 37, hands defiantly on hips.

Lomax took a step toward her. "Just stay in the room." He pushed her hard and slammed the door.

In the doorway of Room 32, Dolyacki smacked the palm of his hand on the peeling paintwork in frustration at finding it empty.

"Inspector!" The shout came from the alleyway below.

Dolyacki crossed the room to the window, opened it fully and leaned out. "What is it?"

The voice called up from the darkness. "We've got him, sir. He came down the fire escape."

"Bring him around to the front. I'll be right there."

The crowd surged into the small lobby of the Chelverton, uniformed policemen, FBI agents, their prisoner almost lost in the middle of the throng. Dolyacki, descending the stairs two at a time, stopped dead. "Who the hell's *that?*" His voice rose close to screaming pitch.

Agents and uniformed men went silent and fell back from the patrolman handcuffed to the prisoner. Collarless, the lapels of his pinstriped jacket ripped, Baker tugged at the handcuff. "There's been some mistake," he said, terrified by the speed and violence of the events of the last few minutes.

"Get back outside," Dolyacki yelled at them. "Goddamn flatfoots." He turned to Lomax. "We've lost him!"

From his position at the top of the fire escape Horn had seen the man below arrested, had heard one of the patrolmen calling up to the inspector and had watched the man handcuffed and hustled around to the front of the hotel.

Moving down the fire escape now, he flinched as his weight carried the last section with a squeal of rusted rollers down to street level. Jumping clear, he let the counterweight take the iron fretwork back into place and ran to the back of the hotel, where a brick wall divided the railroad property from the line of stores and cheap hotels that backed onto it.

He knew there was no time for caution. Covering the width of the backyard in eight steps, he threw himself upward and reached for the far edge of the brick wall. Scrabbling to get a toehold in the crumbling mortar, he hauled himself up. The first patrolmen, racing to cordon off the hotel, saw him silhouetted for a second against the hanging arc lamps of the freight yard across the tracks.

Horn hit the cinder-strewn grass below the wall and ran. Two hundred yards ahead, across a network of crisscrossed rail tracks, some low warehouses and repair sheds offered hope of cover. And before that a line of tanker cars . . . an isolated steam locomotive . . . a broken-windowed passenger car. . . .

He reached the broad swath of shining iron tracks and ran on, shortening and lengthening his stride to avoid timber ties and raised rails. After no more than a few yards he found the punishing irregularity of the movement too much for his wearied coordination, but the shouts of the men behind him drove him on until his leg muscles contracted, his ankle turned, and as he pitched forward, his cheekbone hit the cold iron of the rail.

He rolled forward, sobbing and gasping with the pain down the side of his cheek. He found he was facing back the way he had come. Against the lighted hotel windows, with people hanging over the sills, he could see the outlined figures of the police dropping from the wall and other, darker figures with flashlights, already running across the scrub of rusting junk and heaped cinder toward the beginning of the belt of tracks.

He lay on the carpet of cinder dust, his shoulder resting on the split, weathered end of a tie, his chin touching the sharp edge of one of the massive steel bolts. More restful than sleep, defeat swept over him.

"Hey. . . ."

Horn half raised himself to the voice behind him.

"Over here, boy. . . ."

The line of tank cars stood black against the distant hanging lights.

"You can make it, boy. . . ."

He thought he saw a movement in the shadow of the end car. The blanket weight of hopelessness lifted. Like a drunk, he staggered to his feet and stumbled, tripping and reeling across the tracks.

At the rounded butt end of the last tank car a small old man grabbed his arm and dragged him on.

He saw now that the line of tank cars obscured a jumble of wooden huts and siding buffers where twenty or thirty wrecked tank cars stood.

"Thought I'd just take a look at what was going on out here." The old man pushed him toward a tank car with a stoved-in end. "Lucky for you I did."

He jumped nimbly onto the chassis and started to climb the iron ladder past the peeling Standard Oil of New Jersey sign on the rounded flank. Horn followed him up and stood on the top rungs as the old man swung the inspection plate to reveal a two-foot hole. With a practiced wriggle he squatted above the opening—and was gone.

Following him down, Horn saw, before his head dropped below the level of the inspection plate, the jerking beams of the flashlights between the wheels of the line of stationary tank cars.

He dropped into a dark, long, narrow tube and stood while the old man climbed onto a crate and swung the inspection plate back. From his pocket he took two metal bolts and screwed them home. They were in complete darkness, and the sweet stench of poverty thickened the air.

"You just stay where you stand, boy, and we'll have a little light in no time," the old man said quietly.

A match flared. A kerosene wick guttered, and a hand brought a glass down on a filigreed brass gallery. The light spread slowly, illuminating two . . . then three . . . then five . . . whiskered, grizzled faces.

"Sit down, Billy," the old man said. "Billy's what all the fuss was about outside," he whispered to the double row of faces. They nodded understanding.

Horn knelt among the jumble of rags in the curved base of the car and stretched his legs, leaning his back against the steel wall. Now that he was growing accustomed to the light, he saw that the old man was a short, spare figure, his face sharp and weather-beaten, the eyes soft and bright in the lamplight.

"Henry," he said, pointing to himself. The men nodded in loyal confirmation. "This here is Billy," He pointed to Horn.

One of the men leaned over on his elbow, his free hand bringing a large gallon jar from the shadow. He smiled, all lips and toothless gums, handing Horn the heavy glass bottle.

From some sense of form or right behavior, learned in timbered halls where wineglasses sparkled and silver glowed, Horn took the glass jug and drank.

The harsh spirit puckered his lips and seared his throat.

"In California," said one of the men, leaning forward, "I know some place they sell Mary Dear at a nickel a bottle."

Henry winked and took the jug from Horn. "Buzz here don't like nothin' stronger than wine. He says his daddy used to be butler to some big man. He says that way he grew up to be a conn'sir."

"Maybe he did at that," Horn said, keeping his voice low.

A bearded shape leaned from the distant shadows. "I heard some place those folks pay upwards a dollar a bottle . . . French," he added authoritatively.

"Women comes cheaper," someone cackled from the shadows, "French."

"That's young Lefty," the old man said. "He went over in the war. Lost a hand. And was goddamn lucky he didn't lose a whole lot more."

The shadowed figures rolled and doubled with laughter.

"French women," Lefty said from the half-darkness,

"is not like all the others. They don't pretend they don't like it."

"They *just* like the others," a black face said. "They like the biggest they can get"—and with an artist's timing—"the biggest dollar!"

The jug passed on around. "You live here, all of you?" Horn asked the old man. And was even then conscious of transgression by asking a direct question.

The old man smiled. "Who lives any place?" he said, " 'cept you want grief and pain?"

"You keep moving, Henry?"

"What else? We not rich folks. We keep on moving. Last week," he said, taking the jug from Horn, "I was in Florida. Cops pick me up and tell me time I settle down. Stop riding the rails and find a good woman." He laughed. "I spent thirty years *losing* a good woman, I tell them. Week before that I was up in Maine. Cold—"

"More trouble with the cops?"

"Always trouble, Billy boy."

They sat silent for a long time, passing the jug without a word. In his hip pocket Horn felt the damp thickness of the wad of notes. He unbuttoned the flap and fingered off thirty or forty dollars. He had no real idea if he was doing the right thing. But he felt the need to leave something.

"I guess things should be clear outside by now," he said to the old man.

Henry shrugged. "See you in California or someplace, Billy."

Horn reached for the jug. In the half-light he raised it to his lips. When he set it down among the rags he had stuffed the roll of bills into the glass neck. If any of the men saw him, nobody spoke. "What happens," he asked, "if anybody catches you here some night?"

Henry smiled. "What *can* happen?" he said. "The jails are full and the work lines ten miles long. We don't have to worry, Billy boy. It's a free country."

* * *

In the shabby, green-painted interview room at Washington Police Department's Station 15, Niewig sat opposite Dolyacki. In the corner of the room Bishop sipped coffee, silently watching.

"Mr. Niewig," Dolyacki said, "if that's your name. You were in that hotel with an illegal immigrant. And that's all that concerns me at the moment."

"I am an official of the German Reich. An accredited attaché at the Embassy," Niewig intoned. "I demand my diplomatic rights."

"Niewig, for all we know you're an illegal immigrant as well. Until we've checked the position with records I have every right to question you. What were you doing in that hotel?"

"I refuse to answer any questions. I protest at my treatment. I particularly protest at being questioned in the presence of an enemy national. . . ." He shot a malevolent glance at Bishop. "Yes, I know he's English. I know that's why he hasn't opened his mouth since he arrived."

Dolyacki ignored the accusation. "I just saw your friend Stratmann at the hospital," he said. "He claims you were at the hotel to look for some official papers."

"Why should he say that? Since it is not true."

Dolyacki glanced at Bishop, who shrugged.

"Okay, Niewig." He stood up. "If confirmation comes through, I'll have a car drive you back to the German Embassy." He smiled without warmth. "And of course, if you are who you say you are, my apologies for any misunderstanding."

The apartment occupied the second floor of an old brick house across the river in Arlington. The wooden steps from street level led up to an unlocked screen frame beyond which a heavy timber door led into a dark, cool hallway.

It was early morning as Horn let himself into the hall, and the gray-haired colored woman had just finished mopping the tiled floor. He saw no mailboxes.

Stepping past her hot-water pail, Horn glanced at the list of residents to see that Captain Ralph P. Hampton and Mrs. Kay Hampton occupied Apartment D, and continued on up the stairs to the floor above.

The cleaner below was collecting her enamel pails as Horn drew from under his coat the short-handled coal pick he had taken from a tender in the freight yards during the night. As the pails clattered together on the floor below, he jabbed the flat end of the pick between the door and jamb and pried hard.

With a muted rasping sound the screws holding the lock casing were drawn out of the woodwork. Horn pushed the door, sweeping aside the four fat envelopes lying in the hallway, and entered.

He felt safe and exhilarated. He had never imagined it would be that easy to break in. Walking quickly through the living room, furnished with early American furniture, a Persian rug on the wall and the intimate bric-a-brac of Kay's life, Horn stood at the window and watched the old colored woman waddle down the street with her mop and pails, heading for the next apartment building.

Clearly she had not heard the lock give.

Horn searched through the kitchen drawer, selected a knife and returned to the front door. A few twists of the knife roughly secured the screws holding the lock. Bending, he picked up the envelopes and took them back into the living room. There he dropped them on the bureau among photographs of Ralph Hampton at Annapolis, on the bridge of his first command, skiing in California. There were no photographs of Kay.

Horn walked into the bathroom and peeled off his filthy clothing. The heat of the shower brought on throbbing pains down the side of his face and in the vague region of the kidneys where Stratmann had hit him. He realized he was totally exhausted.

He stepped out of the shower and dried himself on a heavy dark blue towel. He was too tired even to eat. Trailing the towel behind him, he found the bedroom and seconds later was drifting into sleep in the huge double bed.

He had no sense of time, no sense of the changed angle of the sun. But somewhere, something was troubling him. Through the heavy drifts of sleep he struggled to register alarm. The movement, the voices in the room next door were distant and unfrightening, out there on the edge of consciousness. Then the bedroom door opened, and he was awake. He opened his eyes to see Kay Hampton standing in the doorway. Behind her, piled in the middle of the floor, were suitcases and army duffel bags.

For several seconds she said nothing, simply watched the astonishment on his face. Then she closed the door behind her and came forward into the room. "I thought you'd been arrested," she said, sitting on the side of the bed.

He lifted himself on to one elbow. "I nearly was."

She was looking at the bruise on his cheekbone. "Looks sore," she said. "Is that part of the story?"

Without answering he sat up and reached forward, taking her around the waist with both hands. With a slight pressure in the small of her back he brought her body close to his. For a moment she kept her head down so that his mouth brushed the top of her hair. Then she slowly lifted her head back and kissed him, openmouthed.

His tongue was feeling the even line of her teeth when by some slight pressure on his arms she indicated she wanted to be released.

"I've been put on indefinite leave while my case is being considered here in Washington," she said as if nothing had just passed between them. "What happened to you?"

"General Walker's under arrest, Kay. I saw it happening."

"The FBI are looking for you?"

"Police, FBI, I don't know the difference—but

they're on to me." He got up, wrapping the towel around him.

"That's why you mailed the papers here?"

"You've seen them?"

She nodded. "Just before I discovered a pile of the filthiest clothes I've ever seen on a bathroom floor. I gave them to the cabdriver to take to the Chinese cleaners down the street. They'll be ready in an hour."

He followed her into the living room. Involuntarily he put his hands to his back as the pain swept over him. She had turned to watch him.

"I'll make some coffee," she said. "And I think there's still a little brandy in the cupboard." She looked across the room at the four envelopes, one of them torn open and the linen paper folds exposed. "And then. . . ." She was staring at the envelopes with something approaching revulsion. "And then we'll decide what in the name of God we can do with *these*."

As Dolyacki and Bishop left J. Edgar Hoover's office, the FBI man's fury exploded. "You heard him. You heard the Director."

"I heard him," Bishop said. "He wants results. He's not too pleased with what we've given him so far."

"We've given him *nothing* so far. Listen to me, Major," Dolyacki said fiercely. "I'm working with my hands tied behind my back. What *are* these goddamn papers?"

Some sympathy surfaced above Bishop's dislike of the man. "If your government had believed it necessary to tell you more, they would have. You know I can't do anything about that. All we can do is concentrate on finding Alfred Horn."

"Jesus Christ!" Dolyacki exploded.

"General Walker left a contact behind in Scotland," Bishop said. "An American woman, a member of his staff, Lieutenant Kay Hampton."

Dolyacki watched the other man's face intently. "Where is she now?"

"She was sent back to Washington. She could be arriving any time now."

He buttoned the crisp, clean shirt and continued talking through the half-open bedroom door. " 'It's a free country'—those were the old man's last words before I left. 'It's a free country, Billy boy.' And in some crazy way for an old hobo like him it still is. Free to starve, free to drink rotgut liquor"—Horn walked into the living room—"but free to help each other and to help someone like me, free to travel, free to live without conforming . . . ?"

She watched him struggling to say something. "If you're trying to say you're sorry you went to the German Embassy, don't," she said gently.

He shrugged. "Yes, I guess that's what I was trying to say."

She stood up. "So . . . what now?"

Rested, wearing clean clothes, with three or four glasses of brandy inside him, he felt a sudden surge of determination. "We go on alone, Kay. At least, I do."

She looked at him evenly, rejecting the exclusion. "How? How do we?"

"We have Hess's notebook."

"The conference record?"

"It's all in there somewhere. The final destination of the briefcase was someone Hess called the Ambassador, remember?"

"But that could be anyone. We don't even know if it signifies a *real* ambassador. We don't know a thing."

"Somebody does. Somebody on Walker's staff, his secretary, his wife. . . ."

She stood, biting her lip.

"What is it, Kay?"

"Mrs. Walker, the General's wife."

"You know her?"

"I met her when I was first posted to the General's staff. I could talk to her."

Horn was silent. "It's a hell of a risk, Kay," he said after a moment. "They've arrested the General; they're sure to arrest her next."

In the release of tension she burst out laughing. "Alfred, you've lived too long with the Gestapo for neighbors. There's not one chance in ten billion that Mrs. Walker could be arrested. Questioned maybe, but not arrested just for *being* Mrs. Walker."

"But if the FBI are questioning Mrs. Walker when we arrive. . . ."

"When *I* arrive," Kay said. "I think you're safe here for the moment. They can't imagine we arranged to meet. After all, I never knew I was to be sent back on the next plane."

Fourteen

Washington's Blair Hotel was built at the end of the last century. In its heavy, decorated stonework, its ornamental brick patterning and its multicolored tiles, it reflected a passionate disregard for style on the part of its architect. Here in the lobby, the Muslim East met with Greek columns and Gothic arches; canework sofas and easy chairs were grouped among forests of pot plants and aspidistras.

Mrs. Irene Walker had stayed here while house-hunting when her husband had first been promoted to Washington. And when Kay Hampton had suggested they meet somewhere other than the house, the Blair Hotel came naturally to mind.

She remembered how much she had liked Kay Hampton when she had first met her. The tall California Lieutenant had introduced herself at the first party the Walkers had given in Washington and had immediately helped take the weight of being hostess from Mrs. Walker's inexperienced shoulders.

The news of her husband's arrest had shattered her. She could imagine no possible reason. She sat now, opposite Kay, among the surrounding vegetation, her eyes red-rimmed, her hand shaking as she lifted her third martini. She was small, dark-haired, in her early fifties. Until she came to Washington, she had never spent longer than a month outside her native Georgia.

"I know nothing, nothing about it, Kay. That I promise you. Since he came back from England on Sunday he hasn't been himself. But the idea that he's been corrupt or . . . something else is just ridiculous. Anyone that knows Tom knows that he's the last man in the world to accept a favor for an army contract."

"Mrs. Walker," Kay said gently, "this is political. Your husband made a decision to become involved in a project which at least he believed was right. In the end, he could still come out lionized or"—she smiled grimly—"thrown to the lions. Either way I can't see that he's done anything to make you feel ashamed of him."

"Is there no more you can tell me?"

"I don't think so, Mrs. Walker. But I need your help. I need to know of anyone, probably in politics, that your husband has been seeing in the last month or so. In particular some foreigner, an ambassador maybe."

Mrs. Walker shook her head. "No, no one I can think of. We don't really move in political circles, Kay. Our friends tend to be army people, a few Georgians we used to know back home. I guess John Caspiani is about the only political friend my husband has."

"Senator Caspiani?"

"Yes. The General plays golf with him now and again."

"How did they meet?"

"Early this year, I suppose it was. I don't really know *how* they met. The Senator asked my husband to a couple of parties, but he didn't go. Tom said they weren't his type of party."

"And the golf?"

"I think that started about the same time. The Senator belongs to the best clubs. Tom went four or five times, I guess."

Kay nodded slowly. "Senator Caspiani, he's a Democrat, isn't he?"

"Yes, he's on all sorts of these new Roosevelt

boards—the TNEC, OPM, SPAB—I don't know what they're all about."

"He's an up-and-coming man in Washington, then?"

"Oh, yes, no doubt about it. I even think Tom was quite flattered at first to be seen with him. Somehow they don't expect Generals and isolationists to hit it off together."

"Isolationists?"

"The Senator is one hundred percent against intervention. So is Tom, as a matter of fact. Not all generals are bloodthirsty villains, you know."

"No. I know the General." Kay finished her drink. "Will you excuse me, Mrs. Walker? You've been a great help to me. To your husband as well, I believe."

Kay made her way through the potted plants with a sense of real triumph. An isolationist Senator, highly ambitious, seeks out an aging General to help forward an incredible project. Caspiani had to be the "Ambassador"—the ambassador between Rudolf Hess and the U.S. government.

Through the windshield Dolyacki watched the taxi come to a stop thirty yards down the deserted street. Grunting to himself as he recognized the figure of a woman getting out, he turned toward Bishop in the seat next to him. "That her?"

Bishop nodded. "If she takes that service alley, she'll come out directly opposite her apartment."

Dolyacki was already reaching for the car door handle. "Leave this to me," he said. He was smiling.

As the taxi pulled away, Kay stepped into the partly covered service alley, threading her way through the overflowing garbage and stacked cartons at the back of the small stores which lined Tremont Street.

The bare electric bulb at the right-angled bend provided almost all the light in the alley. She could just read, painted on the brick wall surface, the ancient advertisement for a brand of pipe tobacco unavailable for many years now—Mason's Gentleman's Cut. As she walked forward, she seemed to see a movement among the piled cartons at the right angle which would take her down onto Tremont Street. Her high heels clicked emptily among the dark, silent buildings. She slowed, then stopped. Someone was definitely there.

Out of the deep shadow the shape of a man emerged. She took one, two uncertain steps backward, her heels clicking like the start of a Ginger Rogers dance routine; then she turned fast and screamed as the man came at her with a rush.

He knew he could catch her before she gained the street. Reaching her in a quick, ferretlike movement, he grabbed her by the upper arm and spun her around into an open-palmed slap across the face.

She gasped as he pushed her back against a brick wall. Above them a light went on and a window opened.

"What the hell's going on down there?" a man's voice shouted.

Dolyacki thrust his knee hard into Kay's crotch. "Inspector Dolyacki, Federal Bureau of Investigation," he hissed. She was sobbing from pain and humiliation.

"Shut that goddamn window," Dolyacki yelled. "This is the police."

Fear slipped away from her now as she saw some sort of rationality behind the attack.

The man above them muttered something inaudible and slammed the window. As he did so, Dolyacki relaxed the pressure of his knee and Kay twisted away from the wall. Suddenly she was consumed with anger. "First, show me your ID," she said. "Then I'm warning you I'll be down at the FBI building first thing tomorrow morning to issue a citizen's summons against you for assault."

She gasped and doubled forward with pain as his knee was again driven hard up between her legs. "I wasn't born yesterday. And you have no witness." He pulled her upright. "I want to know where Alfred Horn is. And I want to know *now*."

From behind, Horn hit him with all the strength he had. But it was an awkward blow. Contacting somewhere between the shoulder and the base of the neck, it hurled Dolyacki sideways among the garbage cans and cartons. Dazed, he still grabbed at the Police Special in his underarm holster.

Even through the waves of pain in his shoulder, he knew this was the perfect opportunity. Attacked from behind while detaining a suspect, he had every right to defend himself. He flicked the safety forward. Horn stood three yards away, his eyes fixed on the gun. As Dolyacki aimed, the window above flew up again. "Listen," the man's voice said, "cops or no cops. . . ." The voice trailed away.

And with it the opportunity. Dolyacki released the pressure of his finger on the trigger and jerked his head toward the man above. Before he could speak, Horn's shoulder charged into him, hitting him in the chest, slamming Dolyacki's head back against the wall. Somewhere among the garbage the gun clattered to the ground. On all fours, his head splitting with pain, Dolyacki watched Horn run with Kay toward the end of the alley.

At the corner table of the small Italian family restaurant, Kay found she was still shaking as the waiter served them a bottle of Bardolo. Horn poured them a glass each and lit a cigarette. "Luck," he said. "Or maybe just nervousness. I was waiting for you to come back. I'd poured myself a second or third whisky, and I was beginning to get worried. I found every time a car drew up outside I'd go to the window and look down. Suddenly I found myself looking down on four separate cars. Two men got out of the first one. One was the policeman who was there when General Walker was arrested."

"Dolyacki," she said. "He's an FBI agent."

"The other was an Englishman named Max Bishop."

"You know him?"

"Very well. We were in Berlin together in 1936. But for a car accident a year later he might have married my sister."

"He's the Major Bishop who interrogated me at Prestwick."

"And the man I saw at the hospital the night the SS squad killed Hess."

She put her hand to her head. "It's obviously not coincidence that Max Bishop was assigned to hunt you down."

"No." Horn smiled. "The best hunters know their prey." He paused. "I got out of your apartment just as they came up the stairs. When Dolyacki started questioning the janitor, I was two yards away."

"What did the janitor tell him?"

"That you'd gone out. That as you left, you'd called back to someone in the apartment that you'd be back in about an hour."

She was silent. "He's a rough customer, Alfred. He's not playing by any rules. I believe he would have killed you tonight if that window hadn't been opened just at that moment."

"Those could be his orders."

"To kill you?" She shook her head incredulously.

"Think about it, Kay. There's no other way of silencing me. My only crime in America, remember, is being an illegal immigrant. I could even apply for political asylum."

"You mean to prevent that, Dolyacki has been ordered to kill you?"

"Me, almost certainly. You, I just don't know."

After they had eaten the lasagna they had ordered, she told him quickly about Caspiani.

"Do we still go ahead and deliver the documents, after all that's happened?" Her large gray eyes searched his face. "If you decided now just to hand

252

the Japanese material to the Washington *Post* and burn the rest, I think I'd understand."

He shook his head. "You're tired, Kay, and, like me, more than a little bit scared." He signaled to the waiter for the bill. "But I don't see that's any real reason to change our minds."

The long room hung thick with cigarette smoke. Some twenty men, all in shirt sleeves, sat at telephones on bare desks. To Bishop the staccato of American question and answer was overwhelming. With Dolyacki leading the way they walked down the central aisle to the huge map of the Washington area on the facing wall. Passing the lines of tables, Bishop could hear snatches of the FBI men's instructions to their roadblocks.

". . . might now be accompanied by a woman . . ."

". . . Caucasian, five foot eight, one hundred and twenty pounds. . . ."

". . . aged thirty-five, blond, five foot eight. . . ."

". . . one hundred and twenty pounds . . . possibly wearing uniform of Army Nurse Corps. . . ."

". . . photographs being rushed to you now. . . ."

"You've got an efficient-looking setup here, Mr. Dolyacki," Bishop said as they stopped before the map.

"We'll know how efficient if we catch him," Dolyacki said grimly.

"*If* we catch him . . . ?"

"Listen, Major, like I said, I'm running this operation with both arms tied behind my back. In any normal manhunt we'd have our man's face on the front of every paper on the eastern seaboard. Every radio station would be broadcasting an hourly reminder of how violent, how dangerous, how wanted, the guy was. Within hours he wouldn't be able to buy forty cents' worth of gas without the chance of being recognized."

"So you don't hold out much hope for these roadblocks?"

"We're going through the motions. Hoping that Horn plans to leave Washington. Hoping that if he does, some cop will be bright enough to put the picture to the face. It doesn't always happen, Major. Two, three in the morning, your coffee break just arriving and you wave the next two cars through. It's human nature."

Bishop watched the face of the man next to him as Dolyacki stubbed out his cigarette, the thin, hard line of the mouth, the eyebrows pressing permanently down on the eyes, the total absence of anything in expression but a driving intensity. He wondered where it had all come from, the Middle European name, the command of languages, the hatred that seemed to be at the heart of this man. He knew instinctively that in Dolyacki's hands, Alfred Horn's life would be snuffed out without a second's regret.

"I want to talk to you, Major." Dolyacki indicated a door leading off the main room. "We can't go on running around like a bunch of headless chickens." He closed the door behind him, and Bishop saw they were in a small, comfortably furnished office. The voices of the FBI agents on their telephones penetrated the walls as a low hum.

Dolyacki sat at the desk. "The way I see it we have only two leads, General Walker and Rudolf Hess. Okay, we're not supposed to talk about Hess. But Walker's out. He refuses to say anything until his court-martial. There's nothing we can do in America to force him."

He looked up at Bishop. "I'm going to untie one of my hands, Major. Whether you like it or not, I'm going to talk about Hess."

Bishop remained silent.

"Your country's at war. We're not talking about General Walker here in Washington; we're talking about a Nazi prisoner in Britain. *He* must know where

Horn's heading. Are you telling me your people just don't have the guts to make him talk?"

"I'm listening, Mr. Dolyacki."

"Okay. My way would be to get on that goddamn transatlantic phone and tell them that unless they want Horn to slip through our hands, somebody has to take the gloves off with Rudolf Hess. Tonight."

In Lord Halifax's room at the British Embassy in Washington the green scrambler telephone rang. The ambassador lifted the receiver. The unmistakable voice of Winston Churchill grunted irritably across three thousand miles of ocean.

"Prime Minister, I have an officer here, a Major Bishop. He has asked me as a matter of the utmost urgency to arrange to speak to you."

Bishop watched while Lord Halifax nodded, listening, then turned and handed him the telephone.

"Prime Minister." Bishop found he was dry-mouthed. He moistened his lips. "This is Major Max Bishop, Intelligence Corps. I believe you are aware of my mission here in Washington."

"I am," the voice growled.

"I am advised by my American associate that given the restraints of secrecy, we have little or no chance of securing the German officer in question unless we are able to discover his destination here in the United States."

"What do you suggest?"

Bishop hesitated.

"What do you suggest, Major?"

"I suggest, sir, that in the circumstances, the German official now held in Britain must be forced to disclose that destination."

At the other end of the line there was silence. Then the voice said, "Colonel Henderson will communicate the required information to you by two tomorrow afternoon, your time."

The phone clicked dead. Max Bishop stood in the

ornate room with the receiver in his hand. He had trained for war since he entered the Royal Military Academy in 1931. He had never imagined that its reality would involve asking that a man be tortured for the information he carried.

The tall figure of the ambassador leaned over and took the receiver from Bishop's hand. "Time you got some sleep, young man," he said. "Time we both did."

In front of the spotlit bed the two girls swayed together to the slow wail of the lead cornet of the Jotown Dixieland Band. Tall, black, the girls avidly kissed each other, their pink tongues flickering between even white teeth. As the record changed, the girl in the white dress turned her partner so that she could nuzzle the back of her long brown neck, cup her breasts in her hands and explore the undulations of her hips.

In long sofas, deep easy chairs, on cushions spread about the floor, six or seven men, jacketless and mostly without shoes, sprawled, drinks in hand, among the same number of girls.

Caspiani sat alone in an armchair, his black eyes glittering as he watched over the top of a highball glass the rhythmic contortions of the black girls. As their dresses fell to the floor and they led each other toward the spotlit daybed, the bell rang below.

Among the men there was immediate consternation. The two black girls stood motionless; the young white hookers chewed gum, shrugged or raised their eyebrows to each other. A police raid meant a small fine for them; their professional lives were not at stake.

Caspiani was on his feet. "For Chrissakes," he said, "what's the panic? I asked a couple more girls. Just freshen up your drinks and take it easy till I get back." He turned to the big black girl. "Jasmine, take five, huh? But stay warm."

The girl's mouth tightened in contempt for his clumsy effort at Harlem slang.

Ted Markland, with five large whiskies inside him, was not too drunk to be unconcerned about the visitor. He pushed himself up from the floor and, glass in hand, padded in his socks across to the door.

Outside the elegant Georgetown house, Kay heard a bolt being withdrawn and a heavy chain rattle back. When the door opened, a tall, dark-haired man was looking at her with a welcoming grin.

"Come right in," he said.

She could smell the alcohol on his breath.

"Not entirely by chance," he said, "it's the maid's night off."

She frowned. "Were you expecting me?"

"Sure." He looked at the tall, good-looking woman as she stepped past him into the hall. She was older than he'd asked for, but obviously a quality piece. The madam he dealt with usually sent him really young ones, nineteen-year-olds sometimes, because that was what most of his friends were looking for. For himself he wasn't against a touch of class, and the brash young hookers that flooded into Washington these days seldom had that.

He gestured Kay to start up the stairs. "I'm Kay Hampton," she said over her shoulder.

"Right, Kay," he said.

"Did Mrs. Walker call to say I was coming?"

He screwed up his face. Mrs. Walker? That wasn't the dragon he dealt with. Mrs. Dupont with the phony French accent must subcontract the work. What the hell, he thought, when you get sent this caliber of woman.

"She didn't give your name," he said in answer to her question.

Kay stopped on the half landing of the tall Colonial house. She had heard the music and voices above. "Is there somewhere quiet we can go?"

"Later," he said. "Right now we've got drinks upstairs, music and a nice little thing going. Sort of gets the mood right. . . ."

Before she could respond, she saw a figure blocking her way at the top of the staircase. Ted Markland, too, recognized in the visitor something well above the gum-chewing hustlers in the room behind him. He reached forward, taking her arm. "You call me Ted," he said. "And the first thing I'm going to do for you is to mix you the finest martini you've ever drunk in your life."

He rocked back, his elbow opening the door behind him. Through an eighteen-inch gap Kay stared in astonishment at two elegant black girls, naked but for their high-heeled shoes, talking casually together as they smoked cigarettes. As the door swung wider, she saw a jumble of red middle-aged faces and pale teenaged blondes all looking up toward her. Then she remembered Mrs. Walker's hints about Senator Caspiani's parties, and she burst out laughing.

Markland's eyes narrowed belligerently. Caspiani spun her by the arm. "What's so funny?"

"I think there just might have been a small mistake, Senator," she said. She was not laughing now. "I'm not from some downtown cathouse. I'm from Mrs. Walker, General Walker's wife. I need to talk to you, urgently."

Caspiani reached forward and pulled the door closed. "Let's go down to my study. This is Senator Ted Markland. He's in on this too."

Sobriety had returned to Markland in the short walk down the stairs. In the study he accepted only ice water from Caspiani. "Okay, Miss Hampton," he said as soon as they were seated. "You start the ball rolling."

Kay nodded. "You know that General Walker has been arrested?"

"Yes."

"Until yesterday I was in Britain posted to the Lend-Lease base at Prestwick in Scotland."

Markland glanced at Caspiani, but both men remained silent.

"I believe you know that Rudolf Hess was heading for the base?"

Caspiani stood beside his desk. After a long pause he said, "Yes, Miss Hampton, we knew that. From the British reports he never made it."

"The navigator who flew with him is here in Washington," she said. "He has all of Hess's documentation with him."

Markland drew in a quick breath. He found himself staring at his dark socks, wishing that he had remembered to put on his shoes.

Caspiani sat on the edge of his desk. "It looks as though the hands have been redealt, Ted. We're still in the game. The only problem is, how do we play this round?"

"Alfred Horn is outside," Kay said. "I'd like to bring him in."

Caspiani came off the desk. "He has the Hess documentation with him?"

"Yes."

Caspiani shook his head. "The name of the game's changed since General Walker was arrested. I don't want those documents in this house."

Kay looked at him bluntly. "For Christ's sake," she said. "They contain details of a Japanese attack on the United States."

Caspiani looked sharply at Markland. "What do we do, Ted?" Both men seemed to ignore Kay's presence.

"We stay clear."

Caspiani nodded. "But do we give Miss Hampton here the name of the man Hess was coming to the U.S. to see?"

While Kay watched, they weighed the possibilities. After a few moments silence Markland got up and added whisky to his ice water. "I vote yes," he said. "That way we still get credit if it all breaks the right way."

"Okay, Miss Hampton," Caspiani said briskly.

"Your next step's up in Massachusetts—more precisely, out on Cape Cod."

The second the needle punctured his skin Rudolf Hess's eyes opened. In a moment of waking terror he saw the two dark shapes above him, was aware of the strap tightening on his right arm, felt the sting of the needle entering the vein.

There was no immediate overwhelming urge to sleep. Instead, in a wild flurry of bedclothes he scrambled to his feet, tipping the army cot on which he had been sleeping, flailing his arms at the two men standing over him, snapping the syringe so that only the needle stuck from the vein, welling blood.

The violence of his reaction stunned the two doctors, and the clatter of the overturning cot brought the guard-sergeant into the room.

Rudolf Hess crouched like an animal in the corner of the castle chamber.

Under his heavy black brows his eyes shone with tears of shock. "Honor," he said, "honor. . . ." He pulled the broken end of the needle from his vein and hurled it across the room. The guard-sergeant stood uncertainly, covering him with his pistol while the two doctors watched him warily.

"A gentleman's word!" Hess shouted. But his breathing was already becoming heavy. Crouched, he slipped onto one knee. As he began to fall forward, the sergeant caught him by the shoulder of his pajama jacket.

When the interrogating psychiatrist arrived twenty minutes later, there was no sign of the incident. Rudolf Hess lay in the neatly made-up cot as the two doctors checked his pulse and eye dilation, their confidence returned.

The psychiatrist was no more than twenty-eight, a Captain for a matter of ten months, but his every movement showed a brisk restless intelligence. He turned to the two doctors. "Thank you, gentlemen. My orders are to conduct this interview alone."

Reluctantly the two doctors left, and the psychiatrist opened his bag on the small writing table with which Hess had been provided. David Morgan-Smith had officially been researching hallucinogens since St. Bartholomew's Hospital in London had provided him with a small travel grant to visit Mexico before the war. But there among the peyote-chewing Indians he had begun to stumble on what he had called linear pulses and what would later be known to medical research as neuropeptides, certain substances extracted from animal brains which could increase perception, depress memory, excite sexuality or change by a pulse or message to the brain a whole range of moods or attitudes. The war had cut short his research, but the war had also provided him with the opportunity to remove and once or twice even to place secretions of neuropeptides in human brains. To a man as callously devoted to the extension of knowledge, and his own reputation, as David Morgan-Smith the results had been unbelievably exciting. Now he had been given a living man, fit, his brain undamaged. Within the requirement only that he discover one piece of information, he was free to introduce whatever range of stimulants he chose. No one would ever know. No one would ever ask.

His system with monkeys was to introduce the peptide by nasal spray deep into the sinuses. He chose an extract from the brain of sleeping cats which he called pulse K. So far he had used it successfully in retarded and autistic humans to increase their perception of their surroundings. Again he had never recorded its use on any treatment chart, but he was by now beginning to suspect that it worked in some way to increase the focus and assimilability of dreams. As a side effect his unofficial patients had also showed a marked decrease in their suspicion of the world around them.

David Morgan-Smith thrust the inhaler deep into

the nose of the sleeping Hess and blew two cubic centimeters of the extract of feline brain tissue deep into the sinal cavity. Then he took a notebook and pencil and drew up a chair beside the bed.

He could tell within minutes from the rapid eye movements beneath the lids that Hess was dreaming. Now his problem was to direct the dream—and this area Morgan-Smith knew to be more or less pure chance.

He leaned forward. "Stellvertreter," he whispered. "Stellvertreter. . . ."

Beneath the eyelids the eyes of Rudolf Hess flickered and rolled.

"Stellvertreter . . . your task is not complete. You have failed, Stellvertreter, failed. . . ."

Hess shook his head violently from side to side.

"You have failed the Führer," Morgan-Smith breathed softly. "Unless you can get to America, unless you can meet the man you have to meet there, you will have failed."

The subject's deep distress was evident. Sweat beaded his forehead; his arms thrashed; he moaned miserably. "The Führer must know," he muttered. "The Führer must know the truth."

"The truth?" Morgan-Smith prompted.

"My sacrifice to carry out his will. . . ."

"All worthless," Morgan-Smith said harshly. "To the Führer you're a traitor."

"My sacrifice . . ." Hess whimpered.

"You flew to Britain. You left the Führer."

"No. . . ." His voice was anguished.

"You deserted the Führer to come to Britain."

"To America. . . ."

"Why America?"

"Loyalty is sacrifice."

"Why America?"

"Sacrifice is loyalty." Tears were coursing down the German's cheeks.

Slowly Morgan-Smith's confidence began to wane.

In the next two hours he blew eight cubic centimeters of pulse K into Hess's sinus tract, stimulating a wild babble of talk—the cross, the moment in the Sports Palast when he had introduced Hitler to a hundred thousand cheering Germans—*Hitler ist Deutschland, Deutschland ist Hitler!*—then again the meeting in the headquarters dugout of the List Regiment. Then suddenly the jealousies within the Nazi hierarchy began to unfold—of Goering, Himmler, the enigmatic Bormann. And at the center, the shining figure of Adolf Hitler. When the Cardinal Legate had first brought the message to him from His Holiness Pope Pius, Hess had agreed to discussions. It was Hitler's wish that Britain should join Germany in the coming struggle against the East. It was also His Holiness's dearest wish. A true crusade against the barbarians of the steppes. Blessed by the Pope and supported by the industrial might of the United States.

"And you would be the hub of this whole design, Stellvertreter," Morgan-Smith prompted gently. "Everything would depend on your meeting in America with. . . ."

Hess was breathing heavily, his mouth clamped tight.

"Your meeting in America . . . ?"

The German seemed to be slipping back into a dreamless sleep. Desperate not to lose the moment, David Morgan-Smith shot six full cubic centimeters high in to Hess's sinus and in that second destroyed a large part of the memory regulator in his brain.

He also saw the heavy lips move to formulate the name of the Ambassador.

Fifteen

Joseph P. Kennedy, former U.S. ambassador to the Court of St. James's, recalled from London because of intense British resentment of his isolationist views, sat at his study desk and examined the linen-backed campaign maps in front of him.

He felt a sense of exhilaration which he disguised behind his steel-rimmed spectacles from the two people who sat opposite him.

Horn, for all his own background among the great Pomeranian estate owners, had still never sensed wealth as he did in the Kennedy household at Hyannis Port. Not that it was ostentatious, nor indeed that it was in any way coyly concealed. It was simply present in every corner of every room, in every assumption of the man behind the desk.

Kennedy put the papers aside. "I can't, of course, read German," he said, the Boston nasality strong in his voice, "but what I can see supports your description of these documents."

He placed his fingers together under his chin. "When did you last see Herr Hess, Captain?"

"As I told you," Horn said shortly, "Rudolf Hess is dead. I saw him shot by an SS squad at a hospital near Dungavel."

"The British press claims he is alive and a prisoner."

"Listen, Mr. Kennedy," Kay said impatiently, "the

British could have a million reasons for claiming Hess is alive. But I can tell you I was there at the hospital and heard the shots and Captain Horn was in the hospital and saw exactly what happened."

"I see."

"*I* don't," Kay said aggressively. "Why is it so important to you to know whether or not Hess is dead?"

"It isn't," Kennedy said.

"Then what is?"

"What's important to me, Mrs. Hampton, is to know whether Adolf Hitler wanted him dead."

"Why?"

"It will affect the way I handle this information."

"In what way, Mr. Kennedy?" Horn asked. He felt a strong sense of unease about the man, an awareness of the calculations going on behind the glinting spectacles.

"If Adolf Hitler were one hundred percent in favor of the Hess proposals, I could use this information publicly to force President Roosevelt to abandon Lend-Lease. That is to say, if Adolf Hitler is really willing to offer Britain peace, it is only the President's Lend-Lease policy which is prolonging the European war."

"And if Hitler does not support the Hess proposals?" Horn said slowly.

"Then I shall have to go to Roosevelt with these documents. Either way the result will be the same, Captain—withdrawal of aid to Britain and a peaceful settlement with Japan."

"And the news of my country's attack on Russia?"

Kennedy lifted his head. "It was never any part of Herr Hess's intention to betray Adolf Hitler's military plans. This information is being offered me in good faith, Captain. That is the only basis on which I accept it."

"You don't understand, Mr. Kennedy. My motive for bringing you this information is to prevent *both* attacks described in those documents."

Kennedy looked at the young German in surprise. "That's treason, Captain."

"Yes."

Kennedy shook his head. "Are you a Christian, Captain?"

"I was brought up to be. I've lost a little along the way."

"A Catholic?"

"Lutheran originally."

"Do you know what's happening to Christians in the Soviet Union, Captain?"

"Do you know what's happening to Jews in my country, Mr. Kennedy?"

It had taken a massive effort to say it. Kay looked at him in surprise and admiration.

Kennedy's expression showed distaste. "I know the present situation in Germany is not attractive, Captain. But Germany is at war. There's not much in the way of democratic freedoms visible in Britain just at the moment either."

"I'm sad to say I'm talking about before the war, Mr. Kennedy."

Horn wondered if the desk lamp were specially angled to reflect great circles of light from Kennedy's glasses. Then the man behind the desk moved, and his pale eyes were visible. "Tell me," the American said, "your motive in showing me these documents was to make sure Soviet Russia was adequately warned?"

"Part of my motive."

"Are you a Communist, young man?"

Horn looked at Kay in despair.

"No, Mr. Kennedy, I am not a Communist. I simply believe that if Russia and the United States are warned in time, either negotiation can replace war, or at least the victim of the attack can prepare. And if you or the American government is not prepared to give Russia the warning, I'm prepared to give it to them myself."

"Captain, I'll leave by private aircraft for Washington early tomorrow morning. I suggest you and Mrs. Hampton stay nearby until I get back. I can put you up in a lodge on the shore a few miles from here. I'll have someone bring everything you need for tonight. Tomorrow I'll be back from Washington. Then you can decide what you think it's necessary to do."

Asquith, the Embassy chief intelligence officer, nodded to Bishop as the green scrambler telephone rang. "That'll be your call, Max."

He lifted the receiver. "Washington Embassy, Asquith speaking. Your identification code, caller?" He listened. "I have Major Bishop with me now, Colonel." He moved to hand over the phone, then stopped, listening intently. His mouth opened as if to protest. Then closed abruptly. "I think you should relay this message yourself, Colonel."

Again he was silent as he listened, his face set. From time to time his eyes rested on Bishop. "I understand," he said finally.

He turned and handed the receiver to Bishop. "I'll be just outside."

"Max"—it was Colonel Henderson on the line—"I got your information for you. Quite a surprise. The man our prisoner was planning to contact is Joseph Kennedy, U.S. ambassador to London until a couple of months ago. It all makes sense, of course—anti-British, but more than anything anti-Russian."

Bishop accepted the information without elation. "Colonel," he said, "just one question."

"Yes."

"I'd like to know," he asked slowly, "just how difficult it was."

"To get the information?"

"Yes."

"You've got the wrong idea, Max. Listen, it's nothing as crude as rack and thumbscrew anymore. All that went out with the Inquisition. These days it's done with a simple injection. I talked to the psychiatrist who handled it. He assured me it was a completely pain-less procedure."

"I see."

"So where's the harm, Max?"

"None, I suppose, if that really is the case."

"I'm assured our man will hardly even remember it all happened."

When Bishop replaced the phone, he looked up to see that Asquith was standing grave-faced in the door-way. He came in and crossed to pick up a brandy decanter from a side table. He poured two glasses and carried them across to where Bishop was standing.

"Here." He proffered the balloon glass.

Bishop took it.

"It's excellent," Asquith said. "Prewar stock."

Bishop sniffed the warm fumes. "You have some-thing to tell me?"

"Yes. A change in your orders."

"Something Henderson wasn't willing to tell me him-self."

"On the phone. It's sometimes difficult."

Bishop nodded. "It's about Alfred Horn?"

"Yes. A personal friend, Henderson said, from be-fore the war."

"That's right."

Asquith sipped his brandy.

"Get on with it."

"Colonel Henderson explained as much as he could. Of course I'm not *au fait* with the whole story, but ap-parently even if you do capture Horn, he would re-main a severe embarrassment."

Bishop knew what was coming. "Yes," he said flatly, "a severe embarrassment."

"So I'm afraid your orders have been changed, Max. For a personal friend of this German officer it's very hard."

"I see." Bishop put down the brandy glass. "London is ordering me to kill Alfred Horn."

* * *

They got into the car and drove toward the tall gates. The gateman supplied them with directions and a bunch of keys.

At the wheel Kay drove without speaking.

"This war is going to spread, Kay," Horn said after a few moments.

"I know. Too many people want their own wars for it to happen any other way."

"Kennedy and his Pope want to fight Russia. Churchill and Roosevelt want to fight Germany. Japan wants a crack at the U.S. . . ."

They drove on in silence for a few moments, the headlights sweeping across grassy dunes as they followed the winding road. "A couple of months ago," he said, "I was flying Messerschmitt escorts for the bomber raids on London. Up there in the air I never had a doubt in my mind. The RAF pilots were as good as we were, their aircraft roughly the same. It was a fair, equal fight. It seemed even to have a certain old-fashioned chivalry to it. What I didn't understand was that the nobility, if it existed at all, was in the fighting, not in the cause we were fighting for. I didn't understand that we were fighting for fighting's sake. And there's precious little nobility in that."

A few miles outside Chatham she turned off the coast road. Having headed the car through a wooden gate, she stopped it in front of a white Cape Cod cottage. "What will you do now?" she asked.

"God knows," he said wearily. "I suppose the logical conclusion of treason is to offer my services to the United States, but I don't think I'm ready for that yet. I have cousins, uncles, all in the Wehrmacht."

She opened the car door. The headlights illuminated the house, a long clapboard cottage with shingle roof and green shutters. She flicked off the car lights, and together they entered the house.

It was much more spacious inside than Horn had imagined, with an exposed pine staircase and a great central fireplace. Upstairs there were two bedrooms with heavy oak beds and a well-equipped bathroom.

Within ten minutes of their arrival a delivery man was knocking at the door. In two large baskets he carried steaks, bacon, eggs, bread and half a dozen bottles of an excellent Burgundy. Spirits, he pointed out, were in the sideboard. Before he left, he had laid and set a match to the fire.

Kay looked at Horn as the door closed behind the delivery man. "It must be nice to be rich." She took a glass of Burgundy from him and stood before the fire. "Are you rich, Alfred?"

He shook his head. "Not Kennedy rich. And maybe after all this, not rich at all. Until last Saturday, at least, I owned a hundred-hectare estate in Pomerania, a very pleasant schloss, a stone building like a very small English castle, a stretch of superb fishing water and a very nice boar hunt." He smiled. "Rich enough, until last Saturday. I inherited from my father when he died a few years ago."

She took the steaks into the kitchen and began to prepare them for the grill. "How strange," she said, "it never occurred to me that you were a country squire. A German country squire. Does that make you a Junker?"

He leaned against the wall, watching her cook. "Yes, I'm afraid that's exactly what it makes me. Every last one of the male members of my family were in the army." He smiled. "My father even wore a monocle."

When the steaks were ready, he opened another bottle of the Burgundy and they sat down to eat before the fire. Somehow he felt she had to keep coming back to the estate in Pomerania.

"As a Junker," she asked with a hard edge of amusement in her voice, "I guess you get a sort of *droit de seigneur,* the right to be the first to deflower all the village maidens. Is that the way it goes?"

"It's not all maypoles and fertility rights tumbling the *dörfer Mädchen* in the barns, Kay. When I was a

271

boy just after the First War, we *fought* for the land. Whole villages led by someone like my father or one of his brothers marched out and fought pitched battles with the Poles."

She stopped laughing. "The Poles?"

"In the anarchy at the end of the war no one knew who the peace treaty was going to assign the land to. The Poles decided possession was nine points of the law. It was bloody fighting, with clubs and pitchforks in the dark as much as boar guns and old army rifles."

"What happened?"

"In our area we held them off. I was just a ten-year-old kid when most of it went on, but I can tell you it was the shooting, the broken heads and the swastika armbands of the Freikorps I remember as a teenager a whole lot better than screwing village maidens in the woods."

She looked up. "I'm sorry," she said. "To be with you, you appear so very American, I forget that inside there is a German officer trying to get out."

He made to pour her some more wine, but she covered her glass with her hand. "No, thanks, not yet. I have a phone call to make."

"Who to?"

She stood up. "Ralph, my husband. He was due to arrive home today."

Behind the staircase the telephone had been fitted into an eighteenth-century London sedan chair. She entered the light leather box and put through a call to the Washington apartment. As she listened to three, four, five rings, she thought, in a moment of panic, that he had not got back. Then the receiver was lifted, and her husband's unmistakable voice boomed out hello.

"Ralph? This is Kay."

"Kay." She winced at the concern in his voice. "Are you okay, honey?"

"I'm okay."

"Look, what in tarnation's going on here? I got

back to the apartment to find the place staked out by the FBI. Your clothes are half unpacked in the bedroom, and nobody's prepared to tell me a damn thing."

"I'm in Massachusetts, Ralph. I'll be here a day or two."

"A day or two?"

"Yes."

"What is it, Kay? You've been assigned duty up there?"

"No, Ralph."

"If it's not duty. . . ."

"Don't ask me any more questions," she said quietly.

With a sudden flash of insight he said, "You're saying you're not up there alone?"

She hesitated. "No, Ralph, I'm not alone."

He was silent at the other end of the line.

"I'll be back in a couple of days, Ralph."

She heard him swallow.

"I always promised you I'd tell you."

"Yes . . ." he said. There was no boom in his voice now. "Yes, thanks for that, Kay."

"I'd like to come back, Ralph."

There was a long pause. She waited, holding the phone close to her ear. Then he said, "I'd like you back, honey. Just as soon as you can make it."

He hung up. "What a bitch I am," she said to herself as she thought of all the times she had ever apologized for him to her friends.

She walked through into the living room and poured herself a large glass of wine. Standing in the middle of the room while Horn watched her, she drained the glass.

"Tell me about your husband, Kay."

She shook her head.

"I need to know."

"What do you need to know?"

"I need to know if it's him that's keeping us apart."

"Yes," she said, her lips compressed. "I'm a respectable married woman. I've done nothing to be ashamed of so far. Just treason possibly, murder certainly. Of course beside those two, lust seems a very small sin."

"Lust?"

"You are a younger, very attractive man, Alfred."

He filled her glass. "You don't have to seduce me, Kay," he said slowly. "I told you back in Scotland that when the time came. . . ."

She was shivering. "Oh, God," she said suddenly, "how stupid can I get?" She got to her feet quickly. "I'm going to bed, Alfred. Before I make a real fool of myself. I'll take the back bedroom."

She moved for the stairs, and he caught her arm, spinning her around to face him. "You're safe with me, Kay. I promise you—no sweet nothings. I'll take the other bedroom. But I'd as soon not spend the night alone."

She said nothing. As he released her arm, she turned for the stairs.

He sat alone, finishing his wine, listening to her taking a shower. When she had finished, he heard her footsteps cross the landing. She had entered her bedroom.

He crushed out his cigarette and took a glass and the rest of the bottle of wine up with him. In the front bedroom he took off his clothes and stood for a moment naked by the open window, listening to the sea below.

Then he turned and climbed into the huge carved oak bed.

He was reaching out to fill his wineglass when he heard the step on the landing outside. He continued filling the glass as he watched the door handle turn.

A shaft of light fell into the room, its center shadowed by a woman's shape. He turned his head to look toward the door. She stood there in a long robe.

"Lust, we said."

He raised himself on one elbow and nodded. "If that's the way you want it."

"No sweet nothings?"

"No."

"Just a simple workmanlike performance."

"Okay, it's a deal."

She took two steps forward, and he reached out and drew her by the hand down onto the bed.

"Do I have to apologize for this?" she said.

"No."

"If there is a reason, it's because I haven't enjoyed a man for eight years."

"You deserve better."

"I'm a realist."

"You're a coward." He pulled the cord of the dressing gown. At the front it fell open to reveal her breasts. He cupped one with his hand and drew her down beside him. As he kissed her face her hand came around the back of his neck.

For almost an hour they kissed and touched each other, forgetful of the agreement between them. He was astonished at the full warmth of her body and the moistness of the response to his hand. When he entered her, she gasped with pleasure.

"Lust," he said, lying above her, looking down into her face.

She smiled. "What else?"

As the private charter plane rose above Boston through the rays of the early morning sun and banked south across the Charles River, Joe Kennedy sat alone in the small passenger compartment and accepted a cup of coffee from the single steward. He knew he was on the most important journey of his long career. For once the disparate threads in his life would be drawn together in a single ambitious design.

He had no time, outside his family life, for sentiment, either with his own projects or with those of others. And for days now he had been convinced he had failed. When the news of Hess's capture in Scotland broke, he had no further room for doubt.

So the Grand Design had seemed to crash in ruins. The "Secret Crusade," as his friend Eugenio Pacelli, Pope Pius XII, had called it: that startling act of the Pope's creative imagination which had seen the opportunity in Britain's defeat to range the British Empire and Germany as allies against the godless Soviets—and the opportunity, too, to keep America out of the war.

Through his immensely wide contacts in the Germany he loved, contacts built up in the long years he had lived there as Nuncio, Pius XII had sought and found the weak link. In the vague romantic mysticism of Rudolf Hess, in his intense loyalty to his own conception of the Führer's real wishes, the proponents of the Secret Crusade had found their man. They had worked on him unmercifully throughout 1940, playing on his desperate sense that he was losing his high place in the Führer's esteem. Losing it to Himmler, even to his own Party deputy, Bormann, losing it to the Panzer generals who had crushed Poland and France.

They had played on his long association with the Führer, on the fact that he alone, among all the Nazi Party leaders, had known Hitler when he was fighting the British in Flanders in the First World War. And they reminded him constantly of the Führer's belief that Britain and Germany belonged together. And that the Russian barbarian was the real enemy.

Then, after the months of preparation, after the risks of an unescorted flight across the North Sea, a broken ankle, it seemed, had been enough to destroy this chance to seize history by the scruff of the neck and force it to do their bidding.

And now, incredibly, it seemed to Joe Kennedy, a young idealistic German flier, confused in his own motives, ignorant of all the facts, might just be God's chosen instrument to advance the great crusade. And not only would the Christian world be saved. In his briefcase were the papers which could bring him, Joseph P. Kennedy, to the highest position in the land. It was the sort of deal Joe liked best—a perfect balance of public benefit and private gain.

Horn awoke to the reassuring, metallic clatter of a lawn mower and a bright square of sunlight filling the window. Kay lay beside him on her stomach, one leg bent at the knee, one arm draped out toward him on the pillow. For the moment Horn didn't move. A filter of birdsong played as a background to the steady whirl of the mower. Careful not to disturb Kay, he slid from the bed and went to the window.

From the lodge he could see the long, parallel lines across the lawn as the old gardener pushed the machine with a steady, unhurried tread. He stood at the window as the old man stooped and removed the bag to empty it under a line of clipped ornamental bushes. Horn opened the window. The sun, from a cloudless sky, had a real summer warmth. Nothing had been normal about the last few extraordinary days. After the confusion, tension and cold fear he felt he had emerged back into some sort of natural existence.

Kay moved in her sleep, then turned and opened her eyes. He went back and sat down on the edge of the bed beside her.

"Hello."

She rolled onto her back, pulling the sheet up under her chin.

"Hi." Her voice was husky with sleep.

"Werd' ich zum Augenblicke sagen: Verweile doch. Du bist so schön."

"What's that?" she asked.

"It's from Goethe."

"What does it mean?"

"I'm not sure I should tell you."

She was silent.

"It means, I speak to the moment—stay now. You are too beautiful to go."

She brought herself up on to one elbow, her large shapely breasts curving under the sheet. "I thought we agreed last night: no sweet nothings."

He looked at her grave, even worried, expression and reached out to run his hand down her warm arm. The movement exposed the lower curve of her breast. *"So schön du bist—diese Augenblicke werden nicht verweilen."*

She lifted her eyebrows in a question.

"Don't worry, Kay—this sort of moment never returns."

He stood up. His throat contracted. Facing the window, he said, "It's a hell of a nice day. Let's enjoy it."

They had slept late, and it was almost noon as they drove into the summer tourist town of Chatham. On a side street they stopped and watched a man in a yellow shirt making candles outside a tiny crafts shop. Then at the corner drugstore Kay bought a pair of sunglasses and Horn idly picked out a map of the area. As they came out on to the sidewalk, the sun blazed from a brittle blue sky and the air was warm with the tang of the sea about it.

Main Street was quiet and uncrowded but with an air of bright expectancy. The shining, newly painted signs and shopfronts stood waiting for the flood of summer Cape Codders who owned or leased the houses along the beaches and who would start to come in at the beginning of June. By then both Kay and Horn knew they would be long gone.

When Joseph P. Kennedy entered the Oval Office as the first appointment after lunch on Saturday, May 17, Roosevelt beamed a welcoming smile from the wheelchair positioned in the middle of the room. Extending his hand, he said, "It's been too long, Joe. Far too long."

Kennedy's eyes glittered. "If it has, Mr. President,"

he said coolly, "it's been none of my making. I'm ready to move to Washington the moment you say. Just name the new job, and Rose and I will be here."

"Not quite so easy, Joe." Roosevelt smiled regretfully. "I've got to find just the right slot for you—and top jobs don't come up every day."

"Maybe we can talk it through when I've shown you this." Kennedy took a bulky set of documents from an alligator briefcase and laid them on the desk at Roosevelt's right hand.

"Have you managed to get down to Florida this winter, Joe? I know how you and Rose like it down there."

"Yes, once or twice." He adjusted his glasses. "Mr. President. . . ."

"It'll be good to see you in Washington, Joe. These new federal agencies are growing like mushrooms. We could do with a good solid business head among all these economic theoreticians."

"Mr. President, the documents I have to show you are of transcending importance."

Roosevelt smiled broadly. "Give or take a phrase, Joe, that's what somebody'll say in my next five meetings this afternoon."

"They'll be wrong then," Kennedy snapped. "Compared with these documents, I can assure you they will be wrong."

"What do you have for me, Joe? You sounded pretty mysterious on the telephone."

It frustrated Kennedy that he could never tame this man. If one tried to produce a sense of occasion, he would cut it down with an apparently artless grin. He was determined always to be the only actor on the stage.

"I've flown down here to Washington, Mr. President, with the gravest possible information for the United States. Last night a young German Luftwaffe officer delivered certain documents to me."

"Go on, Joe."

"Mr. President, I'm laying before you a blueprint for a world war. I believe if you act now that war can be avoided."

"Where originally does this blueprint come from, Joe?" Roosevelt's pale eyes never left Kennedy's face.

"It comes direct from Herr Rudolf Hess. He was on his way to see me here in the United States when the British captured him."

"I see. And did you *know* he was on his way to see you?"

"Yes. The contact was arranged through His Holiness the Pope."

Still Roosevelt left the papers untouched. "This must have been a long time in the brewing."

"I visited His Holiness when I was ambassador to Britain. We naturally discussed world affairs. In particular the appalling possibility of a world war in which the United States would be on the side of godless Russia."

"I don't recall your dispatch on the subject, Joe." There was a perceptible edge to Roosevelt's voice.

"It was a private discussion, Mr. President."

"While you were still an ambassador of the United States, none of your discussions was private. Certainly not discussions on this level."

Joseph P. Kennedy was not accustomed to being talked to this way. His face hardened. "Are you going to examine those documents, Mr. President?"

"They will be microscopically examined by experts. In the meantime, Joe, I'd like you to tell me what they contain."

"They contain the information that, as His Holiness predicted to me, Germany is about to attack Russia. Second, that the Japanese Empire is planning an air / sea surprise attack for the end of this year on the U.S. Pacific Fleet."

Kennedy found it impossible to gauge Roosevelt's expression. He watched the President's mouth pucker in what in other circumstances might have been almost a smile. He watched him nod to himself. "If Japan attacks the United States," Roosevelt said, "I assume Germany will, as Japan's ally, declare war on us, too."

"This is the catastrophe that Herr Hess was trying to avoid—the United States being forced into a position of armed support for the British imperialists and the Soviet atheists."

Roosevelt scratched his eyebrow. "Support *against* Fascist Germany, Joe. And Imperialist Japan."

Kennedy again had the fleeting sense that Roosevelt was laughing at him. "We'd be backing the wrong side," Kennedy said harshly. "Britain's done for. Finished. I saw that when I was in London."

"Too bad London didn't see it the same way."

"Mr. President, as U.S. ambassador in Britain I reported the situation as I saw it. I'm not surprised the British government would have preferred a more whitewashed version to have reached you."

"These are old chimes, Joe. Let's get back to our discussion. Your belief is that Britain must surrender to Germany."

"Herr Hess's proposal was that the surrender terms should be generous. Britain would be required to supply no more than ten full divisions for the Russian campaign. And she would be left in complete command of her fleet to defend her Far East Empire against Japan."

This time Roosevelt smiled. "I see, Joe. The two imperialist powers cancel themselves out in long-range naval warfare. Germany invades Russia and annihilates Communism. And the U.S.? What part does the arsenal of democracy play in this grand scheme, Joe?"

"The U.S. negotiates a settlement with Japan and stays clear."

"That's quite a hypothesis, Joe."

"Only one man stands in the way."

Roosevelt took a cigarette from the box on the table. Tapping the end, he asked, "And who's that, Joe?"

"You know who it is, Mr. President—Winston Churchill. In 1940 he was willing to fight to the last Frenchman. Today he's just as willing to fight to the last American."

Roosevelt lit his cigarette and with one hand wheeled himself across the carpetless floor until he stopped inside the window looking out over the lawns.

Kennedy watched him in profile, the confident, jutting jaw, the narrow cheekbones and the well-shaped mouth.

Roosevelt inhaled the cigarette slowly. "Joe," he said, "the United States is going to have to enter this war."

Kennedy looked at him incredulously. "After you were elected on a no-war platform, after I spoke for you as a no-war President, after these documents offer you a chance to negotiate a peace with Japan before it's too late, you still tell me we're going to have to go into this war?"

Roosevelt swung his chair. "Last November I made a deal with you, Joe. I wanted the political support of the leading isolationist in the Democratic party to secure my last term as President. In return I promised you my support for the 1944 nomination. Now what are you doing, Joe? Are you throwing away that ticket? Are you throwing away the chance to be the next President?"

Kennedy was silent.

"Well, Joe?"

"I don't understand what you're saying, Mr. President," he said uneasily.

"If you publicly oppose me on the issue of war, you can hardly expect my support in three years' time."

"I see no need to oppose you publicly. What I've sketched out is right for America, and I expect you to see it my way. Germany must be retained as a buffer against the Soviet Union."

"Not this Germany, Joe. The price is too high—whatever His Holiness says."

"If we enter the war against Germany, the Soviet Union will emerge as the most powerful nation in Europe."

"In ten years' time we'll have to tackle that," Roosevelt conceded. "But right now it's not the problem that faces democracy."

"Exactly what is?"

The pale eyes raked Kennedy.

"What is the problem that faces our democracy, Mr. President?"

"The economic collapse of the United States."

Kennedy stared openmouthed.

"Not more than four men in my administration know this yet, Joe, but the New Deal has failed. It won't show for a year or two, but it's failed. The latest unemployment returns stand at twelve million; two million more than when I took office in 1933. Unless we fight for democracy, Mr. Kennedy, there will be no democracy to fight for."

"You mean American industry needs this war?"

"I mean American democracy needs it. If you succeeded in forcing the United States to keep out of this war, Joe, you just might still make it to the White House in 1944. But the America you inherited would be a second-rate power. The Soviet Union would not just be the most powerful nation in Europe; it would be far and away the most powerful nation in the world."

He wheeled his chair across to the desk. "I'll have these papers assessed by the military. Premier Stalin will, of course, be informed. I will be releasing no statement to the press on the coming Japanese attack. We will, of course, make all possible preparations, but we must expect an initial setback. It will in any case serve to destroy isolationist sentiment overnight."

He held out his hand. "The choice is yours, Joe. You can oppose me publicly or go back to Hyannis and await the call. You have it in your power, by 1944, to be leading the richest, most confident and most widely victorious nation the world has ever seen."

Kennedy shook Roosevelt's hand. "To do that, I'll need to keep my face before the public, Mr. President. I'd need a senior position in the administration. Let's say State?"

"As soon as we are in the war, Joe. Until then keep your head low. And no contributions to the America First movement. Come next year it'll look as if you were betraying the 'boys at the front.'"

As Kennedy reached for the door, he heard a movement behind. Turning, he saw that Roosevelt had propelled himself across the room and had brought his chair to a stop a few feet from Kennedy.

"Something you forgot to tell me, Joe."

Kennedy blinked behind the steel-rimmed spectacles.

"Where is he, Joe? The Luftwaffe officer who brought you the documents?"

After Joseph P. Kennedy had left the Oval Office, the Secretary of State, Cordell Hull, entered.

The President was smoking another cigarette, his chair positioned to allow him to look across the broad lawns. "These businessmen," he said to Hull, shaking his head. "They all think if they understand money, they understand people. In the political arena, Joe Kennedy would be crushed underfoot."

Cordell Hull was silent.

"You know," Roosevelt mused, "he just told me that as preparation for the 1944 nomination he was going to have to have your job." Roosevelt spun his chair from the window. "Yes, crushed underfoot. Still, he's got a fine crop of boys there. He'll never make it himself, of course, but who knows? Joe Junior might. If I were a gambling man. . . ."

"Who would you put your money on for the 1944 election?"

Roosevelt smiled. "If I were a gambling man, Cordell, I'd put my money on *me*."

* * *

Saturday May 17, 2:30 P.M. FBI telephone transcript. J. Edgar Hoover to Inspector J. Dolyacki. One copy for retention in the Director's private files.

Hoover:
> Dolyacki, the President just called. He has received information locating our suspect on Cape Cod. The precise location is a cottage Mr. Joseph Kennedy rents, between Hyannis and Chatham.

Dolyacki:
> I'll leave right away, sir.

Hoover:
> I want you to fly up there . . . (and Dolyacki, I want you to make damn sure you keep the British out of this). Section in parenthesis deleted in FBI file copy.

Sixteen

They were, Kay knew, engaged in that most painful process between man and woman: they were killing time. The time until Kennedy returned from Washington, the time she herself had allotted to them from her marriage. They were killing time because they were both afraid to go to bed again, to recognize what had happened between them in the week since they met.

After lunch the afternoon sun had a veil of haze, but the fine white sand of the long, deserted beach was warm and dry underfoot, and the sea lapped in with gentle monotony. Horn and Kay had walked through the town and followed a sandy track along the shoreline to find this place. They had spent the afternoon running barefoot along the water's edge, chasing the waves in and out like a couple of teen-agers on their first date. It was easier that way.

Standing on the top of a large dune, Horn looked out across the deep calm of the Atlantic. Behind him a line of trees rose like sentinels along a low ridge, and for a moment he caught their piny scent. He looked down. Kay lay in the sand, her hands clasped behind her neck. She waved for him to come down. He signaled back, then took a last look out to sea. Like people, its mood could change. Tomorrow great mountains of rolling surf might be crashing in along the shoreline. But then, unlike people, the sea itself remained unalterable. As he walked toward Kay, she stood silhouetted against the low sun, and with a slow quietness that seemed to match the gentle lapping of the shallow waves he realized what he felt for her was something close to love.

In Moscow it was after midnight. A cold mist had gathered in the drab side streets and had begun to roll across the deserted expanse of Red Square.

Even at this hour the lights still burned in the windows of a dozen ministries. In their high offices ministers waited—some dozed; others played chess or drank endless cups of coffee. Some harassed their subordinates, and a few tried to work. But all waited for the telephone to ring. Joseph Vissarionovich Stalin suffered from insomnia, and summonses to his presence were normal until two or three in the morning.

Below the crenellated walls and red-brick towers of the Kremlin, in an underground study he used at night, the man whose word the ministers waited on reclined on a low couch; his personal secretary, Poskryobshev, tidied the small writing desk. The ministers enjoyed the joke that the secretary's name derived from the Russian word "to fawn," but they knew at heart that it was a joke against themselves.

"Is there anything else, Comrade Stalin?" Poskryobshev asked, his head inclined submissively.

Stalin thought for a second or two, knocking the cold ash from his pipe. "Not for the moment, Sasha. Send Comrade Beria in the moment he arrives."

After the secretary had left, Stalin stretched over to a switch and reset the electrially operated lock on the only entrance to the room. As he reclined on the couch, the heavy jowls, never allowed to show in official photographs or portraits, relaxed into folds beneath his chin, and the eyes closed halfway, like a vulture.

Suspicion and distrust were the consuming characteristics of this son of a Georgian shoemaker. Aided by the bland, bespectacled Beria, he had eliminated all serious political opposition in the great purge of 1936, and in 1937 he had decimated the army leadership to preclude any possibility of revolt from that quarter. Stalin was internally secure in his position as ruler over one-sixth of the world's land surface, and his uncertainty was concerned now with external elements. He saw knives aimed at his back from all directions. Japan worried him constantly. He was suspicious of Roosevelt, highly suspicious of Churchill. Only one man he felt he understood: Stalin had put his faith in his assessment of Adolf Hitler.

After a few moments the warning light glowed above the door, and a familiar voice spoke in unmistakable Georgian accents.

Stalin operated the door lock, and Beria came into the room. Stalin greeted him warmly, then asked, "What do you make of this?" He handed the head of his secret police a sheet of paper from the ornate writing desk.

"From Sorge?"

"Yes."

Beria read the few typewritten lines, then carefully read them again. He knew of course about Richard Sorge, a German Communist and the Tokyo correspondent of the *Frankfurter Zeitung,* one of the Soviet External Services' most effective men.

"A German invasion," said Beria slowly.

Stalin stroked his mustache.

"Can this information be relied upon?"

"It is difficult to say," said his subordinate carefully, suspecting that Stalin had more to reveal.

Stalin went and sat down heavily at the desk. He wanted to believe Sorge's news of Hitler's treacherous intent, but a customary suspicion clouded his thoughts. He pointed a finger at another sheet of paper before him with a movement of almost physical accusation.

"We've also had a message from Churchill."

Beria looked suitably surprised and wary.

"He too warns us of a German attack. He even mentions the code word for the plan—'Barbarossa.' " He looked at Beria, waiting for his comments.

"There seem to be two possibilities. First, the information is correct." Stalin watched him, the lids of his eyes again half closed, waiting for the second alternative, which Beria rightly judged was the one he wanted to hear.

"Second, Churchill has fed Sorge the information so that both have given us the same false warning. Germany is not about to attack."

Stalin nodded in agreement, pulling at the flap of flesh under his chin. Beria pursued his own logic. "But why would Churchill do that?"

"The reason is obvious," said Stalin. "If we thought we were about to be invaded, what would we do?"

Beria waited for Stalin to explain.

"We would recall Zhukov from Mongolia—move, say, thirty divisions to the German border. . . ."

Stalin began to pace the room as the orchestra of his own thoughts began to play. "We'd take up defensive positions, construct a line of fortifications. . . ."

The orchestra swelled, and Beria saw the light in the other man's eyes. "We might even preempt the attack by making one of our own. One fast crushing advance. Well planned, carried out with speed and precision, sweeping all before it."

The idea appealed to Stalin; the strategy always had. Strike first, deal your opponent a telling, stunning blow before he can get one in of his own. He noticed Beria was looking at him, his mouth half open. "Well?" he snapped.

Beria closed his mouth.

The orchestra had faded. Stalin sat down again and stared at the translation of Churchill's cable.

"No. As I've already said, the reason is obvious. That's exactly what Churchill wants us to do."

He glanced at Beria. "Look into it, will you?"

They embraced, and Beria left.

Stalin felt a nagging unease. He considered phoning one of the ministries, but that would be pointless. What did any of them know? Even Beria had been little help. He felt alone, bearing the heavy burden of final responsibility, forced to make all the decisions. Who else could? He sighed.

Soon he began to pace the room again, his heavy brow in a thoughtful frown. Then in an instant of inspiration he felt he saw the Churchill trap. If Russia sent a new army to the German border, Hitler would interpret it as an act of aggression. It was how Stalin would react himself. Hitler might well invade. Now he could see the detail of Churchill's intentions. It was transparently obvious.

Zhukov and the armies would stay in the East.

In the low wooded hills of East Prussia, construction workers had for some weeks been building a complex of timber huts and bunkers near the small town of Rastenburg. Only a handful of senior officers knew the purpose of the construction work and even fewer the code name of the new Führer headquarters: the *Wolfsschanze,* the "Wolf's Lair."

In his small private bathroom in the central block, the Wolf himself examined his face in the mirror. Running a hand down the left side of his face, he found yet again it felt slightly dead to the touch. Last November, he recalled, the room had swum before his eyes, and he had collapsed into a chair, unable to move his left side for fully five minutes. He felt certain he had suffered a stroke of some kind, and although the doctor who examined him had said he was in perfect health, he had noticed the stethoscope tremble in the man's hand as he sounded his chest. Since then, however, all food, even his favorite trout, had tasted like cardboard, and he seemed almost constantly gripped by a terrible lethargy. Then again, his horoscope, compiled in 1933 on the day he became Chancellor, clearly stated he would live to be eighty, and he was just fifty-two.

Hitler came into the room to find the combined officers of the OKW, the Wehrmacht High Command, standing around the maps spread out over the large central table: Colonel General Alfred Jodl, OKW Chief of Operations Staff, General Franz Halder, Chief of the General Staff, Field Marshals von Leeb, von Bock and von Rundstedt, General Warlimont, Jodl's deputy, and von Thoma, Chief of Mobile Forces at Army High Command.

He nodded a grim greeting, clasped his hands behind his back, and walked to the table.

"Gentlemen. . . ."

The officers gathered around, and Hitler leaned forward and stared at the map for fully thirty seconds. Finally, he straightened. "We have only to kick in the door, and the whole rotten structure will come crashing down."

Von Thoma studied the map again, trying to see something he had missed.

"It will be a war of annihilation," Hitler continued, waving his hand in a sweeping gesture across the map. "There will be no question of soldierly comradeship with the Russians. The Soviet is a subhuman."

"Are we to take it the decision has been taken?" asked von Rundstedt.

Hitler looked at him. Gerd von Rundstedt was the doyen of the Officer Corps. He was now sixty-six years old and had never lost a battle. The son of an aristocratic, military family, he had an austere, abrasive dignity.

"Decision?" queried Hitler.

"To implement Barbarossa," said von Rundstedt calmly.

Hitler turned away and walked to the wall. Staring at the blankness, he suddenly remembered the main purpose of the meeting. Jodl had told him that unless a date for the attack were set now, the main objectives of the first onslaught could not be guaranteed before the onset of winter.

He turned back into the room. "What would be our armor situation?" he asked.

Von Thoma took an almost involuntary step forward in his eagerness to answer. "Seven of the nineteen panzer and three of the twelve motorized divisions were sent to the Balkans," he said.

"How many tanks would be available?"

"In a month we could put twenty-five hundred tanks into the *Schwerpunkt*."

Hitler returned to the map and leaned over it again, but his thoughts were elsewhere. If only Goering's promise to bring Britain to its knees had been fulfilled, or if Churchill had agreed to an honorable peace and joined forces with Germany against the Bolsheviks . . . it would all have been so much easier. Then another question crossed his mind.

"What of Hess?" he said, almost to himself.

"It has to be faced," said von Rundstedt evenly. "The Stellvertreter knew about Barbarossa and may well have told the British. They would, of course, warn Stalin."

"The evidence points to the contrary," said Halder. "Our latest reconnaissance shows little or no troop movement by the Russians toward a defensive position along the border."

Hitler smiled. Operation Barbarossa would take place.

Later he ordered his German shepherd, Blondi, be brought to him and announced he would take a walk. A detachment of SS was sent to check the woods around the compound. Twenty senior German officers waited for his return.

As he strolled in the half-light under the pines surrounding the compound, Hitler's thought returned to Hess. Clearly he had told the British nothing. So be it.

He stood watching the strong, lithe dog running back and forth through the dark trees. He had just committed three million German troops to an attack on Russia. The dog stopped for a moment and stood silhouetted against a patch of light. He noticed the thick neck and powerful jaws. How wolflike it appeared! His spirits returned. He called the dog, and it bounded toward him. He patted its sleek head. They were brothers. He, Adolf Hitler, was a wolf, too: a German wolf poised to savage the Russian bear.

They arrived back at the cottage to hear the phone ringing. Horn walked through the hallway to answer it. Standing, bent forward in the low doorway, he raised the receiver. It was Joe Kennedy.

"I promised to call you, Captain, the moment I got back."

"I'll get the car and be right over," Horn said.

Kennedy hesitated. "It's been a long day, Captain. I'd just as soon leave it till tomorrow."

It was something in Kennedy's tone that totally alarmed Horn. "Mr. Kennedy," he said coldly, "there are certain assurances I require *tonight*."

This time Kennedy was silent.

"Tonight, Mr. Kennedy."

"What is it you feel you have the right to know, Captain?" Kennedy's voice was more thinly Boston nasal than ever.

"I want to know, first, if the Japanese information will be used in negotiations for peace."

"I think you can rely on the President of the United States to defend the interests of the American people."

"And Russia?" Horn was trembling with anger.

"The Soviet Union will be informed of Germany's intentions."

"You can assure me of that?"

"I can."

"Does this mean there will be no war with Japan?"

"Who can say?"

"I thought *you* could," Horn exploded. "I thought that's why I was delivering the documentation to *you*."

"I have done my best, Captain Horn. And now if you'll excuse me, I plan to get some sleep. It's a long flight, Washington and back in one day. Good-night."

Horn replaced the receiver and joined Kay beside the fire. She was sitting on the thick rug, her back against the leather sofa.

Horn slipped from the sofa onto the rug. "Kay, darling"—he had never used the word before—"I think you should go back home."

She turned her head toward him. "You mean leave tonight?"

"I mean right away. I've just spoken to Kennedy."

"I heard."

"The politicians have taken over, Kay."

"I want to stay with you. More than anything I want to stay with you tonight."

"Somehow," Horn spoke slowly, "however much we want it, I think it's far too dangerous."

"What will you do?"

He shook his head. "I don't know. Strangely enough, my first thought is to get in touch with Max Bishop. I could rely on him."

"Then come back with *me* to Washington. Now."

"I have to see Kennedy—just once more. I have to know what *really* happened when he took the information to the White House."

She stood up and warmed her hands at the fire. "If I drive back to Washington now, do you want me to take a hotel room? To wait for you there?" She was looking down into the yellow and blue flames dancing high from the birch logs.

He turned her around to face him. "I think we both know how it is between us. . . . Don't we?"

She looked at him, her eyes holding his, then nodded. "I thought I was immune to such things. I thought my age was all the protective clothing I needed."

He took her lower lip between his finger and thumb and gently drew her mouth to his. Then he moved his head away. "I want you to go back to Washington. To Ralph. I want you to stick close, obviously close to him. I think I've already learned enough to know that if you keep your head down you'll be safe."

"And you?"

"Max Bishop. There are worse ways of sitting out this war than in a prison camp in Canada. Take the car now, Kay. Drive straight back to Washington. And make it obvious as hell to any FBI surveillance that your only interest is in Ralph."

Dolyacki's convoy of limousines pulled away from the Kennedy compound and headed east. In the lead car Dolyacki sat with a map on his knee next to the driver. "A cottage on the shore here," he said. "Fifteen or twenty minutes at the most."

Without looking up at him, she switched on the ignition and put the car in gear. Still not turning her head, she mumbled good-bye into the steering wheel. Then the headlights flicked out across the neatly kept garden, and the car began to roll toward the gate.

"When this war ends, Kay. . . ." He had tried to extend some half hope for the future, but she had cut him short. She had held him tight for a moment, then climbed quickly into the car. When this war ends, she said to herself—and it hasn't begun yet for America—I'll be way into my forties. For all the difference it'll make to you and me, this war might just as well last *forever*.

She turned onto the road and, careless of her own safety, allowed the car almost to follow its own course along the sweeping curves of the shore road, touching brake or accelerator only to accentuate the sensuous rolling of the suspension. Twice the big car gathered enough speed to carry it into the soft sand by the roadside; twice she asserted some residual interest in braking quickly enough to control it.

The third time she skidded, the rear fender was flung hard against a solid clay step lining the road. Completely out of control now, the car hurtled across the road plunging through the dunes until its hood buried itself in a drift of fine white sand. When Dolyacki's convoy swept past two minutes later, it remained unseen by anybody in the four crowded cars.

In the dark driveway Horn had crossed to the hedge that fenced the garden from the surrounding dunes to watch the headlights of Kay's car as they swept from bend to bend. From where he stood he had no idea of how she was driving, how almost suicidally erratic, but when suddenly the headlights disappeared, his jaw tensed with anxiety, and he counted off the seconds, waiting for their reappearance around the next rising dune.

If she had crashed, he had heard nothing. Yet the wind and the surge of the sea made it unlikely that the sound would reach him. He began to work out how long it would take him to go on foot when he saw sweeping the bald hillocks where he had last seen Kay's car, the headlights of maybe four or five approaching vehicles. There could be no doubt where they were heading; from this point on there was nowhere else for them to go. Kay, he guessed, must have seen the lights approaching and pulled over, killing her own lights. Any minute now she would be safely on her way back to Hyannis and south off the Cape for New York and Washington.

He stood for a moment watching the car lights, aware that in some sense Joseph Kennedy must have been responsible. For too long he stood at the hedge, the wind off the sea tugging at his clothes. He knew he should run. But he had no idea where to . . . not even a clear idea that there was any point in running.

Behind him the rising sea lifted and flooded in across the beach. Kay was on her way to Washington. If he allowed himself to be taken, it would relieve the pressure on her—there would be no questions, no harassment and, after a short while, probably no surveillance. They would have him; the main leak would be sealed.

He turned from the hedge and had just started to walk toward the gate when the leading car swung off the road, its lights blazing full into Horn's face.

As he flinched away from the light, he heard a shout from within the car and the double crack of a revolver. The bullet passed above his head. From that moment his reflexes took over. He hurled himself forward into the dark zone beside the car, crossed the road, briefly in the headlights of the second car, and plunged into the dark undulations of the dunes rising on the other side. Four, perhaps five shots pursued him, but he had reacted too quickly for anyone to sight a shot. Within five seconds of Dolyacki's first shot, Alfred Horn was scrambling down a sandy gully which would bring him back across the road behind the cars and finally down to the beach.

She was no longer unconscious, but the ability to focus her thoughts still eluded her. She knew that several other cars had passed by on the road to the cottage—and Alfred Horn would need some warning. She turned on the engine and put the car into reverse. The rear wheels seemed to scrabble for a hold on the loose sand. For a second the whole automobile began to slip sideways; then the wheels bit and the car jumped backward with animal nervousness.

She sat for a moment, trying to recover her breath. A little blood was trickling from her forehead down her face, and shock and fear had left her trembling. She remembered that Horn had bought a small bottle of whisky on their drive up from Washington. Rescuing it from the glove compartment, she unscrewed the cap and took two large mouthfuls. The liquid coursed over her cheeks.

In the cottage, Dolyacki had carried the phone out to the middle of the room and set it up on a table. As he spoke into the receiver, he ran his index finger across a large map that two of his agents had laid out for him.

"If you could bring searchlight teams up to cover the canal, Colonel, we'd have him sealed off."

His finger traced the sickle of land sticking into the ocean and the wide canal that effectively cut it off from mainland Massachusetts.

He replaced the phone and turned to one of the agents. "Get me immediate roadblocks on Routes Six and Twenty-eight where they cross the canal. Let the coast guard know in case he tries to make it by boat. And there's a couple of small airfields. . . ."

"You think he'll try to fly out?"

"Why not? He's a goddamn pilot."

The agent picked up the phone. As he began to dial, he watched Dolyacki's face. It was flushed to a hot red around the cheekbones, the eyes seeming to glisten with something close to tears, his mouth moving constantly in anticipation of the chase. Goddamn it, the guy's crazy, the agent thought. Then, with a grimace, he returned to his dialing.

Outside the car, the wind thumped hard against the bodywork, and a slash of rain appeared across the windshield. She had no idea how long she had been sitting there. She felt better now. More clearheaded, less stunned with the overwhelming sadness of parting. She would have to go back. And yet what could she do? The four cars would have reached the cottage by now, but at least she would find out what had happened to him.

Somewhere far down the shore road a car's headlights glowed and disappeared. Then seconds later they glowed again as they followed the bends in the road. And half backed across the road as she was, there was no chance of the occupants of this last car failing to see her.

Caught in the headlights, she covered her eyes, listening to the car brake and the driver's door open and slam closed. Then someone was opening her own car door, and an English voice spoke her name.

She looked up to see Max Bishop standing above her. He glanced quickly at the front of the car and helped her out of the driver's seat. "You're not hurt, are you?"

She shook her head. "No. I'm okay."

She stood in the cold wind and rain as he got into the car and drove it off the road. He came back, the rain, heavier now, streaming down his face. As he led her to his own car, she realized she was still clutching the bottle of whisky.

Once seated in his car, she offered him the bottle. He took it and placed it on the back seat. "Where is he?" he asked.

"Does it matter now?"

"Yes. A great deal."

She was silent.

"The FBI inspector on this case has orders not to take Alfred Horn alive," he said quietly.

He heard her intake of breath.

"You're children, both of you. What were you expecting? Fair play?"

"No longer." She was crying.

"So where is he?"

"I left him up at the cottage. Four police cars passed me on their way there ten, fifteen minutes ago."

The car jerked forward. Through the slanting rain Bishop pushed it into the turns, braking dangerously. Kay hung on grimly, the tears streaming down her cheeks.

Swinging the car through the open gate, Bishop

brought it to a halt. As it rocked on its suspension, she saw a man running through the rain toward them. A moment later the driver's door jerked open, and a young agent, his light gray hat dripping water, thrust a gun at Bishop. "Okay, get out."

He peered forward and hesitated. "It's Major Bishop, isn't it?" He had once seen Bishop with Dolyacki at the FBI operations room.

"What's happening here?" Bishop asked peremptorily. "Have you got Horn?"

"No, sir. He got away from us. We guess he made it down to the beach. The inspector's taken the rest of the team down there now. He won't get far. The way the inspector sees it, on a beach you've only got two ways to go. Unless he feels like a long swim in *that*." He jerked his thumb in the direction of the rollers breaking against the shoreline.

"Okay." Bishop closed the car door and, to Kay's surprise, reached over and took the bottle of whisky from the back seat. As he unscrewed the cap, he said, "From now on it's up to you."

"I don't understand."

"Put yourself in Alfred's shoes. Down on that beach. Which way did he go? Where did he make for?"

"How can I be expected to know?"

"That man Dolyacki'll shoot him down like a dog. Is that what you want?"

She shivered, and he handed her the whisky. "Think, Kay. For Christ's sake."

She drank some whisky. "Dolyacki's orders are to kill him . . .?"

"Yes."

"And yours?"

He hesitated. "The same orders."

"Are you saying"—she turned in the seat to face him—"are you saying that you'll give him a chance?"

He screwed the cap on the bottle and dropped it over the back of his seat. "Yes," he said quietly. "I'm saying that if I find him first, I'll give him a chance."

"The lighthouse," she said. She pointed along the beach. "Just around the headland there's a cluster of old fishermen's cottages. And a lighthouse standing out by itself. It's empty. We looked over it this afternoon. I can't say why, but I think he just may have gone there."

"Stay here, Kay."

She began to protest, but he had already leaned across her and opened her door. The wind blasted rain across her face. She climbed out and slammed the door behind her. The next moment she was watching Bishop reverse the car and head for the gate.

The young FBI man approached her through the driving rain. "Better come inside, ma'am."

For a few moments she watched Bishop's taillights receding; then she turned to the agent standing uncomfortably beside her. He could have no idea who she was. "I want to use the phone," she said.

"Sure, ma'am."

"I guess it's not too late to raise a cab in Chatham."

Dolyacki stood in the middle of the beach. Using the powerful portable searchlights from the cars, his men were probing the dunes—dark, scurrying figures like the wreckers for which the Cape was once notorious.

He knew he had been overconfident. Among this expanse of rolling dunes a man could hide and move silently on the fine sand. In half an hour they had worked their way along almost a mile of beach without a sign of him. They rounded a headland now, and while the beams of light played along the beach, Dolyacki examined the cluster of white Cape Cod fishermen's cottages among the pine trees. Some of them still showed lights burning; the others stood white and silent against the blackness of the night. Then suddenly the headlights of a car flared. Dolyacki's teeth clamped tight. He had examined the map. There was no road past the cottage, nothing more than a narrow track, leading . . .?

He tried to picture the map on the cottage table. He had checked it for possible escape routes and rejected the track because it was obviously far too exposed. But where did it lead?

Suddenly the image returned. At the same instant his eye caught the black outline of the lighthouse farther along the dunes.

Bishop ran the car to a stop along a length of wooden fence below the lighthouse, killed the lights and climbed out. Above him the stone tower rose to a height of fifty or sixty feet. He took the path up to the doors, watching for any movement at the small broken windows above.

He could see nothing. He tried calling Horn's name, but the wind whipped the words from his mouth and carried them away. He was at the door now; playing his flashlight across it, he saw it gaped on rusting hinges. He stepped inside.

The stone chamber was cathedral-quiet after the howling of the wind outside. Even the shrieking of the gusting wind penetrated only dully into the dank interior.

He called. "Alfred! Alfred. It's Max Bishop. Max Bishop, Alfred." His voice echoed away into the darkness above.

Somewhere up the stone spiral staircase he thought he heard a movement. He shone the lamp up and followed the curve of the steps. Alfred Horn stood looking down, his sweater sparkling wet in the light, his dark hair plastered across his forehead.

"Are you alone, Max?"

"For the moment. Not for long. You don't seem in the least surprised to see me?"

"No. I knew from Kay that you had been assigned to find me. I saw you when you entered her apartment in Washington. What will happen to her, Max?"

Bishop leaned against the wall, shining the flashlight down on the slab stone floor so that Horn was in darkness. "I can't be sure. If she keeps her mouth shut, possibly nothing. She's an American citizen. It makes a difference."

"And me?"

"My orders are to make sure you never talk."

"To kill me?"

"Yes."

Horn came down and sat on the bottom step. "Do you have a cigarette?"

Bishop took a pack from his pocket, gave Horn a cigarette and lit it.

"I've done a lot of growing up in a very short time, Max," Horn said. "If I'm dead, Kay will become the main danger to your people."

"My people?"

"The British government, the American government and everybody else concerned with keeping this quiet. While I live, there's not much point tackling her. The way I see it I have to stay alive to protect her."

Bishop was silent, probing the stone blocks of the wall with the beam of his flashlight. "I promise you, Alfred," he said at last, "to do all in my power to look after Kay."

"That means you've already made your decision."

"Decision?"

"To carry out your orders. To kill me."

"No. I can't do that. I can't kill you, Alfred. But there's no way out for you. Dolyacki, the FBI man, will find you by morning at the latest. Maybe even before."

"If you can't kill me, Max . . . if you can't carry out these orders, why did you come here?"

Bishop reached into his raincoat pocket. He placed the gun on the step between them. "I came to give you a chance. You're a German officer. You should not be shot down like a rabid dog."

"An honorable death," Horn said from the darkness. There was irony in his tone.

"Yes. If you'll take it."

Horn reached forward and picked up the gun. "I suppose I should thank you, Max. But, you know, surprisingly I'm not overflowing with gratitude."

"No."

"Good-bye, Max."

Bishop nodded in the darkness and turned for the door. Where the hinges gaped he pressed against the heavy timber and opened a large enough gap for him to step through. "I promise you, Alfred, I will insist she knew nothing. I will insist that the help she gave you was for purely personal reasons." He stepped through the gap out into the blustering wind.

Dolyacki's searchlight picked up the figure in the light raincoat as it walked toward the car. For a brief second, before his eyes focused clearly, he felt a lift of elation, convinced it was Alfred Horn. Then, as the man in the raincoat continued to walk slowly toward him, he realized his mistake. He ran forward and grabbed Bishop by the lapel. "How the hell did you get here?" He spat the words into the wind.

Bishop wrenched his hand away. "Let's forget the mutual recriminations, Dolyacki. You kept me in the dark; I did the same for you."

"Is he in there?" He pointed to the lighthouse.

"Yes."

"You left him in there?" He started at a run for the door.

"Dolyacki!" Bishop called.

As Dolyacki half turned, the shot came echoing from the lighthouse. Dolyacki's face twisted in contempt. "You goddamn officers," he said slowly, "you goddamn honorable *officers . . . !*" He wrenched himself around and ran for the entrance.

Dragging aside the hanging door, Dolyacki pushed his way inside. The powerful searchlight illuminated the whole room. He pointed it at the base of the staircase. There, lying on the step where Bishop had placed it, was the revolver. There was no sign of Alfred Horn.

As Bishop pushed through the sagging door behind him, Dolyacki lurched around, his eyes protruding, his mouth moving uncontrollably. "You *officers*," he screamed, "you fucking *officers*." The revolver was in his hand without his knowing he had retrieved it from the step. As he pressed the trigger, one part of his mind had already decided that the Englishman had been shot by Alfred Horn.

He stood at the water's edge, consumed with an anger from which all self-pity had been excised. Yet he felt infinitely cheated. The route of honor had ended in a deserted lighthouse on Cape Cod with Max Bishop laying a loaded pistol at his side.

He knew that his life was being sacrificed—by the feebleminded romanticism of Rudolf Hess as much as by the hard-eyed ambition of Joseph Kennedy. He felt an overwhelming urge to fight back, but he knew no way of doing it. No way that would not be a threat to Kay, too.

Since childhood he had accepted the soldier's credo: *Dulce et decorum est pro patria mori;* to die for one's country is an honor to be welcomed. But now he angrily rejected it. A country was just not reason enough. But to die because there was no other way . . . that might be different.

He looked out at the black heaving waters. Behind him he could hear shouts and see the flickering flashlights moving down the beach. He walked forward to the water's edge and let the waves break around his feet. Then he ran forward into the water.

The great seas swelled and heaved under him, pressing against his body, making every stroke a struggle to remain conscious. He knew from the map that the ocean currents streamed past the elbow of the Cape and swept far out into the Atlantic. He knew that if he could reach the pull of the main current, his body would never be recovered. He knew that if any chance existed that Alfred Horn was still alive somewhere, they would never dare proceed against Kay. But he knew, too, that he was doing this at least as much for himself.

To Hess, to Churchill, to Roosevelt and to Kennedy he was a pawn, a dispensable life. Very well; they would pay for it. They would never know what really happened to Alfred Horn: whether he was alive, and still dangerous, or dead and forever silent. They would never be entirely sure of the place they had reserved for themselves in history.

With a will he had no idea he possessed he drove his aching, straining body through the mountains of black water until he felt the first tug of the great current that would sweep him out into the Atlantic.

Epilogue

"A cowardly surprise attack. A date which will go down in infamy."
—*Franklin Delano Roosevelt on the Japanese attack on Pearl Harbor, December 7, 1941.*

＊

"Thank God. We've won the war."
—*Winston Churchill on hearing the news of Pearl Harbor, December 7, 1941.*

＊

"If Hess is mad, the whole world is mad. And Hess could have saved the world."
—*Goering, the night he took his own life.*

＊

Joseph P. Kennedy, the most unpopular U.S. ambassador ever to present his credentials to the Court of St. James's, never achieved high position again. Throughout the war President Roosevelt continued to block him from any public office in which he could become nationally known. It was left to Kennedy's second son, Jack, to achieve the Presidency in the election of 1960.

*

The world never gave Dr. Carl Diem full credit for his organization of the 1936 Olympic Games—perhaps because his most spectacular contribution had to be kept secret. The world believes in the ancient tradition of Greek runners carrying the Olympic flame. But the Olympic flame is a fake, a pure creation of the propagandist genius of Dr. Diem, designed to link the glories of the past with their Nazi reincarnation in Hitler's Germany. In 1936 the world believed. It believes still.

*

For Rudolf Hess, May 10, 1941, was his last day of freedom. In 1971 he became the sole inmate of the three-hundred-cell Spandau Castle Prison, his memory erratic, his sanity continually in doubt.

*

Captain Kay Hampton is recorded as one of the few American servicewomen killed in action. She died on December 30, 1944, in the Battle of the Bulge, during a panzer thrust into the advanced headquarters area in which she was serving. The battle group Commander of the German forces in the area was Colonel-General Karlheinz Horn. Alfred Horn's uncle.

The most fascinating people and events of World War II

International Intrigue from BALLANTINE BOOKS